Who Sleuthed It?

Edited by
Lindy Cameron

Clan Destine
PRESS

First published by Clan Destine Press in 2021

PO Box 121,
Bittern Victoria 3918
Australia

National Library of Australia Cataloguing-In-Publication data:

Editor: Lindy Cameron

WHO SLEUTHED IT?

ISBNs: 978-0-6450021-2-6 (hardback)
        978-0-6488487-6-9 (paperback)
        978-0-6488487-7-6 (eBook)

Cover & Internal Illustrations by Judith Rossell

Cover typography by Willsin Rowe

Design & Typesetting by Clan Destine Press

www.clandestinepress.net

This book is for all the animal-loving mystery readers
who *know* their fur-kids – and their feather,
fin, and tailed ones – would help
solve *all* the mysteries.
Or happily create them.

Contents

Introduction

'What's up, Skip?'
'Tchk-tchk-tchk.'
'Oh no, the bad guys have kidnapped the headmaster and thrown him down a mineshaft? Show us where, Skip.'

Back in the 1960s we Aussies just rolled with the idea of a super-smart native marsupial macropod. After all, why couldn't an Australian bush kangaroo be smarter than the average bear, or any evil mastermind?

L ike many of the authors I know, I grew up reading The Famous Five, so it was a given, when I grew up to be a writer, that I'd be a crime writer; a writer of mysteries. The kid that I was, also wanted to 'be' George so I could 'have' Timmy – a super-smart scruffy mut to sleep on my feet and help me and my friends solve mysteries.

When I was ten-years-old I even formed a club – the Secret Seven Avengers Club – for my sister and besties to be in. We never had a crime to solve but had lots of fun not doing that.

I also grew up *with* television, from the late 1950s, and with Saturday matinees at the local picture theatre. My childhood – which I admit I have never grown out of – was filled with swords-and-sandal epics, and shows like *The Samurai, Prince Planet* and *Lost in Space*.

But my TV viewing was also populated by a host of animal sidekicks: *Rin Tin Tin*, the German Shepherd who protected young Rusty and the soldiers of Fort Apache; *Flipper*, the intuitive bottlenose dolphin who saved the day with his human, Sandy, in Key Largo; and *Skippy*, the eastern grey kangaroo, who bounded the outback with her best friend Sonny and the team at the Waratah National Park ranger station.

Of course there was Lassie – after Lassie, after Lassie – always devoted to one kid at a time. A Rough Collie, she first appeared in Elizabeth Gaskell's 1859 short story 'The Half-brothers', which established the "Lassie to the rescue" concept. She next featured in 'Lassie Come Home', a short story then novel then film (1938/1940/1943) by Eric Knight; and has since been in over 50 books, 12 movies (including a musical!), a radio show, comics, and long-running TV shows.

And then came the long-serving police dog Reginald von Ravenhorst – aka *Inspector Rex*. The 17-season police-procedural comedy-drama was first filmed in Austria where Rex solved crimes with his human partners for the Vienna Kriminalpolizei homicide unit, (1994-2004). And then, when Italy took over the rights (2008-2015), Rex moved to Rome to work with Italian homicide detectives. As a good dog would.

The character also spawned Portugal's *Inspector Max*, Russia's *Muhtar's Return*, Slovakia's *Rex*, Lithuania's *Inspektorius Mazylis*, and Canada's *Hudson and Rex*. Rex in any country is smart, playful and ready for anything – but he's a dog; he doesn't talk. At least not in Human.

But there *are* countless animal sleuths – cats, dogs, birds, rodents – mostly in animated shows and movies, who do talk to us the reader/viewer, or to other animals, either with or without the knowledge of their human friends. There are the kids' TV characters that 'everyone' knows, from the beloved *Scooby Doo*, and *Rocky, Bullwinkle, Mr Peabody* the dog and his human boy Sherman, to the *Octonauts*, and *PAW Patrol*. They're out there, hard at work rescuing their friends, solving crimes or saving the day.

Even *Doctor Who*, and Sarah-Jane had a dog, albeit the mechanical K9.

But, if you search the internet for books featuring cat sleuths, dog detectives, parrot private eyes, your mind will explode.

While there are countless serious crime novels and procedurals featuring the realistic pairing of 'working' dogs – police dogs, search and rescue hounds, bomb disposal canines, cadaver dogs – with their human counterparts, there's also a whole world – *so many worlds* – in which mysteries are solved, often incidentally, by human-owned cats and dogs simply doing what they do.

And that's before we even get to the gazillion books in which anthropomorphic animals do the sleuthing.

These animals, whether 'realistic' or 'chatty', populate a myriad of animal detective series set in bookshops, bakeries, libraries, guest houses, cafes, magic shops, small towns and big cities.

Rita Mae Brown, US activist and ground-breaking feminist novelist, also writes three animal sleuthing series including: 30 books, *cowritten with her cat* Sneaky Pie Brown, featuring a Virginian postmistress and her cat Mrs Murphy; and 13 in the 'Sister' Jane series with their talking foxes and hounds.

Another beloved and best-selling series are *The Cat Who* mysteries by Lillian Jackson Braun, starring ex-newspaper reporter James Qwilleran, and his Siamese cats, KoKo and Yum Yum. The first three books were published between 1966 and '68; then another 26 from 1986. Braun was

94-years-old when her last book, *The Cat Who Had 60 Whiskers* was published in 2007.

It seems worth noting that writing cat mysteries may contribute to a long life, as Shirley Rousseau Murphy wrote *her* twenty-first and final *Joe Grey Cat Mystery* in 2019 at the age of 91.

Another thing: these thousands of mysteries are not children's books, any more than *Inspector Rex* is a kids' crime show. Yes, many of them might be cozies (more often than not) in a humungous 'niche' market, but they are written for the adults who wanted to go adventuring forever with Timmy the dog; or who always wanted a talking cat.

Which brings me to *Who Sleuthed It?* and the stories herein.

I approached my animal-loving writer friends – in Australia, Ireland and the USA – and said: 'I want stories where the animals help each other – or their human sidekicks – solve crimes.'

No one I asked said no; and 18 authors came back with such variety – having had so much fun in the process – that I knew immediately there will be a sequel.

Six authors gave us new adventures featuring their ongoing human/animal characters.

From **Kerry Greenwood** we have a *Phryne Fisher* mystery in which the famous human sleuth is aided by her trusty cat and dog.

We have a new story from the world of *Spam the Cat*, by US writer, **Elizabeth Ann Scarborough**; **Narrelle M Harris** has penned the second in the *Kearney and Sminth* series; **David Greagg** gives Dougal and Shadow, of *When We Were Kittens*, a new adventure; **Craig Hilton** offers up a story from the world of *Whimper*, rat detective; and **Louisa Bennet**'s short story fits neatly between her book *Monty Dog Detective* and its forthcoming sequel (from CDP) *The Nosy Detectives*.

And then there are the stand alones. **Fin J Ross** gives her felines, Sherlock and Watson, a jolly good London adventure; **Livia Day** proves that cats can do anything when they work together; and **Chuck McKenzie** pairs his put-upon human with a cat *for* a conscience.

Vikki Petraitis shows just how protective a Labrador can be; **Atlin Merrick** reveals what wild things there are at large in modern-day Dublin; **LJM Owen**'s clever dog is a must-have for every bookstore; **Jack Fennell** gives us a 'familiar' fox; a penguin holds the vital clue in **Meg Keneally**'s *other*-pandemic tale; and I conquer my own fears of the *sparassidae* family.

Meanwhile, in the world of investigator birds: **Kat Clay**'s rousing tale stars Inspector Reggie Starling of Scotland Yard; **GV Pearce**'s one-eyed harrier hawk escapes for a rollicking adventure; **CJ McGumbleberry** supplies his Great Horned Owl with a chipmunk of a mystery; and in **Tor Roxburgh**'s world, an Australian magpie and a human cop learn to give and take, to help each other solve some murders.

There is no reason kids can't read the stories in *Who Sleuthed It?* – but they were written for grown-ups; for those of us who grew older but never grew up; who believe that animals really do understand us; and for whom *Puff the Magic Dragon* is the saddest song ever written.

Enjoy their adventures.

Lindy Cameron
Australia, 2021

Sidebars

1: For non-Aussies viewers of the 91 episodes of *Skippy*, kangaroos cannot untie ropes, or operate two-way radios. Skippy's famous *tch-tch-tch* sound is also not a kangaroo thing. She was played by nine or more kangaroos – in each episode.

2: The original German Shepherd nicknamed Rinty was a real-life survivor of a WWI French battlefield, rescued by American soldier Lee Duncan and thrust into Hollywood movies as himself, the heroic Rin Tin Tin, in 24 silent and four sound movies. TV's Rinty did a bit of time-travelling, as the show was made in 1952 and set in the 1870s. Rinty also had a Canadian TV reboot in the 109-ep *Katts and Dog* (aka *Rin Tin Tin: K9 Cop*).

3: The 19-season (1954-1973), 592-episode TV show *Lassie* is the fifth-longest-running US primetime TV show (after *The Simpsons, Law & Order/ SVU*, and *Gunsmoke*). All the dogs who have played Lassie are descendants of Pal, the male Rough Collie who played her in 1953's *Lassie Come Home*.

4: *Flipper* was always portrayed by female dolphins, who were less aggressive; and 'his' trademark voice was actually a doctored kookaburra's laugh.

5: *Inspector Rex* was played by four different dogs over the 17 seasons.

A
Rascal
in
Academia

Fin J Ross

A Rascal in Academia

MY NOSTRILS FLARED WITH THE UNMISTAKABLE WHIFF OF VERMIN. I am never wrong about such things. From the moment he darkened our portal like some creepy Nosferatu three days ago, I was suspicious. I could smell the fishiness when he eyed me with that disdainful look camouflaged in a smile. It didn't ring true. I sensed it in his tenuous pat on my back; his hesitant greeting as Mrs Hudson introduced us as her devoted companions. But Mrs Hudson didn't seem to notice it. I put it down to too much wine. She'd fallen into his embrace like a long-lost dog, her eyes closed, her body floating. Under his spell. His eyes, on the other hand, were surveying the room like a searchlight. Like a criminal scanning for a surveillance camera.

Jim Romtiary. Shifty. Up to no good. Why couldn't she see it?

They'd disappeared into the bedroom. The sounds of passion behind the closed door kept me awake for hours, as I sat outside, bereft as a jilted lover. In the morning, he'd kicked me in the side as he scurried down the hall and out the front door in a state of half undress. No accident. No apology. Deliberate.

He'd returned that evening, armed with a bottle of red, and a smarmy swagger. He'd nodded to us as someone would flies on a windowsill. Another night relegated to the passageway. Another quick Romtiary exit in the morning, though I'd got my own back and given him a nasty bite on the ankle as he passed.

Thankfully, he hadn't appeared last night and so we were content to share the sofa with Mrs Hudson in our usual late-night-movie, popcorn-crunching fashion.

But what worries me more than Romtiary himself, is my buddy's apparent lack of interest. His benign casualness. I put that down to too much of his abiding drug of preference. But it's time to shake him out of his boredom-induced indifference. He always becomes maudlin like this when there's nothing to set his intellect afire. I saunter into the snug, his 'consulting suite' if you will. There he reclines, blue as ever, on the chaise. Lost in a fug of self-indulgent woe, fiddling away at some mournful dirge. I glance out the window. At least two customers wait outside, kneading the paving stones with impatient feet.

'Come on Sherlock, snap out of it.'

He eyes me disinterestedly, like he can only discern me as a silhouette. I tip-toe over and jump up beside him. Give him a head butt and lick his ear. He pulls away.

'Will you quit with the fiddling. And pong, it stinks in here. You and your darn catnip. Smells stronger than usual. Can't fathom what you see in it. Has no effect on me at all. I'll open the window. Get some fresh air.'

Sherlock grunts. 'Watson. I have made a remarkable discovery. I can't believe it's taken me so long.'

'And what is that?'

'Rubbing catnip on the strings heightens the euphoria as I play. It's so…so liberating.'

Incredible. I shake my head. 'The world's foremost feline detective and you behave like some stoned sixties rock star. Mrs Hudson won't be impressed at what you've done to her violin.'

'What's there to say, Watson? I need a fix. If I don't have a case–'

'Ah, but I believe you do. You've two customers waiting and then there's this Romtiary to investigate.'

Sherlock swipes a disinterested paw at me. 'Seriously Watson, your suspicions have got the better of you. He's just another in an entourage of would-be suitors. She's lonely you know. So, he doesn't like cats. Doesn't make him a villain.'

'If there's one thing you've taught me, it's how to smell a rat.'

Sherlock rolls his amber eyes. 'Yes, I can smell a rat at fifty paces, yet I remain unperturbed at his presence.'

'Not when you're high on catnip you can't. Your sense of smell goes all fliff-flaff.'

'Fliff-flaff? Really?'

'Really. Now pull yourself together and I'll call in your first customer.'

Sherlock sets the violin aside, rolls onto all fours, spills off the chaise in a blue fuzzy blur and heads for the door. 'I must go pee first.'

So that's going to take a while. Always does. I swear to Bast that he spends half his time in there trying to sculpt the kitty litter into the Great Pyramid or the Venus de Milo. I mean really, it's then up to me to smooth things over again so that Mrs Hudson remains unaware she has a budding Michelangelo as a house pet.

Mind you, she's no more aware of Sherlock's (and dare I say my) eminence in the realm of super-sleuthdom either. We're quite content to perpetuate her delusion that we're just a squishy pair of laid-back, though occasionally mischievous, British Shorthair couch potatoes. How's she to know what we get up to when she's not around?

I beckon the first customer through the window. 'Mr Holmes will be just a moment,' I say as a perfectly-tailored specimen of chocolate-footed, coffee-muzzled fluff, complete with diamante collar pounces onto the windowsill. Birman or maybe Ragdoll. Never can tell the difference. 'And your name?'

'Irene. Irene Adler. I am holidaying temporarily at number 232, though I suspect it may become a permanent arrangement.'

'Baker Street?'

'Yes, just opposite and down a bit.'

'That accounts for my not having met you before. Number 232, Miss Regina Markwell's residence.'

'Oh, you know her?'

'Not to speak of. But I am acquainted with Monty. A very street-smart young tabby that Monty.'

'Indeed. He certainly gives Miss Markwell moments of hysteria. And me. He does like to chase for no apparent reason, but I have learnt, in short order, that atop the armoire in the guest bedroom is a relatively safe haven. I have been here in Baker Street a mere three days, but imagine how honoured and fortunate I am to be staying in such proximity to the great Sherlock Holmes just when I find myself in need of his acclaimed expertise.'

'Ah, here he is now.'

Sherlock minces in the door and oblivious to our guest's presence, adopts his treble-clef pose to lick his fiddlydibs. Then he spots young Miss Adler. His eyes widen like Tom Bowlers and, mid lick, he springs back to a four-footed stance and assumes his debonair genius pose. First time he's looked interested in anything for days.

'And to whom do I owe the pleasure?'

That's it. He's smitten. He advances, somewhat coyly, I note. Presses his nose to hers, then sidles around to sniff her derriere.

This is too much. 'Sherlock. Really.'

'You're new. I take it we haven't met before.'

I short-circuit the pleasantries. 'Irene Adler, temporary resident at number 232.'

'Ah. Welcome to the neighbourhood. You have come from the country I observe. Tunbridge Wells, if I am correct.'

Miss Adler looks stunned. 'Indeed, you are correct. But how can you tell?'

I do like to extol his virtues. 'There's not much the great Sherlock Holmes cannot surmise from a mere glance. He will probably now tell you it comes down to your certain smell, or some such thing which only the most astute and observant nose can detect.'

Sherlock dismisses my remark with another swipe of his paw.

'There is that. A definite air of cod liver oil about yourself. I have it on good authority that a certain Tunbridge Wells veterinarian, Dr Ronald Silverton, is one of the few remaining who still prescribes cod liver oil as a remedy for furballs.'

Irene nods, her jaw slack.

'Ah, but there's more,' Sherlock continues, 'I also know that that very same veterinarian snubs the norm of using a particular shade of shamrock green for those ear tattoos awarded to you when you become, how shall we say, not fully female anymore, and instead uses a distinctive shade of turquoise, known to those in the know as Galapagos turquoise. Observe, Watson.'

I inch closer, without invading Miss Adler's personal space, and indeed observe the unusual hue of her tattoo. 'Marvellous. Mark my words Miss Adler, our Mr Holmes does not miss a thing.'

'He, Dr Silverton that is, is evidently left-handed.'

I laugh at the notion that Sherlock can discern such information without being in the presence of the man. 'Sherlock, such an assumption is surely going too far.'

'Watson, I never assume. It is obvious to me, though evidently not to you, that Miss Adler's claws have been clipped from left to right.'

I shrug in disbelief. As does Miss Adler.

'And,' says Sherlock, 'there is one more thing.'

'Yes?' Miss Adler and I say in unison.

'Your owner, quite evidently, has not yet changed the phone number on your identification tag. 01892 is, of course, the area code for Tunbridge Wells.'

'I say,' says Miss Adler. 'You are, indeed, observant.'

Sherlock reclines smugly. 'Now, Miss Adler, is this a mere casual visitation?'

She bats her eyes at him. Seems quite overcome by his renown. 'Ah, well on the one hand, I am delighted to make your acquaintance–'

'As am I in return.' His tone ingratiating.

Ugh. The charm. Doesn't turn it on very often, but when he does… well pure schmaltz.

'But on the other, I do have a matter of some importance to impart.'

'Yes,' Sherlock replies with a tone of intrigue.

'You must be careful of that man, Romtiary. I have seen him come and go from these premises in the past few days.'

'Hmm, interesting.' Sherlock nods. Looks sideways at me. A tacit acknowledgement of my – in this case – superior judgement. 'Come, sit. Tell me more.'

Miss Adler takes position on the brocade pouffe; sits demurely. 'You see, my human, Constance Nethersole, has had some unfortunate acquaintance with this man, which accounts for why we have been compelled to move from our country manor house, albeit temporarily, to this modest neighbourhood. Miss Markwell is my human's sister, you see.'

Sherlock's eyes are hooded, his paw in swipey mode. That's how he assimilates information.

'Go on.'

'You see, my other human, Professor Bertram Nethersole, passed away quite recently and most inexplicably–'

Sherlock's head snaps up and, in a whirr, he flings himself off the chaise and up onto Mrs Hudson's desk. Miss Adler and I look at each other quizzically.

'It will be something you said,' I whisper, by way of explanation for Sherlock's sudden interruption.

He paws Mrs Hudson's Teledex and the lid flies open. Scrolls the tab down, I presume to 'N'.

'Aha!' he announces with a flick of his tail.

'Are you going to explain Sherlock?'

'I knew the name was familiar Watson. Professor Nethersole is listed right here in Mrs Hudson's contacts. Miss Adler, would I be correct in saying your Professor Nethersole was Dean of Biomedical Engineering at King's College?'

'My gosh, but you are so astute,' Miss Adler says.

Sherlock waves his paw nonchalantly. 'Elementary, my dear. One either knows things…or one doesn't.'

'But how do you know these things?'

'One must keep up with the times. And therein lies the answer.' Sherlock launches himself off the desk and is out the door and halfway down the hall before either I, or Miss Adler, take another breath.

'What the–?' Miss Adler says.

'Beats me, but I suspect he will return momentarily with some gem of wisdom.'

We remain silent amid the sounds of rustling paper in the living room. 'Perhaps I'll go and see.' I leave Miss Adler on her perch, her face still all a-quandary, and hot foot it in Sherlock's wake. There he is, scrummaging through the newspapers on the dining table, flicking the top dozen onto the floor. He's making an unholy mess which will turn Mrs Hudson's face to one set upon by Medusa when she arrives home.

'What on earth are you doing Sherlock? Mrs Hudson will have your guts for racquet strings.'

'It's here somewhere. I know I saw it.'

'I'm not following you. You said something about keeping up with the times.'

'No, *The Times*, I said. It was in *The Times* a fortnight or so ago.'

I'm still mystified. 'I would offer to help if I knew what you were looking for.'

'An obituary. Professor Nethersole's obituary.'

'Oh.'

'You're not making the connection are you?'

'Ah–'

'Do you not recall that our Mrs Hudson left here dressed in black on the afternoon of June 27?'

'Yes, I agree that was not her usual attire.'

'How can you be so obtuse?'

'Ah–'

'Which means she was going to his funeral, which therefore means,' Sherlock flips two more papers off the pile. 'Ah. June 23. Yes it was indeed a Monday I now recall,' he kicks three or four pages with his back paws. 'As I was saying, which means that our Mrs Hudson knew him and–'

'Was perhaps working with him?'

'Ah, now you're catching on. Here it is.' Sherlock runs his paw down the column as he reads aloud.

PROFESSOR'S DEATH A MYSTERY

Pioneering scientist, Professor Bertram Nethersole, 59, died suddenly at his Tunbridge Wells estate yesterday in what investigating police have deemed a suspected suicide.

Professor Nethersole, Dean of Biomedical Engineering at King's College, had spent the past 15 years perfecting an artificial pancreas, which could potentially cure Type I diabetes. Known as the Panclone 12, the technology has been successfully tested on pigs and is now set to go to trial on humans.

It is expected his research will be furthered by his colleague, Prof Victoria Hudson. Prof Hudson, who is said to be shocked and extremely upset by the sudden passing of her associate and mentor, told police she thought suicide was 'highly unlikely'.

'Professor Nethersole was in high spirits and was looking forward to the imminent human trial study of Panclone 12, despite a recent setback due to interference from an unknown third party,' Prof Hudson told The Times.

I nod wildly in recollection of Mrs Hudson's erratic and distressed behaviour a fortnight ago. 'So Mrs Hudson thought suicide was unlikely.'

'Yes Watson.' Sherlock nods. 'And so, we must investigate. Back to my consulting suite. We can't let poor Miss Adler languish there in uncertainty.'

Sherlock licks his paw and smooths out his whiskers before leaping off the table and heading for the hallway with uncharacteristic alacrity.

'Ah, Miss Adler,' he addresses her as he enters the snug, 'according to The Times, your male human committed suicide.'

'I don't believe that to be true. He was not depressed or melancholy,' Miss Adler pauses to scratch her ear, 'though his visitor did have him quite agitated.'

Sherlock looks at me knowingly. 'His visitor you say'.

'Why yes. Your Mr Romtiary was there when my dear Bertie died. Oh, I called him Bertie, as did my female human.'

'Indeed.' Sherlock rubs his chin. 'And how, may I ask, did he, Bertie, meet his fate?'

'Why, he fell from the drawing room balcony and cracked his head on the marble lion.'

'Aha. And where were you when this unfortunate incident occurred?'

'I was performing my morning ablutions on the front porch when Bertie crashed beside me. It gave me such a start. I believe, which is of some comfort to me, that he died instantly. His head was such a mess of blood.'

Sherlock's eyes narrow. 'So you did not actually see him falling?'

'No.'

'And did you look up? Was somebody else on the balcony? Mr Romtiary perhaps?'

'A shadow. A mere shadow was all I saw. I think I saw. I may have imagined that.'

'Mm, and Mrs Nethersole, where was she at the time?'

'Out the back in the rose garden I believe.'

'Was she aware that this Romtiary chap had called?'

'I don't believe so. He left very shortly afterwards. Kicked me and spat at me as he descended the front steps. And then he was away in his motor vehicle.'

Sounds familiar. Evidently not a cat person. 'Sherlock, a question if I may.'

'Provided it is pertinent to the case Watson.'

'How did you come to know this Romtiary's name?'

'Oh, some moments before the…accident, I heard my Bertie shout, "Romtiary what are you doing here?" I then heard raised voices, a scuffle and a thud.'

'Oh, so Romtiary had come uninvited, though evidently Bertie knew him?'

'Yes, he strode in the front door, bold as brass.'

'Aha,' Sherlock says. 'And, to your knowledge, was anything disturbed in his study?'

'Now I come to think of it, yes. I adjourned to his study – I did so love to sprawl on his desk and that was most often where I groomed myself – while Connie awaited the police, and noted that things were not in their usual place. If my memory serves me correctly, I believe Romtiary had a file of papers under his arm as he left.'

I note that Sherlock has a glint in his eye.

'Watson, come. The game is afoot.' He flings himself off the chaise.

'Where to Sherlock? Surely we're not to travel to Tunbridge Wells at this late hour.'

'No, I think we can skip that. I do not believe we will solve this mystery there.'

'Then where to?'

'The Diogenes Club my friend.'

Oh no. Not Mycroft. I do so find myself out of my depth when Sherlock and his brother pit their intellects against each other. My first acquaintance with Sherlock's corpulent older brother – he of the ridiculously expansive jowls – in that haven of intellectual anti-sociability, was one I shall not forget. Why, I was almost expelled from the establishment by a gruff, yet tacit, Maine Coon, for daring to speak in that hallowed cone of silence.

Sherlock had neglected to advise me that one should not make eye contact with any member present, nor utter a mew, save for in the Stranger's Room. Sherlock appears not to notice my sigh. 'You believe Mycroft can help?'

'Perhaps not Mycroft himself, though I feel sure he might offer some insight should he not digress from the matter at hand as is his wont. But he has, as you may be unaware, an acquaintance at King's College – the caretaker's Burmese no less – who I believe may be of great service to us. Now, Miss Adler, you take yourself off home and await our return. I expect to have some insight into your human's fate before the day is out.'

Miss Adler bounces off the pouffe and skips to the window. 'I bid you adieu and thank you for taking up my concerns.' She pounces to the windowsill and turns. 'Don't forget you have another customer waiting.'

Sherlock waves his paw dismissively. 'He'll have to wait. Your concerns are of greater import. Come Watson, we must be away, so as to return before Mrs Hudson arrives home.'

I wave my paw to indicate that he should, as usual, exit the window first and I follow, landing beside the still waiting customer, a black long-haired chap with a pained expression. 'Sorry,' I say to him, 'we have an important case to attend to. Your audience with Mr Holmes will have to wait.'

'Actually, it is you I have come to see. You are, I take it, Dr Watson.'

Oh, such a pleasant change for me to be the sought-after one. 'Yes, yes I am. I can be of assistance if it is an emergency only, otherwise you will need to wait.'

'It's my paw. A thorn.' He lifts his front paw and I clearly see the offending instrument of torture. I get my teeth into it and pull it free. 'Best off home now and get some soap onto that.'

'Thank you so much doctor. Already I can walk on it again.'

'Come Watson,' Sherlock hisses impatiently.

He strides off down the street and I quicken my pace to keep up. It's a good three blocks to the Diogenes Club but we cover the distance to Pall Mall in short order. Sherlock scans the street to satisfy himself we're not being observed and taps the two-three-two password on the door. Momentarily the cat flap, by way of magnetic magic, flips open and we squeeze ourselves through.

A svelte Russian blue greets us in the hall and bows in deference to Sherlock, before nodding our way into Mycroft and his associates' exclusive quarters.

There's no missing Mycroft sprawled in his usual fashion along the windowsill. He yawns at us distractedly; no doubt as high on catnip as was his younger brother prior to Miss Adler's visitation. He puts his paw to his lips, flops off the sill and beckons us to follow him to the Stranger's Room. I stifle a sneeze at all the shelves of musty books, as Mycroft leads us to the bow window.

'Ah, little brother, come for a lesson in the artful power of deduction?'

Sherlock snarls. 'I defer to your superior intellect. Such a shame you do nothing with it.'

Mycroft tips his head to me. 'He knows I am the sharper blade but honestly, who can be bothered with all that sneaking around and problem-solving?'

I nod in agreement.

'I note little brother, that you did not consult me in the instance of the Cornish fishmonger, but I see we arrived at the same conclusion. One cannot assume to substitute pollock for wrasse; leastways not to a discerning clowder of cats. You could have saved yourself an arduous journey had you sought my counsel in advance.'

Mycroft so loves to belittle his brother, yet Sherlock, as usual, takes it on the chin and brushes off his remark. 'My dear colleague Watson and I were in need of a change of scenery, that is all. Weren't we Watson?'

'Why yes. And a fine time we had of it.'

'So what brings you here today?' Mycroft asks with feigned interest.

'What do you know of a malefactor by the name of Romtiary?'

Mycroft shrugs. 'Can't say I have heard of him. What's his game?'

'You have no doubt heard of the untimely and somewhat suspicious death of Professor Bertram Nethersole.'

'Ah yes. Terrible affair. Wasn't suicide, I'd bet the last of my kibble on that.'

'Indeed. He was, of course, the head of our Mrs Hudson's faculty.'

'As I am aware.'

'We now believe our Mrs Hudson to be in imminent danger. This Romtiary fellow has made his presence felt at our abode of late.'

'He sounds fishy indeed. Have you observed any untoward behaviour from this chap for whom I have developed an immediate and suspicious dislike?'

'It appeared to me his intrusion was of an amorous bent, given that he spent all his visitation time in the bedroom,' Sherlock replies, 'yet Watson thought it more, shall we say, opportunistic; or underhanded even.'

Mycroft plucks some dried catnip from a tortoiseshell box beside him, inhales deeply, and turns his orange-eyed gaze to me. 'And you thought this why?'

'Something about the look of him. Like he was up to no good.

Like he was looking for something.'

'Hmm. You are sure he remained in the bedroom for the duration?'

'Yes,' I reply. 'I was outside the door…wait a minute. He did exit the room during the night, on the second visitation. I assumed it was for a call of nature except, now I think on it, he went to the dining room and not to the lavatory. What was he doing in the dining room?'

'Aha. The plot thickens,' Sherlock announces. 'You neglected to mention this to me, Watson.'

'I did Sherlock, but you were too strung out on that stuff,' I point to Mycroft's box, 'to pay heed to my concerns.'

He ignores my remark. 'How long was he in there?'

'Afraid I can't say. I must have fallen asleep.'

'I deduce he was looking for something,' Mycroft says, stating the obvious. 'What do you suppose that was?'

'Oh gosh, I feel so stupid. I now recall Mrs Hudson's frantic search for her research papers after his departure.'

Sherlock rolls his eyes at me. 'So, he steals papers from Nethersole before presumably throwing him off the balcony and–'

I don't give Sherlock the chance to finish his train of thought. 'He doesn't get what he's looking for so he sweet-talks his way into our home to–'

'To steal the patent application for Panclone 12,' Mycroft states smugly.

Sherlock's and my shoulders droop in unison, but Sherlock is the first to ask. 'How did you know?'

'Evidently, little brother, it's not what you know but who you know. Right there in the other room is The Bard, the inexplicably beloved – given his recalcitrant nature – Devon Rex of one E.B. MacBeth.'

Mycroft awaits a flash of recognition from Sherlock. It doesn't come.

'You're not following me, are you?' Mycroft says.

Sherlock shakes his head dejectedly.

'E.B. MacBeth is just London's foremost patent attorney.'

The penny drops. Sherlock's eyes dilate. 'Pray continue.'

'Just today, in fact shortly before you arrived, The Bard had me aside in here, telling me about a visitation at his human's premises yesterday by a furtive-looking chap lodging a patent application for the Panclone 12 artificial pancreas.'

'By gosh,' Sherlock exclaims. 'One Mr Romtiary I'll wager. Claiming the invention as his own.'

Mycroft nods slowly. 'Yet the name Romtiary didn't ring a bell when you mentioned your interloper. Wait just a moment and I shall fetch The Bard.'

Mycroft slouches out the door and returns momentarily with a funny-looking chap who appears to have had an argument with a set of hair curlers. The Bard looks less than pleased at making our acquaintance. Looks at Sherlock with an air of hauteur and me with plain everyday contempt. Mycroft explains our mission to him.

'The man you saw yesterday, his name was Romtiary, yes?' Sherlock asks.

'No.' The Bard laughs scornfully. 'The great Sherlock Holmes has it wrong. The gentleman's name, I believe, was Moriarty. Professor Moriarty to be precise.'

So much for our powers of deduction.

Sherlock sighs, but not to be outsmarted he replies, 'An accomplice perhaps.'

But then...

Mycroft laughs heartily. 'Oh Sherlock, little brother. Catch on, catch on, before I beat you to the punch.'

I can almost see Sherlock's brain cogitating and then he and Mycroft doff their heads in synchronicity. Me, I'm still in the dark.

'Rom–ti–ar–y,' Sherlock pronounces the syllables, 'Moriarty!'

I still don't get it, and my face obviously shows it.

'It's an anagram Watson. An anagram.'

'Oh, of course,' I say, though I'm still not sure I get it.

'So what do we know about this Moriarty?' Sherlock asks.

'Evidently you're not abreast of the latest news this week,' Mycroft says. 'According to a report in *The Times* yesterday, one Professor – although that title is somewhat dubious given that he allegedly studied at CATS College, and yes such a place really exists – James Moriarty has been revealed as the mastermind behind a series of theft and fraud-related crimes in our fair city.

'According to New Scotland Yard's Inspector Lestrade, this Moriarty was the instigator of the Notting Hill jewel robbery, the London gold bullion heist, and last week's Wembley Stadium ticket fraud.'

'Ah yes,' I say, 'all those people left dangling outside that concert with dud tickets.' My comment falls on deaf ears.

'Now it appears he is assuming to take credit for a world-first medical patent which could ostensibly earn millions,' Mycroft observes.

'Not if we have anything to say about it,' Sherlock says.

'Aren't we forgetting something?' I ask.

Sherlock and Mycroft stare at me. 'And what is that?'

I swear they're like twins, saying the same thing at the same time. 'He killed, or presumably killed, Professor Nethersole, so what's to stop him killing Mrs Hudson? Though admittedly he has had at least two opportunities.'

'Perhaps he was witnessed entering or leaving our premises by someone other than Miss Adler. A human personage perhaps rendering the opportunity for murder too risky,' Sherlock offers.

'Or perhaps,' says Mycroft, 'perhaps, he is, in fact enamoured of your Mrs Hudson. He is, I believe, a man of great intellect and it is therefore not unthought of that he might seek a companion of an equal mind. And your Mrs Hudson is not to be considered an unlikely matrimonial prospect.'

That's Mycroft for you. Always speaking in negatives when a straight out 'she's quite attractive' would suffice. 'The other possibility, which is borne out by reading yesterday's article further, is that he is seldom witnessed at the scene of a crime, which means–'

Sherlock interjects. 'He has others do his dirty work.'

'Precisely. So the potential risk to Mrs Hudson may not come from the man himself, but I dare say it is imminent. Moriarty's claim to the patent will not succeed once Mrs Hudson becomes privy to the application.'

I'm already turning for the door. 'Oh gosh, we must warn her.'

'Wait Watson,' Sherlock looks at the clock on the wall, 'we don't know whether she'll be on her way home, or at the university. Wednesday. It's Wednesday, which means–'

'She'll be working late. Come Sherlock.'

'Patience Watson. Mycroft, your friend, the Burmese who frequents the university–'

'Should be here any moment. Always arrives at 4.15. I could set my clock by him.'

'We may need his assistance to gain entry to the university.'

'He'd be happy to assist. Ah, there's the password. Here he is now.'

Allowing for the fact that it's a brisk half-hour walk to King's College and we have little time to spare, we decide to head the Burmese, with the unpronounceable name of 'Hlaing' – which upon Mycroft's introductions we learn means 'Plenty' – off in the foyer. It seems it's only my tongue that finds it hard to say; Sherlock has no problem.

In turn, we pop through the cat flap. Hlaing immediately stops and waits, unconcerned at our apparent urgency.

'Quicker to catch the bus,' he says, 'the N550 or N551 should be along any minute.'

I confess I'd never thought of that, but just as I'm about to mouth my thought, the bus appears. We wait for an impatient horde of humans to embark and disembark, carefully avoiding their brogues and lethal-looking stilettos, before we hop aboard, plopping ourselves on the lower step as the door closes.

'Why walk when you can ride,' Hlaing says rhetorically. 'Besides, it does wonders for the psyche to have so many humans fuss over you. Just ensure no-one snatches you up under the assumption that we're lost, stolen, or strayed. Humans can be so dim.'

I tell Hlaing that I don't mind a bit of fuss, some head scratching and the occasional belly-rub from strangers but Sherlock, well what can I say, Sherlock won't even raise a purr for Mrs Hudson. Her advances are entirely unrequited and yet she loves him so. Humans are mysterious.

We cover the distance in a mere 12 minutes, during which time Sherlock has picked Hlaing's brains about the university's security systems, establishing that they leave much to be desired. We follow Hlaing through a maze of ugly grey buildings, thankful that the place is now almost deserted, until we arrive at the medical engineering faculty.

I have but one recollection of the place, though I saw it through the bars of my carrier the day Mrs Hudson collected me from the vet and brought me here to recover while she finished for the day. A dose of the 'flu you understand, so I was feeling poorly and barely cognisant of my surroundings. I am no more impressed this time.

'Your Mrs Hudson is in Room 334, just along here a bit,' Hlaing announces as we scamper down a nondescript corridor. 'Darn it. Her door is closed, but I can sort that.'

With that, Hlaing flings himself into the air and grasps the handle. 'Push with your head, one of you,' he instructs.

I oblige and Sherlock pushes his way past into the deceptively sizable office. To say that Mrs Hudson, sitting there wide-eyed, is surprised to see us probably goes without saying.

'Shirley, Wattie (yes, that's what she calls us), what on earth are you doing here? And what are you up to Hlaing, you naughty boy?'

You know, life would be much easier if Mrs Hudson – or any human for that matter – understood cat speak. We could warn her to be on the look-out for suspicious characters appearing out of nowhere with malice aforethought.

I jump onto the desk and she scratches me under the chin just the way I like it. 'Oh, Wattie,' she says (adoringly I might say), 'stop drooling'. I hate to be embarrassed, and so I prop myself on the furthest corner of her desk. Nothing untoward seems to be happening here and my relief is palpable.

Sherlock springs onto the desk, right on top of today's edition of *The Times*. He scrummages through a few pages, much to Mrs Hudson's disdain, until he finds the mugshot of Moriarty, grainy and indistinct though it is. He stamps on the column until Mrs Hudson finally glances down. She shoos him off and peruses the article; her hand over her mouth as she reads.

And then…

A shadow in the corridor catches my eye and Sherlock's also. We freeze as a jockey-sized man, with a ski-jump nose and onion weed hair, clad in a trench-coat and wielding a scary, glinting knife, crosses the threshold. It is manifest that this man means to inflict harm on our dear human, and I take a second to praise myself for being so astute. But there's no time for self-aggrandisement.

Sherlock, I see, is all winks and blinks – his brain formulating a plan. The would-be felon's gaze is transfixed on Mrs Hudson as he inches closer. Then, from the corner of his eye, I see he spies me and then Sherlock. His face collapses into a grimace, his eyes all squinty, and then it happens. His head tilts backwards, his mouth opens and he lets fly an almighty sneeze.

Sherlock seizes the moment. 'Haha,' he laughs. 'He's allergic. Attack now boys.'

Without a second thought, I launch myself at the miscreant's chest, dig my claws in. Sherlock flies at his wrist and bites down hard, compelling him to drop the knife. Hlaing springs on his back and scratches through his coat.

I tell you, I have never heard such screams – Mrs Hudson's included – and then we're being spun around as the recreant bids a hasty retreat to the corridor. We let go our holds and chase him, ignoring Mrs Hudson's pleas for us to come back. His forward progress is punctuated by occasional stops to sneeze. He exits the building and heads at speed south along Strand Lane, then veers right into Temple Place towards the river, the mighty Thames.

Hlaing is the fastest of us and manages to keep up the pace, while Sherlock and I seem weighed down by our short legs and flopping girths, to say nothing of our advancing age.

Oh no! He's heading for a boat, just a rowboat mind, moored there beside The Yacht dock. How can we follow? We skid to a halt. Defeated.

'Wait and see which way he goes,' Sherlock instructs. 'If he heads across to Bankside Pier, we can cross over Waterloo Bridge and accost him on the other side. But it's more pertinent to follow him. He may well lead us to Moriarty.'

'Sounds like a plan,' I say short-breathed, 'given that I don't feel up to a swim.'

I turn to see Mrs Hudson, standing there on Victoria Embankment shouting into her phone. No time to determine who she is talking to. Hopefully the police.

As we set off, I hear her shriek, 'If you can't follow the rowboat, follow the cats.'

As we cross Waterloo Bridge, dodging the traffic, pedestrians, and cyclists, we observe our boatman veer past Bankside Pier and disappear under the bridge.

'He's heading to Festival Pier,' Hlaing calls out. By the time we arrive on the other side, our quarry is disembarking his watercraft.

'Stay back,' Sherlock says. 'Don't let him see us. He'll think he's given us the slip.'

We, being experts in the art of tailing a perp by ducking under parked cars and hiding behind lamp-posts, fall in step fifty metres or so behind, but Hlaing seems overcome with excitement at the chase and is at risk of betraying our pursuit. Sherlock admonishes him, yet he seems intent on skipping along a few paces ahead.

We pass the concrete dogbox of Royal Festival Hall and follow jockey-man across the forecourt of an apartment complex to Sutton Walk, traversing beneath the railway line.

I make the assumption that our quarry is heading to Waterloo Station, and I prepare myself for the prospect of a train ride. But my assumption is incorrect, he changes tack and heads along Mepham Street. He stops suddenly and Sherlock just manages to snag Hlaing by his collar and pull him in behind a rubbish bin.

Sherlock peeps out, his paw to his lips. 'He's heading into the Hole in the Wall,' he whispers. 'Quiet now. You two stay here. I'll case the joint, see if I can get a glimpse of Moriarty.'

I hear a siren approaching, just as Sherlock crawls, belly to ground, towards the Hole in the Wall – an uninviting drinking establishment set under an arch of Waterloo Bridge. Its reputation as the waterhole of choice for London's low-life element precedes it, though I have never entered to ascertain that for myself.

Hlaing and I watch as Sherlock slips through the grille and disappears from view. But I realise, all too soon, that our cover is blown as a police car pulls up right beside me.

'There, there, two of the missing cats,' a man calls from the car window.

Missing? We're not missing you fool.

'Quickly,' I say to Hlaing, 'follow me. We can cut through this alleyway and check out the back.'

I hear footsteps approaching behind and turn. I spring onto a pile of wooden pallets to avoid being scooped into an officer's arms.

'Keep going. Round the back,' I call to Hlaing. But it's too late. He's been nabbed by a second uniform. He protests wildly. Gosh, I never knew a Burmese could holler so loud. Even a train passing overhead doesn't drown him out.

I scoot around the back and jump onto a windowsill to see what I can observe. The glass is grimy. The kitchen I expect. I make my way along to another window and peer in. There, sitting at a table with his back to me in a small room is Moriarty. Even from behind I can tell it's him; his slick hair a dead give-away. Jockey-man is there before him, all a fluster, jabbering away.

'You mean to tell me you failed in your mission?' Moriarty shouts.

'I, I…yes, I failed.'

Moriarty shakes his head. 'It was so simple. Go there. Kill her. Leave without being seen. What am I to do with you?'

'I, I–'

'Did she attack you? You're covered in blood man.'

'No. 'Twasn't her. It was, oh my goodness, I was pursued by a bunch of crazy cats.'

Moriarty roars with laughter. 'Cats you say? You stupid man. I can think of 101 ways to deal with cats. You can kick them, step on them, poison them, stab them, starve them – though that might be a touch slow – throw them under a bus, a train; need I go on?'

Just then I see the door open a tad. In strides Sherlock, bold as a lion.

No, no. 'He'll kill you,' I scream. I wave frantically but he doesn't see me; his eyes are fixed on Moriarty. I swear, sometimes his bravado is foolhardy.

Moriarty leans forward menacingly. 'And who have we here? A tiger? A lion? No, it's just a wee garden-variety cat. A domestic I believe. Where are your balls man, that such a blob of fluff should scare you so?'

Blob of fluff? How dare you malign the great Sherlock Holmes?

Oh-oh. He has a pistol. I didn't see that coming. He's waving it from side to side, aiming first at his gopher and then at Sherlock.

'Now, who wants to go first?'

'Drop your weapon Moriarty!' The shout comes from behind the door.' The voice is deep, authoritative, but Moriarty appears to ignore it.

Another voice. 'You shoot my cat and I'll have you put away for cruelty to animals, on top of your many other crimes.'

It's Mrs Hudson!

Moriarty raises his hands in mock fear. 'Oh, so the little lady is afraid for her pussy cat.'

The scenario plays out before my eyes in slow motion, and I can do nothing to influence the outcome. The door flies open and there stands the inimitable Inspector Lestrade, his gun pointed at Moriarty's chest. Another officer and Mrs Hudson hover behind him.

Realising the opportunity of the diversion, Sherlock leaps at Moriarty. A gun goes off. And then another shot. All is a blur. Through the cloud of gun smoke, I see Sherlock flopped on the table.

Motionless.

Oh, my giddy aunt. My companion is dead. My colleague is dead. My friend is dead.

My Sherlock is dead.

Moriarty is…not dead. Merely wounded and protesting wildly as

Lestrade wrests the pistol from his injured arm and snaps handcuffs onto his wrists.

Mrs Hudson rushes to Sherlock. Smothers him so that I can't see.

Oh tragic day. I am bereft. Too stunned to think. I have to get in there. I paw wildly at the window and an officer comes forward and opens it. I leap from the sill to the table. Mrs Hudson is sobbing. I lick wildly at Sherlock's rump, the only part of him free of Mrs Hudson's clutches. What will I do without my buddy?

'What will I do without my Shirley?' Mrs Hudson sobs.

I head butt her arm – as consolation, but also to remind her that I am here. She pats my head and lifts her body away from Sherlock.

And then I see it. He is breathing. He is still breathing! Blood trickles from a tiny wound on his right leg, but he is alive. He lifts his head and winks at me.

'Sherlock. Really. It's just a flesh wound. You're such a drama queen,' I say. 'A bit of patching up and some well-earned catnip and you'll be right as rain.'

He sits up and we watch as Moriarty and his now-handcuffed accomplice are hauled to the door. I notice that Moriarty is limping, just as he spits at Mrs Hudson, 'you need to do something about that darn cream cat. He bit me and it's caused a nasty infection'.

'No less than you deserve, you appalling scoundrel,' Mrs Hudson replies.

'Pooh,' Sherlock echoes at Moriarty's departing back.

It is but an hour later and Sherlock and I are happily ensconced on the chaise in our shared consulting suite. Mrs Hudson has stopped her fussing now. I swear that both of us have been patted, scratched, and combed to near Nirvana. Honestly, these humans do carry on.

The veterinarian anaesthetised the wound, popped in a single stitch and bandaged Sherlock's paw in an unsightly, gaudy tape. He's floating on a cloud of fresh catnip, while I am studiously watching the six o'clock news, as Mrs Hudson prepares a hearty dinner of tuna, rice and carrot for us.

'There, Sherlock,' I say, as the visage of our nemesis appears on the screen.

'Tell me, tell me Watson. I can't focus on the screen,' he drawls sleepily.

'It would seem that Moriarty has been charged with at least a dozen offences. Murder, attempted murder, burglary, theft, fraud, threatening police, fire-arms charges…oh, yes, and animal cruelty. I should think he will be locked up for some considerable time.'

'Another successful case, Watson. All in a day's work. I say, would you mind popping over to advise Miss Adler of my brilliance in solving her human's murder puzzle?'

'Oh but of course, though I was sure you might hanker for a further acquaintance with her.'

Sherlock has not the energy to raise a paw. 'Trivialities my dear Watson. Trivialities.'

I am smug, snug, and contented.

Sherlock is snoring.

The
Tiger Mothers
of
Bethlehem Maternity

Vikki Petraitis

The Tiger Mothers of Bethlehem Maternity

T HERE WAS A STRANGE SMELL AROUND THE MATERNITY WARD TONIGHT. It fought against the slightly lingering odour of dinner on trays, strong notes of antiseptic, the bloom of fragrant pink lilies near where I sat, and something else. And then it hit me.

Fear.

As an ex-cop – police dog retired to service dog – I could smell fear.

I raised my head, closed my eyes and drew in a deep breath. Yep, definitely fear. Sure, I'd smelt fear here before. It's on the women who wobble and shuffle in here, afraid, trembling, nervous, hands protectively cradling their impossibly large stomachs. But that fear smells different; it's mixed with excitement as well.

Of course, the Coronavirus lockdown had added another layer to that. But still…

I climbed to my feet and padded softly down the dim corridor. In the small hours, human shapes beneath blankets in the four-bed wards were mostly still, but the night was peppered with the occasional moan or painful turning. No one ever slept comfortably in a hospital bed. In the restlessness was a yearning for home, for their own beds. The desire to go home and form a family with their new baby was strong. I walked past unit A, then B, then C, and the smell got stronger. I predicted I'd find it in D.

And sure enough, I did.

Three dim spaces, half hidden by drawn curtains and a light shining in the fourth. I moved into the room silently as I always did and walked towards the light. Sarah was standing next to the bed, scrambling with her bag, pulling things into it. Her breathing was heavy and she was no longer wearing the nightgown I'd seen her in earlier. She had on a pink tracksuit, smudged and stained.

I'm not one to stand on ceremony and I made a noise in the back of my throat to announce my presence. She jumped and let out a cry, looking quickly at me and then at the sleeping baby in the crib on the other side of her bed.

'Oh, it's you,' she said, 'you gave me a fright.' She put a finger to her lips. 'Shhhh. Don't make a sound. I have to get out of here.'

I raised my eyebrows in question. Why was she packing in the middle of the night?

She opened the top drawer of the bedside chest-of-drawers and took out a mobile phone. She clicked it to life and tapped Settings then scrolled down to Privacy, then to Location Services. She clicked Off and tucked the phone into the side of her bag.

For a moment, I was at a loss. I couldn't stop her – what could I do? Stand in her way? Growl? Block her path? And anyway, I sensed this wasn't a job for brute force, it was a job for subtlety. I needed to strengthen my numbers.

Without making a noise, I stepped backwards, giving her space. She ignored me and went on gathering her things. I backed into the bed next to Sarah's with a jolt and woke up Fiona. I knew she was a light sleeper and it wouldn't take much. It did the trick.

'What–' Fiona sat bolt upright and turned to the Perspex crib by her bed. It only took a moment to clear her head, check her baby, see me, then notice the light on behind Sarah's curtain. She looked at me. A question. I looked meaningfully towards Sarah's closed curtain and she got the picture. Something was up. Fiona struggled out of bed with the same slow pained movements that most women used in the maternity ward – 'straddling broken glass' I'd heard one new mother call it.

I decided to let Fiona do the talking. She'd been with us for a couple of days and I liked her. She was strong and forthright. Spoke her mind. 'Don't take shit from no one,' is the way I'd heard her describe herself to Belinda in the third bed.

'What are you doing?' Fiona asked in a voice louder than a whisper.

Sarah jumped in fright. 'I… I have to get out of here.'

'Why?' Fiona moved to the foot of Sarah's bed. 'What's going on?' And then she stopped suddenly. She knew. Just like I did. 'It's Tim, isn't it?'

Sarah's eyes widened and she rubbed her left wrist. The act pushed her sleeve up a little and in the dim light from above her bed, even I could see the bruise. I was sure Fiona could too. She moved gently around to Sarah and took her hand. Sarah flinched at the touch. Fiona rolled up the sleeve. At first Sarah tried to pull her hand back, but I sensed a small relief in the sharing of her problem.

I heard Belinda and Audrey coming before they did. I stepped aside as the shuffling women closed in. When Sarah saw them, she said, 'Oh

God.' She pulled back her arm from Fiona and fumbled with her sleeve to cover the bruise.

'I knew it,' said Belinda. 'I knew he was no good.'

I'd known it too. We'd all seen Tim visit. We'd all noticed the wiry agitation, the short temper. It was hard to miss. Thankfully the virus had kept him away except for short visits, but mask or not, it was easy to see that Tim was not a natural father. He had none of the puppy-dog eyes that I saw in most new dads who stared at the little ones in delighted wonder. And he certainly did not gaze at Sarah with admiration like the other dads did with the mothers of their babies.

Before Sarah could stop them, Fiona, Belinda and Audrey perched themselves like pigeons around her cubical. Fiona on the visitor's chair and the other two on the bed. I opted for the floor, sank down comfortably, and tucked my legs under me. Years of downward dog made me more flexible than most.

Audrey, quieter than the other two – an earth mother – asked the question we were all thinking. 'Where are you going to go?'

Sarah stepped away from her packing and crossed her arms in front of her in a lonely hug. I noticed she was trembling. 'I don't know,' she said at last. 'I just need to take my baby and leave. Tonight.'

Belinda looked at her watch. 'It's after midnight,' she said. 'How will you even get away? The curfew, remember.'

Sarah looked horrified. I guess that in this closed world of muted hospital dimness and soft nightlights and babies and bathing and feeding and no visitors, she had forgotten about Melbourne's lockdown curfew. Easy to forget, I supposed.

For the first time in the years I'd been here, aside from fleeting visits from masked fathers during the day, Bethlehem Maternity was mostly just mums, these lumbering women swaying gently on their slow walks, cocooning newborns in soft arms.

'Bloody hell.' Sarah slumped, the fight gone out of her. She moved her bag to the floor and sat down heavily on the bed. She manoeuvred herself painfully up against the pillow and faced the four of us. Her quivering lip broke my heart.

In the shadows of the night she told us tales of sorrow – of a bright young women drawn to a rebel called Tim. She worked hard, saved for a house deposit, supported Tim in his quest to become a musician. She ignored his growing temper (it was because his ambitions were frustrated) and cried after the increasingly nasty verbal attacks (not during because Tim said only weak women blackmailed their men with tears). She was powerless when drug taking became drug dealing. When Tim smashed her most prized possession in front of her (a china teapot she'd inherited from her grandmother) when the tea wasn't to his liking, she'd silently cleaned up the pieces and put band-aids over the blisters on her legs where the burning tea had splashed and left tear-shaped scars. She'd accepted his apology when he'd first hit her (Babe, it's only because I love you so much that you can make me so angry) and covered the bruise with makeup. Hiding the truth from the world, protecting her shame.

Her words floated and prickled in the still hospital night. It was death by a thousand cuts. The slow realisation that she was trapped. The growing embryo that good luck (not good judgement) had saved from his fists and boots. The baby – she gazed over at it with love and tears – was not safe. A baby to her. To him, a bargaining chip. A 3-kilo Sword of Damocles.

'So, he's living in your house and you want to run?' Fiona. Queen of summaries.

Sarah nodded.

And then our secrets were revealed.

I was surprised when, like I had been, Fiona said she was in the police force. Belinda was a lawyer. Audrey was a crime novelist. And in the blink of an eye, Sarah went from floating aimlessly in space where no one could hear her scream, to gazing heavenward, watching the stars align.

The new mothers and I sat long into the night. Discussions were had. Plans were hatched, and – in between – babies grew drunk on milk, burped, shivered as their nappies were changed, and slept once they were re-wrapped in their cocoon of blankets. Just before dawn, we all returned to where we belonged.

To take our places.

I had always admired the strength of the new mothers I saw every day. They shuffled in, gave birth, and then became…warriors, tiger mothers. A desire awakened in each of them to protect and serve their babies. The babies squawked like newborn pandas and the mothers hurried to tend to their every need. I had been taken from my own mother when I was just ten weeks old so I had never truly known what mothers were until I was retired from the police force and took the placement here. They didn't call my job 'security' – Bethlehem Maternity was more subtle than that. The label on my vest said 'Wellbeing Consultant'.

I watched as the plan played out. Sarah gave a statement to a nice woman who no one would have guessed was a detective. A search warrant was issued. In quiet moments, Audrey the crime novelist pushed her baby's trolley over to Sarah's cubicle and the two women made lists.

'It's like plotting,' Audrey said.

Change the locks

Change all passwords

Remove Tim's access to her bank accounts

Family violence order

'Oo, I can do that for you,' Belinda said as she joined them with her own baby trolley. 'Consider it my christening gift – like the fairy godmothers.'

Sarah's eyes sparkled. For the first time, we saw the woman she had been, and the one she could be again soon.

Fiona and her badge helped expedite some of Audrey's to-do list. But like a rat flushed from a drain pipe, locking the bank accounts brought Tim to their ward. We got forewarning because, thanks to Fiona, he was under surveillance. She got the call the minute he turned in the direction of the hospital.

As synchronised as a murmuration, the women of Ward D all pushed their trolleys to the nursery where the babies were locked away. They returned to their room with lies on their tongues.

Tim signed in, barely acknowledged me, and stalked off to Ward D. I followed at a discrete distance. He ignored the other three and went straight to Sarah's bedside.

'Where's the baby?' he said.

Sarah seemed calm, but from where I stood, I could sense her nerves. 'They give the mums a break and take them to the nursery.'

Tim looked suspiciously at the other three women.

'Best hour of the day,' said Fiona loudly, then laughed.

Tim seemed to relax when he saw they didn't have their babies either.

'Look, there's something wrong with our—' He stopped when he saw all the women were staring at him. He walked around the bed, grabbed the curtain and it zinged around the rail, blocking off our line of sight.

Murmured words float around the curtain. '…bank accounts… blocked…' And then an angry, 'Get on your phone and fix it!' The clatter of a hospital tray, pushed. The flap of the curtain. Tim stalking out of the room.

'Gee, he's a peach,' said Belinda once he had gone.

Fiona laughed. Then Audrey, then finally, Sarah.

'I should have swiped left.' Sarah struggled off her bed and came to stand closer to the others. She looked at Audrey. 'The bank account block worked. He's furious.'

A message pinged on Fiona's phone. 'The warrants are ready.'

'We need theme music,' said Audrey as she struggled from her bed. 'Like Eye of the Tiger.'

Belinda found it on Spotify and the tinny lyrics floated from her phone as the four tiger mothers walked slowly back to the nursery to retrieve their cubs.

What a difference a day makes. I could sense a shift in the energy before Tim even reached the nurses' station. He scrawled his name and address on the sign-in sheet, then looked up as the unformed cops – three of them – approached him. He put down the pen, stood straight, then slowly, casually reached into his back pocket.

Luckily, I was watching his every move like a hawk. I knew about the switchblade he carried in his back pocket and I'd been there when Fiona had telephoned her colleagues to brief them on the arrest. Suspect will be armed.

As the three cops approached from the corridor, I moved in behind. I could see the shape of the knife as he grasped it with his fingers and began sliding it slowly from this pocket.

Not on my watch.

Before the cops reached him and before he got the chance to pull out the knife, I pounced. My full weight – slamming into him from behind – made him fly forward and clip his chin on the desk as he went down with a satisfying thwack.

As soon as I made my move, so did everybody else. Tim grappled to retrieve the knife, wriggling like larvae on the floor. The cops all joined me, trying to grab bits of him.

Suddenly, Tim screamed like a chimpanzee – a high screech – and the knife went skidding across the floor. Then I moved back and let the cops do their job. Handcuffs. Grabbed. Dragged to his feet.

Tim looked at me. Murder in his eyes. 'She bit me!'

One of the cops grinned at me. 'You bite him?'

I blushed slightly. Looked up at the ceiling. Didn't answer. Old habits were hard to break.

'Good girl,' said the cop with a wink.

Suddenly, Fiona was there next to me, her hand protectively on my collar. 'She used to be a police dog,' she told the cops as they marched Tim off towards the exit.

Blood and Bone

Narrelle M Harris

Kearney & Sminth: Blood and Bone

L UCIUS KEARNEY WALKED THREE TIMES AROUND THE BURNT OUT SHELL of The Haymarket Theatre, senses alert, but nothing emanated from it but the acrid smell of cinders and a faint whiff of pitch. Only its Bourke Street façade still stood: the theatre's iron roof had caved in, exposing broken and scorched timbers, and its eastern wall had collapsed and crushed a handful of market stalls. Nearby, the barroom of the Haymarket Hotel hadn't burned but only because it was waterlogged from the efforts to save the site.

The destruction was a shame, but perfectly natural. It wasn't the source of the uneasiness Magnus Sminth swore was creeping into their adopted city. Their guardianship had lasted twenty years so far. Various things had stalked the Melbourne streets during that period. Lucius and Magnus made it their business to stalk them back. At the end of it, they'd acquired a large house and a reputation, in certain quarters.

After his clockwise walk, Lucius turned and walked three times anti-clockwise, but it revealed no hidden power and only exposed him to the stink of the sewerage in the drains on either side of the road. He hoped an early October rain would give him and the city some respite in the next few days, but didn't fancy his luck. The air promised sun for a week or more. Perhaps they would bake the muck and seal the stink in.

Magnus, his partner and, in his way, family heirloom, had been walking clockwise and widdershins around the church in Richmond that had met a similar fiery fate. Now Magnus stepped out of the night to meet him at the corner of Bourke and Stephen Streets.

Though one was tall and wiry and the other short and stocky, they looked remarkably alike: blue-eyed, dark-haired, pale-skinned as they were. Though unrelated, once they had passed for brothers. Now, Magnus – 300 years old and simultaneously an un-ageing 22 – appeared so young as to be Lucius's son. One day, the magician would seem to be Lucius' grandson, and then in time Magnus would mourn his loss, as he had lost so many of Lucius's clan over the centuries.

'The church's outer roof burned only; though the little House of God is wet through now,' he reported. 'I asked the rats, but the flames had an innocent enough beginning. How fare thee?'

'No sign of devilry. Are you sure you felt it?'

Magnus looked down his long, thin nose, haughty and hurt in equal measure. 'Something brews here, my Luke, never doubt me.'

Lucius grimaced. 'Sorry. Stupid question. What now?'

Magnus' shoulders twitched. 'I will continue to walk. I will ask the rats. Some cats also may speak to me.'

'I'll come with you.'

'No. You sleep. Something comes. The world winds up, coils. You must be rested.'

Lucius left Magnus to his investigations. Still, although their home was only a block away down Stephen Street, he decided to walk the longest way, marking tiny sigils in chalk on the brick walls as he passed. Three times clockwise, three times widdershins, around the Flinders, Collins, Russell, and Stephens block. Coiling, as Magnus said, the portents sitting heavy in the energy of the world. Better to call it close and deal with it on their own terms than let it burst randomly free, not knowing what brutal damage may result.

The protection of Melbourne was their chosen calling, after all.

The first day of October was as sunny as expected, and nothing dread had occurred overnight. Lucius and Magnus both greeted the day in better moods than in last night's tense patrolling.

Perhaps Magnus had spent too long conversing with Melbourne's creatures, however. He'd fallen easily into his other shape. Lucius was beginning to worry about how often Magnus did this now, and how often he forgot to hide parts of his rat self when he was on two legs again. He was on four legs now, sitting on Lucius's shoulder and squeaking at the window. Lucius' grandfather had once conversed with rat-Magnus, and when Lucius was an infant, the enchanted rat would curl beside his soft baby face and sing falsetto nursery rhymes. But speech in this form too was a diminishing skill, and another reason for Lucius to worry.

Lucius pulled aside the sitting room curtain to see a woman pacing the footpath below. She hardly seemed a Messenger of Doom, but he was almost certain she was here because of the previous night's efforts.

The rat on his shoulder squeaked approbation of their visitor, the sound barely recognisable as the words *fair maiden*.

'None of that, Magnus,' Lucius admonished him. 'I hardly think she's knocking door to door for a beau.'

Magnus ran down Lucius's arm to the windowsill, then down the curtain to the floor, and a moment later his wiry human self stood in the rat's place.

'Yet deny not the possibility,' he said. 'Love's vi–'

'Whiskers,' said Lucius.

Magnus' long fingers felt his upper lip, where ratty whiskers still sprung out. They vanished in a trice and he continued with his observations. 'Love's visitation cannot be foreseen, and–'

'And if you start on about how I'm losing my youth and my looks, and must marry while someone will still have me, Magnus, I'll hex you. We've other concerns today, at any rate.'

The woman on Stephen Street rapped abruptly on the door and waited, back straight as a poker. Lucius could only see the top of her elegant hat, but he approved of her posture and the determined way she awaited an answer to her summons. He'd give Magnus this much: he knew the kind of woman that Lucius found appealing.

He stood by the fireplace and affected a commanding nonchalance, never an easy feat as a short, stocky man of middle age, born in East London, even if he had mostly shed the accent. Magnus, whose manners fluctuated between man and rat, stood on the carpet, alert and curious. They heard footsteps on the steps and a moment later, their maid Emma opened the door and bobbed a curtsey.

'A visitor for you, sir. Miss Muriel Frisk, Sir.'

'Tail,' snapped Lucius sharply, sotto voce.

Magnus, with an alarmed look down at the tip of his pink tail still visible under the hem of his trousers, muttered, 'Go to!' and it vanished just as their visitor was ushered into the parlour.

The young lady was perhaps in her mid-twenties, and of resolute and regal bearing. She was taller than Lucius, with smooth brown skin, elegant gloved hands, a sensitive full mouth, and dark, clever eyes – and she was the most handsome woman Lucius had seen in a long time. Her curly black hair was piled high under her dark blue hat, and her penetrating eyes observed him and Magnus from under the brim.

'Welcome, Miss Frisk. I'm Lucius Kearney, and this is my partner, Magnus Sminth. Thank you, Emma. Some tea, please?'

Emma bobbed and departed, leaving Miss Frisk coolly assessing the men of the house.

'You're not what I was expecting,' said the lady at length, her accent revealing her American origins. New York, Lucius guessed, though he only recognised three American accents – east, west and south.

'What were you expecting?' Magnus asked immediately, his blue eyes gleaming with interest.

Miss Frisk, hands folded primly in front of her, replied, 'Fortune tellers are usually artistic older ladies wearing many scarves, too much lace, and redolent with the scent of roses and disrepute.'

Magnus burst out in delighted laughter and Lucius found his approval of their disdainful visitor increasing.

'Well, as you may know,' he responded, 'fortune telling is illegal in the Australian Colonies. The law says it's obtaining funds by fraud.'

'Are you suggesting that your reputation is unearned and your work a deception?'

'Hardly,' Lucius responded with a quick grin. 'The police come to us from time to time, as it happens, though they don't like to. It makes them uncomfortable, especially as we aren't frauds.'

Emma arrived with the tea things and bustled about the table, setting down cups, teapot, sugar and milk. Miss Frisk unpinned her hat and took a seat at the little table; for all her scepticism obviously intending to stay.

Niceties were observed. Lucius turned the pot three times clockwise; Magnus turned it three times widdershins, then Miss Frisk declined Madeira cake, sipped her tea and addressed her business.

'I'm told you may help me find my brother,' Miss Frisk said. 'His name is Braybee Frisk and he vanished a week ago. At first I thought he had gone on a jaunt with friends, but he would never leave without a word to me.'

'Wouldn't he?' Lucius asked. He knew many a young fellow who wouldn't hesitate to take off on a lark. He and Magnus had come to Australia on a lark of sorts, at the start of the gold rush.

'He would not,' she replied brusquely. 'We are musicians and perform together for our livelihood. His violin is still in our rooms. Even if he'd leave me, he would never abandon his instrument.'

Magnus leaned towards her, his long, lean fingers laced together and his nose fairly twitching with interest. 'What say the constabulary?'

'That he's gone to the goldfields, in all probability. They're not very interested in my opinion to the contrary. Of course I investigated the possibility. Nobody admits to selling him passage or a horse, or any equipment. I spoke to his friends, who only know he was intending to meet a particular friend. None of them knew this fellow's name, so I conclude he's either responsible for Bray's disappearance or he's likewise vanished.'

Lucius turned his cup in the saucer three times, clockwise first, then three times in the other direction. 'I read about your brother's disappearance in *The Argus, The Advertiser,* even *Melbourne Punch* gave his disappearance a few lines. You were quoted, though nobody took you very seriously.'

'No,' said Miss Frisk. 'I'm triply cursed: as a woman, as an American woman, and as a black American woman at that. Your newspapermen give me little credence. They said I was hysterical.' Her ladylike snort was decisive on her opinion of Australian newspapermen.

Lucius couldn't help a laugh, but sobered in the face of her glare. 'You're the least hysterical and most straightforward woman I've yet met in Melbourne,' he said. 'Which is why I wonder why you're here, to see the likes of Magnus and me.'

'Desperation,' she replied crisply. 'Your name was suggested in the wariest of tones by Sergeant Dayton, who at least has some compassion for my fears. All other avenues of investigation have led nowhere. The papers think I'm having hysterical fantasies, and Bray's friends are all useless. I know my brother is still alive, but–'

'Why?'

Miss Frisk stared primly at Lucius before admitting, 'I feel it.'

'Where do you feel it? In your heart? Your head? Your bones?'

She fixed him with her black eyes. 'In my blood, Mr Kearney. In my soul. He and I are twins and I've always known when he was in trouble, as he knows when I need him. I can't find him, but I know he's alive.' She tilted her chin up then, defiant, expecting mockery.

Magnus helped himself to Madeira cake but ate it with his fingers instead of a fork. 'Ah, my Lady. I see in thine eyes the conviction of your declaration. Yet so many mothers and sisters cry out that they would know if harm befell one they love. For most 'tis but a heart's deep wish and no true Art. To know if your blood calls to his needs some other proof. What more does your blood tell you?'

He turned his teacup three times widdershins with one hand, ate cake with the other. 'Tell me all.'

Miss Frisk spoke as she watched how Magnus ate his cake in nibbles from between his fingers. 'I know he's warm and fed but imprisoned. I know he's afraid. I know he's angry.'

Magnus' nose twitched. Lucius held out his hand to her, palm up. 'Remove your glove for me, and I'll see what else your blood has to say.'

The command was alarming, but Miss Frisk obeyed. She tugged her glove off and held her slender hand out to this strange man. Lucius took it and examined the lines of her palm, the shape of her knuckles, the ridge of tendon and the lines of her veins beneath the delicate skin of her wrist.

He handed her a knife – not the blunt cake knife, but his own sharp pocket blade. 'I need a little blood. Not much. I could cut you but I thought you might feel safer doing it yourself.'

Miss Frisk met Lucius's steady gaze. 'You are mad and I should leave.'

'So you should. But you came to suspected fortune tellers on the advice of a colonial peeler because your blood tells you Braybee Frisk is a prisoner. You already knew you'd get no ordinary help here. Human agency has failed you. Something more arcane may prove worthwhile, if his blood truly calls to yours.'

'Is this black magic?'

'Dark magic, yes,' Lucius conceded. 'That's not the same as wicked magic. Sometimes dark deeds need dark magic to bring them into the light. Magic can't all be sunny spells for safe travels and banishing warts.'

Muriel Frisk laughed then, a breathless bark. 'Sergeant Dayton warned me that your family would be frightening.'

'I'm not his father,' said Lucius. 'More like…'

'Brothers,' said Magnus.

'Or cousins. Only not.'

'And yet, we are,' said Magnus. 'For I have served Luke's family, and they have served me, for almost three hundred years.'

And he promptly, there on the table, turned once more into a rat. His clothes and all vanished into the curious space where he kept all his human bulk, and as an abnormally large, sleek, grey-brown Norway rat Magnus stood on the dish with the remainder of his cake. He took up a piece in his clever paws and nibbled away. His blue eyes were now black beads, but they held the same expression of delighted curiosity.

'Are you frightened yet?' asked Lucius in a tone of mild curiosity.

'I feel as though I ought to be, but he's a dear little thing.' With that, Miss Frisk took Lucius's offered knife and jabbed the pad of her forefinger. Lucius took her hand and turned it so that blood dripped into his tea, and then onto the Madeira cake. He gave her a cloth napkin in which to wrap her tiny wound.

He turned his cup three times widdershins, then sipped the tea in which her blood swirled. Magnus' ratty fingers turned the plate three times, also anti-clockwise, and then he nibbled the blood soaked cake.

The air around them swirled indefinably – an eddy of dust motes; a twist in the reflection of light; the energy around them wound up tight by all the twisting of the brew.

Miss Frisk held her breath.

The man and the rat raised chins, lifted noses and fingers into the swirling motes, inhaled. They drew something from the eddy that Muriel Fisk couldn't see. And then, with the slight scent of tea and rust, the coiled air-and-light unfurled.

The man and the rat exchanged glances. 'Well, that's a rare gift and a true one,' Magnus said.

'He's alive, as you say, Miss Frisk, but you're correct that something's very wrong,' Lucius said. 'I recall from the *Punch* article that your brother had been to visit Melbourne Zoo on the day he disappeared?'

'I believe so. He told me he was to meet there with a friend. They wanted to see the marsupial wolves.'

'We'll begin there then. As luck would have it, we have an avenue of inquiry there not available to the police.'

'I shall accompany you,' Miss Frisk said, and promptly rose and reached for her hat. She slid the pin through hat and hair and her expression was such that Lucius felt sure she knew how to use it as a weapon, should circumstances call for it.

Truly, he liked her very much, but he knew better than to believe that she was a manifestation of love's visitation. In all his 38 years, love had visited but rarely, and had never stayed.

Being a gentleman by hard-practised habit if not by birth, Lucius paid Miss Frisk's entry fee to the Zoological Gardens, though his generosity was undercut by the fact he smuggled Magnus-as-rat through the gates inside his deep coat pocket. Miss Frisk cast a speculative glance towards that pocket from time to time – Lucius detected apprehension but also curiosity in that look. Her lack of outright alarm was intriguing.

Under the guidance of director Albert le Souef, the gardens had become a much more densely populated place in the last year. His new acquisitions – monkeys, birds, lions, and the like, could be heard calling from time to time as they walked to their destination.

The animal held in this enclosure was, according to the sign, a male American Black Bear. The enclosure was a sorry circus cage and the great black bear sleeping behind the bars can't have enjoyed its limitations.

'Bern,' Lucius called to it. 'Bern, wake up!'

The bear lifted his great shaggy head and yawned at them, displaying all his many teeth and long, long tongue. Then he lay his head down on his great clawed paws again.

'Bern, you lazy beast, I want a word!'

Magnus chittered in Lucius's pocket. Lucius extended his arm towards the bear cage, fingers dangerously close to that savage maw and, to Miss Frisk's obvious disquiet, Magnus ran from pocket to shoulder and along Lucius's outstretched arm until he could take a leap into the enclosure and landed on the bear's face.

Miss Frisk gasped.

The bear awoke and stared cross-eyed at the man-rat perched on his nose.

'Bern,' said Lucius impatiently. 'We'll let you get back to allowing horrid little tykes to throw nuts at you soon, but we've some questions.'

The bear opened his mouth and spoke. 'Get off my face, Magnus, you bastard, or I'll snap you in two.'

Magnus merely spread his ratty self out to grasp the bear by his eyebrows and pulled.

'Ow, ow, ow,' complained the bear. He shook his head, sending Magnus flying into the straw. 'You little shit.' And then the bear saw the mortified face of the young woman outside the bars. 'Bloody hell, Luke, some warning. There's a lady.'

'I know there's a lady,' said Lucius. 'We're looking for her brother, who came here a week ago, so his friends say. I don't suppose you've noticed anything odd?'

Bern the talking bear huffed and sat on his haunches. Stretched. 'Odder than me?'

'You're just a damned lazy wizard who can't be bothered unravelling the charm that trapped you,' said Lucius. 'I could do it for you, if you ask nicely. Probably,' he added after a beat.

'Nooo,' said Bern in his gruff voice, his snout unnaturally forming words never meant for a mouth like that. 'It's not bad here. Plenty of food. Sunny days. Old Man le Souef says he'll make a proper bear pit soon, so that'll be nice.'

'Mr le Souef knows you're not really a bear?' asked Miss Frisk in surprise.

The bear laughed. 'No, Miss. I think his eyes would pop out if he knew. It was a fair transaction though, and he paid good money to the sailor who brought me in. What the sailor knew, that's another matter. I'll settle that score later. Maybe.'

Lucius sighed and added, 'Bern is the laziest person of power I have ever known, apart from the energy he expended on the fool experiment that transformed him.'

Magnus had begun to climb up Bern's flanks towards his face again. Bern looked at his progress from under his bear arm. 'I'm not the only one for fool experiments,' he said. 'Hey, Magnus?'

'Enough,' said Lucius. 'Miss Frisk's brother. Any ideas?'

Bern leaned towards her, stuck his snout through the bars and took a long sniff. Miss Frisk gave him an affronted frown.

Bern laughed, which was deeply alarming given his shape and his gravelly growling voice and his teeth. 'You're a brave one,' he said.

'Do you know what became of my brother?' she demanded.

'No,' he said, withdrawing, 'But I know he was here. Your scent is something of a sibling to another that's been hanging around, but it's strange. You're strange too, but it's not the same strange.'

'Being a bear has addled your brain,' Lucius said lightly. 'Do you have anything more useful for us?'

'A man has visited the zoo every day this week,' Bern said. 'He brought a wriggling bag with him the first time and it was empty when he left. He's an odd-smelling thing too. The magic on him smells out of balance. Rotten, maybe. I could tell you better if I was human, but then I don't think I'd smell it. You can have clarity or you can have instinct, but not both.'

'What about this man?'

Bern rose up and grasped the bars with his threatening claws. He lifted his chin and grunted into the sky. A flock of sparrows flitted past, chirping, and he lumbered back to all fours.

'You speak with birds?' Miss Frisk asked.

'Sometimes,' said Bern. 'They're mostly idiots. They've been keeping an eye on this man for me. I don't like him and I think he knows what I am. He's at the monkey cages, even now. He goes there every day and leers at the poor things. You can hear them screeching back at him most days. They're peculiar too. I don't know if he's involved, but where one off kilter scent goes, others gather, as you well know.'

'Aye,' Lucius agreed. 'Strangeness attracts strangeness. It's how I found you, after all.'

'Yes, and you keep disrupting my sleep. Away with you, little warlock. Speaking makes this jaw ache.' The bear held out a paw and Magnus ran down the dark fur and leapt onto Lucius's shoulder.

'I'll bring you some apples tomorrow. And maybe one of Magnus' books on transformations?'

'Later, later. Let's find a new bear for the Old Man first. He's been very nice to me and I don't want to leave him a bear short.'

'Lazy brute.'

Bern just grunted and settled back down to sleep.

Muriel Frisk was very quiet as she walked beside Lucius towards the screech of the monkey cages. Magnus had run off to the grassy verge and returned a moment later in his human form. Miss Frisk cast him a brief glance then continued on, introspective.

'How are you?' Lucius asked, because he genuinely didn't know. This mighty woman with Art in her blood seemed to be taking flesh magic in her stride.

'Chastened,' she replied quietly, which was more puzzling than her acceptance of things.

Before he could formulate another question, the three of them came upon the cluster of circus cages containing the monkeys. Different breeds were held in the pen, though most had retreated to the far reaches, clinging to tree trunks and high up bars in favour of the two white-faced capuchins at the front of the cage. Those two held onto each other and bared their teeth at the man who stood before them on the path, leaning on a silver-topped cane.

'You degrade yourself and your family name,' said the man evenly, inflexibly, to the angrier of the furious pair. 'I shall restore you when you've restored your honour. So I tell you again: you must eradicate him, with your own hand. I've made it easy for you.'

The capuchin so addressed wrapped its arms more tightly around its companion and very deliberately planted a puckered kiss on the other's white face.

The man's ruddy face went almost purple in response. 'How dare you defy me?'

'Forsooth, tis a churlish monkey indeed,' said Magnus, making the man jump. He glared at the wiry, whiskery stranger at his elbow. Magnus grinned at him. 'Thou art a commander of apes, I see, or would be, if only you can induce the poor beasts to listen.'

Lucius would have been happy to see what Magnus did next – he was not always predictable, and he'd forgotten to reel in his whiskers and tail again – but Miss Frisk bypassed all that by running to the cage, hands outstretched.

'Bray!'

The second capuchin, receiver of the defiant kiss, leapt onto the bars and screeched. One long, skinny, hairy, black arm reached towards her. Its tiny hand met her fingers and all of Miss Frisk's careful control was blasted away. She turned on the ruddy-faced man.

'How dare you, sir! Restore my brother to his true form at once!'

The man sneered. 'All I see here are monkeys.'

Magnus bumped the man's shoulder with his own. 'Thou art not a natural dissembler, for the lie falls heavy off your tongue. I see here two transformed boys, and it's clear to any eye of power that this one is kin to the lady. The other is…' Magnus arched an eyebrow. 'Kin to thyself? Ho, Luke, what a beast is here, who would curse his son as easily as a stranger!'

'What else is a father to do,' growled the man, 'when his son lies like a beast with another man?'

'Why, let love take its course,' said Magnus, who had lived a long life and treasured his fleeting loves too well to be much concerned with such paltry matters. ''Tis hardly against nature, and such as we care not what men say is against God.'

'Says another beast,' was the angry response. 'You are neither rat nor man but something far less than either.' He raised his cane in one hand and muttered words in an arcane language.

'Hold on, you,' started Lucius, swiftly raising his own hands and summoning the magic at his command.

A coil of energy warped the air between the man's cane and his forehead: where a cold grey eye opened horribly. The warping air arrowed then between that awful third eye and Magnus.

Magnus twisted away from the channel of energy, changed shape and dropped with a heavy thud to the path; the capuchins both shrieked fury. Lucius grasped for the cane and so put himself in the sightlines of that unpleasant, bulging, supernatural eye. The air warped between them and Lucius, unable, like Magnus, to make himself a smaller target, began to murmur a wall of protection that he wasn't sure would hold.

But before he could utter more loudly, Miss Frisk beside him gave voice to a sudden arpeggio of rising and falling notes, high and clear, that augmented Lucius's forming spell. Even as the song and spell bound together, Miss Frisk lunged at their assailant's third eye with her hatpin. The point of it penetrated to the bone through the awful thing. He roared in pain and rage, dropping his cane, covering his forehead with both hands. He fell to his knees, howling and cursing.

Between his yells and the screams of the capuchins, it was a wonder that everyone in the zoo wasn't running towards them.

Well, thought Lucius, they are running *away* and that's a better thing.

Miss Frisk stood over the man, breathing heavily. The flurry of notes she'd sung still hung in the air, reverberating with magic.

'Miss Frisk, you are a revelation!' Lucius declared, carefully picking up the cane. 'Did you know you could do that?'

Miss Frisk panted. 'No,' she said. 'That is to say, yes. Or rather.' She held the hatpin in a tight grip. 'I have suspected but not known. Not for sure. I don't know how I know to sing like that. I don't know what I am, that I can do that.'

'Hush, my lady, hush, be not afeared,' Magnus had regained his form and patted kindly at her wrists.

'Make him give me back my brother!' Miss Frisk demanded, in tears for the first time.

Lucius weighed the cane in his hand and eyed its former wielder. 'Magnus, best give us some room to work, if you can.'

'Oh, aye, that I can,' said Magnus. He walked around the little group, clockwise, then widdershins, clockwise, back again, muttering protection spells as he went, making a shield of the air around them. He walked the boundary as Lucius dealt with the warlock.

'You, sir.' Lucius poked at the man on the ground. 'What's your name?'

'Smith.' A snarl.

'Oh, don't,' said Lucius, annoyed. Magnus sometimes used a similar name when one was required of him. 'I don't need your name for anything more than manners: Magnus has for years being trying to teach them to me. All I need now is blood and bone, and the latter is already in here.' He gripped the cane firmly.

The man glared his defiance. 'I am Henry Ruben and I will turn you into a toad.'

Lucius snorted. 'Not likely, you won't. Not without this. Whose bone is in the cane, by the way?' He examined it, then held it to his ear as though it spoke to him. 'Oh you barbarian,' he said, glaring at Ruben. 'A child's arm bones are sealed in this cane. You really are the slimy rot at the bottom of the corroded casket, aren't you? There, there,' he addressed the cane again. 'He won't keep you, I swear. I shall lay you to rest, as you ought to have been. May I ask for your help, though? It isn't the son's fault, much less Bray's.'

The cane twitched in his hand. Ruben twitched on the ground.

Lucius took out his pocket knife and opened the blade.

'I require the blood of the mage who conjured the transformation, Mr Ruben,' Lucius continued. 'I should prefer not to cut your throat for it. That would be distressing to everyone, and most especially Miss Frisk, despite her magnificent courage and splendid aim with a hatpin.'

'Go to hell.'

'You first, Mr Ruben. I'm not an amateur, you know. Transformation magic is done with blood and bone; therefore your victims must be released with blood and bone. I've asked the bones in the centre of your cane if they will share their power, and I'll settle for only blood from you. I'll take both from you, though, if you insist. Some fingers or your hand would be enough, I think. The poor dead child you've trapped in here has been forced to enough wicked magic.'

Mr Ruben blinked at him with his two human eyes, assessing the threat, but there was no doubt. Lucius's ruthless expression did not speak of kindness or squeamishness. Not to squander upon him, at any rate. Still, Ruben curled his hands into fists, refusing to make it easy.

Magnus gave Miss Frisk's wrist a final pat and he said, 'Fear not. Your brother is at hand. Perhaps if you would give to Luke your weapon?' He gently took the hatpin from her, gave it to Lucius.

'Don't look, Miss Frisk,' said Lucius.

'I will,' she said defiantly. 'I haven't hidden yet and I won't start now.'

Lucius beamed at her, proud of her even though he had nothing to do with her courage. Then he plunged his knife into the fleshiest part of Ruben's left bicep and pulled it out again so that a gout of blood spurted out. While Ruben cried out in pain and anger, Lucius wiped the cane handle over the bloody wound as well. Then he drew the hat pin over the bloodied handle before pushing the point of it into the wood. Despite the sturdiness of the cane, the pin slid easily into its centre, coming to rest against the concealed bones, tip scraping against the ivory.

He drew it out again and carefully handed the pin back to Magnus.

The monkeys had become very quiet, waiting expectantly for Magnus' assistance. He became a rat again, holding the pin in his teeth by the unbloodied head, and scurried into the cage. He sat with them on their perch by the bars. His tail wound around their tiny capuchin hands, linked in a worried grip.

Then he took the pin in his little ratty paws and jabbed it quite through their joined hands.

As one they shrieked and then suddenly two young men – one milk-pale, the other dark-skinned – were lying in the bottom of the monkey cage, naked, spots of blood on their hands, but human again.

Magnus rose up between them, whiskery and with his tail out, but clothed. He'd had long, long practice at where to put the rest of himself when he shrank to rat size, and how to fetch it back again.

His eyes twinkled at Lucius through the bars of the monkey cage. 'I am forgetful. I should first have unlocked the gate,' said he.

Poor Mr le Souef was so scandalised by so many things at once – the disruption to his zoo and the families who attended it; the naked men in the monkey cage with the peculiar, whiskery fellow; the bleeding, belligerent, red-faced gentleman on the path and the grim little man with him; the attractive, dark-skinned young lady being subjected to these appalling insults to her sex and sensitivities – that he hardly knew where to begin shouting.

He chose instead to guide the discomposed young woman away from the indecent scene. When he turned back, however, the caged men and the grim fellow were gone, leaving only the heavy set man bleeding from head and arm, who refused to say a word of what had been happening.

Miss Frisk watched Mr le Souef dash about, hand in his hair, demanding explanations. Two of his burly keepers arrived and, taking the truculent Mr Ruben by the arms, hauled him to the office for medical aid and interrogation.

'Psst.'

She turned. Lucius Kearney gestured to her from along the path. She didn't move.

'How is it that these people don't see you?' she demanded in a hissing whisper.

'Perception magic,' Lucius whispered back. 'It will hold long enough for us escape attention, but we mustn't dawdle. We need to get your brother and his sweetheart away from that evil bastard, Ruben. Pardon my language.'

At mention of her brother, who stood looking shaken behind Lucius and Magnus, Miss Frisk ran to him, embracing him briefly but fiercely. Then, nose wrinkling, she drew back.

'Did Magnus conjure these clothes for you?' she asked, puzzled, at the smelly, shabby clothes in which Bray and his friend were now clad.

Magnus' bright-eyed grin was back. 'I summoned them, my lady, from nearby. The keepers will be astonished at the theft from their hut, but their need is greater.'

'How did you escape the cage?'

'Luke has a charm which turns iron to air, for a time. We must be away, my lady.'

'Come along while Magnus' deflection spell holds around us,' said Lucius.

Miss Frisk, her brother and his friend dashed along the path between the two wizards, and out through the gates, where Lucius summoned – more correctly, compelled – a cab and they piled inside. Through the roof they heard the cabbie complain about their combined weight but the carriage lurched away and took them back to the city.

The rescued men sat, twitching slightly and still disconcerted, in Lucius's parlour. Their appropriated clothes emanated the reek of unwashed skin and compost. Miss Frisk had taken on the duties of a hostess, sending Emma for tea and adding plenty of sugar to the cups she poured for her brother and his friend.

Lucius had laid the confiscated cane on one end of the table where he and Magnus regarded it speculatively.

'Tell me, Young Ruben, where did your father get this cane?'

'Orlando, please. And he obtained it early last year. Just before our fortunes changed.'

'For the better or the worse?' Magnus asked.

'Better, at the start,' said Orlando, hands clasped about the teacup, looking much younger than his 21 years. Braybee Frisk sat close by him, not quite daring to hold the boy's hand for comfort.

'Our family found old rivals falling on bad times, lifting my father and his business dealings up in equal measure. And then the tide began to turn. Some angry men began to visit us in the dead of night, and in the dead of night my father bundled us out of the house and onto a ship for Australia. The vessel docked in Melbourne a month ago.'

'I told thee so,' said Magnus, thoroughly vindicated.

'Yes, Magnus. I know. I'm sorry.' Lucius's confession didn't keep the smug grin from Magnus' face.

Lucius went back to questioning Ruben's son. 'What business is your father in?'

'I'm not entirely sure. He traded on the stock market and in merchant vessels. Other ships sank at sea, but never the ones he had invested in. Stocks fell when he wanted to buy, rose when he wanted to sell. It was uncanny good luck.'

'Uncanny forsooth,' said Magnus, his fingers skittering along the table beside the cane. 'He stole innocent bones and made a tool to feed his greed. But he forgot or did not understand the cost. The greater the imbalance in his favour, the greater the swing in fortunes to reset the scale.'

'Ha,' Orlando's laugh was feeble and still half afraid. 'He always said he made his own luck. What will happen to him now?'

'After the zookeeper has turned him out and the officers of the law have had their say? Well, we shall have to call on him to discuss that. Perhaps you'd be so kind as to escort us to your house for that conversation.'

Orlando groaned and buried his head in his hands. Bray's strong hands immediately reached for the lad, bravely giving comfort, for he hadn't realised yet that nobody in this room would censure him. 'Oh leave him alone; he's had enough of that old brute. See what he did to us? I was a *monkey*!'

'A very charming little monkey, too,' said Magnus, amused.

'Don't,' said Miss Frisk suddenly. 'I know it's nothing to you to be a man one moment and a beast the next, but it's not nothing to us. Whatever we are.' Her voice dropped at the end and she studied her fingers.

'Oh, my lady,' Magnus said gently. 'Know you not what you are? You have the Minstrel Tongue.'

'And what's that?' she asked sharply.

'You know,' Lucius told her, just as sharp. 'In part, at least.' At her defiant look, he added, 'You said you felt chastened, and I've been wondering what you meant. What were your expectations when you came to us? How did we fail to meet them, that after conversing with a shape-shifted bear you felt chastised?'

The brave young woman raised her chin and met his eyes. 'I thought you would be amoral at best; or malicious. I thought you would want a high price for helping me, but I had nowhere left to turn. I know that I have some kind of magic in my voice, but I was sure when I came to you that I would have to guard against how you might corrupt me. But you're...ruthless, but just. Kind to those who need it. And...not at all menacing.'

'Go to, my lady, you will offend his keen professional pride!' Magnus' eyes were gleaming with humour again.

'And you,' she said, looking at Magnus, 'are unnatural but you are no more evil than I am. Indeed, I find you curiously sweet.'

'Now, my girl, you offend mine!' But he was still brimming with laughter. 'But in truth, you should understand that the power Luke and I wield comes of study and intent. We have Art in us, and use it to bend nature to our will. That is very unlike the Minstrel Tongue, which is a gift of nature Herself. She is mindful of her own balance. Where she grows the poison, she also grows the cure.'

'Minstrel Tongue?' Braybee interjected. 'Does he mean the music, Muriel? Your voice and my violin?'

'He does.'

'When our home in Manhattan burned down in the '64 riots,' he told Magnus earnestly, 'Muriel sang to the flames and made a path out of it. We'd have burned to death along with our parents if she hadn't. I suspect my violin has some power in it too, but I've been wary to try anything.'

'Lucius could show you better how to channel it,' offered Magnus, a little slyly.

'In the meantime,' said Lucius pointedly, rising, 'Magnus, you should take Orlando home for fresh clothing at least, and to ensure that Ruben senior has no more nasty artefacts hidden in his study.'

'Don't make me go back there, it's an awful place,' wailed young Orlando. 'I can't live in it a moment longer. He turned me into a monkey! He wanted me to kill Bray!'

'We have so many empty rooms,' said Magnus, waving his long fingers about, indicating the weight of the whole building hanging above them. 'We long ago thought to have filled them with Luke's children, but alas, we have only the cook and maid below, Luke above and me as I rattle about the attic with my books. I shall have Emma shake the dust out of a chamber and you may stay as long as you like. May he not, Luke?'

'Of course,' Lucius assented. 'As soon as we have removed any cruelly made devices from his father's lair.'

Orlando seemed distracted by the notion of his father having a lair. Bray insisted that he would accompany his anxious lover, though he wished to stop at the lodgings in Powlett Street he shared with his sister, for clothes that fitted and did not smell like the zoo.

'Come with us, Muriel.'

'I'd like your sister's aid, if she'd be so kind,' Lucius said.

'If I can be of any help,' she said, inclining her head. She had set her hair and then hat to rights again, though without the pin which had been used so brutally to gain such noble results – the restoration of her brother and his lover. Muriel knew what the world thought of such assignations, but she knew Bray had a good and loving heart. If he chose to love a skinny, pale English boy, then let him love.

Once they had gone, Lucius placed his hand on the cane. 'I want to set the little one free, and I think a song from a Minstrel would help ease its way. Do you mind?'

'I would be honoured to set the poor mite to rest.'

They walked to the Yarra River, which flowed past the end of Stephen Street, with the cane wrapped in clean white cloth. They turned east, then crossed the river at Prince's Bridge and into Muller's verdant Botanical Gardens.

'Shouldn't we take it to consecrated ground?' Muriel asked.

'I don't believe the child Christian,' Lucius said, 'though I can't work out if that means it wasn't baptised or whether the poor little thing was from another faith. It doesn't communicate in words, exactly. But I think some wholesome earth under God's blue sky and a song to see them off will be ceremony enough. Don't you?'

Put like that, it seemed the most natural thing. Beneath a leafy English Oak, Lucius knelt and conjured a narrow but deep hole. With his strong hands, he cracked the knob of the cane and split the whole along one side until two slender bones, the radius and ulna of a child no more than seven or eight, were revealed. These he gently tipped into a silk handkerchief he took from his pocket, then folded the corners over the remains.

'I release you, little one. Return to the earth, return to the world. You did no willing harm and the penance will not be paid by you.'

He lowered the makeshift shroud into the hole and looked to Muriel, who began to sing, not a church hymn, but something simpler and older. She hadn't even realised she knew the words until she sang them.

> *'Be at peace 'neath sun and moon,*
> *Be innocent of pain*
> *The bosom of our mother earth*
> *Holds her child once again.'*

Lucius waited until the last note faded, and then ran his palm over the ground. The hole sealed up after him, leaving the rich soil, the green grass, exactly as it was.

'Do you feel it?' he asked.

'I feel…peace.'

'Aye, you feel it.' He rose and offered her his hand. She took it and rose after him.

'I would be very honoured to tutor you, as far as my skills allow, if you'd like,' he said.

'I might,' she said. 'Magnus seemed keen that you would.'

'Magnus has romantic ideas.'

'Does he?'

'I'm afraid so.'

Miss Frisk readjusted her hat, inspected her hands and said, 'I may have some notions of my own.'

Lucius brightened. He offered her his arm and Miss Frisk took it for the walk back to the city.

'I should like to court you, if I may, Miss Frisk,' he said, not looking at her.

'Yes, that might be acceptable. You must promise there'll be no love potions.'

She may have been joking but Lucius was horrified. 'Oh no, that's far too cruel a magic, to induce love against one's will. Nasty. How could anyone be satisfied with love that isn't real? You should know, Magnus and I do not cast spells willy-nilly. We don't read the future, we don't play tricks. We found a vein of gold with our own digging so we could buy our house. Even dark magicians, and one a part time rat at that, need safe lodging. That is to say, we do very little magic on our own behalf and we strive, in our way, to keep the balance. We're not nature's remedy, as are the Minstrels, of course–'

His nervous rattling was cut short by Muriel Frisk's laugh. 'Oh my dear Mr Kearney, I didn't mean to sting you. Of course you have too much respect for me to use charms. Other than the ones you naturally possess.' She blushed then, and Lucius was so startled by the notion that Miss Frisk believed he had charms that he fell utterly silent until they'd crossed the bridge back onto Flinders Street.

'So I may walk out with you?' he said, 'and teach you what I know of the Minstrel Tongue?'

'I'll allow it,' replied Miss Frisk. 'You can begin tonight by taking me to the theatre.' She tucked her hand more firmly into his elbow.

'I know of several that have not yet burned down,' he said.

'You are odd,' she replied, but she kept firm, affectionate hold of his arm, and Lucius decided it was the best compliment he was ever likely to receive on this earth.

The Flotilla

Meg Keneally

The Flotilla

Sydney, 1900

JEAN WATCHED THEM, WHENEVER SHE COULD. THEY AMBLED DOWN TO the shore, waited, inspecting the water before suddenly plunging in. She liked standing on a rock so she could see their small black shapes gliding underneath the surface, ducking down in pursuit of a fish or weaving around each other, navigating their way out of the small bay.

Jean Harkness' days were usually defined by pustules and moans and the rattling chests of the nearly departed. She could turn away from the water and see the infirmary on the hill where, right now, people were dying. Some days she found it comforting to know that nearby, these creatures were going about their business, insensible to that horror.

The little penguins did not seem to object to her presence, as long as she mostly kept to herself.

When the birds were safely embarked on their day's hunting, Jean would put on her own wings – those which extended on either side of her head when she wore her starched white nurse's cap – and trudge up the small beach towards the luggage shed and the laundry room, the carbolic showers and the full infirmary.

It wasn't unusual to find someone dead here. This was, after all, perhaps the greatest concentration of the ill in the country. In a quarantine station in the middle of a plague, you might say a day without death was far more unusual.

The first year of the twentieth century had brought with it an old enemy: a delivery man who ferried goods to and from Central Wharf had been the first to develop the characteristic welts which every doctor in the world recognised as the calling card of the bubonic plague. Then a sea captain. By the time he was brought to the quarantine station, he was dead. Hundreds more followed him, dead and alive, leaving behind them emptied streets punctuated by piles of rats, killed by rat trappers, and awaiting disposal.

It was hard enough to care for those already ill, and for the hundreds more sent here out of fear they had been exposed. But more were coming in by ship.

And when the ships came, they came here.

The quarantine station sat within the northern lip of Sydney's harbour, its new concrete pier jutting into the water, waiting to receive the healthy and the sick, the first class passengers and those from steerage, all stepping onto the wharf, blinking away the sun on the water, looking up at the squat wooden buildings which dotted the hill above them, as their luggage was taken to the baggage shed into which no guests were allowed, in case they saw the waiting coffins, unloaded at night so as not to cause alarm.

Jean kept waiting to get used to it. The other nurses seemed to be doing far better than she was. It was not that they did not care, did not grieve. But they seemed to have a carapace which enabled them to continue to function after draping a cloth over the closed eyes of a child.

It wasn't only the young she mourned.

There was Mrs Cloverfield, for example, who was well into her eighth decade. Her clothes were expensive, but those who cared about such things would probably sniff at them, as they were the height of fashion twenty years ago. Her hair was often undone, and occasionally she entered the first class dining room in her nightgown. She had an open, friendly face, smiled shyly at anyone she encountered, her eyes crinkling and emphasising the heart-shaped mole high on her left cheek.

The elderly lady was wealthy, certainly. But there was nothing in her of the arrogance which marked many of the other first-class denizens of the quarantine station – people who had left lavish cabins to find themselves restricted to a small patch of bush.

They didn't seem to notice the tents which had been hastily set up on a patch of lawn nearby, which housed some of their less wealthy travelling companions. Instead, many of them complained, insisted their importance merited their release, as though sickness would never dare visit someone like them.

Mrs Cloverfield was different. She could certainly afford the nicest accommodations the site had to offer, for herself and her son. But she smiled whenever Jean brought her a glass of water, thanked her, reached out and patted Jean's hand. Many nurses flinched when patients tried to touch them, even one such as Mrs Cloverfield. But Jean could not begrudge her the contact – especially when little in the way of affection was coming from her son.

Gerald Cloverfield's father must have been huge, because his mother was a diminutive little bird of a woman. He scraped six feet, barrel-chested with a voice like a ship's horn, which he used to complain at the lack of speed in responding to his requests.

He clearly saw Dr Saxon as the pinnacle of social respectability here. 'Dear old fellow,' he boomed across the table one night, making Jean wince at the thought of all the spittle flying through the air. 'We had quite a lovely talk about cricket. Though he's somewhat old-fashioned. Do you know, I saw a cloak hanging on the back of his door, which must be at least as old as I am.'

By virtue of their ability to afford first class accommodation, with private rooms, four-poster beds and French doors opening onto broad verandas, the Cloverfields seemed to have avoided the pox which was blighting many of those in the third class quarters. Jean had hoped that the old lady would be able to retire, in her faded gentility, to the comfort of her own home. But Mrs Cloverfield was never to see her home again.

'Don't stay,' said Matron Halloran, as Jean sat by Mrs Cloverfield's body. She'd gone to check on her when she'd not shown for breakfast.

Matron was a woman of barked commands and bitten-off sentences. Formidable. Heartless, Jean had thought, until she came upon her sobbing quietly in the laundry room after a child had passed away.

'But she did not have the plague,' said Jean.

'You do not know that. Perhaps the disease had not yet had time to raise buboes on her skin before it took her. She was elderly. And it is often quick.'

Jean nodded, but continued to sit with Mrs Cloverfield for a little while, holding the cold hand with its papery skin.

It wasn't simply a courtesy. Jean knew – Mrs Cloverfield had told her in one of her moments of lucidity – that there was a box hidden somewhere in this room. It contained jewellery – every piece Mrs Cloverfield had ever been given by her late husband. Jean hadn't seen it, but she guessed it would be valuable. If she couldn't save Mrs Cloverfield, at least she could guard what was left of her memories.

'It's just odd, is all,' said Jean. 'When did you last see someone die of the plague without buboes, doctor?'

Normally she would never have dared address a doctor in such a manner, even one as kind as Dr Saxon. But when you had stood beside someone else watching a person slip away, the barriers tended to break down.

Dr Saxon had come in to examine the body, but had found nothing to tell him what had killed her, beyond age and her presence at a place of sickness.

'It can be hard, when someone dies, not to know why. And we don't, Jean, not always. We must accept it. Mrs Cloverfield, God rest her, had a long life. And perhaps it was not plague which took her. But speculating on what did will do her no good, and we have plenty of living patients who need our attention.'

The rebuke was mild, but it stung coming from him, a man who greeted nurses and patients as he walked down the hill from his quarters every morning, his old-fashioned black cape draped over his shoulders.

Now, he opened the door, and gestured, ushering her out of the room.

As she passed him, she noticed a sheen on his face.

'Are you feeling quite well, Dr Saxon?'

He smiled, nodded.

'Quite all right, Nurse Harkness,' he said, signalling by the use of her last name that he invited no further familiarity. 'Although the next time I accept an assignment, I will make sure it is at a place without quite so many hills.'

Jean had seen Gerald Cloverfield in the first class dining hall with its high ceiling and leadlight windows, sipping from dainty, coloured glasses and eating off Wedgwood platters, while the second class residents were served on white crockery, and the third class got enamel trays. He often retired to the gentlemen's' smoking room afterwards, trying to cajole the more distinguished of his fellow diners to come with him.

Mrs Cloverfield had always sat very straight, her shoulders pulled back, as a governess had taught her in her childhood. She would look around the room, a benign look on her face, but never aiming her glance at any person in particular. Sometimes, when her eyes would pass across Gerald, she would frown slightly.

Gerald would smile at her, and pat her arm.

'Who are you to claim such familiarity, young man,' she would say, an edge to her voice which came as an almost physical shock the first time Jean heard it.

'It's me, mother,' he would say. 'Your son. Your little boy.'

On one of these occasions, Jean saw a woman sitting at the same table wince.

Mrs Smithers, who had come on the same ship, was not much younger than Mrs Cloverfield, but had as much mental acuity as anyone Jean had ever met.

Jean had approached her, one day, when she'd been down at the beach, looking at the penguins. Jean was certainly not the only person here who drew comfort from the little birds.

Mrs Smithers had turned and smiled at Jean when she heard her footsteps.

'Lovely little fellows, aren't they?' she said.

'Yes,' Jean had said. 'I'm not sure how lovely they think we are, though.'

Mrs Smithers had laughed.

'Well, I imagine they didn't appreciate the construction of a plague palace on their shore.'

'Mrs Smithers—' said Jean.

The older woman looked at her sharply.

'You want to ask me about Gerald,' she said.

Jean nodded. 'I just worry,' she said. 'I don't wish to be indelicate, but – do you think he treats his mother well? There are times when she looks so worried, in his presence. I am sure it's not my place even to raise it, but I wanted to make sure...'

Mrs Smithers nodded slowly.

'I do not know much about him,' she said, 'despite sharing passage from England. His mother, she seems a very gentle soul. Sometimes a little...well, distracted. I didn't see the two of them together much at first, but after a few days he was always at her table, always reminding her that he was her son.

Jean had seen it, in elderly patients. People dipping in and out of the present moment, much loved faces known for decades, suddenly disappearing from memory.

So Gerald's continual insistence to his mother that he was her son probably didn't mean much. Mrs Cloverfield was surely not the first charming person to have a less than charming child.

The penguins did not seem to find Gerald Cloverfield particularly charming either.

Hours after she had held his mother's lifeless hand, as she was welcoming the penguins back from their day's adventures, he strode onto the beach. She wanted to scream at him for injecting himself into a part of the world which she saw as hers – not Nurse Harkness's, but Jean's.

He strode towards her, and the birds still remaining on the shore scattered.

'Where are they? Her jewels?'

'Mr Cloverfield, I'm afraid I don't know. I am sure all will be resolved once your mother's will is read. If you'll excuse me, I must attend to patients.'

She began walking towards the boiler house which squatted on the edge of the beach, but he grabbed her arm and yanked it roughly back.

She looked down, and saw his hand was covered in a creeping red rash. She looked up to examine his face. There was a sheen of sweat, and less hair sprouted from his head than had when he first arrived.

Rashes. Fever. Hair loss? She had not heard of hair loss as a result of the bubonic plague. But she needed to find Dr Saxon, enlighten him as to Gerald's symptoms.

'You've stolen them, haven't you?' he hissed.

He pulled harder, nearly sending her down to the sand.

'You little bitch, you've taken them! Where are they?'

Jean struggled to free herself, lifting her sturdily shod foot and driving it down onto the top of his. Even on the soft sand, it would have hurt, and he yelped and let go of her arm. She ran around the side of the boiler house, towards the road which led up to the nurses' quarters.

He followed her, not quickly, not as though he was intent on catching her there and then. If anything, it was more as though he was stalking her.

As she began to climb the hill, shouts spilled down it towards her. A moment later, a wild-eyed man rounded the corner. His tie was askew, and he was sweating heavily in his fine wool jacket.

Despite his disarray, he was well-dressed. He wore a high, starched collar, and a well-made waistcoat, which she could see underneath the coat which was flapping behind him. A fine gold chain extended from one pocket of the waistcoat to the other.

'Where is she?' he yelled. 'You can't keep me from her!'

Some of the men who guarded the entrance to the quarantine station were pounding down the hill after him, shouting at him to stop.

'Stupid bugger!' one of them called. 'Once you come in here, you don't leave!'

Jean stood to the side of the road, not moving. She had seen this before. The relatives of those kept here made occasional incursions on the place, worried, desperate to see their loved ones, fearful it would be their last chance and insensible to the risk to themselves, and to those they might infect in the outside world.

'If you don't go now, you can't go,' one of them said.

'Tell her I came!' the man shouted. 'I'm at the guesthouse on Addison Street. Tell her to send me a message! I just wish to know she still lives!'

As the group disappeared around the corner, Jean turned back to see if Gerald Cloverfield was still following her, but he had disappeared.

Later, with the station lit by a full moon and lanterns shining from the windows, Jean came out of the infirmary. Her eye snagged on some movement on the road – unusual, after dark.

The man was walking up, towards the entrance. She couldn't see, for a moment, who it was. As her eyes adjusted to the dark, though, she recognised the distinctive swish of Dr Saxon's cape. Unusual to see him leaving at this hour. But in the middle of this outbreak, she was no longer sure what usual was.

She had only dipped briefly into sleep. She would begin to drift, only to be woken by the memory of the papery skin of Mrs Cloverfield's dead hand, or the vague smiles she would scatter around.

She was not sure why this woman was haunting her dreams, not when she had seen so many others die.

It soon became clear that sleep was too ambitious an undertaking. She stood, dressed and left without waking anyone. She might as well farewell the penguins this morning.

She watched as they approached the water, some ambling, some angling their bodies forward and aiming themselves at the bay.

This morning, though, there was something waiting for them. Something pale, rolling its way towards the sand.

The jacket was gone. So was the waistcoat. The high starched collar, now sodden, was still there, though, the tie still askew. The eyes open, staring at nothing as the body was tumbled by the waves.

Jean wasn't squeamish. The number of substances she had seen, the appalling conditions of bodies, both living and dead, had burnt through her and left no room for delicacy. Now, though, she felt bile rising into her throat, and clapped her hand over her mouth as she ran up to the gate, to tell them that the man they had removed yesterday was back.

'It's a matter for the authorities, Nurse Harkness,' the matron said. 'The man was not killed by disease, but by another's hand. Quite a nasty dent in the back of his head, I'm led to believe. I suggest you stop speaking of it.'

Jean had run up to the matron as she had stepped outside the infirmary. She had felt a pang of guilt – Matron Halloran, thinking she was alone, had looked up, let out a juddering sigh, balled her fists and forced them into her eye sockets. Jean often did the same. She did not want to interrupt the matron at such a personal time – almost as rude as intruding on someone at prayer – but did not feel she had a choice.

'It's a terrible thing, matron,' she said now, 'but I've something else on my mind as well. May I ask, have you ever known those who sicken with the bubonic plague to lose their hair?'

The nurse frowned at her, without responding – a clear signal she wasn't quite sure whether the question warranted an answer.

'Only, I've observed a bit of hair loss on one of our guests,' she said. 'Together with a rash.'

Matron Halloran pursed her lips.

'I can't say I've observed those particular symptoms, no.'

'Perhaps I could ask Dr...'

The matron shook her head.

'I'm afraid that won't be possible. He is, well, indisposed.'

Jean fancied she heard a small catch in the matron's voice.

He is not – is he sick?'

The matron turned away, busied herself with rearranging her veil.

'I fear so,' she said. 'He started shivering. Could barely keep his eyes open. He took himself off to bed yesterday afternoon. I checked on him a short while ago – no sign of buboes, as yet.'

'Oh my,' Jean said. 'What if it takes take him? When he has helped so many?'

'This is no time for sentimentality,' the matron snapped, although Jean could see her eyes were beginning to shine.

'It must have come on very suddenly,' said Jean. 'He was up and about last night.'

'He was most certainly not. He started experiencing symptoms yesterday. He has been in bed since yesterday afternoon.'

So he could not have been leaving the quarantine station yesterday evening. But someone did. A thickset man. One who knew where Dr Saxon kept his cloak.

The fear was always there, of course. That the disease would jump into them from those they were helping. It had happened already. Girls as young as Jean, younger, nurses now buried in the clifftop cemetery.

If you wanted to stay sane, though, you pushed away the thought of infection. It was that, or madness.

It was a lot harder to accomplish when one of their own was lying ill. And harder still, when a murderer was in the area. Perhaps even in the quarantine station itself.

For the rest of the day, she thought about who could have been underneath that cloak. She asked the men on the gate if they knew who the dead man was, but if they did, they did not share the information with her. She went about her duties, all the while running through the list of symptoms she observed in Gerald Cloverfield. Sweats, maybe a fever. Rash. Hair loss.

She was just able to get to the beach in time for the penguins to return that evening, and here they came, tumbling over each other in hurling themselves at their burrows, parting to navigate their way around her as though she was a tree.

She looked absently, as she always did, for any little bird requiring disentangling. None of them, today, were adorned with seaweed. But one of them was adorned with gold.

The bird stood on the water's edge, seemingly in no great hurry to run towards the bushes at the back of the beach, the fringes of which hid its home. A fine gold chain had wrapped itself around its body a few times, both under and over the wings. It could not be comfortable, with a large gold disc at one end snagged and acting as an anchor.

Jean went over, slowly. The penguin made no attempt to walk away from her, so she carefully, gently disentangled the gold pendant from the chain and unravelled it.

She watched as the penguin ambled away, and then looked down at the chain in her hand.

It was not, as she had thought, a pendant. It was a locket.

She slid her finger underneath the catch, and it popped open – a well-made thing, which had not allowed too much water inside. At least, not enough to obliterate the faces in the two small photographs, which stared up at her.

One of them was Mrs Cloverfield – younger, but unmistakable with her distinctive heart-shaped mole.

The other was the man who had washed ashore this morning.

She waited outside the first class dining hall before lunch, watching passengers who were used to far finer fare walk in with something of a heavy tread. Gerald noticed her, and frowned as he walked past.

She wasn't waiting for him, though.

'Mrs Smithers – I wonder if I might have a word?'

Mrs Smithers glanced towards the group filing into the dining room, looked back towards Jean, nodded. They walked a little way away.

'I wonder,' asked Jean, 'if you could tell me what you observed of Gerald Cloverfield's relationship with his mother. During the voyage, I mean.'

Mrs Smithers shrugged.

'Much the same as you see here. She either seemed not to know he was there, or occasionally asked him who he was.'

'And Gerald boarded the ship with her? They were together all the time?'

'Well…I do remember thinking, the first couple of days, that it was a shame that a lady like Mrs Cloverfield was having to travel alone. That she clearly needed some assistance. I was going to ask, actually, if I could be of any help, but then I saw her with Gerald. Constantly reminding her he was her son.'

'And did you see anything, or hear anything, that you felt proved that he was her son? Apart from his own insistence, I mean?'

Mrs Smithers frowned.

'No – but why would you insist you were the child of an elderly woman, sit with her for hours and days and weeks, if she was not your mother?'

When Mrs Smithers went in for lunch, Jean quickly glanced into the room, where Gerald was having a conversation with a newly arrived couple, who looked as though their capacity for politeness was wearing thin.

There would not be a better time than this to see if his quarters could shed any light on the situation.

She had a lot of questions which lacked answers. But she was fairly certain she could answer Mrs Smithers' question. It all depended on whether the woman you claimed was your mother happened to have a fortune in jewellery hidden away.

Gerald's quarters could have been a little bit neater. It was clear the man was used to others cleaning up after him, and expected them to do so.

His pyjamas were still draped over his bed, and the straight razor he had used on his cheeks that morning still bore traces of soap and flecks of hair.

Jean told herself she was being ridiculous as she bent to look under the bed. She didn't have the foggiest idea what she was looking for, and found nothing.

She moved over to his steamer trunk, eased it open. Clothes which should have been hung began to spill out onto the floor. She nudged it open little further, opened a small built-in draw, and reached inside.

She pulled out a sheaf of papers. Letters, addressed to men of different names. John Burton, Alfred Howarth, Henry Butler. More. She scanned them quickly. They all seemed to be from different women, either promising their undying love, or reproaching him for failing to respond to their letters, fretting whether he was all right. And at the bottom of the pile was a piece of sticky, yellowish paper.

It was the sort of paper that could be found all over the quarantine station, with the black dots of flies' body stuck to it.

This piece had not been cut. It had been torn, and its edges were discoloured as though part of it had been soaked in water.

Jean read the newspapers whenever she could find one, whenever Dr Saxon or one of the temporary residents left one lying around. And she had read the story of a man in London who had slowly poisoned his lodger with arsenic.

He had extracted the poison by soaking flypaper in water.

She heard voices in the distance. Lunch, it seemed, was over. She quickly replaced the letters and the flypaper, slammed the steamer trunk shut and walked as quickly as she could towards the infirmary. She passed Gerald on her way, inclined her head in a polite nod. He did not nod back, and as she walked, the prickling on the back of her neck told her he was, in all likelihood, staring at her.

'This is fanciful nonsense,' Matron Halloran said. 'There is flypaper in my room, as well. Am I a murderer? And as for this,' she tapped a fingernail on the locket, which lay open in front of her. 'Can you be certain that this is Mrs Cloverfield? This woman, really, could be anyone.'

'I don't think so, matron,' said Jean. 'You see, here? That heart-shaped mark, just underneath her eye?'

'Lots of people have marks, freckles or moles or what have you.'

Jean knew the matron was wrong. Perhaps she simply disbelieved Jean, or perhaps she was trying to avoid any further upheaval. Whatever the reason, Jean had to think of a way to talk to the police.

As she always did, she decided to do her thinking down with the penguins.

They were just beginning their march back from ocean, and she sat on a rock and watched them for a little while. She wondered if they had concerns she was not aware of, beyond survival. If they argued, in their own way, or hurt each other, or deceived one another. It did not seem possible – but there were many things, now, which she hadn't thought possible.

'The least you could have done was tidy up after yourself.'

Gerald had moved more quietly than she would have expected, given his bulk. Now, he was standing just feet behind her, arms crossed.

'An unfortunate mistake people sometimes make,' he said, 'is assuming that just because something is not arranged in their version of order, others won't notice if it's disturbed. What were you doing in my room?'

'Nothing, I…'

He smiled. 'So you were there. I knew it was you. I've seen those little whispered conversations that you have with Mrs Smithers, the nosy bat. And you know where it is, don't you? The jewellery?'

Before she could stop herself, her hand went into the pocket of her pinafore, where the locket lay.

'Oh, we have secrets of our own, do we? What do you have in there? Let's have a look first.'

He started advancing on her, and she walked backwards as slowly as she could, casting a glance behind to make sure that she didn't trip over a penguin.

He kept walking, and pulled out a pistol. Sarah could see the rash snaking around his hand as he extended it.

All those letters from women. The hair loss, the sweating, the rash.

Syphilis, perhaps.

'Mr Cloverfield,' she said. 'I have some concerns for your health. I believe you may be suffering from a condition which may be interfering with your mind.'

He laughed.

'There is nothing wrong with my mind, young woman,' he said. 'Or my aim.'

He swung the gun to the side and fired. Jean looked the direction of the shot. One of the penguins squawked, blood staining the sand at his little feet.

Until this moment, Jean had feared this man. Now, she hated him.

She ran at him as fast as she could. He clearly was expecting her to cower, not charge him, and the force of the blow when she collided with him knocked him off his feet.

'They have done nothing to you, nothing!' she yelled, as she grabbed for his gun.

'Yet you come here, with a pocket full of false names, and shoot one of them! And it's not the only life you've taken, is it? You are not the only one who is aware that flypaper contains arsenic. That it can be used over a long period of time to send someone on their way. Your best hope is to convince the authorities that your mind has been addled by your disease. That you don't know what you're doing.'

She tugged at the gun, trying to wrest it from his hand. But he tugged harder.

'Oh,' he said, pointing the gun at her, 'I know exactly what I'm doing.' He laughed, and pulled the trigger.

Jean had always thought the infirmary was a little dim. That there would be no harm in larger windows, which could let in fresh air and a bit of sunlight.

Now, though, she was grateful for the half-light – it was all she could bear as she opened her eyes.

Matron Halloran was there. The older woman smiled when she saw her patient was awake.

'You are fortunate that Mr Beams, or Mr Cloverfield as we knew him, was not a military man. Had he aimed a little further to the right, you might have been in somewhat more trouble than you are.'

Jean tried to sit, felt the pain in her left shoulder.

'Lie down and don't be foolish,' the matron said. 'You lost a lot of blood. And I would rather have one of my best nurses back on duty, as soon as I possibly can.'

Then she smiled at Jean, a genuine smile of delight, an expression Jean had never seen on the woman's face before. The smile widened further when a disgruntled squawk emerged from towards the foot of Jean's bed.

'Well, his highness is awake,' Matron said, with an indulgent tone Jean had never heard before.

She sat up, saw a cardboard box on the end of her bed. Matron smiled again, rose and brought it closer so Jean could look inside.

The penguin stood on a folded towel. Its wing, where the bullet had clipped it, was expertly bandaged.

'I tended his wounds myself,' Matron said proudly, as though she was a newly-minted nurse who had just been given charge of a patient for the first time. 'And yours, of course.'

Jean looked at her own dressings. It certainly seemed as though the same amount of care had been taken of her shoulder and the penguin's wing.

'Some men unloading baggage heard the shot,' Matron said. 'They saw that rogue running up the hill, and they were able to tackle him. Then you were found. Bleeding into the sand, mumbling about a bird. I came down and found him a little later.'

The penguin squawked again, and Matron looked at it in mock severity.

'And I must say, the manners could stand improvement.'

She leaned over and patted Jean's knee.

'We are all quite concerned,' she said. 'Dr Saxon will be delighted to hear that you have regained consciousness.'

'He is well, then?' asked Jean.

Her voice rasped, and her tongue felt as though it wanted to stick to the roof of her mouth. The matron held out a cup water to her.

'Thankfully, yes,' she said. 'Seems to have acquired a nasty flu, but not the plague.'

Jean sighed. 'And Mr Cloverfield? Beams? Whatever he is called?'

'Ah. Turns out he is many people known by many different names. Type of fellow who likes to latch onto rich women, seduce them or find any other way he can to part them from their money, and then disappear. He did so with the maiden aunt of a member of the House of Lords, and things in London were getting a little, shall we say, uncomfortable.'

'And then he saw a golden opportunity in poor old Mrs Cloverfield, no doubt,' said Jean.

The matron nodded. 'From what I've heard, his plan was to find her jewelry and try to leave the quarantine station before enquiries could be made as to her next of kin, or a will located.'

'The next of kin – the man who washed up on the beach.'

'I'm afraid so,' said the matron. 'Apparently, Mr Cloverfield – or Beams – snuck out of the station and found the fellow. A blow to the back of the head, and he lugged the body to the cliff and tumbled him into the water. The currents brought the poor fellow to us.'

'He took Dr Saxon's cloak,' said Jean. 'That's how he did it, that's how he got out of the station at night. I saw him – although I didn't know it was him.'

'You see a lot,' said the matron. She cleared her throat, as though surprised it could produce such indulgent words. She stood, smoothed down her dress, and nodded at Jean as though they had just passed each other in the street.

'Mind you follow the doctor's instructions, Nurse Harkness. We can't have you malingering any longer than necessary, and those who are really ill have need of this bed.'

It was another week before Jean could get back down to the beach, scanning the water for the little black forms as they returned for the night.

She carried with her a cardboard box, from which increasingly insistent squawks were emerging. Perhaps the little creature could smell the sea, and was anxious for something fresher than the sardines Matron had pilfered from the first class kitchen.

She wanted the bird to have the beach to itself for a time. She put the box down, gently and slowly tipped it over, and the penguin waddled out onto the sand. She took a grease paper parcel out of her pinafore pocket and opened it – strips of snapper, caught that morning. The first class diners would hopefully not notice their portions were a little smaller this evening.

They sat there, the two of them, waiting for the flotilla to return.

And here they came now, a black line behind the small waves, some of them surfing ashore on their bellies, righting themselves and walking back to their burrows in a journey they had been making for millennia.

Manly is home to the last breeding colony of Little Penguins in mainland New South Wales. If you're lucky enough to see one, please do not approach it.

For more information visit the Foundation for National Parks and Wildlife at support.fnpw.org.au.

Carpathia
and the Case of the
Vanishing
Chipmunk

C J McGumbleberry

Carpathia and the Case of the Vanishing Chipmunk

SITTING IN THE CORNER STUDY OF HER SPACIOUS APARTMENT IN THE oversized hazelnut tree, Carpathia contemplated the last half hour's rotten turn of events.

She had lost, yes, lost the chipmunk she was keeping a weather eye upon for her lunchtime meal. First it was there and then it was not.

'Maybe,' she thought, 'I'm getting old and my eyesight is starting to decline.'

But no, it was nothing of the sort! That freaking chipmunk had literally vanished, she was sure of it. There was more here than met the eye, and Carpathia could not shake the feeling that something odd had happened.

As a Great Horned Owl and proud member of the order Strigiformes, Carpathia would not take this lying down.

Well, as an owl, she would never take anything lying down. Owls do not lie down. They stand up their entire lives. Okay, okay, unless they are baby owls who cannot yet support their heads when they sleep, but the point remains, generally you will not see a parliament of owls lounging around a vole carcass, legs akimbo, talons unkempt. No siree, these are a proud carnivore, with a level of decorum and certain standards to be upheld!

Be that as it may, the mystery continued to gnaw at Carpy. At first the chipmunk was there, prowling near the base of Douglas fir tree #762,951 – or as she liked to call this particular tree, Squiggles the Snow Leopard – and then the little striped thing was just not there.

(What? Yes, Carpy has numbered and nicknamed every one of the many trees in her part of the forest, the list scrupulously documented with extensive notes by Carpy's asthmatic personal assistant, Cecil the Praying Mantis.)

Now of course Carpy was not about to go strolling around on the forest floor near Squiggles to try and see if the little chipmunk disappeared into a burrow right at the base of the tree. Loping about on the ground could put her in danger of being another predator's next meal, so nope, this was a job for a fellow forest friend.

Lizard the Blue Dasher Dragonfly would definitely be the best operative to help Carpy solve this vexing mystery of the vanishing chipmunk.

What? You think it odd an owl would have a dragonfly as a friend? Let us not forget they share the special power of flight, which many forest creatures do not. Couple that with the fact that dragonflies do not eat owls, and the Great Horned Owls of the Fern Ridge Wilderness Area do not eat dragonflies, and it's not such an oddity after all.

And make no mistake, Carpathia needed Lizard's big, iridescent blue-green eyes. Those striking compound orbs helped Lizard see in almost 360 degrees, and it was this very fact which put Carpy on course to the nearby body of water and her friend's favourite hunting spot.

As it so happened, at that precise moment Lizard hoped to see Carpathia. It was about a very important insect problem that needed to be dealt with in a speedy and stern manner.

An amiable sort of dragonfly, Lizard was always polite and willing to lend a leg or wing as the situation dictated. However, lately their regular food spot had been bereft of morsels worth munching and it had not taken long for Lizard to figure out why.

It seems a competing dragonfly had moved in on the buggy buffet Lizard had been enjoying, and Lizard would not take this lying down! You see, dragonflies also do not lie down! They stand up their whole short lives, so they are not taking any guff!

Right, so Lizard set out to the mammoth hazelnut tree where Carpathia lived to see if she would agree to pull some intimidation moves on this joker dragonfly, jostling the interloper and getting them to bug off out of town. As it so happened, they were in midair when Carpathia and Lizard spotted one another, each immediately having philosophical thoughts about coincidental timing and the far-reaching implications of a universe where fate can be altered by just a few seconds of flight.

'Hello my visually-challenged friend!' shouted Lizard. With over 30,000 optical receptors per eye, Lizard felt that every other creature who did not possess compound eyes was at a distinct disadvantage. (Yes, even gross flies! Gah!)

As soon as she heard Lizard belting out her insult-greeting, as only that tiny winged marvel could, and spotted her friend's chalky-blue body, Carpy swooped down onto Douglas fir tree #211,221, whom she called Pepper the Adverb Queen.

Carpathia spoke first, in her elegant, dulcet tone. 'Yo, Lizard, what be the haps?'

Lizard was uncharacteristically still for a moment before they got right into the meat of things. 'Well, I feel a fool for asking, but I have a problem and need your help very much. You see, I was wondering if you could harass, possibly slightly injure, a food-stealing dragonfly. Only just enough to force the cavern-stomached lout to permanently depart my feeding spot?'

Make no mistake, Carpathia felt she was too regal and deadly an aerialist to bother with bum-rushing a bug, but she did need Lizard to surveil the area near Squiggles and so she said, 'Lizard, I believe I can intercede with your buffet-busting bug quandary.'

Carpathia paused in the dramatic way only owls can and added, 'In turn I would like to request you do a bit of surveillance for me at the base of Douglas fir #762,951.'

Lizard gave Carpathia a blank stare. 'Say what?'

'You know, Squiggles.'

If Lizard's eyes weren't already wide, they'd have gone so. 'Are you telling me all the trees in this forest have a specific name and number?'

Smart as she was, it was only at this moment Carpathia realised her system of tree identification probably was not used by all the insects of the forest. No wonder her PM PA (praying mantis personal assistant) Cecil had at first been confused. 'Um, it's the tree on the southeastern bank of the reservoir, the one scratched by a bear?'

Now *that* Lizard understood. And speaking of bears, Lizard also understood they needed to know one more thing before they agreed on anything. 'Is there danger in what you need me to do for you?'

For many in the forest, danger lurked around every pinecone and each fiddlehead fern. For some creatures, every moment of every day was filled with danger, and for a creature like Lizard...well there was always the danger of being eaten by predators who enjoyed the rich Mediterranean flavour it is said a Blue Darner Dragonfly imparts to any meal.

'For sure there will be danger!' Carpy answered honestly. 'But it is really quite the interesting mystery. Maybe I should tell you what happened.'

Carpathia let her mind drift back to what she had seen a day ago, trying to put herself into the mind of one of the family Sciuridae, of which the chipmunk was a member.

Now Carpy had never once spent a moment thinking about what might go through the mind of what she was having for lunch, she killed deftly, and without remorse because a gal has to eat, right? Do not hate the player boss, hate the game.

But now, as she tried her level best to imagine being a tiny rodent and to explain how the little bugger might have vanished before her very eyes, she had a notion. Maybe, just maybe, all little rodents were not complete idiots. While she did not stray into thinking that they were her intellectual equal, the fact that she was thinking of them as anything other than a hot meal, was a level of personal growth she was not used to experiencing.

Why did she have any need for personal growth? She was already Great. It was in her species name! Now how many other of God's creatures have such a qualifier right in their very name? I will tell you, two, the Great White Shark and the Great Dane breed of dog.

'Well, here it is Lizard, one moment I was looking right at this delicious-looking chipmunk and then the next moment they disappeared right before my eyes.'

To be fair, Lizard was still far more interested in 'for sure there will be danger' than in vanishing chipmunks, but Carpy continued talking, providing her small friend with a smorgasbord of praise.

'I know you can hover all darned day if you want to, and fly backwards and upside down, something I could never do in my wildest dreams!'

Carpathia hadn't even begun on Lizard's field of vision capabilities, unmatched in the Aves class, before the small insect was drawing up a contract. Penning a lean list of action items and a few detailed drawings, in moments they'd hammered out a contract that kept both parties happy. Tiny contract in tow, Lizard was swiftly on the wing and set to surveil.

With Lizard's exceptional sight and manoeuvrability on heightened alert, they took a direct route towards the Douglas fir tree known by Carpathia as Squiggles the Snow Leopard, and had a speedy but detailed look at the ground around the base of the tree.

The first deliverable, per the contract, was a detailed artistic rendering, in correct scale, in triplicate, of all facets of the terrain from the broadly-defined base of the tree, stretching outward for six feet in every direction. Lizard was good, but also only had a hard drive the size of a dragonfly's brain, so this reconnaissance was going to take several trips. Yet that notion was soon exploded like a faraway star going supernova.

Getting within twenty feet of Squiggy, Lizard could see something was not right, the forest floor seemed at odds with its surroundings. Like most all dragonflies, Lizard has added visual acuities other woodland residents do not possess, specifically polarised vision and the ability to detect ultraviolet light. So, Lizard could tell some part of the forest floor was not in accordance with its surroundings, the vegetation did not have a proper visual rhythm. There were patterns out of order and this discovery had Lizard feeling a tingle of excitement.

'So, Carpathia may possibly be on to something here,' thought Lizard, hovering just 24 inches above what was most assuredly the entrance of a chipmunk burrow. However, there were multiple objects in the vicinity of this particular burrow entrance, and Lizard did not have the life experience to know what they were. You see the flying portion of a dragonfly's life is only six months to a year on average, so there were many things that Lizard would never know or understand.

Still, Lizard quickly made mental notes of those objects and once back at the office, and in just the better part of a morning, Lizard was flush with contract deliverables – a tidy group (in triplicate of course) of detailed drawings and darned fine artistic renderings of the ground around Squiggles the tree.

Since Lizard was no CH-53K King Stallion military cargo helicopter and could not possibly carry all these drawings, Carpathia was going to have to come by Lizard's business office to review the intelligence requested. And hopefully Carpathia would be able to report to Lizard that the interloper who has been scarfing up delicious water nymphs had been run off, or better yet eradicated, if that was how things finally went down.

Lizard alit for the short flight to Carpathia's palatial rooms in that obscenely large hazelnut tree to share the news of what the reconnaissance had uncovered. Nearing the hazelnut, Lizard could see what appeared to be the offending dragonfly sitting on Carpathia's lanai sipping a berry smoothie!

Landing smartly, putting Carpathia directly between the food-stealing fiend and themselves, Lizard said casually, 'Uh, hey Carpathia. Who's your smoothie-sipping buddy?'

'This is Epithelial Duct, an itinerant survey specialist from down south,' replied Carpathia.

Unimpressed, Lizard pressed on with the most pertinent question. 'Itinerant? That means he'll be moving on soon?'

It was at this moment that EpiDuc, as he liked to be called, spoke up. 'I plan on moseying along before sunset today. Never meant you offense Lizard, I sure did not know that swell feedin' spot was under your jurisdiction, or I would not have helped myself the way I did.'

Lizard remained stoic, saying dryly, 'I wish you well on your surveying, now if you'll excuse us, this owl and I have some important business.'

Epithelial Duct swilled the last of the smoothie and took flight with a nod and a tip of his wing, heading into the afternoon sky.

'Well you sure are gruff, Lizard,' observed Carpathia.

'Time is of the essence Carpy, and I've not any time for niceties towards a grubby food stealer! If you want to look at what I have found, and get a look at the location yourself before nightfall, we had better make this march my friend.'

They easily winged over to Lizard's business office together because, despite their noticeable difference in size, a Great Horned Owl's average top speed is 40 miles per hour, while a Blue Darner Dragonfly can average 35!

As they stepped into the main conference room where Lizard had laid out the myriad artistic renderings, Carpathia said, 'What in the name of the Grand Budapest Hotel is all that stuff?'

There were drawings, 3-D renderings, written documents, sculpted items from reservoir clay, even a tiny diorama of the entire layout of the eastern side of the forest floor at the base of Squiggles the Snow Leopard aka Douglas fir tree #762,951.

'These are the agreed upon deliverables,' said Lizard, 'my visual intelligence rendered in easy to understand formats for the pertinent data. What? No good?'

Quite the contrary, they were great! Carpathia immediately began asking questions in hopes she'd soon know what had happened to that chipmunk.

'What are these things over here,' inquired Carpathia, pointing one very sharp talon at a group of small sculptures.

'They very well may hold the key to your mystery,' Lizard said excitedly. 'You see, as I got closer to the base of Squiggy, my super dragonfly vision was immediately drawn to these because they were not in synch with the other shrubs, grasses, or soils that make up the forest floor. Nothing else at the base of Squiggy was odd or out of the ordinary except these things, set up in close proximity to the burrow entrance. That is why I think you need to take a look for yourself, so that with your greater life experience, you may be able to figure out what they are, and thereby perhaps solve the mystery of the vanishing chipmunk.'

After the presentation, Lizard ran through a list of recommendations and even offered the security of extra air support for Carpathia if she chose to get a close look at these strange objects.

'You know, I really would like to get this puzzle solved,' said Carpathia, 'so I am accepting your offer to keep an eye out for predators who may try and jack me while I get a better look at these things on pages 14 through 16 of your marvellous sketchbook.'

With that said and the afternoon wearing on, thus making the whole endeavour that much more dangerous, the two cohorts took flight toward Squiggles.

As they arrived, Carpathia motioned to Lizard to take up a hover position 40 feet above the base of the tree, the best place to keep a lookout for any animal who thought owl burgers should be on the evening's supper menu. Armed with Lizard's protective gaze Carpathia made a deft descent, followed by a very rare forest floor drop down, finding herself standing right at the chipmunk's burrow entrance and looking at the items Lizard had described as 'not fitting' with forest floor décor.

Now Carpathia was a Great Horned Owl, who as rule do not usually kick the bucket before the lucky age of 13. If you have good owl genes like Carpathia, well then you could possibly see another couple of years tacked on to that gaudy baker's dozen assigned the 'average' Great Horned Owl. (And isn't that an oxymoron? An 'average' Great Horned Owl?) All of which is to say that though Carpy was not old for owls, she was still a pretty sharp knife in the drawer of sharp knives, to use a cutlery analogy. Yet she was not sure what these not-fitting things were, thought she meant to find out.

Without wasting another moment she spread her mighty wings, wrapped her talons around two of the strange objects and took flight back toward her laboratory, deep within the bowels of the gargantuan hazelnut tree she called home. Calling back over her shoulder, 'Thank you Lizard, I have to get some analysis done!'

Yet after quite awhile back at the lab, Carpy just could not put her talon on what these things were or how they made a chipmunk disappear. There really was only one thing to do now: check with the oldest owl of any of the owls living in the Fern Ridge Wilderness Area – possibly even the oldest owl in all of Oregon – GiggleToes, a spry old dude already two years outside the 20-year average for a Northern Spotted Owl.

Now Carpathia had met him a few times over her years, and recalled him living by the longer skinny part of the lake, in a large Western Red Cedar on the Elmira side of the reservoir. (Carpy only kept track of the Douglas fir trees – Cecil was already overworked – so she had no nickname for GiggleToes' cedar.) If any owl in this part of the Willamette Valley would know what these things were, he would be the one.

It was only a few minutes by wing to GiggleToes' roost, and since Northern Spotted Owls are mainly night hunters, Carpathia could see that he was in as she approached.

'Happy mouse hunting Sir GiggleToes!' she called out, 'It is Carpathia from the other side of the reservoir, of the Great Horned Owl tribe, I seek your counsel on a strange conundrum. Would you be amenable to looking at clues I have gathered in my mystery-solving efforts?'

Always an inquisitive owl, Carpathia had immediately piqued GiggleToes' interest with her counsel-needing problem, so he asked her to alight on the branch just across from the bejewelled roost on which he had a throne. Yes, you heard right. This owl had his very own, ornately-carved throne, made just for an owl his size!

Carpathia landed as requested and tried not to stare, but it was difficult, especially since it seemed he had a tiny sceptre under his wing and even a tiny crown sitting jauntily on his head. The fact that Northern Spotted Owls have black eyes added to GiggleToes' striking look. Willing herself to concentrate, Carpathia went about presenting her case.

'Mr. GiggleToes, I have been vexed by a recent experience. You see, I had been keeping a weather eye on a chipmunk at the base of a Douglas fir recently, and without a single blink, I saw the creature disappear. I have an exceptionally keen eye your highness, and know the rodent did not run away. It was there, and then it was not there. My friend and I feel these items found in close proximity to the chipmunk's burrow may be part of the key to how it vanished. Is there anything you might be able to tell me about these?'

Carpathia flew over and deposited the items on the little carved dais next to GiggleToes' throne. She felt like she was an attorney presenting evidence.

Squinting and blinked at the objects, GiggleToes sat and he thought and eventually he said, 'You know the way you can sometimes see yourself in the still water as you get a drink?'

Carpathia nodded. She often admired her superb plumage in this fashion.

'Well did you try to look at yourself in the shiny side of these discs? Because my friend these are like the lake, they are some sort of mirror.'

Ookaaay.

'But sir, could you kindly unravel the mystery of how these mirrors, as you called them, could make an entire chipmunk vanish?'

GiggleToes took a deep, deep, deep, deep breath and went very still. For a very long time. So still, for so long, as a matter of fact, Carpathia believed maybe he'd expired in front of her. She was just about to clear her throat, when the old owl turned his head and said, 'Sorry about that blank spell, I had to go into my mind palace to check my archives since I had an old owl's gut feeling I know the answer to your conundrum.'

Carpathia went breathless, tightly clenching the branch she was on in anticipation of GiggleToes' learned response.

'It was magic!' he burped editorially.

Oh great, Carpy thought in disappointment, he's off his rocker.

'That is to say, it was something a magician might do to make an object appear to vanish. You see, if you know what you are doing, and you have a number of mirrors, you can set up little 'blind spots' on the forest floor. When you are up in a tree dozens of yards away, it can be difficult to tell if you are seeing something that is actually in your direct line of vision, or if what you are keeping your eye on is instead actually a reflection.'

Carpathia sat there, dumfounded.

'You see, when mirrors are arranged in the correct configuration they can trick your eye into thinking you are seeing something straight on when in fact you are looking at the reflection of something that is not actually in your line of sight.'

GiggleToes could see the wheels turning as Carpy tried to process his explanation, so he pressed on. 'I know this sounds outlandish, but it is true. I was a house owl once, living with a wannabe magician and I saw a lot of videos and films studied by my host. Then too there were the endless practices by this inferior being as he tried to elevate himself to the age-old arts of the alchemist or necromancer.' GiggleToes trailed off with a faraway look in his deep, black eyes.

Continuing to feel like she was a DA trying a case on one of those criminal court television shows, Carpy leaned forward to ask the most vital question in the Mystery of the Vanishing Chipmunk. 'So, Mister GiggleToes, you are saying these mirrors reflect images of what is in close proximity to them, correct?'

'Yup,' giggled GiggleToes.

'And if these mirrors were arranged in a certain configuration they could easily fool the eye, rendering a chipmunk in proximity to them invisible, is that correct, sir?'

'Yes'm,' GiggleToes said.

Wow.

Wow, wow, wow.

It was as simple as that. Though not really simple at all! While Carpy didn't know why this mystery had taken Squiggles-like root in her subconscious she did now know there was a hyper-intelligent chipmunk in Lane County's Fern Ridge Reservoir Wilderness Area.

So, with one mystery solved, she already began ruminating on a chipmunk that was smart enough to know how to use these mirrors to camouflage its burrow at the base of Squiggles the Snow Leopard. Was this the only overly-intelligent rodent living in this part of the forest? Were there more super rodents she had heretofore been unaware of?

Before her brain possibly started smoking from the myriad of new questions, she brought herself back to the moment and thanked the kindly old owl for his help.

Carpy knew she owed GiggleToes a bit of tonight's hunting efforts in repayment for his wisdom, so before leaving the impressive cedar lodge this magnificent owl called home she said, 'Mr. GiggleToes, if I may repay your kind counsel, after hunting tonight, I would like your permission to fly by and deliver a number of tasty morsels. I would never have solved this mystery without your years of life experiences.'

Delighted that he could take the night off from hunting himself to enjoy his first ever dinner delivery, GiggleToes said, 'Hey Carpathia, that would be super cool if you wanted to do that.'

The sun was now close to setting and Carpathia knew that for her tribute she would find the most prey in the crepuscular part of Thursday. She again thanked 'King' GiggleToes, gave him her tree information, and invited him to visit any time he was in that part of the forest. Taking flight, her mind was now at ease. At least about the mystery of how the chipmunk disappeared. Carpathia would definitely have to have Lizard over for berry smoothies soon to explain it all.

Meanwhile, just south of Dougie fir #762,105 aka Quagmire the Painstaking, and just a pinecone's toss from #762,221, Dendrite the Zoo Sweeper, a super-intelligent rodent named KoZe was hard at work in the 'ideas' room of his burrow, perfecting the system which had so far prevented him from falling foul of some forest carnivore's desire for lunch.

A highly intelligent chipmunk, KoZe was well-versed in employing forest floor camouflage techniques, but hiding under a big leaf or standing still in a stand of ferns was, he knew, far from foolproof, so as he noshed his fir cone seeds, he'd brainstorm unique ways to safeguard himself.

As part of his never-ending quest for knowledge, KoZe would drag back to his burrow many strange things, especially from the areas where the people went. This was how he had amassed a small collection of cosmetics mirrors with pretty tortoiseshell covers.

It had taken KoZe a long time to determine the placement of the mirrors because, as brainy as he was, he was also a more juvenile-minded chipmunk than most, and as such, he was full of energy and had that amazing ability human children seem to have to spin around in a circle for as long as they want without getting the urge to revisit what they had for lunch.

It had been at one of KoZe's spinning breaks that a radical idea had formed in his mind. (KoZe had a theory about freeform spinning and the expansion of the pineal gland along with creative neuron stimulation. Yeah, not your average chipmunk.)

You see, KoZe had been a big fan of Doug Henning, the Canadian illusionist famous for his signature trick, televised on 23 December 1976, of making an elephant disappear. KoZe considered himself an astute, amateur student of the illusionist genre and was fascinated by the different ways in which the eyes of any creature could be deceived into either seeing something that wasn't there or not seeing something that was actually visible.

KoZe, hoping to be the first recognised chipmunk illusionist, had been pouring over the footage of the disappearing elephant illusion to inform his own efforts at visual trickery, and came to understand the rare knowledge of using mirrors to fool the eye. This had led KoZe to gather his small tortoiseshell collection and start figuring out their proper tilt and angle, painstakingly factoring in the light, the direction of that light, and the shadows which would be cast along with half a dozen other variables.

After much trial and error, KoZe had arranged his mirrors around the entrance to his burrow in such a way that, when he stepped up close to the entrance, he could be behind a mirror on all the sides where a predator might have a line of sight to him. He could be within a couple inches of his burrow entrance, easily seen by a predator, but with one lightning-quick step he could be behind a mirror and vanished from sight. The mirrors themselves were reflecting the leaves of the undergrowth all around them, and so from a distance nothing on the forest floor appeared out of the ordinary.

KoZe had gotten this configuration into place just a few weeks ago and had been pleasantly surprised by how well it was working. On the forest floor, every rodent knows that flying predators and quadruped predators are always hungrily looking for their next morsel. KoZe had not gotten to be a four-year-old chipmunk by following the same old standard actions that were taught to him by his parents, no.

While the average chipmunk in the wild will likely live for only two or three years, an above average chipmunk can live up to eight years. KoZe was not even your above average chipmunk. He was extraordinary and he would be ten on his next birthday.

And he still had a lot of energy for spinning. And collecting more mirrors.

He wondered if he could make an entire tree vanish?

This small tale of a large forest contains herein a very good lesson, the wisdom of which every one of us might do well to remember.

What we see, we might not actually be seeing. Not everything is what it might appear at first. Try not to jump to conclusions or to judge things on a single fleeting glance.

And absolutely positively do keep an eye out for super-intelligent rodents in the Fern Ridge Reservoir Wilderness Area.

Kidnapped

David Greagg

Kidnapped

I WAS SITTING ON MY CHAIR, AS IS MY WONT, ENJOYING THE MORNING SUN. The comfy chair on the front veranda is better, since it has the winter fluffy on it. Some days you want a fluffy yourself, and on those days I claim it very early in the morning. But mostly I leave it to my sister, since she has short black fur and feels the cold.

I'm a Viking Forest Cat, with long fur more suitable for colder climates than this. My chair is a plain one with no sides and just a woolly jumper on it. From there I can oversee my neighbourhood. I suppose you would call me the Top Cat, or the alpha male, of the neighbourhood. I really don't care about it; but I don't like bullies and some days you have to administer chastisement.

I can still remember one night when we went for our walk and I saw White Cat come out to try to bully my little sister. Again. I chased him all the way back to his house and gave him a thumping. I didn't see it, but Shadow told me afterwards that poor little Luna – a timid girl-cat who lives next door to him – crept along the footpath and looked through the hole in the fence, agog at seeing the neighbourhood bully getting what was coming to him.

But mostly I don't bother. Boy-cat fighting is for losers. You see them around sometimes: battered old toms with scars all over them and missing bits of ear and tail. I cannot see the point. You give bad cats a thumping when you have to. Otherwise, live and let live is best. Since I'm the biggest and strongest cat around, all I have to do is sit down, stretch out my front paws and look at them. We don't have to do this! I tell them. Just go about your business and no-one gets hurt. Mostly it works. And today I was curled up with my eyes closed and my paws stretched out, blissfully happy and content with my life.

'Dougal! Wake up!' Instantly I was awake and watching. It was my sister, standing on the comfy chair with her fur fluffed up. Such as it is, since short-haired cats can't manage much of a decent fluff-up. I don't bother with that. I'm big enough to intimidate anything short of a dog. I followed her eyes and saw what she was facing off. It was a dog, and I tensed. They can't get in unless our humans are silly enough to leave the gate open, and today they hadn't. I relaxed, just a little. I'd seen this one before: a black and tan medium sized hound with a leather collar. Usually he walks on by, content to wag his tail and fawn over his human the way dogs do. Today he was out without his human, and he had plenty to say for himself.

I heard my sister tell the dog to sod off. She is such an alley-cat. And she really is. We weren't kittens together. She turned up in my cage at the Bad Place With Cages and our humans picked both of us. So I call her my sister even though we aren't related. I grew up in a proper house; but she was a wild cat. She sounded pretty wild right now. Such language! She insulted the dog, its ancestors, and all dogs in general. She told it to go back to its rubbish dump and leave us alone. She didn't stop until the dog barked at her. She subsided, muttering.

'Well, Dog?' I inquired. 'Are you trying to tell us something important, or are you going to stand there all day being annoying?'

'Bark, bark, whine?' it said. And here is the chief reason dogs and cats don't get on. We can't really speak each other's language. But we can read body language, and what I saw disquieted me. Because he was doing his best impression of I'm A Good Dog: sitting up, all four paws together, not being aggressive. So I hunched down and put my paws out. He looked at me and gave a little nod.

'All right, you are trying to tell us something,' I said. 'Please give us a hint?'

'Bark, whine, small cat, down, black, brick?' he managed to say.

'Cat?' I asked. He stared at me and gave me a look which indicated I was the stupidest thing he had met all day.

'Dirt! Hole, dirt, housebrick!'

'Look, Dog, I don't understand you. Are you saying there's a lost cat somewhere?'

'Bark, bark! Fear! Cat! Housebrick!'

'All right,' I said. 'You lost me at housebrick, but I get the idea. Where is it?'

'Road! Lamp-post! Housebrick! That way!' He pointed with his nose and walked off in the opposite direction. I exchanged glances with my sister.

'I think there's a lost cat somewhere,' said Shadow.

'I guess so. And I suppose we should find it. Considering that the dog thought it worthwhile to tell us. We can't ignore it now.'

We got down off our chairs and set off down the road.

We saw a few other cats out in the street. I even asked Audrey if she'd seen anything. I needn't have bothered. Audrey is a small black and white cat with similar markings to me, but much smaller. She's an Only Cat, and has forgotten how to talk to other cats. She blinked at me and ran back into her yard without telling me anything. I got a glimpse of White Cat, but he took one look at me and jumped the fence back into his yard. Then we saw Kitty, who's a stripy boy cat living down at the corner. He looked scared, so I sat down on the footpath with my paws outstretched and let my sister handle the negotiations.

It's a funny thing, but Shadow, who has very little time for boy cats in general (with the possible exception of me), has a curious relationship with Kitty. Several times when we go walking with Man at night he comes bounding up to her, exhibiting challenging behaviour. The first time it happened I expected her to chase him away. Or belt him. But she didn't do either of those things. She sat down next to him and they had a silent commune. I asked her what they talked about but she wouldn't say, except to tell me that she thought Kitty was lonely. Thereafter, whenever we see Kitty on our walks she sits down with him. And Man and I have to wait for her. But perhaps today their unusual friendship might come in useful.

Presently my sister returned. 'Well?' I inquired. She touched noses with me.

'Kitty says a strange human came to the house across the road last night. They knocked on the door, the human who lives there opened the

door, and then there was a thump noise, some banging, and a later the stranger came running out again.'

'That doesn't sound all that strange,' I told her.

'Well, no, it doesn't sound much. But Kitty thought it was odd.'

'Odd, as in bad?'

'He thinks so.'

'We may as well go and have a look at the house, then.'

So we did. There were the usual cars outside in the street. There seemed to be a light on, but there were no sounds coming from inside. It's an old-smelling house, and we like to browse there sometimes because there's lots of grass growing all around it.

'Shadow? Remember what the dog said? There's a lamp-post here. Maybe this is the place he meant.'

'I can smell kitten,' Shadow told me. I lifted my nose and inhaled.

'So can I. And it's scared. I think we're at the right house.'

We padded around the house, but the scent was very faint. Eventually Shadow looked at me. 'What shall we do now?' she asked.

'What did the dog say, Shadow? Something about dirt, hole, housebrick?'

'Assuming that the dog wasn't talking nonsense. It's just a dog. Do they even know what day of the week it is?'

'Shadow, there's nothing else to go on. Can you see any holes here?'

'No. It's a big house and yard. It will take a long time to search it all.'

I sat down, tucked my tail around my paws and had a quick think. 'Can you do the Kitten Call?'

'I don't think so,' she answered. 'My mum didn't talk much out loud.' And that made sense, since Shadow and her mum were wild cats. So it was down to me. I tried to remember how our mum used to call us.

'Mrowl?'

Shadow sat down and gave me a pitying look. 'I don't think that's right,' she observed. 'I think that means Bring Food Immediately.'

'All right then. You try.'

She blinked. 'Mraaawwwwllll?' Abruptly she shut her mouth. 'That's no good either, is it?'

'I'm afraid not,' I told her. 'I think that was Lady Cats? I'm heeeere!'

Shadow looked away in embarrassment. She doesn't like amorous tom-cats and has a very short way with them. Now you may ask why we didn't just call the kitten with our minds. Most cat conversations are silent. But the problem with that is that the other cat needs to be in sight, and able to move. It's mostly done with gestures. Your face and ears make a small movement one way or the other. Where you put your paws says a lot as well. And your tail does a lot of the talking. The silent mind-to-mind stuff is just on top of everything else. What we needed was vocal mother cat calling her kittens, and I couldn't remember how it went.

'Mrrrrrrp?' I tried.

Amazingly, it worked. Shadow's ears pricked up immediately. And there it was. A small kitten-voice was calling us.

So we searched the whole yard. I tried the call again and I could hear a faint mewing, coming from near the side of the house. And there she was: down a wet, smelly hole, and hiding behind a house-brick. Just like the dog had said. A little round face, jet-black like my sister, staring wide-eyed up at me.

'Come out, little cat,' I said. She eyed me off and shrank further behind the brick. Fear was pouring off the poor little girl. I wasn't going to get anything out of her, so I backed away and sat down. 'Shadow? I think you'll have to try and get her out.'

My sister sat down at the top of the hole and put her nose down it. Presently she reappeared. 'No good,' she told me. 'She's cold, wet, hungry and thirsty, and scared out of her wits.'

'So what do we do now?' I asked her. She gave me a steady stare.

'Dougal, you are going to stand guard until I get back. I've told her you won't hurt her.'

'But – ' I got no further. My sister had disappeared. So I sat where I was and tried to send warm, loving thoughts down the hole. All I was getting back was a steady pulse of fear and distress. But this might pass, with time. I hoped so.

It was quite a while before my sister came back. And she had a sausage in her mouth. She dropped it down the hole. I have to say it smelled wonderful. Presently I could hear tiny sounds coming from the hole, as if little teeth were busy at work. I touched noses with my clever sister.

'I don't know how you do it,' I told her. 'But if you don't mind my asking, where do the wild sausages grow?'

'I always was a good hunter,' she said evasively. I sniffed at her mouth, which smelled very strongly of stolen sausage.

'Were there by any chance other sausages?'

'There may have been. But I can only carry one in my mouth.'

I let it go. I was sure my sister had probably eaten at least one more at the scene of the crime. I hoped the humans who had suddenly found themselves short of lunch wouldn't mind. And Shadow had certainly brought one back.

Both of us backed away from the hole; and presently the little trembling kitten came out. She still looked terrified, but she blinked, and licked her lips with considerable appreciation. She padded past in front of us towards a metal water-dish and sat herself down in front of it. I watched her tiny pink tongue lapping at the water and felt all warm inside. Then she turned to us and sat down, her shoulders hunched forward, her body tense and ready to run away.

My sister told her to stay put and walked straight up to her, and began to wash her.

It was wonderful to see. Little by little Shadow seemed to be washing the fear out of her. The little cat began to purr, and Shadow pinned her down and gave her a thorough wash all over. By the end of it the kitten was ready to talk.

'All right, little friend,' said Shadow. 'Is this your house?'

'Yes.'

'What happened to make you so scared?'

The kitten licked her lips some more. 'A new human came, and did bad things to my human.'

'I see. Have you ever seen this human before?'

'No, never. But he plays with his plastic thing sometimes and then his lady human comes to see him. She makes noises on the front door.'

'And what happens then?'

'They play together for a while on the bed, and then the lady human goes away again.'

'So how was this time different?'

'It was the same noise on the door, but it wasn't the lady human. I like her because she's kind and strokes me. This was a Bad Human. And I got scared and ran away and hid.'

All this was interesting, but I had a question of my own. 'Little cat, where's your human now?'

'Still there, I think.'

'Still where?'

'In the house. He's sitting in his chair, but it's all wrong. I don't think he's happy.'

Shadow and I looked at each other. We'd have to go and look, wouldn't we? 'Has the bad human gone?' I wanted to know.

'Yes. Last night.'

'I'll go, Shadow. You can come too. I assume you have a cat door?'

Yes, the house had a cat door. It was a bit of a squeeze for me, but I got in all right and had a look around. It didn't take long to find the human. There he was, sitting in a chair. The kitten was right. I've seen happier humans. I sniffed at him, but he'd fallen asleep. There were funny plastic things on his front and back paws, and these seemed to be pinning him to the chair. I went back through the cat door to have another talk with the kitten.

'You didn't mention your human's clothes?'

'What are clothes?' she wanted to know.

'You know. Cloth things they put on themselves. Except he's not wearing any. You might have mentioned this before.'

'Oh,' she said, and blinked. I had a quick think about this, realising that cats don't usually notice clothes. Shadow does, of course, because she sits on the side of the bath while our humans are in it. She's fascinated by humans and everything they do; and she watches the clothes come off and get put back on again. But I have to admit that I don't pay much attention to them. Still, there was a mystery to be solved here, and we were the cats to do it.

'All right, small cat. When he plays with his plastic thing and the lady human comes, does he ever take off his outer fur things before she comes? Like maybe he's ready to play with her?'

The kitten was sitting up, paws tucked in and desperately trying to be helpful. 'Sometimes. But mostly they do that later on. When they're playing on the bed. Oh, but this time he did, yes. But it wasn't her. It was the bad man. And he knocked my human down and put him in the chair.'

'I see.' I looked around just in time to see my sister emerging from the cat door. She didn't look happy.

'Dougal, I could do with some help here,' she told me. 'Let's try and get the human free before we work out what's going on.'

Well, that was telling me, so I followed her back through the cat door. What we found in the main big room was disturbing. There he was, straining at the chair's long bits, but he couldn't get himself free. There was some funny grey stuff stuck to his face, and covering his mouth. Strange noises were coming from inside the grey stuff. It seemed like a strange thing for anyone to do to themselves. Fear and anger was pouring off him, so I sat down with my paws tucked in. 'Human? Would you like some help?' I asked.

Shadow didn't wait. She jumped straight onto his lap and he yelped. 'Shadow, you might want to stay off his private bits,' I called out.

She shifted a little and began to bite at one of the plastic things. Her strong jaws gnawed away it, and I was trying to tell him to calm down and let her help. But I wasn't getting anything back from him except generalised pain. A pity, because some humans do speak Cat. Ours do, especially Man. But this one couldn't understand us.

Shadow jumped down and walked up to me. There was a little streak of blood in her mouth. 'You'll have to take over, Dougal. My teeth hurt.'

I was as gentle as I could be, jumping onto his chair. The human squirmed and managed to make room for me. I could see his point. I'm a big cat, and nobody wants heavy weights on their tender bits. I've noticed this with Man, which is why I stopped trying to sit on his lap when I was still a kitten.

I saw that my clever sister had almost chewed through the white bit. I sank my teeth into it and began to gnaw. It took a long time, but I felt the white thing come apart. I jumped down to the floor and looked up at him to see what he'd do next. And it was really interesting. First he tore off the grey stuff from his mouth and spat. Then he waved his paw in the air and shook it. He looked down at us and said something that sounded like 'MPHBLCX!'

We looked at each other. 'Any idea what he wants now?' I asked my sister.

'I have no idea. And I'm not going to try my teeth on any more of those plastic things,' she said.

I didn't want to either. But we'd got one of his paws free, so that was something. Perhaps he could manage by himself from now on. I didn't feel good about staying in a house with an angry and embarrassed human with no clothes on.

'Mrrrew?' said a small voice behind us. We turned to see our little friend come into the room. She jumped up into the human's lap and began to wash his sore paw. She turned to us. 'He wants his flat plastic thing,' she said. 'The thing he talks into.'

That made sense to us. We've all seen humans talking to their plastic things. Perhaps he could call somebody to help out. So we divided the room between us. Shadow found it lying on the floor in the corner. 'Human?' she said. 'Is this what you want?' She pointed with her nose.

'MMMRAGH!' said the human. We looked at him again. Shadow pointed with her nose. Little by little the human managed to push himself, and the chair, towards the plastic talking thing until it was in reach. His paw reached down and he put it on his lap and began to play with it. We sat down and watched as he seemed to to talk to several different people.

Then things began to happen. A big car drew up outside with flashing lights. Humans came to the front door and knocked. Our human dragged himself to the front door and opened it. Two humans came in and talked to him. They got his other paws free. The human put on a big fluffy and then he called to us. We didn't understand any of it but Shadow looked at me. 'I think he was saying thank you,' she said.

Then the front door was flung open and a female human rushed into the house. She grabbed hold of the man and hugged him. And Shadow and I decided it was time to leave.

'Mew?' said our new friend. She came and touched noses with us both. 'Thank you.'

'It was our pleasure,' I told her. 'Take care, little friend.'

We made our way slowly down the street back towards home. Taking our time, and smelling the flowers and browsing on occasional bits of grass. We felt exalted, as well we might. Suddenly Shadow stiffened. 'Look, Dougal! There go the loud humans!'

The big car with lights had pulled up outside another house, and the blue-coat humans knocked on the front door. There was some angry human talk, and then one of the blue humans turned the other human around and tied his hands with a metal clip thing.

We went home ourselves, had some munchies and some water, and sat down on Man's bed to discuss our morning's adventure.

'You know what I think, Dougal?' my sister said. 'I think they must have caught the bad human. Did you see what the blue humans did to him? They put ties around his front paws, just like he did to Small Kitten's human. I think that's fair enough.'

'So do I. But what was it all about?'

'Small Kitten said that the bad human took his man's plastics away with him.'

'Plastics? Not the talking box? You found that on the floor.'

Shadow shook her head and flicked her front paw over her ears. 'I think she meant the flat plastic things humans carry in their leather things. I think they help humans to get stuff. You know when Man comes home with all the food bags? I've seen him putting his plastic thing away in his leather afterwards.'

I thought this over. 'That would make sense. Humans can get anything they want. I've always wondered how it works. So you get stuff using the little flat plastic thing? And the bad human took it away, and pinned him to the chair so he could get stuff using the plastic.'

'Small Kitten was right. He really was a Bad Human. But how did he get into the house?'

I looked at my sister. 'I think I know that. Small Kitten said that he likes to invite his lady human to come and play with him. And he uses the plastic talking thing to talk to her. Only you don't really know who it is, because there's only voices, right? So Bad Human was pretending to be the lady human and made the same noise on the front door. And I bet he told our human to meet him with no clothes on. Because they play with no clothes on later.'

'That was a bad trick to play. Do you think they'll give the Bad Human a thumping?'

'Maybe.'

Shadow leaned forward and began to wash my face. She still smelled of wild sausage.

'We're a good team, Shadow,' I told her. 'And you are a very clever cat.'

'And so are you, Dougal.'

And then we went outside to lie in the sun and listen to the birds playing in the trees.

The Fox
and the
Phantom

Jack Fennell

The Fox and the Phantom

M Y FOX WANTED A LOLLIPOP.

Dr O'Donnell glared at me. 'What's he saying?' he asked.

'Maybe if he gave out lollipops, his patients wouldn't be so afraid of him,' said Sproggett. 'Tell him.'

'He says you make him nervous,' I said to the vet.

Dr O'Donnell was a huge man. He knew perfectly well that he had that effect on some of his patients, and on other people. He found it useful, so he leaned into it.

'Hmm. Well, the problem is obvious: you're feeding him crap that foxes shouldn't eat.'

'I've been a brave boy. I deserve a lollipop.'

I swallowed. 'Really? I thought that foxes could eat pretty much the same stuff as us. I mean, urban foxes eat out of bins, don't they?'

'You know a lot of healthy urban foxes, do you?'

'Can we stop and get a lollipop on the way home?' Sproggett asked.

'This is a common problem with familiars,' the vet continued. 'You get intermittent flashes of whatever he senses, so you've been feeding him things that are palatable to you.' He scowled. 'Haven't you.'

I thought about lying, but only for a second. 'Well, yeah. Last year he ate a dead shrew that he found under a bush. There was projectile vomiting.'

'I can imagine,' said Dr O'Donnell, not sounding very sympathetic at all.

I cringed. 'How bad is it?'

'It's not serious yet, but you need to take his diet more seriously. Ideally, you should be feeding him mice, crickets and mealworms—'

My stomach lurched, and he heard me gag despite my best efforts.

'Or you could feed him on lean meat, rice, and bones; plenty of fruit, too.'

'That sounds doable,' I said, feeling a little bit better.

'It has to be raw, by the way.'

My stomach dropped again. 'All of it?'

'No – you can cook the rice. Just be thankful you didn't bond with something more exotic.'

'Is there any advice you can give me about how to deal with tasting what he's eating?'

Dr O'Donnell shrugged. 'I dunno. Yoga?'

Fossamore, a city in everything but an official charter, gets its name from the Irish Fosadh Mothair, meaning 'the encampment of the wooded swamp,' so the North-Western is probably the closest residential building to the site of the original settlement. There used to be a load of theatres in the North-Western's general vicinity, which established the edge of the wetlands as an artsy, bohemian neighbourhood in the early twentieth century; it was still a fairly groovy place to live when I had a flat there, if you didn't mind stepping around clumps of poets and bongo-players sitting on the stairs. One of them stopped me on the way up to my flat on the third floor.

'Hey, Jo – there's a guy outside your flat. He was askin' about you, but he wouldn't say why. Everythin' okay?'

'Don't worry about it; I'll be grand.' On the third-floor landing, I gestured for Sproggett to stay behind me. The man at my door was tall and slender, with jet-black hair and a bronzed complexion – a Returned Hy-Brasilian, by the look of him.

'Joanna March?'

'Yes, hi.'

He held out a laminated ID card. 'Sitric Edson Ó Gríofa. I work for Obsidian Securities. May I come in?'

I was between jobs, and opportunity was knocking. Obsidian were one of the largest private-sector security companies in the country; my dad had consulted for them a couple of times after he retired. I quickly opened the door, ushered my visitor inside and drifted towards the kettle. 'Lovely to meet you, Sitric! Please excuse the mess. How can I help you?'

He smiled. 'I think you've already guessed. We need a contraphysics consultant to look at something for us.'

"Contraphysics" – the polite, legal euphemism for "magic."

Sproggett paced around cautiously. 'What does he want?' Though I heard his voice in my head, I could only respond vocally, so as a general rule I had to ignore him around other people. It didn't stop him trying to join in on every conversation, though.

Sitric glanced at Sproggett, bemused. 'Your familiar's a fox?'

'Yeah. That's not a problem, is it?'

'I was told you had a dog,' Sitric said. Then, seeming to realise how abrupt that sounded, he added, 'Not that a dog would be a deal-breaker, mind.'

'Who referred you to me, if you don't mind me asking?'

'An old colleague of your father's.'

I chuckled. 'Dad would be delighted to hear that. So tell me, what's the story?'

Sitric shrugged. 'We're swamped at the moment, but we've got a heap of pro-bono and lower-priority cases on our books that we can't just drop, so we're looking for outside contractors to help us out.'

'This isn't just consultancy, then,' I said.

'You can see my issue, right? Nobody takes any notice of a woman walking a dog. A woman with a fox, on the other hand…not exactly inconspicuous.'

'We have ways to get around that issue,' I said.

'What ways?' Sitric asked.

'I prefer to keep that private,' I said. 'Nothing illegal, I assure you.'

'You're just making stuff up,' said Sproggett.

I turned to my familiar and squeezed his face. 'Yes, baba! We have our secwet ways!' Annoyed, he flounced off to the living room.

Sitric cleared his throat and took out his phone. 'Okay. The client is a union. It's a workplace negligence case.'

'With a supernatural element.'

'An apparent contraphysical element,' Sitric corrected me. 'Which you may be uniquely qualified to prove or disprove. Are you interested?'

'Yes.'

'Excellent. Four months ago, an investor named Neil Carnahan bought an old mansion called Vanderleigh House – it's up in the hills, about a mile off the dual carriageway between here and Limerick. The plan was to renovate it into a classy hotel. It's been empty since the seventies, and for a long time before that there were parts of it that weren't used at all.'

'It's haunted,' I guessed.

'Just listen for a minute,' Sitric said. 'Anyway, after he hires an architect and visits the site, he realises that the east wing is unsalvageable. So, he hires a crew to demolish and rebuild it entirely.'

'One of the workmen spotted a ghost.'

'I'm getting to it. So, on April thirteenth, while the demolition is underway, Carnahan suddenly asks the crew to leave one corner of the east wing alone. The architect, Monty Quilligan, calls the foreman, and says it's okay to leave it standing. Then, boom – those old walls collapse a few days later, on the sixteenth. Four men end up in the hospital. Their union wants to sue.'

I paused, waiting for him to continue. 'And there's a ghost involved somehow?'

'Oh yes,' he said, smirking. 'Carnahan is now maintaining that the site is haunted, and arguing that the resident ghost brought down the old walls. Legally, that would make it force majeure, not negligence, meaning nobody would owe the injured workers anything.'

In the wild-magic days between 1890 and 1930, it was established in Irish law that hauntings have a human origin: most unquiet spirits were people once, and they tend to be volatile because they came to a bad end at the hands of other people, which'll make anyone cranky. This puts hauntings into the category of force majeure, alongside war and political uprisings: circumstances beyond the policy holder's control, but caused by people rather than "Acts of God."

'So you want me to prove that the ghost isn't real?'

Sitric nodded. 'If you could prove that the "haunting" story was dreamed up after the fact, even better.'

'I'll probably need to visit the site.'

'Whatever you feel is necessary. Bear in mind that we want to keep this hush-hush, so if you approach these guys, try to do it surreptitiously.'

'*Surreptitious* is my middle name.'

'Liar,' said Sproggett from the living room.

It was an easy solve. Ghosts do not destroy their own habitats, for the same reason that goldfish have no vested interest in smashing their bowls. When they make a nuisance of themselves, it's usually because they're defending their territory to a point beyond what the living would consider reasonable. If there was a spirit in Vanderleigh House, the crew would have spotted it when they first entered. All I'd have to do was visit the site, and note the complete absence of evidence.

It was more practical to check the site out under cover of darkness – firstly, ghosts are more inclined to come out at night, so nocturnal reconnaissance was called for on the tiny off-chance that the ghost was real. Secondly, this investigation had to be covert. If I were to visit the place during the day, I'd have to sign waivers and wear protective gear, and I'd be escorted around the site: none of which is good for "surreptitious" snooping, and all of which is a massive pain in the arse when one has a symbiotic companion animal to consider.

'Are you gonna call the security person?' Sproggett asked as we got out of the car and started walking up the unkempt country road.

'Why? I don't see any signs up to say we have to keep out. Far as I can see, this is a public walkway, and I'm out for an evening stroll.'

We trudged forward in the dark – well, I trudged, and Sproggett nimbly scampered – expecting to run up against a perimeter fence sooner or later. The closest we got to such a thing was a wooden gatepost, onto which a handful of plastic signs had been tacked.

'Do we keep going?' Sproggett asked.

'Hmm… "Beware: Heavy Machinery"; "Protective Gear To Be Worn At All Times". Nope, I see nothing forbidding public access.' A few moments later, the gravelly ground underfoot had given away to muddy earth rutted with tyre-tracks, and we were standing in front of the old building itself.

'That was way easier than I thought it was gonna be,' Sproggett said. 'It's weird, right?'

I dialled the number Sitric had given me for the security coordinator: *Sorry; the number you have dialled is not in service. Please check your contact information, or try again later.*

'Yeah,' I said. 'It's weird.'

The churned-up earth was sprouting ferns and briars. The heavy machinery was long gone. There were sickly patches of vegetation to show where the cabins and portable toilets had once squatted, but the grass was well on its way back to full strength. The destruction of the east wing was unmistakeable, though: it would take the undergrowth years to cover over the jagged mound of broken brick, mass concrete, planks, and rebar.

'Okay,' I said. 'Let's move from the outside in.'

The ground had been exposed to four months of weather and new growth, but I kept looking for a print that stood out – alas, no sign of a smooth slipper-sole, a high heel, running shoes, or anything else that didn't belong in a construction zone.

One side of the front wall was covered in old ivy. I've hated ivy since the summer when my dad and uncle press-ganged my cousins and me into helping them pull a load of it off the back of my granddad's house. It sheds dust that you'll be washing out of your eyes for weeks, and it plays host to every kind of spider and bloodsucking midge you can imagine. The windows upstairs would have succumbed to its creep eventually, if local kids hadn't shattered them already. The downstairs windows were broken, shuttered and locked from the inside.

Sproggett was putting more distance between us than I liked.

'Get back,' I said. 'You're coming through too faint; you're gonna leave me fumbling around here.'

'You told me to scout around,' he answered. His voice was faint and echoey in my head.

'Where are you?'

'I'll be quick.'

'Tell me where you are!'

He didn't answer. His presence registered as a hum on the horizon. It felt like there was a magnetised needle in my head, pointing in his direction. I couldn't tell if he was too far away to communicate with, or just pretending to be.

At the rear of the house was a sunken courtyard, with a path leading off into the undergrowth and little sheds lining the walls, all overgrown and crumbling. There was no back door. It had fallen, been broken in, or rotted away long ago. There was nothing to bar my entry to the darkness beyond. Inside, I'd need Sproggett to stick closer to me. I was relying on his eyes, ears and nose to pick up anything that looked, sounded or smelled out of place.

Eventually, he wriggled out of the undergrowth and trotted to my side.

'Good of you to show up. See anything back there?'

'Old sheds,' Sproggett said. 'Maybe places for big animals, like horses or cows. The smells are all gone, though. Weeds everywhere, walls falling down.'

'Right.' I gestured to the dark doorway. 'Shall we?'

The inside of the old ruin was deathly still. With an entire wing destroyed, there should have been a bit of a breeze, but even the motes of dust that hung in the moonbeams were motionless, like drifting particles in deep-sea caves that never see a current. Every step I took echoed through the whole structure. The walls were covered in graffiti, decades upon decades of it, going back to a time before spray-paint, when teenagers carved things into wallpaper with any sharp implement they could find. Everywhere, I saw the tell-tale signs of copper thieves, too – hacked-up floorboards, the marks of sledgehammers and pickaxes on the walls, ripped-out light fixtures.

Sproggett had his nostrils to the ground, snuffling this way and that. 'Piss,' he muttered as he trotted back and forth. 'Mostly rats and mice, but plenty human, too.'

I kicked an empty beer can out of the way and shone my torch into a couple of corners. There were mounds of rubbish bags and old household appliances everywhere. The grand staircase had been destroyed along with the rest of the east wing, but the servants' stairs in the west were still intact. We ascended to the upper floors, which had been just as thoroughly defiled, though it was clear that truant teens were the most frequent visitors there. There was nothing left to distinguish one room from the other, except for the love-hearts and libels left by kids who were probably living responsible lives elsewhere by then.

Repeat visits from teenagers, fly-tipping neighbours and who knows who else: all of it stacked up against the presence of a ghost. Generally speaking, if a place is for-real-no-fooling haunted, people stay away. You might get legend-trippers stopping by for the thrill of it, but if they ever encounter something, they don't come back. You definitely don't get people spending the night more than once. I was more certain than before: this place had never been haunted.

That's what I was thinking, anyway, before I emerged from an empty room on the third floor, and found myself looking at a ghost.

The thing blocked the whole third-floor hallway: its tangled hair brushed against the ceiling, and its glowing rags billowed out to touch the walls. Its face and arms were skeletal, the bones charred. There were manacles around its wrists, lengths of rusted chain still attached. Sickly lights shone in its eye-sockets, and it was enveloped by a swirling miasma, like a cloud of grey water and shredded toilet-paper disgorged from an unblocked sewer.

There's a lot of lore about how to properly address a spirit, most of which is useful only if you can remember it in the chill of the moment. The best I could manage was, 'Shite.'

The thing unhinged its jaw. 'I'm the Sinners' End,' it said, its voice fluctuating and raspy.

'Lovely,' I said, backing up. 'We were just on our way.'

'What would you have done with your life, if you'd known that I'd be coming to end it?'

If ever there was a sign that we had to run, that was it.

'Split up,' I said to Sproggett. 'It can't focus on both of us at once.'

'Way ahead of you,' he answered back. He was being literal; I could sense him descending the stairs already.

The floating skeleton bastard ignored him, and came swooping after me. There was just one very stupid exit left. I sprinted to the last of the front rooms in the wing, shut the door, and ran to the westernmost window – where the old ivy was hopefully growing thick enough to support my weight. The empty, worm-eaten windowframe crumbled as soon as I laid hands on it, and I exited feet-first with all the grace of a cow trying to go backwards down a flight of stairs.

As I toed around for a secure-ish foothold, the door exploded off its hinges and slammed into the opposite wall. The thing came at me with its arms outstretched, jaw opened wide, shrieking.

I let go of the sill and trusted to simian instinct to guide my way to the ground. However, I don't have thumbs on my feet, and as far as modern science can determine, my distant monkey ancestors never wore boots while they were hastily ascending or descending trees in primeval Africa. My progress was mostly made up of slips, screams, and frantic grasps – less a "climb" than a fall with frequent interruptions.

Above, the thing was slamming itself against the wall. The impact shuddered through the ivy, raising clouds of gnats and desiccated leaves. I tried to rub my face on my sleeves to get the grit out of my eyes, when I felt something rush past my head – a brick.

I glanced up, and between the moonlight and the spectral luminescence, I could see the wall around the window buckle and bulge outwards as the ghost pounded on it from within. The ivy was the only thing stopping it all from crashing down on top of me, but it was starting to crack and creak under the weight. I felt a wave of terror rush at me from below: Sproggett was watching everything, panicking. I shouted at him to get back as slates started to slide off the roof and drop like guillotine blades.

The thing kept shrieking throughout it all. It only seemed to get louder as it realised I was getting away.

I jumped the last ten feet to the ground, scrambled to my feet and hobbled away at speed, with the noise of smashing masonry and spectral screaming rising to a crescendo behind. When we got out of range of the flying debris, we understood that the thing had not followed us out of the house, though it continued trying to break through the wall.

'You okay?'

'I'm fine. Are you?'

I picked Sproggett up and held him tight as I continued back to the car. 'It's okay, baba. Let's go home now.'

I was pointing my eyeballs at my coffee at the kitchen table the following morning, staring through it into nothingness. Sproggett sat on a chair beside me, resting his head on the table. I could feel him looking at me sidelong.

'That was a real spirit,' he said.

'Yeah,' I said. 'It was.'

'If that was a real ghost…then the case is open-and-shut. The lads who got hurt get nothing.'

'Yeah,' I muttered into the heel of my hand.

'It wrecked the place. You said that ghosts don't do that.'

'Yeah, I did.'

'So that's that, then.'

'Yeah. I suppose it is.'

I was on the sofa, staring at the ceiling. I had my laptop streaming a 24-hour internet goth-rock station that I wasn't really listening to. Sproggett slowly snaked his head over the back of the sofa to look into my face.

'You still have a lot of stuff to pay off.'

'I'm aware.'

'So you still need to rack up loads more billable hours. Even though you already know the case is a bust.'

'Sproggett, I'm thinking about all of that right now. You're pulling it directly out of my head. That's the only reason you even know what a "billable hour" is.'

'So…are we gonna have a "research" day?' He made his voice sound all plaintive, but a whump-whump noise behind the sofa told me that his tail was wagging.

Sometimes private investigators or consultants take a day off, then write it up as "archival research" and bill their clients for the time. I am not for one minute admitting that the thought ever crossed my mind, nor that Sproggett and I ever enjoyed a subsidised day of TV and junk food.

'No,' I told him. 'Obsidian's gonna follow up on every item on any invoice I send them.'

'We risked our lives, though.'

'And it's still only a few hours' work.'

'So if we wanna see a decent return for the danger we put ourselves in–'

'We're gonna have to go through the motions of a full investigation anyway,' I sighed. 'Yeah. I know.'

So, I was going to have to put in more legwork than I originally intended. For a start, I'd have to do some research so that I'd be at least as well-informed as the people who'd hopefully be paying me. Vanderleigh House was inside the county bounds, so a small fee to the local council got me a digital copy of the building's record from the Register of Derelict and Dangerous Sites; hopefully it would contain details of any suspicious deaths or disappearances that had taken place there.

Nothing. The family who owned it had left the country years ago, and when the last former inhabitant died in Malta in 1977, the probate proceedings lasted for decades after. By then, there were so many potential heirs, and so little interest from any of them, that the house just hung in limbo until someone offered to take it off their hands. There was nary a gruesome murder to be seen or inferred anywhere.

Surreptitiousness nearly got me squashed and decapitated by the world's angriest floating skeleton, so Plan B called for something a little less subtle. I made some calls, and started digging out old clubbing gear that I hadn't worn since I dropped out of university.

Most of Neil Carnahan's businesses were based in Dublin, but he wasn't the kind to put down just one root when he invested outside the Big Smoke. He had a restaurant in Fossamore, *The Ringleader*, and he was in the process of converting the floors over it into a vaguely defined "philosophers' club," a long-term project that had him making repeat visits. A search for his name in the newspaper archives revealed that he had been buying heaps of witchy antiques to decorate it at auctions across Ireland, Britain and the Democratic Republic of Scotland.

'You look stupid,' Sproggett told me as I checked myself in the mirror.

The performance of gender is a human concept, so even though we were conjoined at the psyche, it was pointless trying to explain to him that goth-ness was how I pushed my femininity to the point where it became a spiky forcefield.

In all fairness, though, I had laid on the war-paint a little thick that morning. I looked like a black-and-white photo of a mime playing the wicked stepmother in a vampire pantomime.

'I have to look the part,' I said, trying the number for Carnahan's security coordinator again, in vain.

'You're pretending to be a journalist.'

'A specific kind of journalist.'

I'd taken a guess that Carnahan would agree to an interview with a magazine that shared his interests, and the guess had paid off. My efforts to arrange a meeting with Monty Quilligan, on the other hand, were all in vain; by then, I was sure that the architect's secretary was screening out my calls.

'There's only one reason a guy like that moves to this town and sinks thousands into a wizards' social club,' I said, pulling on a vaguely Victorian faux-leather jacket. 'He's a wannabe.'

Magic – or contraphysics, or "the antithetical field" or whatever you want to call it – has been declining since the Great Depression. I know people want to believe it will come back one way or another, and I hate to be a dry-shite about it, but all the indications are that we will never again see magic of the kind that flared up around the world between the late Victorian era and the Roaring Twenties – hence the persistent nostalgia that has influenced interior design ever since.

The Ringleader restaurant was full of art deco patterns with Ogham and Celtic spirals woven in; every wall radiated an aspirational swinging-sorcerer vibe. I had a feeling that Neil Carnahan wouldn't have a problem with me bringing my familiar onto the premises outside of opening hours.

Sure enough, Carnahan made a beeline for Sproggett rather than introduce himself to me. He was a big, broad-shouldered, ruddy-faced man in his early forties, with a pair of hands on him like something from the Natural History Museum. I thought the back of his jacket was going to burst open as he doubled over, knelt down, and started smooshing Sproggett's face.

'Ah, isn't he dotey!'

Sproggett flashed annoyance at me, a demand for intervention.

'He says you're fairly dotey yourself, Mr Carnahan,' I said.

Most people get awkward when it's pointed out to them that animals can observe them back. Carnahan released Sproggett and hauled himself upright, hiding his embarrassment behind a wide grin. 'You're connected to him?'

I smiled back. 'It's like having a backup brain.'

'Dead handy when it comes to doin' interviews, I'd say.'

I laughed. 'He is indeed. I'm pure disorganised with my notes sometimes.'

Carnahan laughed back. 'I doubt it. Anyway, Miss Hartigan – tell me what I can do for you.'

'Please call me Fiona,' I said. 'I'm here, Mr Carnahan, because a little birdie tells me you recently hired an exorcist for a property you've acquired nearby.'

He raised an eyebrow. 'You talk to birdies too?'

It was time to chance my arm. 'Our readers are into gossip as much as anyone else, Mr Carnahan; they just happen to be more interested in hauntings than celebrities. So, when we hear that a well-known investor has retained the services of an exorcist, we naturally think that there's a story there that might be worth following up on.' If I had guessed wrong, the worst that could happen was that Carnahan would tell me so.

Carnahan pursed his lips and tried not to look too pleased with himself. 'Who did you say you worked for, Fiona?'

'*Let's Talk About Hex*. I'm just a freelancer really, but I think a story like this would look good on my CV.' I gave him a pleading look. 'What do you think? Might you be able to comment?'

'Hmm. All right. I can't go into everything, 'cause there's law at the moment, but about the haunting itself, ask away.'

'So it's true that you've hired an exorcist?'

'Of course I did. Have to be responsible, y'know. Hired him myself; didn't wanna roll the dice with the county council, an' end up with some chancer hired off the bleedin' internet.'

'Is this your first haunting? How does it make you feel?'

'Are you asking if I'm scared?'

I bit my lip and tucked my hair behind my ears. 'Well…that's the kind of thing our readers are interested in most of all. How people react to it. The feeling of being alone in a dark place, when an icy finger runs up your spine.'

Carnahan's jaw dropped a bit, and he shivered. 'Good Jayzes! Not my cup a tea, but sure, each to their own.'

A wave of derision erupted from Sproggett, who was watching from a safe distance beyond the reach of Carnahan's hands. 'Mission accomplished; he fancies you.'

I cleared my throat. Sproggett kept his thoughts to himself once more.

'I wasn't there,' Carnahan continued. 'Sorry to disappoint. I only heard about the ghost after word of the accident got out; a local historian got in touch to warn me.' He forced a laugh. 'Look, I don't wanna be blowin' my own trumpet here, but I've dealt with scarier things than bleedin' ghosts.'

I raised an eyebrow and smirked. 'Oh yeah? What's scarier than the unquiet dead?'

'I've had people threaten to make *me* one a' the unquiet dead, if you get my drift!' He shrugged. 'This is a rough game. If you don't make enemies, then you're not playin' it right.'

'So…if you haven't seen the ghost yourself, how do you know for sure it's even there?'

'Look, all I know is what that historian fella told me; he emailed me this long story about the shite that used to go on in that house an' the things people have seen there, an' I took him at his word.'

'I'd like to talk to that historian, if I could. Do you have his email?'

'Yeah, totally. I'll forward that on to you. In the meantime, here–' He reached into his inside jacket pocket and handed me a business card. 'If you don't land yourself a column with that magazine, giz a call. I think you'd fit in with the Ringleader Philosophers' Club. Come back for the big opening, an' see what you think of it.'

'How do you mean, "fit in"?'

Sproggett burst into peals of high-pitched chuckles, cutting Carnahan off before he could answer.

There was a new gelateria with outdoor seating in the town centre, and a certain someone was keen to try it. For the sake of keeping the peace I agreed.

'I'll have my usual,' Sproggett said.

'Sprog, we've never been here before. You don't have a *usual*.'

'Hazelnut with a dribble of chocolate sauce.' He was doing his laughing-face, and wagging his tail.

'Fine. But you have to be good and eat proper fox-food for the rest of the week. This is a treat, understand?'

'Love you, Jo.'

I kept glancing around as I waited in line, fearful that Dr O'Donnell was going to spring out of nowhere to kick my ass. Back outside, I let my mind wander over the ins and outs of the situation, staring vacantly at the distant monument to the Famine-relief workers who built this town.

'Maybe we should look into Carnahan's insurance policy,' I said, as I wiped the ice cream from Sproggett's muzzle.

'Why?'

'If Carnahan and his mates are claiming force majeure to avoid paying compensation to the injured workmen, they have to prove that the ghost died by human action, and not by some tragic accident.'

'You said there's nothing like that in the file.' Sproggett tilted his head to the side. 'But that doesn't make a difference, because there is a ghost. We're just going through the motions here, remember?'

I drummed my fingers on the table. 'I know. But there was just too much human activity around that place for it to be haunted by such a dangerous spirit. The bloody thing could've crushed me, but people were dumping their rubbish in that place, and kids were in there dossing off from school! No way does something that violent go unnoticed for fifty years. Someone would've said something.'

'What does that leave, though? D'you think the ghost was somehow transplanted from somewhere else?'

My phone chimed out an email alert. It was from Carnahan, and there was a document attached, purporting to be the history of Vanderleigh House. There was no contact information for the local historian who supposedly wrote it. I skimmed through it, baffled: there was a lot about the spirit calling itself the Sinner's End – who it was in life, how it died, and why it was floating around now – but there weren't any details that corresponded to the known history of the house. It wasn't exactly compelling to read, being a list of short bullet points with phrases capitalised, underlined, bolded, or all three.

I downloaded it and checked the file properties. I snorted when I saw the name of the author.

'Here's an epiphany for you,' I said. 'Carnahan's source for the ghost story was Horace Emmet Gubbins. Looks like we're heading to the magic shop.'

If the *Tenebrazon Emporium of the Arcane* had been around when I was sixteen, it would loom large in all my embarrassing memories today. When teenage counterculture started to go vaguely weird and witchy all those years ago, any shop could break even by putting a few pentangles and contorted willow twigs in the window. The Emporium came along just a little bit too late to catch that wave, and in a few years had faded away to a basic head-shop. Sproggett had never cared much for that kind of establishment, and he held its proprietor in particular contempt.

'People like this used to kill foxes and cut out their tongues,' Sproggett said. 'Their tongues, Jo. You know why?'

'A magic charm for removing sharp objects from a person's flesh,' I replied.

Sproggett seemed surprised. 'How'd you know that?'

'You bring it up a lot.' I glanced around and hunkered down next to him. 'By the way, the rule about not talking to each other in front of other people goes double in here.'

'You think he might be able to hear me, too?'

'I don't think so, but it doesn't hurt to be cautious.'

A bell tinkled over the door as we entered. Horace Gubbins, master of the arcane, was leaning on the counter, head resting on one fist, flipping through a magazine.

'Vaping gear and supplies in the cabinet to your left,' he said in a flat, bored Limerick accent. 'Lava lamps and novelty ashtrays on the right; we don't sell seeds, heat lamps or blacklights, and the bongs are for decorative purposes only.'

'Actually,' I said, 'I'm looking for information about ghosts.'

He looked up, straightened himself, swept the magazine off the counter and brushed down his velvet jacket. 'Oh, I see,' he said, switching to a sonorous, Oxford-accented voice. 'My apologies; these days, I do not receive many visitors inquiring after the unknown.'

Professionally, Gubbins called himself Dr Dorchadas, from the Irish for "darkness." Sproggett called him Dork-Ass.

'Maybe it'd help if you opened during witching hours instead of regular business hours.' I held myself back from doing finger-guns.

He frowned. 'Hmm.' Then his gaze alighted on Sproggett. 'Why hello there, Old Soul!' He came out from behind the counter. 'Are the two of you...bonded?'

'No,' I said. 'I do wish I could talk to him, though.'

Dork-Ass arched an eyebrow. 'Of course, the subtle language of foxes is a tricky thing to master.' He smiled at Sproggett. 'Isn't it, my friend?'

'I'm not your friend, you bollocks,' Sproggett answered, in his subtle language.

The wizard chuckled, as if at a private joke, and nodded. 'How true, Master Fox. How true.' He reached out and tried to pat Sproggett on the head; Sproggett flinched and growled.

'So,' Dork-Ass said as he returned behind the counter, 'you wanted to learn about ghosts?'

'Yes.' I glanced over my shoulder and leaned in closer. 'In fact, I'm wondering if you know anything about the one in Vanderleigh House.'

'Vanderleigh House?' Now he was doing that elongated 's' thing beloved of cult leaders, ASMR performers, and cartoon snakes. 'I'm afraid I'm not familiar with that one.'

'Really? Because I heard that Neil Carnahan hired you to perform an exorcism there, only the ghost is still around.'

'What did you say your name was?' His real accent was starting to leak out.

'It's okay,' I said. 'I already spoke to him.' Note the technical absence of any lie in that statement.

He narrowed his eyes. 'Sometimes, exorcisms must be performed several times. It's not an exact science.'

Sproggett snorted. 'Not when you're just making it up as you go along, anyway.' He walked around the shop, sniffing at the various display cases, then stopped at one, alert and intrigued. 'Ask him about the giant spider with the upside-down human face. Trust me.'

I kept my expression neutral. 'So, this hasn't happened at any of your other exorcisms?' I paused, and steeled myself for a leap of faith based on Sprog's not-always-reliable insight. 'Not even...that incident with the giant spider?'

Dork-Ass peered at me, and then looked over my shoulder in

Sproggett's general direction. I looked too: Sprog had thrown himself down inside the door, the picture of boredom. The wizard turned back to me.

'What giant spider?'

'Oh come on, Doctor,' I scoffed. 'Are you saying there are others out there that don't have human faces?'

'You are...very well-informed.' He was still wary, but not as defensive as he had been a moment before. 'That was about six years ago, at the site of a former industrial school where some unsavoury things had taken place. The spider was actually the soul of an abusive teacher.'

I widened my eyes. 'That is so cool! How many exorcisms did it take to get rid of him?'

Dork-Ass chuckled. 'Just the one.'

Sproggett started rolling around on the floor, yowling and whining like a cat caught out in the rain.

'Is he all right?'

'He's fine,' I said. 'I'm afraid that's my cue to go, though. He just gets a bit cranky when he's hungry; it's almost like having a toddler.'

'I can imagine.' Dork-Ass knitted his brows. 'Remember to stay away from haunted sites, though.'

'I will,' I said, as I opened the door and Sproggett scampered out. 'Don't worry – the Old Soul here keeps me on a short leash.'

Dork-Ass obliged me with a beatific smile and a wave of his hand as we left.

We waited until we were safely back in the flat before talking. The first thing I said was, 'Gawd, that man is so full of shite! Thanks for rescuing me with that stroppy-pet routine. I could tell he was gearing up to bore the arse off me for the rest of the day. Now, tell me: where the hell did that stuff about the giant spider come from?'

Sproggett's tail started to wag. 'What's the name of the cereal that's like big bricks of grain?'

'Neet-Weet.'

'That's the one. Look up "Neet-Weet monsters," and tell me what you see.'

I opened up the laptop and did as he suggested. The results were all about a set of six glow-in-the-dark stickers that were given away with boxes of the cereal in the run-up to Halloween in 1986. The images were highly detailed paintings of gruesome-looking creatures; from what I could see, they were now quite valuable collectors' items.

'Okay, there's the spider. It looks badass, actually.' I paused and gasped. 'No bloody way!'

There among the monsters was a picture of the spirit that had nearly killed me in the old house. It was so exact in every detail that it could have been a photograph.

Sprog's tail was fairly whacking the couch now. 'I know. He has the whole set in a display case in his shop; I spotted our friend among them when I was nosing around, and reckoned it was worth taking a punt on one of the others.'

'How did you work out that the spider was the one to ask about?'

Sprog paused. 'I…didn't. I picked it because it stood out. Sorry, I was just excited.'

'Right,' I said, sighing with retrospective relief. 'Well, now we know that this isn't the first time.'

'The first time for what?'

'I don't know.'

I searched for any mention of an old industrial school being haunted by a giant spider, and got no hits; neither was there any result for Dork-Ass being hired to exorcise such a place. However, there were several results for Neil Carnahan applying to redevelop one into a tech hub. The architect named in connection with that project was the same guy connected to the renovation of Vanderleigh House – Monty Quilligan. A search for him and Carnahan together returned mentions of three other developments they had worked on over the intervening six years.

'These aren't ghosts,' I said.

'I know,' said Sproggett.

'No, listen: we know that the look of the ghost came from this image. Plus, there's no record of anything that might have caused a haunting. This thing isn't a ghost – it's a thought-form!'

'You've lost me.'

'It's like an imaginary friend that takes on a life of its own. They're sometimes called "elementals." Back in the wild-magic days, some researchers believed that people could create them by accident, even in their sleep. Some even argued that most reports of spirits and demons back then were just people's repressed emotions coming to life.'

'And these guys brought the Neet-Weet monster stickers to life?'

125

'Not exactly. I think they collaborated on imagining the same thing, with Dork-Ass supplying the imagery and the fake back-story.'

I opened the bogus history document and rotated the laptop so Sproggett could see the layout. 'Look – bullet points and short sentences. The language is really basic too. They made sure that they were all imagining the exact same thing in every particular: three minds focused on bringing an entity into being.'

'Why, though?'

'Well, think about it. We saw no security measures at Vanderleigh House, and the number for their security coordinator isn't working. They've probably done this at least once before, and they might do it every time they start a new project. Dork-Ass writes up a plausible history involving a terrible ghost, and the other two memorise it and study it until they start to believe in it; the imaginary ghost becomes real, and it haunts the site like a paranormal guard-dog!'

My phone rang.

'Hello?'

'Hello, Ms March. This is Monty Quilligan. I need to speak with you. I know you met with Carnahan and the warlock. I have a good idea what you're looking for. Be at the café opposite the train station in ten minutes.' He hung up before I could answer, but his number was there on the screen.

So, I called him back, and I cut him off before he could speak again.

'Hi, Mr Quilligan. You forgot to block your number when you called me just then. I'd be happy to meet you, but I'm afraid that the time you indicated isn't workable for me. I can meet you there in two hours.'

There was a string of muffled curses at the other end. 'I have things to do, Ms March! I can't be hanging around–'

'Another day, then. It was nice talking to you, Mr Quilligan.'

'Wait!' There was a defeated-sounding sigh, and more muffled swearing. 'Fine. See you there in two hours.'

Quilligan was fuming when I showed up to the café five minutes late. His head was as round and as bald as a cue ball, though he was cultivating a little pointed beard to offset it. I took my time ordering and walking over to the booth. When Sproggett leaned on the table, Quilligan re-arranged the cutlery, napkins, empty coffee cup and paper plate so that none of them were touching the fox directly.

'I missed my train,' he hissed. 'They wouldn't let me transfer my ticket; I had to buy a new one.'

I smiled. 'In future, you should remember to get a flexible one.'

Quilligan scowled. 'I'll bear it in mind. Now, who are you working for?'

'I can't tell you – client confidentiality.'

'Am I in someone's crosshairs?'

'Possibly.'

Quilligan looked at me closely, and sneered. 'You know nothing. You're fishing.'

'Mr Quilligan, you should've known that it might have been dangerous to leave that section of the wall standing, and you okayed it over the phone without inspecting it in person. It's fairly obvious that you're partly to blame for those men's injuries.' I took a sip of my tea.

'So someone is gunning for me, then?'

'They might well be,' I said. 'That's entirely up to them. I'm just telling you what I know.'

'Okay. Well, we can't talk here. Let's go someplace with fewer prying–' He winced and massaged his temples, then pointed at Sproggett, who was staring into his eyes and wagging. 'I'm sorry, but could you make it stop doing that? It's really distracting!'

'He's got a gun,' Sproggett said. 'Under his left arm. Brand new. It's got the same kind of oil on it that your dad uses.'

'Thanks, Sprog.' I turned to the architect. 'Mr Quilligan, we're going to stay right here, and you're not going to do anything with that firearm. Do I make myself clear?'

Quilligan's eyes flicked from me to Sproggett and back. 'Just tell me how long I've got. I can leave the country tomorrow morning if need be.'

'What?' It suddenly dawned on me. 'Nobody wants to kill you, you eejit! They're planning to sue you!'

'Oh,' he said. 'Well, when you work with Neil Carnahan long enough… you come to expect the worst.'

'And you thought you'd handle the worst-case scenario by kidnapping me at gunpoint?' I turned and gave the customers at a nearby table a big smile. 'Audition,' I whispered. 'Wish me luck!'

The elderly couple's expressions remained dubious, but they turned their attention back to their own plates.

I locked eyes with Quilligan. 'This meeting was your idea. Is there something you want to get off your chest?'

The architect dithered. 'Okay. Carnahan didn't have permission to tear down Vanderleigh House. There's a Preservation Order on it. The only reason Carnahan got his hands on it at all is that the former owners didn't want to be responsible for it; none of them live here anymore, and they didn't want to be prosecuted for letting it fall apart.'

'Did you and Carnahan know that when you demolished one of the wings?'

Quilligan rolled his eyes. 'Give me a break. Preservation Orders have never stopped anyone. You get around them by working over the weekend, while the council offices are empty and nobody's answering their phones. On Monday they wag their fingers and fine you, then you pay it and get on with your day. Everyone does it; if people didn't break Preservation Orders, nothing new would ever get built!'

'That's what Carnahan was planning to do at Vanderleigh, then?'

'Yeah. He's done it loads of times before. This is the first time he's ever had a problem paying.'

'Let me guess: the fine was really big this time, because he keeps on doing it.'

'Carnahan freaked, and told the lads to stop everything; he thought that if he left part of the wall standing, it might mitigate things. He called me in a panic, and told me to tell the foreman whatever it took to call a halt to the whole thing.' He shrugged. 'You know the rest.'

'Yeah,' I said. 'Your made-up ghost got out of control and seriously hurt people. That never happened before.'

Quilligan gawped, but he didn't ask me how I knew. 'The things get... realer every time we do it. And every time we do it, it's harder to get rid of them afterwards. Practice makes perfect, I suppose.'

'Mr Quilligan, if you have any decency, you'll contact Sitric Ó Gríofa at Obsidian Securities, and give him a detailed account of everything.' I wrote Sitric's number on a napkin and slid it across the table to him.

'Why should I? They have no case. What happened was awful, but nobody's going to take them seriously if they go into a courtroom and say that a fictional ghost attacked them.'

'I've found someone who'll take them very seriously indeed,' I told him. 'The Leeton Grain Corporation – owners and global licensers of the Neet-Weet cereal name, and the ones who commissioned the original paintings that those stickers were based on, back in 1986. They're concerned about potential PR damage, and they're looking into the feasibility of a copyright infringement lawsuit.'

That, I admit, was a complete load of cobblers. It had the desired effect, though.

'They wouldn't! They'd be laughed out of court!' Quilligan's eyes were saying *No, no,* but his pallor was saying *Oh, shite.*

'You know how these big corporations are,' I said. 'They're a bit Sun Tzu when it comes to defending their trademarks: they've got the grindstone in hand, and they're looking for an egg to drop it on. The fact that you're named in the union's lawsuit doesn't bode well.'

'And if you were me?' Quilligan asked.

I shuddered. 'I'd start hormone therapy immediately. If you want my advice, though, I say you need to get ahead of it as soon as possible. Talk to my guy at Obsidian and tell him that you'll be a witness for the union if they agree to go after Carnahan instead. If it's just his name on the lawsuit, he can't pass the blame to you later.'

Quilligan didn't think too long about it. 'Fine,' he said. 'Fine. I was planning to cut ties with him anyway.' He squirmed. 'Now if we're done here, I have to wait half an hour for the next train, so could you get that animal out of here, please?'

I waited a long time for Sitric to get in touch. Obsidian paid me what I invoiced them for, plus a bonus for convincing Quilligan to play ball. I paid my most egregious outstanding bills and continued to draw the dole while applying for jobs I had no hope of getting, being a filthy witch tethered to a semi-feral animal. I did make more of an effort to feed Sproggett properly, and I experimented with different seasonings until I found one that made his approved food taste less horrible to me.

'He's still in awful shape,' Dr O'Donnell said a month later.

'What are you talking about? He's lost weight, he has more energy, and he's feeling better all round!'

'There's something we're not seeing here,' said the vet, shaking his head. 'I'm going to have to order more blood-work, and possibly an MRI.'

In case you were wondering – no, my medical card doesn't cover the fox to whom I'm psychically linked.

'What are you basing this on?' I asked.

Dr O'Donnell sighed. 'On you. I can tell something's not right. You're as pale as a sheet, your eyes look sunken, and your lips are discoloured. It indicates poor circulation, if nothing else.'

It took me a moment to process all of that. 'Is that what you've been relying on all along, to diagnose my familiar?'

'It's a handy indicator of his state, yes, but–'

'It's makeup,' I said. 'Goth makeup.'

The vet's mouth hung open. 'Oh. I didn't…isn't the goth style supposed to be more, uh, pronounced?' He cleared his throat. 'Your look is quite subtle.'

I let an awkward couple of seconds drag out. Then, through gritted teeth, I said, 'Give my fox a lollipop.'

When I got back to my flat, Sitric was waiting outside. 'How're you keeping?'

'All right.' I opened the door. 'I was beginning to think you'd forgotten all about me.'

'Nope, just up the wall, as usual. I dropped by to tell you how everything went. Quilligan went on the record with the union's legal team, and they went after Neil Carnahan instead. Carnahan dropped the force majeure angle and settled. Everyone wins.'

'Except Carnahan.'

Sitric shook his head. 'The compo he paid turned out to be a drop in the bucket. The weirdest thing happened. Y'know the Neet-Weet cereal?'

My stomach dropped. 'Yeah?'

'The people who make it heard about the whole thing, and made an offer on Vanderleigh House. They're delighted that someone brought one of their old promotions to life, and they're going to turn that old pile and its estate into a haunted Neet-Weet theme park.'

'You can't be serious.'

'I am. Carnahan and Gubbins set up a company between them and registered their method as a proprietary technology. Then they immediately sold it all to the cereal people for more money than you or I will ever see in our lifetimes. Gonna be a big economic boost to the county, too.' He smiled. 'So, yeah. Good job.'

'Terrific. So…any other work going?'

'Well, Quilligan is planning to sue Carnahan and Gubbins for what he reckons is his fair share of the profit, and his solicitors have asked one of our subsidiaries to help build his case. I don't suppose you'd be interested?'

'I'd sooner eat my own ears.'

'Yeah, I thought so.' He flicked through some files on his phone. 'Which is why I gathered all the other cases on our books in need of a contraphysics consultant into one handy bundle, in case you'd like to take a look.' He smirked at me, the cheeky git. 'Will I email it to you?'

'You offering an advance on any of them?'

'I'll tell you what I can do.' Sitric tapped on his phone. 'There's one involving a haunted barn that's got about two hours' work in it, tops. Take a research day for it and invoice us; I'll make sure it goes through.'

'I like this guy,' Sproggett said, wagging his tail.

Sitric grinned. 'Cheers, buddy! You're not so bad yourself.' He paused long enough to let me know that I was making a stupid face, and added, 'What? You think you're the only one with secret ways?'

I gawped after him as he sauntered down the hall and around the corner to the stairs, then turned to my fox and asked, 'Did you hear that?'

'Yeah,' Sprog said. 'He gave us the go-ahead to order in the junk food!'

My email alert chimed. My inbox was suddenly full of paying work, and I'd spent weeks trying to disguise the taste of raw chicken and mealworms. 'Yeah,' I said. 'Let's do it.'

'Love you Jo.'

'Love you too, Sprog.'

Time Spent with a Cat

Chuck McKenzie

Time Spent with a Cat

'YOU'RE ABOUT TO GET A VISITOR,' SAID THE CAT, SITTING ON – OR rather, hovering about a centimetre above – the edge of my desk. It directed its gaze to the wall behind my chair, where my framed licence hung. Private Investigator James Carpenter. 'Might want to straighten that up. Can't afford to look sloppy in front of clients right now.'

I hate cats. I really do. Feral, lazy, arrogant creatures. So it does seem unnecessarily cruel that my Conscience took the form of a talking tortoiseshell kitten. Maybe current theory on Consciences being "shared subconscious projections" is crap after all. Or maybe I just really hate myself that much. Four whole months since Everyone, worldwide, got a Conscience, and still nobody can explain a damned thing about it. All I knew for sure is that my previously thriving business had slowed to zero as society worked through the resulting chaos.

'Up yours,' I snapped, and flicked the pen I'd been holding at the Cat. The pen, of course, passed right through the animal and clattered against the floorboards.

There was a knock on the door. Three sharp raps.

I bit down on the follow-up insult I'd been about to hurl at the Cat. I'd already learned the hard way that potential clients get twitchy if they catch you swearing at a kitten, even a possibly-imaginary talking one that everyone can see and hear. I stood up, angrily buttoning my suit jacket. 'Come in,' I called, forcing a smile

Of all the people I might have guessed would be at the door when it opened, Alan Cook wouldn't have been one of them.

Alan nodded. Flashed a smile that vanished as quickly as mine had. 'Jim.' He looked uncomfortable, standing there in full military uniform, with his cap tucked underneath his arm.

I sat down again, carefully considering my response. 'Well. This is a surprise,' I said, eventually.

Alan gestured towards the empty chair facing my desk. 'May I?'

I made a vague gesture. Alan slowly stepped into the office, looking around at the bookshelves and filing cabinets lining the walls.

A tall figure walked in behind him.

'Holy crap!' I said.

Alan's Conscience bowed, treating me to a huge grin that shone blindingly white against dark skin. 'Beautiful day, Boss! Allow me to introduce myself—'

'Baron Samedi,' I interrupted. 'From *Live and Let Die*.' I gave Alan a look. 'Didn't know you were a Bond fan.'

'I'm not. But we both know that counts for nothing.' Alan glanced pointedly at the Cat on my desk.

Samedi laughed delightedly and clapped his hands together. 'Just so, sir! Just so!' His voice was rich and creamy, exactly as it had sounded in the movie

'Well, I'm starting to feel better about being stuck with an animal I despise,' I said. 'Better than being stuck with what probably comes across nowadays as an Uncle Tom routine.'

Alan's pale face turned crimson. 'It's no bloody joke. Half the people I interact with now assume I'm a dyed-in-the-wool racist.'

'You're not?'

The crimson tone deepened. 'No, I'm bloody not!'

I smiled. 'Well, if it's any consolation, in *Live and Let Die* Samedi used the subservient approach to cover the fact that he was a pretty damn scary dude. Powerful and deadly. Almost took out Roger Moore with a machete.'

'Great. I'll send a memo around the office.'

'Alan?'

'Yes?'

'What do you want?' I asked, wishing I hadn't thrown the pen at the Cat, so I could tap it on the desk to indicate how valuable my time was.

Alan drummed the fingers of both hands against his cap for a moment. He looked stressed, but that's what the army does to you. Plumper than when I'd last seen him. A Colonel's insignia on his shoulder-board. Uniform beautifully clean and laundered, which meant he was either in a relationship, or far better domesticated than when we'd been cadets together. It looked like staying with the army had been good for Alan. And that stung. I'd been the one who'd been expected to rise through the ranks, after all.

'I wanted to offer you a job,' said Alan, at the same time as Samedi said 'He wants to apologise, Sir.'

Alan turned sharply in his chair. 'Will you please be quiet?' he snapped. Samedi shrugged. Alan turned back to me.

'Well, which is it?' I asked.

'Both would be good,' said the Cat, and I felt an unfamiliar sense of camaraderie, which faded quickly.

Alan looked at the Cat, then back at me. 'It talks.'

'It does,' confirmed the Cat.

'Well?' I pressed.

Alan floundered visibly for a moment, and I almost felt sorry for him. 'Yeah. Both,' he admitted. 'Look. Jim – I'm truly sorry.'

I waited.

'I never asked you to take the rap for me,' he went on, 'but I should have spoken up. They clearly knew it was one of us, but I guess neither of us thought you'd get booted out over it. And when you were, I should have fessed up. Apologised.' An awkward pause. 'I do understand if I'm a bit too late with this.'

I opened my mouth, having no idea of what was going to come out.

'Apology accepted,' said the Cat. 'How the heck are you a Colonel already?'

I turned to berate the Cat...then realised that, despite the mixed emotions stirred up by Alan's visit, the anger just...wasn't there anymore. 'Yeah.' I nodded slowly. 'It's cool.'

Alan did his best to maintain a military demeanour, but I saw how he sagged slightly in his chair. This clearly hadn't been easy for him. Not that I was ready to actually feel sorry for him.

'So, again, how the heck are you a Colonel already?' the Cat persisted. A fair question, I thought. It takes a minimum twenty-one to twenty-three years to go from Officer Cadet to Colonel, even assuming one has the drive, ability, and suitability for an army career. Last I'd seen Alan – just over fifteen years ago – he'd had none of the above; an undisciplined party-brat, looking for a blokey work culture to immerse himself in while he waited for his inheritance. The polar opposite of myself. Another reason why getting kicked out of the army had hurt me so badly.

Alan cleared his throat. 'Look...what happened to you was a massive wake-up call for me. I knuckled down. Pushed myself. Had some lucky breaks along the way. Rules were bent to get me to where I am now, because it turned out I had a certain…efficiency…in overseeing tech projects.'

'Special Operations, huh?'

Alan said nothing.

'I bet it's Special Weapons,' said the Cat.

Alan gave the Cat a look.

'Definitely Special Weapons,' the Cat fake-whispered to me, loudly.

Samedi inclined his head slightly. 'We can't tell you that, Sir. Unless, of course, you wish to take the job…?'

I drummed my fingers against the desktop for a moment. 'Okay, so what is it?'

'Homicide investigation.'

'What, MPs can't handle it?'

Alan looked down at the desk, then back at me. 'There are complications,' he admitted. 'The deceased isn't military. She's a private contractor, and was about to pitch what she suggested would be a game-changing piece of tech to us. It would look…bad…on several levels if the army went barging in to investigate.'

The Cat tilted its head, quizzically. 'Why not the police, then?'

'Fair point,' I added.

Alan cleared his throat again. 'Well, I convinced a judge that letting non-specialist investigators in on this was potentially dangerous. The compromise we reached was that the investigation would be conducted by a non-military party nominated by myself, and that I'd also remain on-site as a safety liaison. You'd obviously have to submit a full report to the court afterwards, to eliminate the possibility of collusion, but–'

'Okay,' I interrupted. Something just wasn't adding up here. 'But again, why not someone with the specialist skills you need? Surely you could use the vast resources of the army to find and vet a suitable investigator? I genuinely don't see why I'm your go-to guy, here.'

Alan exhaled loudly. 'Because we don't have the time, whereas I knew I could immediately refer the judge to your impressive record as a private investigator.'

I nodded. Once you've been in the army, they never really stop watching you. And I figured maybe Alan had personally kept tabs on me, in the way some people like to check up on ex-partners: a combination of nostalgia, guilt and curiosity. 'Is the judge not aware of our…history?'

Alan clenched his jaw slightly. 'Very much so. Came clean on everything.'

'That must have hurt,' said the Cat.

'Oh, yes indeed!' grinned Samedi.

Alan nodded. 'Yes. But this is too important. I needed to demonstrate to the judge that you were one of the best at what you do, that you weren't going to do me or the army any favours, and…'

I nodded. 'And that I could keep my mouth shut.'

'Just so,' said Samedi, softly. 'Just so, Sir.'

'Okay. So why the need for such speed?'

Alan fidgeted in his chair. 'Ah. Well. The judge has given us a strict time limit on our nominee investigating the scene before she opens it up to the civilian police. She's just as concerned about the military contaminating evidence as she was about the cops screwing with hazardous tech. Police forensics are already on the scene, assisting us, but–'

'How long?' I cut in, impatiently.

'Twelve hours.'

I swore involuntarily.

'From the time that I left the judge,' Alan added. 'Which was an hour ago.'

I actually laughed. 'Oh, okay then.'

'So…what's in this for us?' asked the Cat. 'To take on a full murder investigation on such a ridiculous time limit?'

'Samedi?' Alan prompted.

Samedi held up his right hand, palm out so I could see the dollar value that had materialised there, seemingly in white chalk. Interesting, I thought. Using his Conscience for secure communication. 'Your fee, Boss.'

I blinked. My mouth may have drooped open slightly.

'Great poker face, dude,' muttered the Cat.

'Erm…right. Right. And, er, what if I don't actually solve the case?'

That's just your consultancy fee,' Alan said. The sum on Samedi's palm shifted and changed. 'That's your final fee if you actually close it.'

I swore again.

The Cat gave me a look.

'Okay,' I said. 'Let's…I mean, I'm in.'

Alan extended his hand across the desk. After a moment I stood, grasped it, and shook. 'You can take me directly to the scene?'

'Car's waiting outside.'

I shrugged. 'Okay, then. Let's go.'

'Look,' said Alan, as we took the stairs three at a time down to the street, our Consciences floating beside us. 'The time limit isn't necessarily as grim as it seems, because there's really no doubt about who committed the murder. I was already on premises, with some of my team. We heard a brief, shouted argument, then what sounded like a gunshot. Rushed in, saw the husband standing near the body, nobody else in the room, nobody else on premises, windowless room with a single point of access.'

I frowned. 'Sounds like an open-and-shut case. So, what's the issue?'

It was Samedi who replied. 'Because there's no weapon, Sir. No weapon at all.'

Samedi wasn't wrong; no weapon whatsoever to be found. There was, however, a sizeable hole in Karen Scott's head, right where her left eye should have been.

'My team swept the room from top to bottom,' said Alan. He gestured towards a young woman in sterile duds, who was swabbing nearby surfaces. 'Forensics haven't found much either, other than chemical residues.'

'Guess I won't bother with my own search, then.' I glanced at Scott's body again, then quickly looked away. I'd seen dead bodies before, despite dealing mostly with cheating spouses and internal corporate theft, but most of those I'd seen previously had been nicely laid out on mortuary trays, prettied up for the purposes of identification.

Scott, on the other hand, was still spreadeagled where she'd collapsed, a chaotic jumble of limbs that unpleasantly contrasted the elegant navy business suit and skirt she was wearing. Maybe forty years old? There was a look of faint surprise on her pallid face. No Conscience, of course. Would have vanished at the moment of death, which – if it turned out that Consciences weren't subconscious projections – seemed to me like pretty cruddy behaviour. No kids, Alan had told me. Just Scott and her husband, a lecturer at one of the second-tier Melbourne universities.

'Excuse me?' I called over to the forensic staffer. 'Is there any chance we could…cover her up?' She nodded understandingly, and started fishing some plastic sheeting out of the kit near her feet.

'What did that?' I asked Alan, gesturing towards the crater in Scott's face.

'They were checking when I left to see the judge – hang on.'

Alan addressed the forensic staffer as she laid the sheeting over Scott's body. 'Delgado, was it? Any word on the projectile?'

Delgado shrugged, as did John Lennon, standing just behind her, 'There isn't one. Whatever killed her drove itself well into her frontal cortex, but there's no sign of it in her head, and no exit wound.'

'Firearm?' I asked. 'Or maybe something like a slingshot?'

'No, definitely a firearm,' said Delgado. 'There's powder burn around her eye socket, and across her face. Shot at close range. But no bullet, or even fragments, which makes no sense whatsoever.'

'Imaginary bullet from an imaginary gun,' Lennon intoned. 'Strange days indeed.'

I looked around the room. The building was one of those 1940s-style houses that had been converted to serve as both a workplace, with a foyer at the front for receiving clients, and a private residence at the back. The room in which we now stood had been Scott's study-cum-workshop, separating the foyer from the home: a laminate desk and built-in bookcases full of textbooks on one side, complex arrangements of glass tubing, pipettes, beakers and sinks along a long, linoleum-covered bench on the other. Against the wall opposite the door, a metre-long aquarium full of small, colourful fish sat atop an enclosed wooden stand. Above this, a wall-mounted shelf held a mini stereo system, some CDs, and a photo stand. On the work bench nearest us was a large Plexiglas tank, the back wall of which was thickly coated in what appeared to be ballistics gel. Near the tank was a large serving tray upon which sat a number of champagne glasses, with a magnum of champagne resting in an ice bucket in the middle.

I glanced at Alan. 'So, you and your team rushed in here the moment you heard the shot. No time for the killer to clean up any incriminating evidence?'

'I wouldn't have thought so.'

'The husband does have powder residue on his hands, though,' Delgado piped up. 'But it's not enough evidence to convict him, unless we can find the weapon.'

I nodded. 'Okay, thanks.'

Delgado smiled, and she and her Conscience went back to their swabbing.

I rubbed my chin thoughtfully. 'So. So, so…'

'You have an idea, Sir?' asked Samedi.

'Where are we at?' I asked, more to myself than to anyone else.

'Well,' said the Cat, 'we know she spent a lot of time in here.'

I automatically opened my mouth to tell the Cat to shut up, then paused. 'Go on.'

'Well, the room's set up for both admin and practical chemistry work, so she probably did almost all of her work in here. And the sound system and aquarium suggest she either spent some of her downtime in here, or at least spent enough of her day in here to want to make the room more liveable.'

I looked around. Yes. I could see all of that myself, even if the Cat had pipped me to the post in terms of collating that information into a concrete observation. Interesting. 'So, she was a workaholic.'

'Which could have been putting a strain on her marriage. Or maybe she threw herself into work to escape an already crappy marriage.' The Cat gave a very human-looking shrug.

'Yeah. Yeah.' Good thinking. 'A chat with the husband's in order, I think.' I glanced at the tray of champagne glasses. 'She was clearly prepped for a congratulatory drink.'

I turned to Alan. 'You said that you and your team were already here for Scott's pitch when the murder occurred.'

'Yeah.'

'Did you interact with her in any way?'

'Yeah, briefly. She came out to the foyer to say hello, let us know she wouldn't be long, that sort of thing.'

'How did she seem?'

Alan thought about it. 'Excited. Rushed, maybe a little stressed. But she did say she'd only just gotten back from a week away in Sydney, so she was probably trying to finalise prep for the demonstration.'

'Huh,' said the Cat.

Alan and I both gave the animal a look. 'What?' I asked.

'Well…just seems odd that a highly-successful scientist would be running behind the eight ball to prepare a demonstration with so much financial success riding on it.' The Cat glanced at Alan. 'Unless she was a bit eccentric that way?'

Alan looked at me. I raised an eyebrow.

'Well, no,' said Alan. 'She was always very professional. Meticulous.'

'But obviously excited about the demo?'

'Yeah, but she was always excited about her work, certainly in all the time I've known her. Didn't make her any less professional.'

'Do you think you could find out what she was doing in Sydney? Talk to anyone she might have interacted with there?'

Alan nodded, probably pleased at the prospect of having something to do. 'Sure!'

'Okay, great.'

Alan gestured towards the door. 'Shall I?'

'Not just yet,' I said. 'Still some things I want to run past you before I start trying to put it all together.' I considered for a moment. 'This demo. Would you personally have been able to sign Scott's paycheck, here and now, if things had panned out?'

'Well, I'd certainly have been able to authorise picking up the project. Although, depending upon the price tag, I may have had to tap sources further up the line. Assuming I felt it was worth it.'

'And…what's your gut feeling? Do you think whatever-it-was would have been worth tapping extra funding?'

Alan grimaced and spread his hands wide. 'Well, I mean, she'd told us absolutely nothing about the nature of the project.'

'Educated guess, though? Had she always delivered in the past? On commissioned work? Any other original projects that she pitched successfully?'

Samedi grinned. 'Oh, indeed, Sir! Yes, indeed!'

I looked at Alan. 'What sort of areas was she working in?'

Alan shuffled slightly, saying nothing.

'Just the basics,' I said. 'Areas of expertise, general applications, that sort of thing. Could give us some clues.' I pulled out my phone and glanced at the screen. 'Eight hours and counting.'

Alan sighed. 'Okay, well, most of her work was in defence metallurgical research and design. Producing materials used in fast construction of military instalments. Support structures for bridges, oilfield equipment, deep sea projects, that sort of thing.'

'Actual weapons, though?'

Alan shook his head emphatically. 'No. These materials don't lend themselves to that.'

'Okay, fair enough.' I glanced hopefully at the Cat.

'No idea,' admitted the Cat.

I glanced around the room again, and a thought occurred. 'Alan, how many personnel were with you for this pitch?'

'Five. Not including myself. Why?'

So: six military personnel, plus Scott, plus–

I looked over the champagne tray. Seven glasses. Hubby hadn't been invited. Which could simply mean that Scott had intended this strictly as a work thing. Or…

'Okay,' I said. 'Colonel, if you could start making some calls about Scott's Sydney trip, that'd be great.'

'On it,' said Alan. 'What are you going to do?'

'I think I'll have a chat to Mr Scott,' I said.

'Prendergast.'

'I'm sorry?'

Scott's husband tilted his head back so that, even from his seated position, he could look down his nose at me. 'My wife's surname was Scott. Mine is Prendergast.'

Was, I noted. This guy had already relegated his wife to the past. A small, yellow video-game star spun cheerily above his shoulder, in stark contrast his own cold demeanour. Balding, with what hair remained clearly dyed brown. Oversized fashion spectacles. Expression like he'd sucked a lemon. Full suit and tie. It all combined to make him look like an insufferable twat. I did my best to remember that twat didn't necessarily mean guilty.

'Oh, I'm sorry. No offence intended,' I assured him. 'And I'm genuinely sorry to burden you at what's obviously a very difficult time, but I do need to ask you–'

'As I've explained to every other cretin today,' Prendergast snapped, 'I won't be discussing anything with anyone except for my lawyer.'

I caught the eye of the military guard standing beside Prendergast's chair. Her expression was professionally neutral, although the bluebird on her shoulder was giving me a distinct *If you don't punch him, I will* look.

'Right. Well. That's a shame,' I said, 'because – as I believe has been explained to you already – for the moment you'll have to make do with a lawyer assigned to you by Colonel Cook. A right that you've waived, I note. So, given that you are literally the only current suspect in your wife's murder, you may actually find that answering my questions is very much in your interests.'

'Assuming you didn't kill your wife, that is,' added the Cat.

A tiny smile touched the edge of Prendergast's sneer. The effect was highly unpleasant. 'I'm not saying anything,' he said. 'And when you finally have to release me due to lack of evidence, my lawyer will tear each and every one of you to shreds.'

I caught the bluebird's expression again: *We could make it look like an accident.*

'Excuse me a moment.' I glanced at the Cat. 'Quick chat in the corner?'

We retreated far enough away for Prendergast not to be able to overhear us. Which was a fair distance, as it happened. They'd confined Prendergast to his own study, situated in the residential part of the house, and it was frankly huge: all dark wood and opulent leather, lush carpeting and armchairs, and bookshelves crammed with hardbacked volumes, many of which looked antique. A massive, well-lit aquarium, filled with a dizzying assortment of tropical fish, illuminated the far end of the room

'Clearly guilty,' opined the Cat.

'Absolutely. But super confident that we can't pin anything on him.'

'Interesting.'

'Very,' I leaned closer to the Cat. 'Look, I feel like I'm maybe getting a handle on – you.'

'Oh yes?'

'Yeah. It kinda seems like you notice all the same stuff that I would, only it takes ages for those details to filter through to my conscious mind and percolate into something useful, whereas you process it all straight away.'

The Cat licked a paw daintily. 'Okay.'

'Is that a yes?'

The Cat shrugged.

'Well what I'm wondering is: seeing as how Prendergast's refusing to spill, how much information do you think you could get out of him if I did all the talking?'

'Reading his body language, you mean? Facial tics, breathing, that sort of thing?' The Cat peered past me to regard Prendergast. 'I can give it a go. Keep in mind, though, anything I can tell you would legally be considered conjecture, not proof.'

'Oh, I know, but if we can at least get a handle on the Why, then maybe we can get to the How more quickly.'

The Cat shrugged again. 'Sure. I'm in.'

'Just let me do the talking, okay?'

'You're the boss.'

Prendergast deigned not to acknowledge us as we approached him.

'Sooooo, Mister Prendergast. How did you and your wife get along?' No answer. 'What was the fight about? Can you tell me that?'

I gave the Cat a sidelong glance.

'Financial issues? Maybe you felt she was spending too much time working?' No response. 'Or maybe something more trivial. Someone left the cap off the toothpaste? Jealousy over one of you having a better aquarium display than the other?'

'Was she about to divorce you?' interjected the Cat.

Even I saw Prendergast stiffen at that one. I nodded, and beckoned the Cat to follow me back into the corner of the room.

'You saw his reaction to the divorce question?' asked the Cat.

'Oh, yes indeedy. Did you glean anything else from him?'

The Cat scratched thoughtfully behind its ear. 'Well, his breathing increased when you asked about money.'

'Makes sense if they're getting divorced. Wonder if she has a pre-nup? He certainly has more expensive tastes than I figure an academic's salary can support. Anything else?'

'Well, that crack you made about aquarium fish? I got a pretty strong reaction to that one as well.'

'Huh. Any ideas about that?'

The Cat shook its head. 'None whatsoever. Maybe we should pop back to Scott's workshop?'

'What, and check out her aquarium?'

The Cat shrugged.

The Cat hovered at my elbow as we both peered through the front of the aquarium, which contained around a dozen pretty little blue-and-red fish, some aquatic plants, a couple of small rust-coloured pieces of slate, and an ornament shaped like a sunken galleon sitting on the white gravel at the bottom. Nothing that struck me as significant. I glanced at the shelf above the tank. There was no indication of any music-share accounts on the stereo display, just the CDs stacked beside it. Mostly 80s and 90s Oz Rock, I noted: Baby Animals, Midnight Oil, The Living End, and so on. Music that a 40-something-year-old woman would have listened to in her teens, and probably the actual albums she'd bought back then, judging from the worn state of the jewel cases. The multi-photo picture frame beside the CDs held a number of photographs of presumed family and friend, as well as a couple of a younger Karen Scott – standing on a beach, drinking at a party, posing in front of a small home aquarium – and a far more recent pic of her next to the aquarium the Cat and I now stood before.

'Check the stand?' the Cat suggested.

I nodded, squatted down, and opened the door on the stand. Basic (I assumed) aquarium equipment: the softly-humming motor for the filtration system, a small open-top container that looked like it was being used as a bin, a small net, a container of fish food, and a small plastic box containing vials of aquarium chemicals.

'The net's damp,' the Cat noted.

'Yeah.' I pulled the bin towards me. Inside were a few algae-encrusted tissues, and the remains of a clear, mid-sized plastic bag, a hole torn in one side, the top knotted with a rubber band. The sort of thing you'd bring an aquarium fish home in.

'Bag's wet, too,' said the Cat.

I peered at the brightly-coloured fish in the aquarium. 'So, something's been introduced to this tank within the last day or so. And since Scott only just returned from interstate, Prendergast must have done it.'

'These fish are different from the ones in the picture,' the Cat noted.

'Are they?' I stood, and checked out the photograph of Scott in front of the aquarium. 'Yeah. Looks like goldfish here. And in the older photo, too. So, what are these?' I indicated the current residents of the tank.

'No idea. Is it even significant?'

I shrugged, pulling my phone out. 'Maybe it's relevant to the argument between Scott and Prendergast.' I started Googling. 'I think they might be neon tetras,' I said, eventually.

'Okay. So?' asked the Cat.

'Not sure if that's relevant in and of itself,' I said, slowly, 'but...' I turned towards Delgado, who had moved on to swabbing the sinks on the work bench. 'Hey, Delgado? Did anybody search the aquarium yet?'

She shook her head. 'No. We all figured if a weapon had been stashed there, it'd be easily visible.'

'What if it'd been shoved under the gravel at the bottom?'

'The husband's hands and arms were dry.' Delgado shrugged.

'Okay. Thanks.' I stared through the front of the aquarium again. Dead end.

'Maybe, what if Scott was working on some sort of stealth tech?' the Cat suggested. 'Bends light, or something, so it's invisible to the naked eye?'

'Something that could be sitting right in front of us,' I finished, nodding. 'Yeah. But that line of investigation could be endless, and yield nothing. Although, I guess a quick look at the specifics of her past work might at least give us a clue.'

I Googled Scott's name. Found some articles. Started browsing.

'Oh, hell!' I said, after just a few moments. I showed the screen to the Cat.

'Oh, HELL!' the Cat echoed.

We both peered back into the aquarium

'Delgado!' I called out, as I bent to retrieve the net from the stand. 'Do you have an evidence bag handy? And something I can use to dry off some evidence?'

'Sure,' said Delgado, as she and Lennon hurried over. 'But what—'

I turned to her, shaking excess water from the slate-like fragments in the net. 'Here. I need these as dry as you can possibly manage, and bagged up.'

I turned back to the Cat. 'Okay.'

'Pieces starting to fall into place?' asked the Cat.

'Yeah, maybe,' I said. 'Just need to check Scott's outdoor rubbish bin, then Google the difference between keeping goldfish and tetras. And then we see what Alan has to tell us about Scott's interstate trip.'

'So?' I asked.

Alan glanced at the small collection of physical evidence I'd taken from the aquarium. 'What's all this?'

'We'll get to that,' I said. 'What did you find out about Scott's trip?'

Alan nodded. 'Okay, well, she was up in Sydney for eight days. Spent much of that time catching up with friends – it's where she grew up. Lunches, bars, a couple of nights out on the town.'

'Did you talk to any of those friends? How did they say she seemed?'

Alan shrugged. 'Seems like she's rather different outside of a working environment. You tend to think people will be more businesslike at work, and emotional in their personal life, but Scott was apparently the opposite. Excited about work, in general, but more cool and calm during her downtime. Her friends describe her as being laid-back, even when partying, but not demonstrative or excitable.' Alan paused. 'Her lawyer describes her the same way.'

'Lawyer?'

'She visited her family lawyer. Couple of meetings.'

'Divorce?'

Alan nodded. 'Flew back here with papers ready to serve to Prendergast.'

'I don't suppose the lawyer mentioned whether Scott had a pre-nup?'

'No.'

I sucked my teeth. 'Never mind, easy enough to check, although I'll bet my consultancy fee that the answer is yes. And you say the lawyer described her the same way Scott's friends did, as laid-back?'

'Well, his actual description was *clinical*, but I guess it amounts to something similar.'

'Right.' I glanced at the Cat, who regarded me from the workbench.

'What–?' Alan began, but the Cat shooshed him.

'Give him a moment. He's percolating.'

'He's what now?'

'Percolating,' Samedi supplied. 'Like a fine coffee, Boss. All the elements coming together.'

'Okay, then.' Alan gave me a hard stare, which I ignored.

I steepled my fingers in front of my face, thinking, pacing slowly back and forth. Thinking some more. 'Okay.' I said eventually, rubbing my hands together. 'I think I've cracked it.'

The Cat coughed politely.

I gave the Cat a look, then nodded slowly. 'We cracked it. Together. But it's a pretty long explanation, and not completely linear, so stay with me on this. And no interruptions, because it's all still percolating.'

Alan and Samedi both pulled identical expressions of impatience.

'Okay,' I said, yet again. 'So, first clue was the fish. We figure Scott asked Prendergast to look after her goldfish while she was away; feed them, probably administer chemicals to treat some condition they were suffering from.

But while Prendergast shared her interest in fish, he didn't really give a crap about following her instructions. The marriage was pretty bad by this point, although Prendergast doesn't seem to have suspected that Scott was preparing to divorce him. So he neglected the fish, and they died.'

'Which a quick search of the outside bin confirmed,' added the Cat. 'It was pretty rank.'

'We found a torn plastic bag in the bin under the aquarium,' I continued, 'and realised that Prendergast had replaced all the fish within just the last couple of days.'

'Except that he chose the wrong fish,' said the Cat.

'See, all the personal stuff Scott kept in here was for nostalgic reasons. The music she loved as a kid, photographs, and she kept goldfish because she'd kept them as a child also. But Prendergast isn't nostalgic like that. He wants the best of everything. Trophies. So when he replaced the goldfish, he replaced them with what he considered to be better fish. Neon tetras. More sparkly and exotic-looking.'

Alan nodded. 'I see. And that's what the argument was about, right?'

I held up a finger. 'Yes – but not for the reasons you think. It wasn't the goldfish per se she was angry about. But we'll come back to that.'

The Cat stretched. 'See, from what you've said, Scott was very calm when dealing with personal issues. It was work matters that made her emotional. Ergo, Scott's anger in this case was work-related.'

'Okay,' said Alan, looking nonplussed.

'So,' continued the Cat, 'stick a pin in that for the moment, and let's consider the demo Scott was planning for you. The ballistic gel block over there indicates the demo definitely involved a weapon, despite your assertion that her field of expertise had no applications in actual weaponry. And it seemed fair to assume the demo weapon was the same one used to kill Scott. A weapon that then apparently vanished into thin air.'

'So, I started Googling some of Scott's previous work,' I said, 'hoping to get some hints about what sort of weapon she might have been developing.'

I gave Alan a stern look. 'Why didn't you mention her specific area of expertise was in dissolvable metals?'

Alan gave me a blank look. 'Well, because, I mean, it didn't seem relevant.'

'Why not?'

Alan shrugged. 'I mean– What? You're suggesting that Scott made some sort of firearm out of dissolvable metal, and Prendergast killed her with it, then disposed of it in the aquarium?'

'That doesn't seem obvious to you?' I responded, incredulously.

'Well, no – look, like I said earlier, the materials Scott produced were used to create support structures for military constructions.'

'Sure,' I interrupted, 'that's what you said. But a fuller explanation is that she created materials used to build short-term support structures. So a deep-sea base, for example, could be built in record time using Scott's metal to support concrete or other materials that were still curing or settling, after which those supports would dissolve away, allowing full access to, and functionality of, the base. Yes?'

Alan was looking increasingly frustrated. Even Samedi was starting to give me the evil eye. 'Yes, that's right, but – but – we're talking thick metal, here, dense metal. It takes weeks for supports like that to dissolve in water, if not months. In fact, you need a heavy nitric acid solution to dissolve even a small piece of this metal effectively, and even then it can take anything from several hours to a full day.'

I nodded again. 'But what if you used 3D printing or some such to produce really thin pieces of dissolvable metal?'.

'My friend,' said Samedi, 'I can see where you are taking this. But any 3D-printed weapon strong enough to survive being fired would require a solution far more acidic than aquarium water in which to dissolve.

'Unless that weapon was intended as a single-use firearm,' said the Cat.

I gestured towards the plastic bag on the bench.

Alan's eyes widened. 'Is that–'

'That,' said the Cat, 'is what's left of Scott's weapon. Pretty badly corroded, but a forensic team can probably confirm it.'

Alan pressed his fingers to his temples, as though warding off a headache. 'But how did it deteriorate so fast?'

'Okay,' I said. 'So, Scott hit upon the idea of a single-use, water-soluble firearm, something that could be used for, say, assassinations, and disposed of quickly. At this point, I'm 99 percent sure she managed to create a metal that was both sufficiently strong to hold together during the firing process, and thin enough to allow a reasonably short time to dissolve, by adding some extra element to the 3D printing process; I dunno, maybe titanium, or some such. Again, forensic examination should confirm this. Same thing with licking the issue of dissolvable metals taking ages to dissolve – she developed a mix that could dissolve within minutes rather than hours, and I'll come back to that in a moment,' I added, as Alan opened his mouth to interject.

'So,' the Cat continued, 'Scott organises the demo. And with the promise of a massive payout looming, she decides that this is the perfect time to organise her divorce. She flies out to Sydney, organises the papers, parties a bit, gets back into town just ahead of the planned demo. She rushes around to prep the pitch – only noticing at the last moment that one major element of the demo has been utterly screwed up.'

'The fish,' I added. 'Or rather, the aquarium. And yes, we'll get to that in a moment. So she confronts Prendergast about it, flies into a rage, almost certainly loses her cool enough to blurt out that she's kicking him to the kerb, and Prendergast – in a fit of rage, or more likely desperate not to lose the lifestyle to which he's become accustomed – grabs the prototype off the bench here, shoots Scott in the head, then dashes over to the aquarium and drops the gun in.'

'So, he understood the properties of the weapon,' stated Alan.

'Some,' the Cat agreed. 'Enough to know the weapon was supposed to dissolve in water. Assuming he wasn't already privy to the minutiae of his wife's work, Scott may have clued him in during the argument when she tried to explain why she was so angry.

'You know, tust the basic details: "I was going to use the aquarium to dissolve the gun in! I had everything how I wanted it, and you've gone and ruined it!" That sort of thing.'

'He probably thought she was just being precious about the fish, but that the gun would still dissolve. Which is why he was so damn confident we wouldn't find it.'

I gave Alan a look. 'Which leaves us with two questions; why did Prendergast's replacement of the goldfish lead to a work-related argument with Scott, and what happened to the bullet that killed Scott?'

Alan looked pointedly at his watch.

I grinned. 'Don't be like that. Trust me, you're going to love this.'

Alan sighed. 'Oh, go on, then. You're obviously dying to surprise me.' He glanced at the Cat. 'Both of you.'

The Cat preened. 'So, the issue with making these metals dissolve fast is the need for nitric acid. Fortunately, if you can't immerse it in acid, you can pump an acid gel through the microstructures of the metal.' The Cat winked at Alan. 'Google is our friend'.

'Problem is,' I continued, 'an assassin looking to dispose of a murder weapon immediately after use is unlikely to have access to nitric acid. So Scott developed a metal that could dissolve rapidly in any liquid, so long as the pH – the acidity – was within a certain narrow range. Again, your forensic bods will have to check the debris to ascertain exactly what went into the mix, but the upshot is that she managed to construct an amalgam that dissolved quickly – in minutes – in regular old drinking water, which generally has a pH of seven'.

Alan nodded slowly. 'That's brilliant, if it's true. You could dispose of a weapon like that in a sink, or toilet.' Then he frowned again. 'But the water in the aquarium took hours to reduce the weapon to that state.' He indicated the remains in the bag. 'So why did Prendergast dispose of it there instead of chucking it into one of these?' He indicated the closest sink on the workbench.

'Good question,' I said. 'For starters, if you'd busted in here and seen the tap running, that might have alerted your attention to the sink before the weapon could dissolve. But I don't think Prendergast actually considered that. See, as a result of whatever Scott told him during the argument, I think Prendergast already had in his head that the aquarium was going to be used in the demo, to show your team how easily the weapon could be disposed of. Of course, we also know that he didn't have sufficient info to realise that it wouldn't work – but I'll come back to that. So, in that moment of panic after he killed Scott, he runs to the aquarium and has sufficient smarts to drop the gun in behind the ornaments and plants, where ideally it would have gone unnoticed while it dissolved completely within minutes. Which is exactly the demo Scott had planned for your team.'

'So, why didn't it? Dissolve quickly, I mean?'

'Cat?' I prompted.

The Cat nodded. 'Going back to the goldfish. Different species of aquarium fish require water with different pH. Goldfish, for example, love a pH of around seven. The same as–'

'Drinking water,' finished Alan. 'Holy crap!'

'Exactly. But when Prendergast replaced the goldfish with neon tetras, which prefer a pH of around five-point-five, he added an alkaline solution to the water,' the Cat indicated the box of aquarium chemicals sitting on the bench, 'not realising it was going to ruin Scott's demo.

'Scott, however, realised it as soon as she noticed the goldfish had gone. Which – going by the timing of the argument – was only a few minutes ahead of the demo. She flies into a rage, tells Prendergast he's out on his ear, and gets shot for it.'

Alan and Samedi both nodded, wonderingly. 'Wow. That's – wow,' Alan said. 'Holy crap. So the water was still acidic enough for the metal to dissolve, just not sufficiently so to make it happen fast.'

'Luckily for us,' I agreed.

'But what about the bullet, my friend?' Samedi urged. 'The human head is not filled with drinking water, after all!'

'No,' said the Cat. 'But want to guess the pH of human blood?'

'Unbelievable,' murmured Alan. Then: 'I think we have everything we need, at least to get Prendergast properly charged, and to have a stop put on the intrusion of the police on the scene while the court accesses Scott's files to corroborate your findings.'

He glanced at his watch. 'I'd better run, take Prendergast in, talk to the judge.' Alan stepped up to the bench and picked up the bag of metal fragments.

'Want us to come with?' I asked.

Alan paused, considering. 'Not just yet, no. I mean, we'll get around to all the paperwork you'll need to sign off on. And I'll action the commission fee as soon as I get back to the office, full payment once the judge rules the case closed, yeah?'

I nodded. The commission fee alone would keep me in comfort for a very long time. 'Cool.'

'Besides, my friend,' added Samedi, 'the Boss will be talking shop with the judge, looking to get access to the lady's work. Sensitive information being discussed, yes?' He winked.

I nodded. 'Palms to be greased.'

Alan gave Samedi a stern look. Samedi laughed. 'Just so, my friend. Just so.'

Alan extended his hand. 'Thanks, Jim.'

We shook. 'You're welcome,' I said, and meant it.

I leaned back on against the bench with a sigh as Alan and Samedi left.

The Cat floated over beside me. 'You look happy.'

'Yeah.' I admitted. 'It felt good. Not just having a case after so long, but something that actually presented a challenge.'

'Massive pay check doesn't hurt, either.'

'Agreed.'

We ruminated in silence for a moment.

'So, listen,' I began.

'Mm?'

'Just, um, thanks for everything. Y'know? I mean, frankly, I still suspect you're a projection of my subconscious. But even if that's true, if I really am basically talking to myself, so to speak, then it doesn't make much sense to be treating you badly. So, y'know. Sorry.'

'Apology accepted,' said the Cat. 'Only–'

'What?'

'Well, what if I am, in fact, a magical, immaterial, talking cat?'

I shrugged. 'Well – either way, you were really helpful today. It would have taken me more time than we had to put all the pieces together, and maybe not even then. So, thanks.'

'My pleasure.' The Cat stretched luxuriously. 'Soooo, in lieu of payment for my services, how about giving me a name?'

I blinked. 'Um. Yeah, sure. Any preferences?'

'I quite like...Coco.'

'Cool, Coco it is, then.'

The Cat – Coco – nodded. 'Yay. Has a nice ring to it, don't you think?'

'Coco the Cat, you mean?'

'Coco and Carpenter.'

'Whut?'

'You know, on the door of the office.'

I gave Coco a look. 'Let's not get ahead of ourselves. A name is the best you get out of me for the moment.'

Coco shrugged. 'Fair. How about Carpenter and Cat.'

I sighed. 'That'll do, Cat. That'll do.'

Where the Wild Things Are

Atlin Merrick

Where the Wild Things Are

A LEXANDER 'ALLIE' HUONG MAKES RULES. LOTS OF USEFUL RULES. However, if Allie actually followed most of them, he'd never have discovered his favourite cheese, started fighting crime, or fallen in love with a werewolf.

Dog. Sorry, Vikka is a weredog.

Anyway, if Allie was good at rule following, he'd still be doing little more than teaching at Trinity by day, grading by night, and enjoying occasional day trips away from Dublin.

Fortunately, as stated, Allie emphatically hardly ever only sometimes maybe once in awhile follows his own rules. For example, this afternoon he was running. Not because he was late, he wasn't, but because he's always running. Rule 5, run. Made back when Allie was an undergrad and started making rules to live by.

So, he was running for his bus, close enough to smell exhaust fumes, when two things happened. Three if we're being thorough. Four if we're pedantic.

Allie's mobile rang.

He reached for it as he ran, breaking rule 18.

He stepped on a pile of wet, brown leaves and, as dictated by physics and fate, when Allie fell down, his mobile went up and with a chesty grumble the bus pulled away.

Before his butt hit the pavement he had time to reflect on many things, did Allie Huong.

One: he was glad his mobile had a rubber case.

Two: he thought maybe he should make an addendum to rule five along the lines of if you ignore your own rules expect what you get.

Three: he recalled the woman he saw yesterday, the one who did exactly what he was doing now – running, slipping, falling in comforting slow motion, then–

3…2…1

–landing flat on her back on a pile of muck. He doesn't know if she made a new rule for herself too, because her friends helped her up and he caught his bus to the college. He thought no more of it until now, just now, looking at the tree above, brittle-gray and bare though it was early spring. He wondered if this was one of those dying trees the papers said were popping up all over Dublin.

'Allie!'

Allie stopped wondering about the skeleton tree and groped for his phone. The screen was unbroken. He grunted a cheer.

'Allie! Iss's me, Jaya Jaya fee fia!'

Allie sat up, winced at the pain of his fast-bruising bum. 'Hey there missy, are you drunk?' He began knee-walking toward the lawn of Merrion Square.

'Yes! But for a very good reason! A big log of Burwood Bole broke two of my toes!'

Allie stopped knee-walking. 'What?'

'It's fine now, I'm doped up and I'm fine now. Except those bastards keep arguing about the DOP of my cheese!'

Jayashri Kelly's work took her across the EU, and she could tell you for first-hand fact that gourmet cheese was a cutthroat game.

'I don't know what that means, Jay.' Allie stretched out on the park's squishy lawn. Spring in Dublin was anything from gentle sunbeams to impulsive spurts of rain. Today was spurts.

'It means I'm stuck in Berlin until tomorrow.'

Allie knew where this was going. 'I know where this is going. Okay.'

'I know iss's last minute and – what?'

Two young men came by with an umbrella. One was a student of his last year. Allie smiled and gave them a thumbs up. While lying on the grass. In the rain. Talking on his mobile. Possibly he should get up. There was a rule in there somewhere.

'It's okay,' he said. 'I'll take the dogs out. We'll go to the fort. We'll share some takeaway.'

Jaya squealed drunkenly. 'Ooo, I'm so gonna steal a log of Burwood for you baby! It looks like a scented candle.'

Someone started speaking to Jaya, no doubt drawn by her squeal. Allie presumed it was a new nurse as he could hear her standard introduction. 'Jayashri. Or Jaya. Or just Jay. It's Indian. What? Oh, no I'm fine! I was just talking with—'

Allie disconnected, texted thumbs up, dog, and takeaway emojis, then got his soggy butt up and started toward the bus stop again.

He did not run.

Braya and Ferdinand did. Later that night Jay's two old mutts ran Allie fast toward Phoenix Park, then ran everywhere in the park, hunting deer spoor, answering doggie pee-mail left on the walls of the Magazine Fort, and sometimes sharing Allie's takeaway.

It was well after eleven by the time they got back to Jaya's flat, the ancient pups chuffing happy exhaustion on the sofa as Allie refreshed their water and laid new puppy pads down on the kitchen floor.

He was in the middle of a closing monologue with the dozing dogs – 'and your mam'll be back tomorrow morning with cheese for everyone!' – when the two dogs suddenly bolted from the sofa and shot down Jay's hallway.

Allie followed and found them in three-part cacophony with another dog, yipping on the other side of Jayashri's bedroom door. Later Allie would think he should've called Jay about the surprise canine, but he didn't. Instead he opened the bedroom door and the old dogs bounded in for what was clearly a canine reunion, if their excited prancing was evidence. The new dog returned as good as they got – to Allie. A solid seventy-five kilos, tall at the shoulder with a rangy build, the brown hound looked up at him with such bright eyes and an open-mouthed grin that Allie was on his knees in seconds, crooning.

'Hello baby–' he peeked at the dog's undercarriage '–boy. Who are you? Aren't you a beauty? Look at you, you're such a big lad, such a big pup. Jaya didn't tell me about you did she, no she didn't. Are you a Wolfhound baby, are you?' The dog yipped happily, rubbing his muzzle against Allie's long black hair.

'Oh, what a sweetheart you are yes, whose mam forgot to tell me about you? Who? Are you hungry baby boy? Are you thirsty?'

A quick glance into Jaya's en suite showed most of the necessary supplies, including water and dog nappies on the bathroom floor, but when Allie tried feeding him, the big dog wouldn't even glance at the wet food. Allie tried enticing him by kneeling on the kitchen floor beside the food bowl, but the dog just huffed happily in his face with breath that somehow smelled of curry.

Twenty minutes after leaving it, Allie was back in the park, the brown hound at his side.

Still hurting from his afternoon fall, Allie was happy Jaya's new pup neither pulled at his lead nor lagged, instead he kept a good pace and did what dogs do: sniffed pavement cracks, individual blades of grass; wet paper; old chewing gum; and trees. So, so many trees. Though Dublin's biggest green space – more than twice the size of New York's Central Park – had great, rolling expanses of grass, was dotted with monuments, clubs, a zoo, a mansion, and, Braya and Ferdinand's favourite, a fort, it was the trees which fascinated the Wolfhound. It was about the time he was walking his way around a seventh sycamore, sniffing high and low, that Allie's mobile chimed with a voicemail alert.

'I didn't even hear it ring,' he informed the dog, who looked up at him long enough to appear to wait for more words. Instead Allie listened to his message.

'Allie! So so sorry about this but I forgot my friend was, uh, dropping off their dog. That I'm babysitting. Today. Don't worry about walking him, okay? The dog? Just leave Vikka in the house, he'll be fine until I'm back in the morning, I promise he doesn't need to go out for a walk or anything okay? Call me back when you get this.'

'Vikka!' The dog stopped scenting a copse of big beeches and came right to Allie. 'That's your name Hello Vikka, hello! I think it's too late to call Jaya, don't you? Let's just email her a photo to show you're happy.'

Hey, just got your message and figured it's way too late to ring. Vikka and I are already forty-five minutes into an epic tree sniffing adventure in the park. He is such a sweetheart. Here are five blurry photos of us because I kept falling over laughing when he'd snuffle my hair. Promise I'll have him home soon.

Except Allie didn't.

Because "soon" wasn't on Vikka's agenda, not with. so. many. trees.

After a day giving lectures and a night planned for little more than grading essays, Allie was more than delighted to follow the rangy pup on his slow tree tour, moving carefully from ash to sycamore to the occasional tree bare-limbed and blighted, until eventually they washed up at the edge of Oldtown Wood, and there Vikka stopped dead.

And got…bigger.

Spine straight, standing tall, head canted in a nearly-human way, Vikka took what for all the world sounded like a deep breath, and then did something odd. He turned and looked Allie in the eye. No, not the way dogs do, not with a gaze that met and bounced away and met again, this one was eye-to-lingering-eye, as if the Wolfhound was waiting for Allie to weigh in on something vital.

'What baby, what is it?' Allie murmured, because, somehow, he knew it was time for whispers. He knelt and the dog came close, huffed soft and plaintive in his ear, almost, almost a reply except not, and then Vikka looked again into the shadows ahead. Allie did too and he wanted to tell the dog they shouldn't go further, that city dark wasn't safe, but when Vikka turned and headed toward the shadows again, away from the wide-open deer pasture and walking paths, and into the hodge-podge woods where street and car lights didn't reach, well Alexander Huong followed him.

It was the first time. It would not be the last.

Though it felt cut off in the woods, Allie could still hear distant city noise, rendering the shadowy bulk of trees less otherworldly and dire. He let the now-solemn Vikka go where he would, and that turned out to be toward a rag-tag cluster of large, old oaks; sniffing one, then the next, pausing and circling. Allie began to relax to the familiarity of that until he heard what at first he thought was a fox.

Yet when he stopped behind Vikka, who was now looking hard to his right and no that wasn't eerie (yes, yes it was), Allie realised it wasn't the yip of a fox, it was a high gasp, in and in and then...a hissing, choked cry.

Allie's first instinct was a strange one. He wanted to pull Vikka away, to protect him somehow from the weeping. Yet where before the dog had seemed to ask before moving forward, he became unwavering now; not pulling, but there was no slack in the lead.

Those strange gasps turned into gut-wrenched sobs when the torch on Allie's phone lit up the densely-treed space, showing in its light a white boy of about sixteen, face streaked with dirt, slumped under a rambly old oak. It took a few moments for the rest of what Allie saw to clarify in his awareness, and the rest was a scattering of silver metal, a rucksack, tools. And blood.

Blood soaking fresh and bright through the canvas of the boy's yellow runner, the source clearly, so very clearly the long drill bit sticking out of the centre of the boy's foot. From the dead-still way the kid held his leg, it was a damn good bet the bit continued straight on down into the ground.

Later he and Vikka would learn the boy was lucky, for a certain value of lucky. It would turn out that in his vandalism, when he slipped, it was while using one of the smaller bits to drill a pilot hole, instead of the one he would've used later to bore holes three centimetres in diameter.

Vikka pressed his body against the weeping boy, and as Allie got near he could hear the dog soft-softly huffing into the boy's ear, a comforting, gentle sound of soothing.

'Hey...'

Allie drifted slow, slower, slowest, his torchlight pointing mostly at the ground now and, like the Wolfhound, Allie murmured softly, until he was close enough to kneel beside the boy and say, 'I'm Allie and this is Vikka can we...help you?'

Unsaid was 'we are going to help you, of course we are, we'll get you to hospital, god that has to hurt, let me call an ambulance,' so it was a surprise when the kid sobbed, 'Noooo, noo nooo, my mam'll kill me.'

'Hon, you're bleeding, you're really hurt.'

As if suddenly reminded of the terrible thing running through his foot, the boy began sobbing louder. Vikka started pacing, rubbing against the boy while he continued those soft little comfort exhales.

Allie sat on the wet grass, earlier pains forgotten. 'What's your name?'

It took awhile for the boy to catch his breath enough to stammer, 'S-Sammy,' before sobbing again.

Knowing that in giving comfort, comfort is given, Allie said, 'Hey, could you please hold on to Vikka for me a little? He's uh, scared of the dark sometimes, but when he heard you we came over. I'd really appreciate it if you could help him calm down while I call an ambulance, okay? Your mam's not going to be mad, I promise, so if you'd just hold on to Vikka for a little bit that'd be grand.'

He hadn't even finished talking before Sammy wrapped both arms around the Wolfhound's neck, crooning weepy endearments into brown fur. 'Good dog, good Vikka dog, good dog.'

The ambulance was quick in coming, yet for Allie the waiting stretched toffee long, allowing him too much time to see everything around them: the boy's green rucksack collapsed empty on itself, a rectangular blue plastic box, empty of the expensive-looking battery-powered drill that lay near Sammy's hip, dropped so hard when it slipped that its nose had taken a chunk out of the grass. The scattering of a couple dozen drill bits, probably kicked as Sammy fell, were hefty, thick things winking silver in the light of Allie's phone. And Sammy's runner, its yellow canvas now completely blood red.

While Sammy held him Vikka stayed silent and still, and it wasn't until much later that Allie knew the dog understood the reassurance he offered, and the next morning, talking to Jayashri on the phone, Allie said over and over, 'Vikka's the one that found the boy. It was him. It was like he knew he was in there. You should have seen him Jaya, you should have seen him.'

Come see him.

Allie was running to catch his bus home a few days later when his phone pinged. He shouldn't have checked his texts, no, he should've followed his own rules et cetera and so forth but hey, it wasn't raining this time and his coccyx felt pretty good, and so he did it, he checked his message.

Vikka and I are in town, if you're still at the college come by and I'll introduce you.

Allie looked up. He watched his bus drive away. He texted back.

I've already met him missy, and besides, isn't he your friend's dog?

Two more buses pulled up. That was the way in Dublin. Three at once or none.

We're at The Morrígan. Meet us and I'll tell you something I didn't tell you.

So that was how Alexander Huong found himself crossing the Ha'penny bridge, then turning onto the narrow boardwalk beside it. Not far along was his and Jaya's favourite tiny cafe and at one of its outdoor tables he saw his brown friend sitting with a white man.

'How're your toes?' he asked Jaya, looking at the thirty-something man, at his wavy brown hair and wide smile that Alexander didn't, no he absolutely did not recognise. But a year from now, when they're at this same little cafe celebrating the day they met, Allie will whisper in Vikka's ear that, even though a muzzle isn't a mouth, even though a dog can't smile, not really, no, even so Allie will remember this moment right now as one of recognition.

Jaya lifted and wiggled her booted foot. 'They're taped to each other, like little worms. Or sausages.'

Allie nodded, nodded, kept nodding, then turned and blinked. 'What? Oh! Yes. Can you walk, are you okay? Do you need me to come take the dogs out for you?'

Jayashri giggled, the brown-haired man grinned wider, and after Allie fetched a coffee, he sat beside Jaya, and he absolutely didn't look at the man across from them when he asked about the dogs, but he's going to remember it that way a year from now, when he's crooning endearments in his true love's ear.

'Alexander Huong, meet Vikka Murphy, Vikka meet Allie.'

Love at first sight is really just a cascade of many small, sweet things later remembered as if they happened all at once.

In the case of Vikka Murphy that cascade began on the night he looked up into the eyes of a pretty man as he spoke to him in a high, kind voice. It was sniffing the man as he knelt down, finding he smelled of butter and tasted of salt. It was being talked to for the entirety of their walk together and after the walk, after the bright lights of an ambulance, it was watching the man unwrap takeaway leftovers in Jaya's kitchen and being fed bits of soft bread while his ears were stroked and he was comforted from their long, strange night.

Love at first sight was looking up when Alexander walked up to their table minutes ago, and absolutely recognising the smell of him, the kindness of him, and yes, the pretty prettiness of him. His Vietnamese heritage clear in his black hair, straight dark eyebrows, and cheekbones against which in future Vikka will whisper odes.

Love at first sight is a cascade of many small things and so, when Alexander Huong smiled at him and said sweetly, 'It's lovely to meet you Vikka. Is it a coincidence you share the name of the dog Jaya's sitting? And where is he, where is my sweet boy?' – well it was easy for Vikka to do what he so rarely did.

Tell.

'You mean Were is he.'

Jayashri barked. There was no other word for the yip that came out of her as she giggled, 'Were as in wolf, oh that's good, that's grand.'

'Dog.'

'Hush.'

'What?'

'You know better.'

'What?'

Alexander blinked wide-eyed as they laughed between themselves, his friend and the pretty man, and he said it again. 'What?'

'I'm not a wolf when I change, I'm a dog,' Vikka said, voice low though there was no one near them on the boardwalk. 'People like me, we say dogs not wolves. There's not a lot of scientific consensus yet, but that's how we identify ourselves.'

Allie blink, blink, blinked.

Werewolves...dogs...were only just beginning to be acknowledged in the 1950s, and even then they were more a punch line than anything. 'They're bad sci-fi,' wrote one of the early doctors who wrote anything at all about them. Poorly-done studies mostly just confirmed pre-existing bias that Weres were freaks of nature, with no particularly exploitable talents, that they were aberrant, basal, inferior. The more open-minded called them 'noble beasts'.

It wasn't until the 1990s that Weres became less the source for bad jokes, than just people you might know, though rarely talk about.

'Oh god...' Allie blinked fast some more, it seemed to help cool his over-heating brain. 'Did I...was I...I'm sorry if I–'

Again Vikka grinned and it was the prettiest thing. 'You were very kind, very gentle. When I'm Were my brain works differently, my recollections are largely sensory.' Vikka closed his eyes. 'Usually, those senses are the feel of carpet under me, the coolness of a bowl of water. But the night in the park was different. It wasn't the scent of rain-wet earth or animals in the zoo I remember, it's smelling – knowing I was smelling – blood and pain, grief and desperation.' Vikka sighed. 'That was the first time I've been outside after a change, so I'm still processing what all of it means.'

Allie traded blink-blinking for an eyebrow-raised frown. 'But why?'

Vikka shrugged, watching two little kids throw dead leaves into the low-tide Liffey. 'You know how some people still are about Weres. My ma and da are no different. When the change hit at fifteen they right off taught me to hide, and do you know what? That was fair. We lived in a small town in County Clare, and so hiding was just what I got used to. Even once I moved away. Y'know, eat a good dinner, put down some uh, doggie nappies and water, and just sleep through it.'

Vikka looked at Jayashri, who grinned big. 'Then I met herself.'

Neighbours who a few years ago had bonded over a shared love of the then-craze for bulletproof coffee – 'everyone hates the sound of it until they try it; then only half of them hate it' – Vikka had begun walking Jaya's dogs when she worked late, which over time began a different sort of bonding.

'I told her what I am, and do you know what she didn't do? She didn't ask me the stuff people always ask Weres: "does it hurt, can you do it right now, do you have sex with dogs". She asked me if it got lonely, being by myself when I changed.'

Vikka returned Jaya's toothy grin. 'So now I come over just before, I bring movies and curries and we hang out for the day and night of my change.'

Allie said nothing, his face said everything.

'Weres don't change with the moon like people think,' Jaya said. 'Each has their own calendar, so Vikka gives me a heads-up text when he needs to come over and if I'm late he lets himself in, but–' Jayashri lifted and wiggled her taped-up toes. '–I got a little distracted and didn't check my phone in time.'

Allie said more nothing. His face, however, continued to be quite talkative.

Jaya smiled at him. 'So, I didn't realise Vikka'd be there when you came over, not until I saw his text. I called but you were already out in the wide world taking him for his first walk as a Were and you looked so happy, and he looked so happy and so it didn't seem bad to let you both be happy.'

Allie looked at Vikka. It seemed to be his serve, so to speak.

'You probably wonder why Jaya never took me out, and it's because for nearly twenty years I've been repeating what my parents told me. If I went out when I'm Were, something bad would happen, something terrible. They never said if it would happen to me or by me.'

Jayashri allowed that moment the gravity it deserved, then she leaned over her knees, took them both in with glee-wide eyes, and shouted, 'Instead you fought crime!'

Jayashri tried to stand but grunted in pain, so instead she punched the air with both fists. 'Crime! Crime! You solved a crime! You know how trees all over Dublin are dying right? That no one figured out what was wrong for awhile? And then some bright boys and girls dug down and saw dozens, sometimes hundreds of holes Swiss cheesing their roots, everywhere from Broombridge to Ballyowen to Bray? Well it's been a few hundred trees by now, because how do you find who's doing something like that when they go across the whole city? You don't, you can't.

'But you and Vikka did.'

Allie looked at the beech trees beside the Liffey, at the potted palms between them. Though he'd lived by the Irish Sea for the last fifteen of his thirty-eight years, though Dublin sees twice the rainfall of his native Los Angeles, even so, Alexander Huong damn well respects the sanctity of trees, so he frowned and he asked, 'But why?'

'Because sometimes you lose control to get it,' Vikka said. 'Sammy? I went to see him in hospital yesterday and ended up talking to his dad. Sammy's parents divorced last year. His mam moved out and he... wanted her to come back. How does the son of an arborist get that arborist's attention? Well, to a sixteen-year-old brain it seemed logical to destroy the things she loves.'

At Allie's head shake, Vikka leaned across the tiny table and said softly, 'The first time I turned, and the second, third, fourth...that whole first year...I was horrible. I was rude and impatient, I wouldn't talk with me mam and kept telling myself if my da wasn't an alcoholic I'd be normal.'

Vikka shrugged. 'That made no sense, but I was fifteen and do you know what happens then? I read up on this a few years ago. What happens, is at that age teenagers kind of mentally turn back into toddlers. I had a friend who quit his epilepsy meds at fifteen because the only thing Ruairí felt like he controlled was his medicine, so he controlled his medicine. By not taking it. He had half a dozen seizures a week but there was no talking to him. Then his parents got him some sessions with a weight trainer to give him something else to control and do you know what? Now Ruairí's a totally-jacked drag queen who takes his epilepsy meds.

'What I'm trying to say is, I know why Sammy did it and when he faces a judge for this I'm going to be there for him because...well you don't put toddlers on trial.'

After that everyone looked at the slow flow of the Liffey awhile, saying nothing.

Then someone did, and changed all their lives.

'Could you do it again?' Jayashri squinted against the lowering sun shining off the Ha'penny's white rails. 'Could you find someone else who needs help like Sammy did?'

Two pairs of curious eyes looked at her and Jayashri-Jaya-Jay Kelly knew that seeds... well, at first they seem so small. Yet if well-planted, they don't stay small. So Jay kicked dirt over these particular seeds by saying 'Isn't helping what people are for – whether Were or the boring kind? Aren't we meant to use our gifts to ease suffering, to create joy?'

Jay leaned across their tiny table, grinning gleeful enough for three. 'Yes,' she pronounced, simple and so very sure. 'Oh yes. Changing the world, one desperate-needy-worried person at a time, that stuff starts with us.'

Jayashri knew other things, too. She knew that for this kind of change, these two men must be more to each other than they were right now. So Jay stood suddenly and, with no elegance whatsoever said, 'My foot hurts I'm going home now okay bye.'

She did not wait for acknowledgement.

Still, her decampment was not precisely speedy, so Vikka and Allie watched her gather her rucksack and crutches, watched her wobble round their table, watched her cross in front of their table, watched her walk along the long boardwalk, then over the bridge, before she actually managed to disappear from sight.

Allie and Vikka sat silently for another little while. Both wondered what to say but were for a time too shy to say anything. Then, finally, at last, *hallelujah*, Vikka Murphy said the second-best thing possible at that time. 'Would you like another coffee, Allie?'

Alexander Huong drinks one caffeinated beverage a day. Never more, often less. Suddenly on familiar, comforting ground, Allie smiled and said, 'That would be against the rules.'

Here, right here was where Vikka said the first best thing, the thing that would lead to them spending another hour at the cafe.

'Rules?'

Then two hours over dinner in Irishtown.

'I have this thing I do. With rules. I mean I hardly ever almost never ever follow any of them, but I try.'

Followed by another hour wandering along the docks.

'So, how many rules do you have?'

And then, eventually, the arrival at Vikka's flat and rule 55, which they would not that evening go beyond.

'Two hundred and three.'

Rule 55. That one was about kissing.

Reggie Starling
and the Adventure
of the
Crown Jewels

Kat Clay

Reggie Starling and the Adventure of the Crown Jewels

T HREE GENERATIONS OF CORGIS GLARED DOWN AT ME FROM THE PAINTINGS on the walls. As I flew into the elegant office, I felt their snooty little eyes following me, as if I'd dirty the furnishings with my claws.

Before me, the very real Lady Augustina Flooflebottom the Third sat in a velvet-lined basket by the fire, paws crossed, looking gravely serious – as serious as a dog with fluffy ears can look – and said, 'When I requested Scotland Yard's finest, I did not expect a bird.'

'What you got against birds?' I said. I had been summoned from my nest in the early hours of the morning by a gruff-faced beefeater demanding I go immediately to the home of Lady Flooflewhatsit, so I had quickly smoothed last night's birdseed from my feathers and flitted through the city to Marylebone Gardens. The warm fire made me wish I'd drank some more water before I went to sleep.

'If Scotland Yard says you're the best, then I take their word for it. This case might need someone with a little more of your...street experience.' She sniffed the air, as if she had detected a great big ponging smell. I resisted the urge to sniff my wings.

She continued, 'We are in a grave and desperate situation, Inspector Starling. In the early hours of this morning, the Yeoman Warders discovered that the St Edwards Crown has been stolen from the Tower of London.'

I held back a gasp. The crown jewels were missing!

'The coronation of King William is in two days. We must have the crown returned, otherwise the ceremony cannot take place,' she said.

Not only was the Tower thought to be impenetrable, after Colonel Blood tried to steal the jewels last century, but who would want to steal the crown itself? The piece was instantly recognizable; you couldn't fence it at a hock shop without someone noticing.

'Do you have any suspects in mind?' I asked.

'This was delivered to the palace by anonymous courier pigeon early this morning.'

She gestured to a letter on a low table. I perched on the edge as I read it.

FREEDOM FOR ALL ANIMALS
OR THE CROWN GETS IT

The letters had been cut out from newspaper headlines and pasted down in uneven lines.

'Only anarchists, kidnappers and journalists send demands in newspaper print,' I said.

'Regardless of the perpetrators, we cannot let these agents of chaos interfere with the coronation.'

As much as I didn't like Lady Wooflesnotter, I had to agree. It would be a tough case, but if I could find the crown, it would secure Scotland Yard's reputation with the new king.

'I'll get it back for you, don't you worry about that.'

'Good birdy,' she said.

I was keen to prove my mettle and find the crown. Since the police force started two years ago, us peelers wanted to show our worth to all of London. While animals and humans had worked alongside each other in peace for hundreds of years, there was still a criminal element to the city – both human and animal.

I flew down the Thames, swooping my way through the bobbing masts on the river, dodging flags and moving ropes. The Tower of London loomed in the smog. Its unmistakable square, impenetrable facade looked out over the moat, and beyond that, the river. I flitted down to the ramparts, the yard below humming with guards and policemen. The sounds of animals caught my ears; no doubt it was the menagerie that had been here for hundreds of years. What Newgate Prison was to humans, the Tower's menagerie was to animals. Bear burglars, con-tigers, even a gang of one hundred rattlesnakes who staged a train robbery. The very worst animals of London lived out their days in the menagerie prison.

I spotted the head raven, Agatha, who was in charge of guarding the Tower. She cawed in greeting to me. 'Is that you, Starling? Finally, the Yard's sent someone decent to look after this dog's breakfast.'

I brushed her wing with my own. The ravens were all highly trained ex-military types whose sole job was protecting the Tower. They say that if the ravens ever leave, the Tower will crumble, and England will be plunged into chaos.

'I'm sure you'll want to see the scene of the crime,' she said. 'The jewels are housed in the basement of the Martin Tower. It's quite the tourist attraction in regular times.'

'Could a thief masquerading as a tourist have stolen the crown?' I asked.

Agatha shook her head, her glossy black feathers ruffling in the wind. 'Unlikely. Every tour is minded by at least one guard. Besides which, we suspect it happened in the early hours of the morning, when the shifts were changing. The crown was there last night. The only Yeoman Warder on duty is nursing an awful headache after being knocked out by what he claims was an enormous man.'

I said nothing, but knowledge of guard schedules pointed to one thing. An inside job.

A Yeoman Warder unlocked the door to Martin Tower and led us down to the basement by the light of a bull's eye lantern. When the light hit the remaining jewels, there were more colours in the room than a bowerbird's nest. Rubies, sapphires, diamonds, gold.

'Cor blimey,' I couldn't help exclaiming. 'But why would they only steal the crown, when they could have all this?'

They clearly weren't in it for the money, which would fit with the theory about an anarchist organisation.

The jewels were housed in a glass case crossed with iron bars that ran the length of the back wall. Someone had smashed the glass right through and bent one of the iron bars. Remnants of glass lay on the empty velvet where the crown had been.

'Shine a light here man,' I said to the Yeoman Warder, flitting over to the hole in the glass. Careful not to catch my wings on the shards, I hopped into the hole for a closer look. A tiny tuft of ruddy fur hooked on one of the pointed glass pieces on the inside of the case. It looked like someone had been caught pulling their hand from the hole. It could've been a fur coat or an animal, although the idea of someone wearing my feathers as a fashion statement made me shudder.

'Did anyone report their keys missing?'

'No,' said Agatha. 'They'd protect those keys with their life. I know that sly look Starling, what are you thinking?'

'We're looking for two sorts of creatures. One strong enough to break glass and bend iron. The second, nimble enough to pick a lock. I've seen enough here. Take me to the menagerie.'

The menagerie stretched along one of the moat walls in long rows of cages open to the elements. A lion prowled the length of his enclosure, watching me curiously but saying nothing. His fur was too bright to match the brown of the clue from the jewel chamber.

The usual chatter of monkeys slid to silence as we passed, their grim eyes peering at us from behind bars. The rattlesnakes all twitched their tails simultaneously; I straightened my wings, focused my face forward, and kept flying, knowing full well one of them could probably fit me in their mouth.

I'd been to Newgate, but the menagerie was a whole new level of crim.

Of some repute was the next inmate: Count Federico de Visconti, aka Harry Windham, an Essex con-tiger who'd made the papers for fleecing a thousand pounds of diamonds from an elderly dowager. Harry was wearing a monocle and reading *The Times*. He looked up from his paper and down his nose at me. 'Excuse me, but don't you know it's rude to stare.'

'Reggie Starling, Scotland Yard. I'm here to ask you a few questions about the break-in last night.'

'Oh, that terrible thing. Such a rumpus.'

'That rumpus could affect the coronation of our new king, mind your manners.' The Yeoman Warder held up the tuft of fur we had found so it could be matched against the tiger.

'I would never wear anything that brown,' said the tiger. 'Doesn't go with my eyes. If you ask me, that looks like Old Martin's fur.'

'Old Martin?' I asked.

'The grizzly bear.' Harry flicked his paw at the cage two doors down, where an enormous bear prowled the length of his cell. His gait was off; a slight limp as he favoured his right front paw.

Old Martin growled ferociously at our approach. He stood on his hind legs and roared. Thank goodness for the iron bars between us. When he reached up, I noticed his left paw had shallow cuts on it.

'Settle down you old codger,' I said. 'We're here to ask you about the robbery.'

Despite being behind the bars, he surged forwards, baring his teeth at me. I'd been standing a little too close to the bars and copped a wad of spittle. Shaking myself clean, I said, 'Forgot to brush your teeth today?'

'I'm not talkin' to no pigs,' he growled.

'Good, because I'm not a pig, I'm a bird. A starling to be exact. And I've got a piece of fur from the scene of the crime that matches yours and a witness who says he was knocked out by an enormous man. I figure that's you.'

'I got nothing to say!'

'Spill it, or you'll be telling it to all of London in a court of law,' I said.

The bear stopped growling and sat down on his hind legs, weighing up his options. The threat of public exposure was a sore spot. 'What is it you're scared of getting out to the press?' I said.

The bear clammed up, crossing his arms.

'I'll find out and if you don't tell me now, I'll be sure to tell the papers later.'

The bear slumped, as much as a 700-pound mound of fur and claws can slump. 'They was threatening my cousin in Bermondsey,' he said.

'Who was?'

Old Martin shook his head. 'I don't know his name. I got this message from a courier pigeon who perched on my cage, saying their boss knew what my cousin had done, and if I wanted to protect her, then I'd do what they said.'

'And what had your cousin done?'

He leaned towards the bars so only I could hear. 'They'd caught her with her paws in a honeypot.'

I understood then why he'd wanted to protect his cousin. 'What happened last night?'

'They brought a stuffed bear rug to put in my cage in case the night watch saw that I had escaped. It was 'orrible, seeing a fellow bear turned into a foot mat. They told me that's how I'd end up if I didn't help them.'

'Who's they?' I demanded.

Just then, the monkeys, who had been listening on, burst out of their cages. Chaos broke out in the menagerie's forecourt as the monkeys skittered towards the fortress walls. If you've ever tried to catch a monkey on the run, it's harder than picking a squirming worm from the soil.

If Lady Flooflebottom had been there to see the attempt in apprehending these bastards, she would have been appalled. Bobbies falling over every which way, the slinky creatures slipping out of their grasp, leaving our finest face down in the mud.

When the monkeys reached the open courtyard, Agatha signalled to the other ravens who swooped the monkeys from the sky. It only slowed the monkeys down enough for me to get airborne. I wasn't big enough to mount a direct attack on the monkeys, but I would follow them wherever they went.

Five of them clambered over the north wall of the tower, scuttling to the other side. I followed in the air, watching their small brown bodies nimbly descend the stone walls, finding foot holds in the uneven rock. There was no way they could get past the moat without going over the bridge, now crowded with guards and policemen waiting to catch them with a net.

The lead monkey thumbed his nose at the boys in blue and dived off the wall into the moat. His gang followed suit, plunging after him.

Who knew monkeys could swim?

I chased them as they emerged sodden from the water, and sprinted toward the narrow streets. Agatha and her ravens were close behind me, although one of them had taken a nasty hit to the head.

'Where do you think they're going?' she asked.

'They're heading north to Whitechapel Road. It's not the first time a crim has tried to hide out in the dark recesses of East London.'

It would be easy for monkeys to find a hidey hole in the twisted alleys.

'I'll follow at a distance, see if they lead us to their hideout. Call off your soldiers Agatha, they might spot us if we're too big a flock.'

She gestured to her ravens, who broke off in formation and flew back to the tower.

We swooped low into the alley. Rooftops crowded out the sky, dim light filtering through even though it was the middle of the day. Below came a hubbub, as the monkeys leapt through the back streets of London, leaving a trail of screams, yelps and fist-waving locals.

A washing yard lay ahead, women banging out sheets as they sang. At the sight of the monkeys, the washerwomen began chasing them with paddles.

'No, you don't you dirty little critters! You're not going to ruin my washing.'

They scooted up the washing lines, leaping from wire to wire. We dodged under strings and paddles, flitted past white sheets. I couldn't see for the chaos that was going on. One woman threw a bucket of water, and I had to tumble sideways to avoid getting soaked. When I regained my balance, Agatha was at my side. We'd lost them.

'What do we do now?' she said.

I picked myself up and patted my feathers. 'We go see a magpie about some jewels.'

Fergus the Magpie was an old underworld contact of mine. I'd caught him filching watches at the races one day, and he'd offered me a deal. He'd keep his beak to the ground for anything big going down, and I'd forget that I'd seen him putting his pecker into a gentleman's pocket for a rather nice fob watch.

'It's a habit,' said Fergus. 'Us magpies, we love the shine, we love the glimmer. S'in our blood. Telling me not to pinch things is like telling the sun not to shine.'

I found him in his usual shop, a small hole in the wall – nothing much to look at – which opened to a large nest in the attic of a fruit shop, filled with glass cases of the shiniest tat you'd ever seen. Nothing like the crown jewels, oh no. Sweets wrappers and keys and shards of broken mirror. It was hard to know where to look.

Fergus looked up from examining a piece of jewellery with a loupe. When he saw my face, his yellow eyes widened. He hastened to the door, shutting it.

'Didn't I tell you never to come here, Reggie Starling? Use the signal, and I'll meet you in the skies. Wouldn't do no good to have a copper spotted at my door.'

'Desperate times, Fergus. Someone's nicked the crown.'

'Someone's nicked the crown? You're pulling my wing.' His beak drooped when he realised I was serious.

'And you thought you'd come looking at old Fergus' place, see if I've gots it? Well, I don't. Don't got no crown jewels. Not stupid enough to take something you can't fence.'

Agatha cawed at him, her wings outspread. 'Careful pie,' she said.

'You is one of them ravens down the Tower-like. You don't scare me.'

Agatha turned her beak towards the glass cases full of shiny objects and began pecking on the doors in a rat-a-tat motion.

'No, you wouldn't dare,' said Fergus, his head bobbing from side to side. The glass splintered.

'She's a trained military professional sworn to protect the crown,' I said. 'There isn't much she wouldn't do to track down the jewels.'

'I'm telling the truth,' he said. 'Get her to stop and I'll give you the info I know.'

Agatha withdrew her beak and huddled like an ominous shadow in the corner, watching Fergus' every move.

'Like I said, I haven't seen no jewels about. But if I were gonna steal the jewels – not saying I've thought about this – I'd pluck out the gemstones, cut them down into smaller, less recognisable pieces, and melt the gold into bars. That way you could sell it without too much hassle.'

'Keep talking,' I said.

'There's one more thing,' said Fergus. 'It's not about what I've heard. It's about what I'm not hearing. I've got a steady stream of reliable customers,' he paused and gulped as Agatha stretched her wings in the cramped corner. 'Legal customers,' he added. 'But the last two days it's been dead quiet from one gang – I mean legally-formed group of business entrepreneurs.'

'Who's that?' I asked.

'The pigeons. Not those collared pigeons you see down at the business end of town. No, it's those feral street pigeons, the ones that get into all sorts of trouble over a crust of bread. They've been dead quiet – not a peep or a coo the last week.'

It made sense. The street pigeons were a notorious flock of birds who operated out of the East End, with rackets all over London.

'Do you know who they're working with?'

'Don't make me say his name gov, you want to get us all killed?'

Agatha stretched her wings; Fergus twitched.

'Fine. You didn't hear this from me. He goes by the name of Falco.'

'And where's this Falco's hideout?' I asked.

'If I knew, I'd tell you. Rumour has it, the room is littered with skeletons and stinks of chemicals. He's got every sort of animal in his gang. Even a bruiser of a lion, watching your every move. You either join his gang or get snapped up by his big teeth, and I ain't keen on doing neither.'

We weren't going to get any more from Fergus; he was already on edge after mentioning Falco's name. We swooped out of there, careful to make sure no one was watching before heading back to the skies.

'You think we can trust him?' asked Agatha, as we soared over London.

'His fear was genuine,' I said, remembering the look of panic in his eyes when he said the name Falco. 'Besides which, he knows if he tells me porkies, I'll bring him into the Yard. But still I've got no idea where this Falco could be, and time is running out.'

We flew low, perching on the edge of a metal railing, watching the London street pass by. A newspaper boy called out, paper in hand. 'Read all about it, coppers chumped by chimps, crown still at large.'

There was no way I was going back to the Yard without the crown in my claws. And I certainly didn't want to face the teeny-tiny teeth of Lady Fartbottom.

There was something we weren't getting. Sensing my deep thoughts, Agatha watched in silence, her black eyes flitting from side to side as she assessed the crowd for risks.

Old Martin had been terrified of ending up as a stuffed rug. Fergus' rumour mill placed Falco in a building littered with animal skeletons.

A butcher? No, the lion couldn't easily hide out in a meat-market. And a scientific establishment would have lots of chemicals, but surely, they'd notice a gang of animals coming and going.

I realised that the gang was hiding out in the last place you expected live animals to be.

A taxidermist.

It was late in the day, but we needed some human hands and a copy of the *Post Office Directory*, so we flew to the one place guaranteed to have one: the General Letter Office. A beady little man, who bore more in common with a mole than his human compatriots, thumbed through his copy of the directory, listing three taxidermists in the East End.

Between us, Agatha and I memorised the addresses. I didn't say it, but I was fearful of going anywhere near a taxidermist and their pointy little tools.

'I could be chirping up the wrong tree,' I said, after the first turned out to be a polite older woman who worked for the museums.

'In all the years I've known you Starling, your gut has never steered you wrong,' said Agatha.

I nodded grimly, as the last slip of sunlight dipped below the soot-blackened eaves of the tall houses.

Us starlings have good eyesight during the day, but I'm not a night owl, and the dim shadows lessened my ability to spot the finer details in the houses. We pushed on. There was no time, and I only hoped we could delay the destruction of the crown.

The second taxidermist was a young myopic man whose primary business was restoring beloved domestic animals called Betsykins and Mr Snugglypuff for their devoted humans. Despite the pungent scent of chemicals, there were no lions, no pigeons and no signs of Falco.

The third taxidermist's address was deep in the East End, down Vinegar Lane. The streets became progressively narrower, and we had to swoop low to traverse the laneways. I heard the familiar coo of pigeons first, pushing Agatha and myself back into the shadow of a drainpipe.

A gang of pigeons huddled on the cobblestones, hassling a baker. 'Cough up the dough, or we'll nest in your eaves and crap all over your wares!' said the lead pigeon, a rough-looking grey bird with a jagged wing.

The baker, terrified, held up his hands and dropped several loaves of bread at the door. The pigeons didn't even wait to dig into the food, pecking it to shreds. Fights broke out between the birds, their beaks tussling over the remnants.

Agatha almost rushed to the baker's aid, but I held her back with my wing. 'We need to find Falco.'

As we watched them fight, I noticed the curl of a long furry tail slip into an alley further down the street. The kind of tail that would belong to a primate.

Careful to stick in the shadows, I hopped from ledge to ledge, and flitted up to the roof of the building. I could barely make out the room below through a series of grimy skylights, one of which had a rock sized hole in the glass. Below me, a dark room full of every type of animal. A crucible glowed orange, as two monkeys operated a small furnace.

The crown glinted gold in the firelight; it sat on the head of a terrible looking animal, the largest bird I'd ever seen in London. Rare, but not impossible: an urban falcon.

Falco. His yellow eye held a piercing, terrible gaze.

'Hello Starling,' cooed a voice behind us. I'd been so caught up in spying on the crown I'd not heard the pigeons land. 'Falco will have fun with you two. Get them, boys!'

The pigeons swarmed us on the rooftop. Grey feathers overtook my vision; I pecked at their attacks, but there were too many. Agatha put up a better fight, slashing at the pigeons with her beak, her size a real advantage against the street birds. Still, there were too many, and she took a sharp peck to the wing, rolling off the roof.

'No!' I shouted.

Sharp claws pinned me down. The pigeons clasped my wings and feet together, so I could do no more but squirm in their grasp. I hoped she was all right, but it looked dire. No one knew where we were.

They took me inside the abandoned taxidermist's office, a dusty, high-arched building with only the furnace for warmth. Crows, snakes and hawks leered down at me from shadowy walls; normally I could tell the difference between the living and the dead, but for the noises coming from the shadows. Hissing, caws, roars, a terrifying cacophony of animal sounds. If this was how I would end my career, then at least I knew I would go in service to King and country. Still, I didn't want to share the same fate as Mr Snugglypuff, stuffed in a museum exhibit of the European starling.

The pigeons threw me into a bird cage and slammed the door, the monkeys locking it with their dexterous paws. I glimpsed the lion; it watched on from the shadows. As my eyes adjusted to the gloom, I saw Falco, his wings blending into the darkness.

'You're the bird who's been looking into our little escapades,' said Falco in a deep, rasping voice, his head swivelling towards me. 'You're a smart animal, but you haven't been told the full story about my organisation.'

Keep him talking. It was the only thing I could do while I figured out a way to escape. 'I've been told you're anti-monarchical anarchists. Are you saying you're not?'

Falco chuckled, but it came out more like the screech a bird of prey makes before it devours a field mouse. I gulped.

'It's a very human way of describing us. Anarchists. Animals have lived on these lands for longer than any humans. You've seen for yourself firsthand what humans have done to us: they've stuffed us into cages and enslaved us for their benefit.'

'I seem to be the only one in a cage,' I said.

The cage rattled as I moved – it was one of those collapsible numbers that pigeon keepers used. If I unbalanced it, perhaps the cage would spring open. I started pacing from side to side as Falco kept talking.

'Very astute. We have a simple request: freedom for all animals. Are you here to deliver our freedom, Starling?'

'You want freedom but you're going about it in all the wrong ways!' I said, starting to notice something strange about the lion in the corner. It hadn't moved once. And there was something weird about Falco's movements; his head swivelled from side to side, but his body was still.

'I take that as a no,' said Falco.

I slammed my body into the side of the cage. The hinges split apart at the sides, and I broke free, swooping to knock the crown off Falco's head. It spun across the hard floor.

I hit Falco's head with a thump, colliding with his rock-solid stuffed body and knocking the bird off his stand with a loud clunk. His head rolled off into the gloom. In the darkness, I made out a yellow canary, standing behind the plaque where Falco had been.

'What, you never seen a canary before?' he squawked in a deep voice so unlike the sweet chirping of his kind.

Holding back my surprise, I flew for the crown, grabbing it in my claws, but it was too heavy for me to carry.

A monkey swatted me out of the air. The crown skittered away under the lion's paws.

I writhed under the monkey's grasp, wriggling out and catapulting into the air, my wings unfurling. The monkeys abandoned the smelter and clambered through the rafters, but I dodged their hands, swooping low underneath the lion's belly.

They stopped chasing me.

Because the lion roared, its teeth snapping at my wings. I dodged and darted, turning somersaults in the air, flipping past its tail and in behind a stand of stuffed meerkats.

I was outnumbered, outsized and out-toothed.

Still, I would rescue the crown, even if it cost me my life.

'Stand down,' said the canary. The narrow stand where I hid was filled with a frightening side-show of animals. Further down, a branch decorated with starlings. My poor friends and relations! I crept quietly and perched among the branches, holding still as the lion stalked past, the canary riding on his head.

'Come out Starling. We'll clean you up nice and good.'

My only chance was to take out the canary and get him to stand down his thugs.

I shot across the room, my sharp beak pointing towards the tiny gangster. He tumbled from the lion's head, and we rose into the air in a desperate tussle. His beak ripped a small shred of feathers from my wing. But I fought back, raking him with my claws. I felt his wing snap, and I grabbed him by the feet as he tumbled from the sky. Despite this, I was flying lower and lower towards the lion's mouth, his gullet open to catch us both.

Above, the skylight smashed into a thousand pieces of glass. A swarm of black feathers shot past my vision.

Agatha and her ravens. She'd survived, and not only that, sent for backup.

A vicious battle broke out, the six ravens dashing from corner to corner, claws out. Feathers flew everywhere. The pigeons somehow disappeared in the fight; that sneaky gang knew a lost cause when they saw one.

The monkeys skittered for the door. Tower guards armed with spears burst through the opening, followed by F Division's finest, waving their rattlers and all champing for a fight. They picked the crown up off the floor, holding it with the reverence it deserved, although a little dusty. Nothing a good bit of soap couldn't clean out.

Battered and beaten, I pinned the canary to the floor, his wing hanging at a limp angle, a red streak across one eye.

'You're plucked!' I said.

King William was crowned the next day, in a ceremony that was thankfully quiet, respectful, and devoid of crown-thieving monkeys. I don't do my job for the glory, but as the King walked by, wearing the glittering crown and carrying the sceptre, he tilted his head at me.

I bowed deeply. Who said us starlings don't have manners?

After the grand procession, Lady Flooflebottom stopped by my church perch briefly. 'Starling, I must admit, I didn't think you had it in you. But you proved me wrong.'

'Oh really? Finally come round to the peelers then?'

'It is not my opinion that matters, but his.' She nodded towards the door where the new King had just left. 'And in his opinion, London needs the Yard.'

Chuffed to have secured the good opinions of the King, I flitted out, chest proud. In the cheering crowds outside, I could have sworn I saw a stalking shadow pass through the shrubbery near the church. I shook my beak, and it was gone.

It couldn't possibly have been a lion.

When the Chips are Down

Louisa Bennett

When the Chips are Down

MUD FLIES. WITH MY FRONT PAWS DEEP IN THE HOLE, I CLAW AT THE damp earth, soft and squishy after two days of rain. My furry bottom points skywards, my tail swishing side to side as if it is waving at the birds flying past. Momentarily I pause and, nose pressed into the rich soil, inhale deeply. Ahh. Rotting leaves, earthworms and, oh yes, duck poo. What better smell is there? Distracted, I almost forget why I am digging up the flowerbed, then I spot my deliciously manky, dogishy-smelly, yellow toy duck. I glance back at the wonky cottage where I live with my owner, Detective Constable Rose Sidebottom, hoping that Rose hasn't yet noticed my excavations.

'Monty!' Rose calls from the back door, her hands on her hips.

Oops!

Normally I'm a good dog. A smiley, loyal, obedient Golden Retriever. But when it comes to washing my duck, I have to make a stand. Rose, like other hoomans, simply doesn't appreciate that my duck pongs to perfection. I'm going to bury my furry friend. Then Rose can't put him in the washing machine. I've chosen a perfect digging spot behind a camellia bush, but I guess the clumps of mud flying through the air is a bit of a giveaway. I drop my duck into the hole and paw loose soil over it as fast as I can.

I hear the stamp of boots on paving stones then the soft thud of Rose walking across the grass. I can smell her aroma of vanilla and peppermint and the sea.

'Stop that!' Rose says, almost upon me.

Caught in the middle of my crime, I lie across my half-filled cavity and pretend there is nothing to see here.

'It's no use pretending. Look at the state of you.' She bends down. Her knees crack. She is only twenty-one, the youngest DC in Geldeford's history, but sometimes her knees sound like an old-un's.

I look up at her heart-shaped face and ponytail which reminds me of a fox's tail. She's not frowning. In fact, she's smiling, which is a relief. Rose is hardly ever cross. Even when I stole a McDonald's burger from the man in the park. In my mind the burger was fair game. He put it down on the bench, as if he didn't want it. How was I to know that he wasn't capable of sipping his coffee and holding a burger at the same time? So much for multi-tasking!

The dirt on my muzzle tickles and I sneeze.

'You're covered in mud.' She sighs. 'I'm going to have to clean you too!'

What? No!

She wraps her delicate fingers around my collar and gives it a gentle tug. 'Out of there.'

I reluctantly leave the hole and the camelia bush. Rose tells me to sit, then stay. She plunges her hand into the earth and brings up my muddy duck. 'Got to be washed now.'

I bark twice.

We've practised this, over and over again. Two barks is no. One bark is yes. When she asks me if I want to be fed, I respond with one bark. Do I want to go for a walk? One bark. Do I love her? One big bark.

Rose seems to enjoy this game we play, but when it's over she says, 'You know, it's almost as if you understand me,' and shakes her head.

Do I want my duck washed? Two barks. No!

She strokes my head. 'Why don't you like me washing your bed and your duck? I don't understand.'

That is my point exactly. I have tried to demonstrate as best I can that my duck and my bed are not for washing. Earlier this morning, when Rose removed the cover from my bed and picked up said duck and then headed for the kitchen where the front-loading washing machine lives, I managed to swipe my fluffy friend from her loose grip and run out of the door. She gave chase and we had great fun running around the duck pond, even if the little quackers did kick up a stink about what they called 'the disturbance.'

Rose resorted to treats to lure me close. I didn't see the trap until it was too late. I dropped the duck and Rose snatched it, heading back into the house. So I ran ahead and then sat, head held high, in front of the washing machine, so Rose couldn't load it. I mean, what more can I do to communicate that I like my bed and duck exactly as they are, thank you very much.

While Rose gets the washing machine going, I slink off with my head hung low and plonk myself down in the sun, my back to the ivy-covered shed. It's late February and the English winter has melted away into an early spring. Snowdrops and daffodils have started to sprout through the grass. I rest my head between my paws, close my eyes, and ponder why it is that I understand Rose, and yet Rose doesn't understand me.

The problem, of course, is that I can't show Rose that I do understand her. I'm meant to be a dumb dog who obeys commands – although I'm not very good at the obedience thing. The big secret is that dogs pretend to be dumb so that hoomans don't feel threatened.

I probably shouldn't try to communicate with Rose, but there is so much I want to tell her and it's frustrating that she doesn't understand. Hurrumph!

'Pssst!' The voice is like sandpaper dragged down a rough fence. It's Jake, the three-legged Staffie. I lift my head, trying to work out where his barking is coming from. 'Oy! Over 'ere!'

I trot over to a yew hedge that stays green all year. Jake sticks his scarred face through the dense foliage.

'Jake! Good to see you,' I say.

Jake was rescued from the pound by Ed, a man in his seventies who Rose says fell through the cracks. What cracks? They'd have to be really big ones to get a man through them. Anyway, Ed must have survived his fall because he lives in a caravan in the forest. Jake once told me that Ed lost his job and his house some years ago and he survives doing odd jobs for people who pay cash.

'Is the boss home?' Jake asks.

'Rose is in the kitchen. How are you, my friend?'

'Can't complain.' Jakes squeezes out of the hedge and sits awkwardly, his body shifting to one side, thanks to the absence of a right leg. 'I need your help, mate. It's Ed.'

'What's happened?'

'Pam accused him of stealing.'

Pam owns the village shop that doubles as a post office.

'It's a lie,' Jake says. 'Ed is the most honest hooman I've ever met.'

'Why would she say that?'

'Somebody's getting into the shop at night and eating stuff. Leaving a right mess behind, by all accounts. Ed didn't do it. I know 'cause I was with him.'

'Why does she think Ed did it?'

'She don't like him. Thinks the caravan lowers the tone of the village. She wants us gone.'

'Poor Ed,' I say, recalling his baggy old trousers and the string he uses to hold them up and the welcoming pats he gives me whenever I drop by. 'What can I do to help?'

'You're a dogtective, ain't ya? I need you to find the real thief, then maybe Pam will leave us alone.'

It's true I've helped Rose solve crimes. But I've never tracked a thief before. 'Do you know if Pam called the police?'

'No coppers have come knocking, so I guess not. But she's threatened to. Came banging on the van door this morning. Said if it happened again, she'd get Ed thrown in jail.'

I hear Rose humming a tune inside the cottage.

'If I could get Rose onto it, we'd crack it in no time. But how do I do that?'

I sit and have a think. An idea comes to me. 'I could lead Rose into the store. We haven't been for our morning walk yet and we usually pass the shop. Pam is such a gossip she won't be able to resist bending Rose's ear about the thief. With any luck, she'll ask for Rose's help.'

Jake stands. His bum sways to one side but he manages to get himself balanced. 'We don't have much time. If the thief strikes again tonight, Ed will be arrested.'

'When do the thefts happen?'

'At night.'

'All right. Here's a plan. If Rose hasn't solved it by tonight, we'll stake out the shop.'

Jakes nods. 'I'll see you outside the store at six, then. That's when it shuts.'

'I can't do that Jake. I have to wait until Rose is asleep before I can sneak out of the house.'

'Okay, I'll do the early shift, six until midnight. You take the late shift, midnight until six in the morning. How about that?'

'I'll be there,' I say.

My plan to lure Rose into the investigation failed. Rose was in a rush to get home at the end of our walk and we didn't go anywhere near Pam's shop. The day passed by as fast as a fleeing rabbit and Rose is now tucked up in bed snoring. The church bell has rung twelve times as I arrive at the shop.

'Pssst!'

Jake is crouched behind what appears to be a wooden barrel, cut in half and now full of soil and daffodils. I join him, although the pot isn't big enough to conceal me too.

'All right, mate,' Jake says, keeping his voice down.

I nod.

The shop is red brick, single story, with a tiled gable roof and a white front door. If it wasn't for the red post box on a black metal pole that looks like a sentinel guarding the place, or the blue glow from the fridge and freezer inside, you might assume it was just a house. Pam lives in the newer extension at the back which is on two levels.

'Anything happened?' I ask, in a woof-whisper.

Jake shakes his head.

'Is there an alarmy thing?'

He shakes his head again. 'No cameras, neither.'

Jake struggles to stand, then stretches his stiff body. 'Good luck.' He lollops down the road.

It's a cold night but my thick coat keeps me warm. I decide to explore the shop's exterior. There is a narrow side passage boarded by a picket fence where Pam keeps her bins. I smell fox, probably rummaging for food scraps. At the back, French doors lead to a crazy paving patio and a rectangle of lawn. I sniff the air. A cat has been on the patio recently; a paver is warm beneath my paws and I recognise the tell-tale scent of corn chips that's unique to cats. I have no doubt Pam locks the front and back doors and I see no obvious way a thief could get into the shop unnoticed.

Bored, I trot back to the front and crawl under a rickety wooden table where Pam puts plants for sale. From my hiding spot I can see the front of the shop and the side passage. The street is deserted. Everyone sleeps. My eyelids grow heavy.

There's a snap. My eyes open. The branch of a cherry plum tree dips and its tiny white flowers catch the moonlight. Petals, like snow, float to the ground. I hear the hum of a tune. To a hooman it would sound like a squirrel chittering, but to me it sounds like a squirrel humming Oliver Twist's *Food Glorious Food*.

Rose likes to watch old movies, especially musicals. We sat and watched *Oliver!* on TV over Christmas. Afterwards, I couldn't stop thinking about Bull's-Eye. I hope he found a nicer master. The leaves part and a grey squirrel scampers along a cherry plum branch overhanging the shop. She leaps from the end of the branch and onto the steeply sloping roof with ease, then hops into the gutter. Headfirst, she swings underneath it and disappears through a hole in the underside of the eaves.

Wriggling out from beneath the bench, I press my black nose against one of ten large panes of glass that make up the front window. My nostrils pulse as I try to locate the squirrel inside. The interior is jampacked with metal shelves full of food in boxes and bags and cans, as well as fresh fruit and vegetables. Along one wall is an upright fridge and a chest freezer that hums like an angry hornet. Near the counter at the far end, chocolate bars and packets of sweets are piled high. Even through the glass, the smorgasbord of smells is overwhelming. Drool starts to drip from my jowl. Determined to stay focused, I prick my ears and listen, trying to shut out the freezer's humming motor.

Scratching.

It's coming from the ceiling. High in a corner of the store, a grey head with round eyes and four long front teeth pokes through a gap in the cornice. She appears to look straight at me, and chatters. She's laughing with delight. I'm not surprised.

If only I could get inside.

I test the doorknob, clamping my jaw down on it to see if I can twist it. It doesn't budge. That leaves me no choice but to raise the alarm. I can only hope that by the time Pam gets downstairs and opens the door, the squirrel is still in the shop and I can catch it, although it has to be said that my success rate at nabbing squirrels is not good. Well to be honest, I've had zero success.

I take a wide stance and a deep breath, then let rip with an almighty bark. It's loud enough and frantic enough to wake the whole village. I'm hoping Jake will hear me too and come to my aid, although the forest where Ed lives is a mile away.

Lights go on at the back of the building. There's a slap of slippers on stairs. I keep an eye on the eaves where the squirrel entered the roof space as I keep up the barking as loud as I can.

The neighbour over the road opens a window and yells, 'Shut up!' I can see lights flicking on in nearby houses, their yellow glow reflected in the windowpanes of the shop.

At last, the shop interior lights up and Pam stomps down one of two narrow aisles towards the door. She's in a pink fluffy dressing gown and has what appears to be the cardboard inners of toilet rolls in her grey hair. She unlocks the door and throws it open, her gown billowing behind her as a gust of wind blows into the store.

'You! I might've known it. Get out of here. Shoo!'

I race past her.

'Stop!' she yells.

I hear her next-door neighbour's front door creak open. I need to find the squirrel fast before I'm dragged away in disgrace. I run past cakes and bread and pasta and rice, following the scent of squirrel which is an odd mix of acorns and liquorice. Her smell is strongest where the shelves are stacked with packets of crisps and nuts. My paws slip on what at first I think are little pebbles. Looking down, I discover the floor is strewn with peanuts and salted crisps. I peer up.

There's a rustling sound. A grey tail sticks up above the bulging crisp packets like a flag of truce. When the squirrel lifts her head, she has a Cheezel – a puffy cheesy ring of yumminess – clamped between her front teeth. She crunches down on it. Half of it falls to the floor, the other half disappears into her mouth.

'Can't catch me,' she taunts as she jumps up high, then lands hard on a packet of cheese and onion crisps, bursting it open with such a loud bang that Pam screams.

This alerts me to the fact that Pam is coming at me with a broom. I suspect she plans to sweep me from the shop. The squirrel uses her back legs to scatter the crisps all over the floor.

'You're making Pam angry,' I say. 'Please come down here and own up to your crime.'

'I'm hungry,' she says and scampers along the top shelf, sending packets plummeting to the floor.

'Bad dog!' Pam says.

Thwack!

Just in time I leap out of the way, the broom brushing past the fur on my flank.

'An old man is being blamed for your stealing,' I bark.

I can't reach her. She's too high up.

'Look! There's a burst bag of peanuts here.' I little white lie.

She blinks. 'Nuts?'

The squirrel-thief scuttles down to

where my nose points. My plan is to hold her softly in my jaw until Pam has seen the squirrel and then I will let her go, my job of identifying the thief done and dusted. Golden Retrievers have soft mouths. We know how to hold delicate creatures in our jaws without hurting them through centuries of practice. But the squirrel is too canny. She sees sealed bags of nuts and darts back up to the highest shelf. I snap at her tail and just mange to catch the fur from the very tip of it. Finally, I have evidence.

Smack!

The broom hits me on the head. Luckily my skull is thick. I almost release the fur as I yelp, but I manage to keep hold of it.

I bolt out of the shop to find Pam's neighbour clutching a shovel. I dodge him and turn up the hill, heading for home. Rose's car is speeding down the lane towards me. She slams on the brakes and gets out.

'Oh Monty, what have you done?'

I'm in disgrace. Rose won't even speak to me now we are home. I tried several times to show her the squirrel fur in my mouth, but she is too busy pacing the worn lino on the kitchen floor to notice.

'She's reporting you, Monty,' Rose says, dragging her fingers through her messy hair. 'This is bad. They could insist I muzzle you.'

Muzzle me? No, no. That can't happen. I can't have a cage on my face. It makes me vulnerable to attack. And a laughing stock. All the little dogs will mock me. I can't believe this is happening. I go to my bed and curl into a tight ball, feeling very down. And to top it all my fluffy yellow duck stinks of a floral washing powder.

Rose kneels next to my bed and strokes my head. I keep my eyes lowered.

'It's okay, Monty. I'll work something out in the morning.'

I don't sleep well and soon a pink dawn sky is heralded by the birds' morning song. Rose usually sleeps in on a Sunday but not today. She's up and making herself a mug of tea as she opens a tin of wet dog food for me and puts my bowl on the floor. I have long forgotten about the squirrel fur caught in my teeth and devour my food. Then I suddenly realise I have eaten the evidence. I can't believe it! Could it get any worse? I wander outside for a pee.

Rose watches me from the doorway as if she's nervous I'm going to raid the shop again. I head back to my bed, too crest-fallen to do anything else.

Apart from the foul floral smell, there's something not right with my bed. How come it smells of liquorice and acorns? I stand and do a circle, only to discover I have been lying on the piece of squirrel fur. I must have spat it out during the night. All is not lost after all.

Rose sits at the oak dining table and sips her tea. She notices me looking at her.

'I'll talk to Pam. Hopefully she's calmed down. I'll clean up the mess and pay for the damaged goods. Perhaps then I can persuade her to give you another chance.'

I don't fancy her chances. Pam used words like 'nuisance' and 'the pound' last night.

Rose continues, 'I'm going to keep you inside today, I'm sorry. Best you keep a low profile. I'll walk you tonight when nobody's about.'

I sigh. I imagine all the fun I'll miss out on: chasing ducks, slaloming trees, chasing rabbits, digging holes, eating sticks, going to the drive-through McDonald's, choosing the biggest and the best raw hide bone at the pet shop. Hurrumph! I wander over to Rose and drop the clump of squirrel fur on the knee of her pyjama bottoms.

'Yuck! What's that?' She stares at it. 'Where did you get that? What is it? Rabbit?'

So many questions and I don't know how to respond. I want to say, that's the thief. A squirrel, not Ed. Not me either.

Rose pokes it with a finger. 'Is it a fur ball?'

I sit, tall and proud, and give a firm two barks. No.

She jerks her head up and looks me in the eye. 'That was definitive. Okay, answer this. Is it rabbit fur?'

Two barks. Definitely not.

'Hmm. What else has fluffy grey fur? Squirrel! Is this fur from a squirrel?'

One clear bark from me. Yes!

She smiles. 'You know, sometimes I think you actually understand me.' She shakes her head. 'Crazy really.'

Don't give up on me already. Believe me!

She sips her tea. 'How did you get hold of squirrel fur? Did you chase a squirrel last night?'

One big bark from me. Oh yes!

Rose chews her lip. 'I wonder...oh why not. She peers intently at me. 'Did you chase a squirrel inside the shop?'

I'm so elated I want to bark and bark. It takes all my self-control to give a single bark in response.

Her eyes widen. 'That would explain why you ran up and down the shop aisles. Pam said you looked as if you were chasing someone but there wasn't anybody there.' She pauses. Chews her lip. 'Do squirrels like crisps?'

One bark from me.

Rose looks at her phone. Taps some letters. She raises her eyebrows. 'Would you believe it? Squirrels have been known to eat pizza, iced buns, cheesy puffs, ham sandwiches. A whole variety of human food, even if it's bad for them.'

And crisps and nuts.

'I must be out of my mind…were you trying to catch Pam's thief?'

One bark.

'Okay,' Rose says, springing up from her chair. 'I'll do what I can to appease Pam. Tonight we're going to stake out the shop. Together.'

I wag my tail with joy.

Pam knows we are parked in the street, watching the front of the shop. Rose has a sleeping bag draped over her knees and she's wearing her black, super-puffy coat that makes her look like a blackberry. Rose has allowed me to sit on the passenger seat.

I keep my eyes glued to one spot, where the eaves have a hole, just below the roof's gutter. My fear is that the squirrel won't come back because of her near-capture last night. But she said she was hungry, so I figure she'll take the risk. Although I don't understand why she is hungry. The ground has thawed, and she will have a hoard of acorns buried around here. All she has to do is dig them up.

I see the flash of her bulbous eyes, glinting in the moonlight. She jumps onto the sloping roof from the cherry plum.

'Oh my god!' Rose whispers, seeing it too.

The squirrel swings down from the gutter and disappears into the hole underneath the eaves.

Rose takes her mobile phone from the top of the dashboard and calls Pam who has her phone on vibrate, whatever that means.

'Pam, a squirrel has just entered your roof space.'

'I'm ready for him,' I hear Pam say, with the kind of relish in her voice that has me worried. I don't want her to hurt the squirrel.

The shop's light comes on. Pam throws a net over the section of shelving where she displays her crisps and nuts. The holes in the net are small so the squirrel can't escape. We jump out of the car and join Pam. Packets of crisps writhe and wriggle as if they are alive, then the squirrel-thief pops her head up and starts gnawing at the plastic netting.

'Help me!' she chitters.

'Who would have thought,' says Pam, moulding her neatly coiffured curls into place. 'It was a bloody squirrel!'

'Why did you steal?' I bark, keeping my tone as friendly as possible.

'I told you. I'm hungry.'

'Monty!' Rose says, 'Leave the squirrel alone.'

'I suppose I should thank your dog.' Pam gives me a suspicious look then turns to Rose. 'Help me seal the net around the nasty vermin. I'll get a pest control man to deal with it in the morning.'

The squirrel squeaks in panic like one of my squeaky toys. 'I'm too young to die.'

Rose stares sympathetically at the clearly terrified animal. 'Can't we release it somewhere else? I could take it to another forest.'

'No,' the squirrel shrieks. 'I want to stay with my clan.'

'Let me help you,' I bark. 'Tell me why you're hungry.'

The squirrel stops struggling. With a look of despair, she says 'I can't remember where I buried my acorns.'

The following day, Rose is as good as her word. She releases the squirrel in a forest about two miles away. However, squirrels have been known to find their way home even if they're trapped and taken ten miles away. Sure enough, the following day, the squirrel-thief hops into our garden and plonks herself down next to me.

'Thank you for your help,' she says.

For the first time I notice that she is skinny for a squirrel.

'I can find your acorns,' I say. 'If you point me in the right direction.'

While Rose is at work solving hooman crime, I explore the forest with the squirrel. She shows me one acorn that she has kept safe inside a decaying tree trunk. I sniff it, then nose to the ground, like we're searching for truffles, I locate most of the acorns that she buried in the autumn.

'Promise me you won't go near the village shop again,' I say.

'I promise.'

Feeling happy, I trot along to Ed's caravan. He's cooking pork sausages in a frying pan over a wood fire. Jake hears me coming. Ed doesn't. He's quite deaf.

'Monty!' Jake barks. 'You saved our hides. I owe you.'

Ed doesn't notice me until I sit next to him.

'Blimey, Monty, you gave me a shock,' he shouts. Ed always shouts. He hugs me to him. Ed smells of wood smoke and moss and tobacco. 'What a good dog you are, catching the squirrel, hey? Almost cost me my home, it did.' He jerks his chin at the rusting caravan, propped up on tyres that have gone flat. 'I bet you'd like a sausage, wouldn't ya?'

I bark an affirmative.

'Don't want you burning your mouth.' With a fork, Ed takes a sausages from the pan and drops it onto a plastic plate, then with his fingers he breaks it in half. Steam rises into the cold air. He wags a crooked finger at me. 'Just wait a little for it to cool.'

While Jake and I wait, Ed wraps a piece of white bread around a sausage and takes a big bite.

Two stalactites of drool start to hang from my jowl. They grow in length until they almost touch the ground.

'Oy! Mate!' says Jake. 'You should see someone about that drool problem of yours.' I turn my head, confused. Is he serious? He barks out a husky laugh. 'Got you!'

Ed picks up the two halves of the sausage, blows on them, then offers one to Jake and one to me.

Yum! Life is good!

The Tidings

Tor Roxburgh

The Tidings

EVERYTHING INSIDE MY NATION IS MY BUSINESS, SO I FELT A SENSE OF responsibility when the human and the cockatoo died. I didn't witness either death. I was too busy patrolling the border on the other side of the railway line. But I heard the cockatoos yelling and not long after I heard police sirens. The sound drew me back.

My family and I flew over the houses and saw the dead human lying on his back. I could smell his blood, but I didn't go down because the garden was overflowing with human tidings: police, paramedics, and onlookers. Instead, we landed on the nature strip, which is when I saw the second body.

We magpies get on well with the cockatoos and I had been close to this one. I felt a wave of sorrow seeing my friend lying on the ground, the noise and clatter of humans uncomfortably close. He lay beneath a tree, his feathers crisp and white, his crest a perfect vivid yellow. He was an old bird in his 60s, but I knew this was murder. There had been fifteen other cockatoos who'd died in the past two days and the avian world was alive with the news that a human was responsible. We didn't know who, but massacres are a human habit.

A policewoman wandered over. I was familiar with this one. When she was a new adult, I'd seen her in uniform correcting younger humans at the railway station. She no longer wore a uniform, but she had the same air of being on patrol.

She took a photo of the cockatoo's body. I didn't move away. Humans are insufferable in springtime, but my chicks were already flying. I even stepped a bit closer, wondering what she wanted. They usually ignore our dead.

She waved to someone and another human, a man, arrived with a bag of equipment.

'It's probably nothing, but treat it as a potential piece of evidence.' She pointed as she spoke. 'I know it's just a dead bird–'

I couldn't help myself. I used a particularly choice Old Birdic phrase and to my astonishment she reacted. She looked around uneasily, then walked off, heading away from the dead human's house toward his neighbour's front gate.

I felt a burst of excitement. It wasn't just that she'd understood me. It was the possibility of putting her to work to help find a way to end the deaths. I gave a loud flap of my wings and lifted into the air. I landed in front of her. She stood as still as a field mouse under a hawk.

'So, you can hear me!'

She fumbled with the latch, flung the gate open and raced away from me, running up the path. I tried to follow but had to pull up at my border. I might have found the first sign of intelligence in the species but that didn't mean I could go racing into another tiding's territory.

I called out for her but she ignored me, knocking hard on the neighbour's door. It opened and I lost my chance. I waited for her for several hours, but she must have used a different exit because there was no sign of her by nightfall.

In the morning, I conferred with the cockatoos, told them we might have some way of communicating with the humans. There was a great deal of excitement and screeching and arguing, as there always is with that lot, but we agreed I should try to form an alliance with the human to help us to investigate the cockatoo deaths.

My policewoman reappeared mid-morning, looking flighty: high stepping across the grass that was still wet from the early frost. To give her credit she summoned up the courage to approach me. She said hello, using that ghastly cheery tone they use when speaking outside their species.

'Well hello to you too,' I responded.

She blinked.

'Are you going to run away again?'

For a moment all was still. My family kept a dignified distance, watched us from a few paces away. Then the cockies began to move. A couple of them flew over, landing with thuds and flutters. I willed them to be patient.

'No,' she said. 'I…I don't think so. I… This is amazing. Either that or I'm going mad. No. No, this is amazing.'

'Good girl,' I spoke soothingly. 'Clever girl. We want to work with you. Bird tidings and human tidings together.

'Tidings?'

I hoped she wouldn't be too stupid to deal with but evidently I was going to have to give her a lesson in avian diplomacy. 'I'm being polite. A tiding is the collective name for magpies. I'm using it as a compliment.

I'm indicating that you are magpie-like. I can call your lot a 'group' if you'd rather be insulted?'

She shook her head and I brought the conversation back to the matter at hand, 'These murders—'

'Harvey Macarthur's murder, you mean?' She frowned, then crouched down, got closer to eye level. 'Are you saying there are other bodies we haven't found?'

'I don't know how many bodies you've seen but fifteen others have been killed. The cockatoos have suspects.'

The number of cockatoos surrounding us had grown and with it their noise, but the woman seemed oblivious. She turned and addressed the cockatoos, speaking to them directly as though every one of them was fluent in Old Birdic.

'They can't understand you. I can translate if you want. I can introduce you to his widow.'

She turned her attention back to me. 'Harvey Macarthur wasn't married.'

I couldn't help the little grunt of irritation that escaped my beak, 'No, stupid. I'm talking about the person who was murdered, not the human.'

She stood up, a look of disappointment on her flat face. 'Oh. Right. So, these other deaths are birds? You're talking about birds dying?'

I hopped forward, got closer, looked up at her, my beak pointing right at her. 'There is a serial killer, a human, who has to be stopped.'

Around us, the cockatoos had become noisy, demanding to know what was being said. I translated the exchange and received six different suggestions and various orders about what I should say and what the woman should do. I translated some of it for her, '...so, the cockatoo tiding has a list of suspects, but they need someone to conduct the interviews. If we can do that together, I may be willing to help you solve the human murder.'

She hesitated. I could see she didn't like me asserting my dominance, but she seemed to recognise my authority because she sat down on the grass, rested her weight on her hands and exposed her belly in an extremely submissive gesture. I admit, I was charmed. Humans aren't known for their diplomacy but this one seemed different.

For the first time in the conversation, we introduced ourselves. Her name was Romy. I gave her mine but she just shook her head and claimed the note was too hard for her to parse. She offered me her father's name. And so I became Victor.

Romy isn't stupid. She's quite clever for a human. A little nervous and as ugly and featherless as they all are, with those funny tufts of hair. She tells me she can sing four different human songs, which she thinks is why she understands Old Birdic. I'm curious about whether she could learn Magpie and become an ambassador. Because we need one. But I won't go into all the affronts we suffer during the spring season.

The cockatoos had six suspects. Most lived in and around my territory but there was one, a farmer, who lived further out. Romy's work tiding had examined my friend's body and discovered that the serial killer had used a common farm poison called omethoate so she insisted that the farmer was our priority.

To a human, the journey from one township to the next is a minor affair. For a magpie, a journey like that involves crossing into other territories, which is a diplomatic issue. It's not Romy's fault that she thinks like a human but the trip from Ballan to Mount Egerton was difficult for everyone and full of interruptions. We traversed 31 territories and spent many etiquette-filled hours singing and parading at border crossings.

She joined in, which was sweet, but she lectured me on human cross-border cooperation protocols, which was not sweet. As if I was an ignorant chick. As if she hadn't just participated in a string of protocols.

Then there was the car trip itself, which was taxing. There is almost nowhere to perch in a car apart from the steering wheel, which Romy wouldn't share. Some of the cockies flew overhead to lead the way, but the others wanted to travel in the car so it was crowded and noisy. They pulled at the seats to keep their balance and some upholstery got ripped. I ended up riding on Romy's shoulder, but she was upset about the damage the cockies caused. I gather she has a lowly place in her work tiding.

The disagreeable mood wasn't improved by Romy's conduct during the interrogation; or the farmer's poor attitude. We interviewed the farmer outside her house. The cockies flew up into the trees and shouted at me: endless accusations and suggested insults.

I took up a dignified position on Romy's shoulder and gripped her jacket with my feet. The problem started when she introduced herself with a string of names and titles but told the farmer I was Victor. Two measly syllables. To top it off the farmer mistook me for a pet.

'More like the dog squad,' Romy corrected her.

I gave Romy's ear a sharp peck and told her to watch her mouth. Dogs are disgusting animals whose status is vastly beneath all birds. While it's well known that humans are in thrall to dogs and cats, comparing them with us is an unspeakable insult.

'I'm here to have a chat about your cockatoo management.' She rubbed her ear, unsettling me. I was so busy shaking myself, opening my wings and maintaining my grip, that I lost concentration and missed some of the conversation. Evidently, she told the farmer about the human death because the farmer spent the next few minutes discussing the dead human's social contacts with other humans in the district.

Romy nodded and made notes. 'And there may be an incidental connection with some bird poisonings. So I'm having a chat with people about cockatoo management. I heard you'd been having problems.'

The woman blew out a gusty breath. 'We follow DELWP guidelines. We use onion grass as a decoy to lure them away from the crops. We use cartridges and gas guns.'

'Ask her about the poison,' I spoke into Romy's ear. 'Press her.'

'Likely, we're looking at someone who is a witness,' Romy said, ignoring my advice. 'Do you know of anyone else having problems with cockatoos?'

'Everyone.'

'Specifically?'

'Every farmer. All the sporting clubs. Anyone with balconies or cedar window frames. Seriously half the bloody district.'

I urged Romy to peck at the woman, but she shook her head and I had to satisfy myself with inspecting the farmer's gun safe and visiting her sheds. There was plenty of poison but no omethoate. The entire journey was a waste of time.

It was late, too late for the trip home, so Romy invited me to stay in her roost, which was nearby and not uncomfortable once she locked away her vile pet cat. She fed me a tasty plate of mince on a china saucer and fresh water in a tea cup and after agreeing to disagree about dogs and cats, we broached the subject of names and titles: Detective Senior Constable Romy DuBois, Criminal Investigation Unit versus Victor.

I will admit that she apologised as soon as I pointed out the discrepancy and she offered me her father's full name, Victor DuBois. Unfortunately, calling myself Victory From The Trees would have been a territorial insult. We settled on Victor Au Delà Des Voies Ferrées, which means Victory from Beyond the Railway Line. My pleasure in my new melodic name was short lived because she refused me a police rank. It was hard to let go of the affront, but I made myself focus on the investigation.

'I want you to bring the other five suspects into my territory for interrogation. After all,' I said, 'humans come to the railway station all the time. They won't object.'

She took a sip of her wine and looked up at the ceiling. No doubt she was trying to find some wriggle room, some new way to defy me.

'They will and I can't make them.'

I gave her a soothing warble and walked across the kitchen table, stood right in front of her and tipped my head, looked at her sideways trying to assess the strength of her opposition. 'Your work tiding is powerful, Romy. Don't forget that. Those little humans will be submissive if you fluff up your feathers and approach them properly. Persuade them. You are such a clever woman. I know you can.' I reached forward and gave a lock of her hair a gentle tug, which made her laugh.

'All right, Victor, I'll try.'

'And in return I will ask my family and the other local tidings about the dead human—'

'Harvey.'

'Yes. We will find out what he was up to in the days before the end.'

Romy and I were a good combination. We didn't let our interspecific tensions affect our work but it was soon clear that the cockatoos didn't have a clear grasp of human behaviour.

The first suspect she brought to the train station was a local musician whom the cockies had noticed taking daily walks around town and behaving suspiciously. We soon realised that 'behaving suspiciously', meant sporting a mohawk, which the cockies had interpreted as a raised crest. The birds claimed the man was agitated. Romy said in human terms he was a fashion tragic, working his 10,000 steps.

The next suspect was young, too young to be a serial killer. When I translated the cockies' insults and accusations, they involved flying a kite with 'eyes' near their roost. After that, there was a woman who had nailed spikes to her balcony railing. Finally, there were two children who had thrown stones when the cockatoo tiding was feeding on their parents' newly sown back lawn.

Romy perked up a bit with those two, but the investigation had stalled. Unfortunately, the killer hadn't. Two more birds were found dead under the branches of a chestnut tree.

But I kept my promise about helping Romy with the human murder. When she returned to the station, I told her that several birds had seen Harvey visiting various human recreational tidings. The people he'd visited had seemed pleased with him. Romy felt it was significant. I almost wished I hadn't told her because I had some difficulty getting her to re-focus on the cockatoo deaths.

She reached into her pocket for her car keys and started walking toward her car. 'I'll follow this up.'

I flew up onto her shoulder and had to give her hair a sharp tug to get her to stop. 'We have to find the serial killer first. Eighteen deaths.'

'Yes.' She slowed to a stop. 'You're right. Any ideas?'

'We need a predator's eye on this.'

She held out her hand so I could perch on it. 'Meaning?'

'Imagine you're up in the sky, looking down. When you're up there, you see patterns in movement. You see where things are and how things are.'

'Like avian surveillance? Some sort of stakeout to catch the killer in the act?'

'No. I'm talking about looking into the past from above. Seeing where the deaths took place. Looking for patterns.'

'A map! Of course. I'll get one from the car.'

We walked back to the car park bench with the map and I called down the cockatoos. Some ten of them arrived. They walked all over the paper and yelled at one another, left filthy footprints everywhere. They all agreed about where the bodies had been found but everyone insisted on having their say, so it was noisy and repetitious and destructive.

In the end, Romy and I had a tattered but useful document to work with. The golf tiding, the football tiding, and the bowls tiding all had clusters of dead bodies near their territories. Romy became animated, pointing out that there seemed to be a connection between the locations where the dead human had been sighted in recent weeks and the location of the avian bodies.

'It's got something to do with sporting clubs. I need to do some ordinary police work, Victor. I need to make some calls, ask some quiet questions.'

I let her go but made her promise to report back. She returned the following afternoon with a piece of paper, which she smoothed out on her knee.

'Harvey was giving away cash. Lots of money. Listen to this,' she said: '$8,550 for defibrillators for the hospital; $2,000 for the CFA; $500 each for the Country Women's Association, the Red Cross, Ballan Rotary, the Lions, and the Lionesses; and $3,600 for the Ballan Community House. Not so keen on the arts because Wombat Regional Arts Network only got $135, the film society got just $122, and the pottery club got a measly $72. Then there was $2,000 for the Men's Shed; half that for the Senior Citizens Club; $8,000 each for the Ballan Football Netball Club, the bowling club, the tennis club, and the cricket club; and finally $1,000 each for the RSL, the jockey club, and the Ballark and District Rifle Club.' She looked up and smiled, showing all her teeth. 'Guess which sporting club is missing.'

'The golf tiding.'

'Ex-actly. I don't know whether the bird deaths and Harvey's death are connected but we need to find out.'

I translated the new developments for the cockatoos and they flew down and crowded around us, insisting that we visit the golf club immediately. Romy said she had to gather more evidence. Over the next two days, she looked into Harvey's financial records but was unable to find the source of his funds. She also rang the education department, the sports and recreation department, and the environment department to check on complaints about cockatoos. The golf tiding was a standout complainant. We were getting closer.

The trip to the golf course was easier than our trip to Mount Egerton. News of our work had spread through the avian world and when we began our parade and prepared to ruffle our feathers, the magpies in the other tidings bowed and invited us to cross their borders.

Romy met the golf elders inside the club house and once everyone was seated, I walked in unnoticed. I wanted her to ask about poison, but of course she started with Harvey.

The elders confirmed that he had been planning to make a major donation to their tiding.

'We were getting quotes. Eighteen new greens. He hadn't played for a few years, but he was a terrific golfer,' the president explained.

'Beautiful swing,' another man added.

Romy kept her attention focused on her little notebook. I kept motionless in the shadows.

'How much are we talking about?' she asked.

'Something over $60,000.'

I heard her heartbeat pick up. 'There must have been a bit of envy from the other organisations. Was he planning to make the gift in cash? That's a lot of cash.'

'That's what I said to Clem,' the treasurer nodded at the club president. 'I said we were walking a fine line.'

Clem glared at the woman.

'Does anyone know where he got the money?' Romy asked.

The humans all glanced at one another, their naked faces looked as though they were signalling something shared and obvious, but I couldn't parse the meaning. I wondered when Romy would bring up the bird deaths, how she would trap the killer.

The president cleared his throat. 'It was gossip but there was talk that in his younger days he was a bagman for a prominent Melbourne family.'

Romy's pen stopped moving and she looked up, her face very still. The humans avoided her gaze. 'Which family? When was this?'

'If it's true, and I doubt it was, it was a long time ago,' Clem answered. 'Harvey's gone to his maker and the club didn't receive the money so I think we can say that case is closed.'

Romy asked again about envious humans.

The treasurer spoke up, 'Ivy thought the town was taking advantage.'

'Ivy?'

'His neighbour,' Clem said.

Romy's heartbeat picked up again as she checked through her notebook. 'Lives next door? Behind that ornamental gate?'

The treasurer nodded. 'That's her. She did Harvey's shopping for him. You get people who think they have a right to get involved if they do someone a favour.'

Then, finally, Romy asked about poison. She told them what she'd told the farmer: that there was a possible connection to some recent bird deaths. She spoke mildly. She said she was talking about a witness and that she wasn't focusing on any contravention of the Wildlife Act.

There was that same shifting feeling in the human group. Faces stilled; too much silence. This time some of the heartbeats raced. Loudest was the woman, the treasurer.

I almost warbled, sure that we'd found her. I waited for Romy to pounce but she seemed oblivious. She closed her notebook and smiled at everyone. Showed all her teeth. Then she stood up and started shaking their hands.

I stalked out of the building, furious that I'd been fool enough to imagine there was such a thing as an avian-human alliance. I opened my wings and flew to the edge of the car park and was immediately surrounded by noisy cockatoos demanding answers. I was too angry to explain and, thankfully, they retreated to the crowns of the trees. I watched Romy walk across the bitumen and it occurred to me that her hearing could be the problem. She might not have heard the woman's heartbeat. I flew over, put my beak in her ear and explained.

'I think you're right,' Romy whispered as she continued walking. 'She's feeling guilty.'

'Not feeling guilty. Is guilty!'

She shook her head. 'No. I think we were wrong. There are two crimes and two killers and the golf club connection is coincidental. It's a small town, Victor. Coincidences can happen in small towns. I'm almost certain the president, Clem, is your serial killer but I can't act without evidence. Let me do a bit of door knocking and ordinary policing. Something will shake loose. As for Harvey, his neighbour is probably the murderer but I need to find out where she's hidden the money before I can arrest her. It won't be in the bank.'

'A bird will have noticed. Someone will have seen her. I'll ask.'

Unsurprisingly, my network was more efficient than Romy's, so she and I were able to approach the human's killer the next day.

Ivy opened the door to us with a smile on her face, displaying all her ageing teeth. You had to wonder at the ugliness of humans. I kept quiet and watched from my perch on Romy's shoulder as they exchanged border protocols.

'So you've made friends?' Ivy led us into the kitchen. 'You were a bit nervous about that maggie when you knocked on my door the other day. They make fine pets.'

'She's as wily as your cat,' I spoke into Romy's ear, 'and just as vile.'

Romy pretended she didn't hear me. She took a seat but turned down the cup of tea. She used her official voice but inflected it with a touch of warmth. 'I wondered whether you could tell me a bit more about Harvey. I've heard that you used to give him a hand now and again.'

The old woman adjusted her glasses. 'Just a little shopping. He had difficulty walking. Had heart problems.'

I hopped off Romy's shoulder and walked across the table, pretending fascination with a spill of sugar crystals. Then I flew over to the sink, landing a little unsteadily on the faucet. The old human followed me with her eyes, still smiling, but I heard her heartbeat increase. She didn't like me moving about in the room.

'Yes, he didn't have long,' Romy said, drawing the old woman's attention again. 'That was why he was giving away so much cash. Did he give any to you?'

The murderer shook her head. 'I would never take advantage...'

I flapped my wings loudly and flew over to the top of the fridge, scrabbling slightly on the polished surface.

'Perhaps you could put him outside?'

'Of course.' Romy stood up. The move gave her body camera an excellent view of the room: the cracked windowpane, the water-stained walls, and the three ceramic canisters on the mantelpiece containing the stolen cash that a local crow had seen her hide.

'I imagine it would have been hard to refuse. A windfall would have come in handy. Make things a little more comfortable?'

The old woman's shoulders went back and her chest filled with air like a bird on border patrol. 'I have enough to pay my bills, not to go wasting money on appearances. We're not all made of money, like some.'

Romy tucked her hair behind her ear, the signal for me to do my part. I let out a loud call and flew over to the mantelpiece, this time scrabbling purposefully. I hoped it looked as though I was trying to find something to grip. Instead I knocked over the canisters. The old woman let out a cry as they fell to the ground, scattering cash and broken china across the floor.

'That's mine,' she shouted.

'So our forensic services won't find Harvey's DNA and fingerprints on the notes?' Romy stepped forward and peered down at the money.

'Come on Ivy,' Romy's voice was kind, but her song was the song of a more powerful bird to its subordinate. 'I think we both know this is Harvey's money.'

Ivy sat down and her body sagged. 'He'd promised that money to me. Did his shopping. Paid his bills. Fetched his wretched pills.' She took a breath and sat up straight again, glared at Romy. 'He had no right.'

We confronted the serial killer two days later, on a balcony overlooking the golf course. Romy hadn't wanted me on her shoulder but the golf club president's veranda railing was covered in spikes. He stood across from us, feet wide apart, hands on hips, flat meaty face.

'So with the statement from your treasurer and a local witness, there will be proceedings against you,' Romy said.

Out of the corner of my eye I saw the cockatoos moving in the trees, jostling for space. Two of them landed on the roof ridge. I wasn't translating. Not yet, but they could sense that Romy and I had found the killer.

'Tell him it's for murder,' I spoke into Romy's ear.

The cockatoos screeched and I heard Romy's heartbeat race. She turned on her body cam and used her formal voice to describe the offence and the penalties. I lost my footing when she outlined the meagre penalties. Had to grip a lock of her hair.

Clem blew out a derisive sound. 'A fine? Okay. Sure. Fine me. You try and deal with that lot.' He waved a hand toward the trees and the cockies shouted back at him, shifting branches, flapping wings, screeching.

'A jail term is possible.'

I spoke into her ear, reminded her it was murder. She tried to brush me aside and I grabbed hold of her collar to steady myself.

'I'm not going to jail for killing a few birds.' Clem turned and shouted an insult at the birds in the trees.

I waited for Romy to peck him but she did nothing. Nothing! I shouted at her to charge him with murder but she was mute. So, I left her. Flew to the trees and called out to the cockatoos, translating the poverty of human justice.

For a moment, all was silent. Then the noise of the cockatoos burst from the branches around me. Small groups took flight like smoke lifting from a fire. Others joined them in the air. Soon they numbered some forty birds.

Clem and Romy stood watching. The cockatoos broke apart and then re-joined, broke apart and re-joined, as one, two, five, ten, twenty, thirty and more flew in from over the river. In a matter of moments, there were several hundred birds in the air. They pivoted and flew across my line of sight, disappearing behind the house.

I heard Romy suggest that she and Clem should go inside but he refused.

With a rush of air and a clatter of wings, that made the humans spin around to face the house, the cockatoos rose above the roof ridge and filled the sky. The killer looked up and took a step back, pressing up against the balcony's spikes. The birds dove, hitting him like a white and yellow wall, the rail broke, and the man tumbled through the air.

Romy raced down the wooden stairs and into the garden with her phone to her ear. I landed near the dead man. She felt for the killer's pulse. I could have told her there was none.

She turned off her camera and crouched down near my beak. 'Tell those cockatoos I never want to see any of them in my district ever again! Tell them they'd better find somewhere else to roost.'

I answered with an old song that blended with the approaching sirens. Then the cockatoos and I left the humans to their corrupt and lawless world.

Ours was not so inhumane.

Cats
Are Better
Than
Humans

Livia Day

Cats are Better than Humans

FIRST, CHOOSE YOUR HUMAN.

In this skill, as all things, cats are superior.

Take my Tiff, an excellent specimen. I knew she was special when she first walked into the Cat's Home to claim me. I felt it all the way down my three-quarters tail (I could tell you what happened to the other quarter, but then I'd have to kill you). She wore a coat with many pockets (not a trace of dog hair), fragrance-free cosmetics, and she had the well-padded behind of someone who knows how to sit still.

I knew then and there that she must be mine.

Despite being the cream of humankind, Tiff herself has terrible taste in humans. Her last three boyfriends were entirely unworthy, and every employee she has hired to help in the shop (yes! I'm a bookshop cat!) has been a wastrel, a student, or a dog person.

Still, she has me to save her from the worst of her mistakes.

And, of course, to assist her with the murders.

No, no, we do not commit murders together, not unless you count the slightly regrettable incident surrounding the mysterious demise of That Mouse Behind The Dresser.

(Mysterious might not be an entirely accurate adjective. I know exactly what happened to that mouse, and I regret nothing.)

We solve murders, Tiff and I. We're rather good at it. Most of the ingenious detective work comes from my general direction, but she is competent at providing regular meals and doing the boring legwork.

Our first murder came as something of a surprise. To the victim, I imagine, as well as everyone else in the town of Hollow Creek. But when the second-best butcher in town met his terrible end at the hands of his second-cousin Pete (who had been disappointed in an inheritance involving a family ute and a beloved guitar), Tiff and I discovered our calling. Tripped over our calling, we might say, as the body fell out of said family ute and ended up on our bookshop's literal doorstep.

Discovering a corpse in a small town meant making many cups of tea for many people. Neighbours and other humans kept popping around for a chat, trying to pick up gossip. It was during this time that Tiff discovered the need for a larger kettle in the bookshop, along with a toaster for English muffins. She also discovered that she had a knack for assembling gossip into proper clues.

(She remains mostly unaware that her cat is ten times better at assembling clues into genuine theories, which is for the best. I do not require praise, nor credit. I only require a warm lap, the best lean kangaroo mince, and sometimes a bit of fish.)

The second murder did not happen in our town, but at a small hotel up in the hills. It involved several members of a rather famous former rock band, and several Golden Retrievers. While human justice was ultimately served, the Golden Retrievers went on to live full and happy lives. But you can't win them all.

These days, Tiff has something of a reputation for making helpful suggestions about mysterious crimes. Sometimes she helps the police with their enquiries; more often, she helps locals who have got themselves in hot water. Always, always, she has me by her side to assist her.

Not a bad life.

My only complaint is that Tiff has a social club which I do not at all enjoy. Largely because this social club takes place in front of a computer, on a chair that does not supply a sufficient lap-to-cat experience.

Also, because of the other cats.

Tiff belongs to The Feline Detectives Club, a group of humans who make an occasional hobby of solving mysteries in their home towns. They all live in different towns around Australia, several hours apart, necessitating the technological marvel known as The Zoom Chat. Every third Sunday without fail, Tiff pours herself a large glass of wine and calls up these people of hers to talk about inane things like boyfriends, vegetarian recipes and, occasionally, murders.

I sit on her lap, of course. The chair might not be ideal, but I have my pride. While Tiff talks shop with her human friends, I have the opportunity to eyeball my own greatest rivals in the art of criminal detection: Princess, Bootle, Ginge, Darcy and Frodo Baggins.

They are a most irritating assortment of cats, each convinced that they are the greatest detective genius of them all. All are wrong, except myself.

On this particular Sunday afternoon, Tiff was the last to connect, which gave the others plenty of time to gossip about me behind my back.

'Your Highness, gentlemen,' I greeted them icily as we arrived.

'Mr Bramble,' they all replied in an array of low purrs.

One of our number was missing. 'Has Darcy's owner sent her apologies?' I asked, a perfectly normal question.

The other cats shared uneasy glances.

'I think perhaps,' said Princess, licking her whiskers. 'Just this once, we had better listen to the human conversation.'

Darcy's human was dead.

A stunning tragedy for Darcy, who took such pride in having a human who never skimped on the treats, and rarely complained at having her lap punctured in twelve places when the doorbell rang.

According to our humans, with their complex web of hearsay, Darcy's human had taken too many of those little pill things, like the kind the vet sometimes likes to pretend are necessary for cats. Tiff and her fellow mystery-solvers all believed this was wildly out of character, and definitely Suspicious.

The nephew who inherited all of Darcy's rightful possessions, thanks to the flimsy excuse of being related to her human, was not a cat-lover. Everyone agreed this was Even More Suspicious, but at least it meant that he did not put up any resistance when Bootle's human turned up on his doorstep a few days later, to suggest she take Darcy to live with her.

Next time the humans opened their group chat, Darcy was there, tail twined companionably around Bootle's. Bootle clearly enjoyed the opportunity to be magnanimous about sharing his human with another cat, especially one he considered to be a professional nemesis. He had never quite forgiven Darcy for solving the Great Dane Danish Mystery before he did.

'My dears, it was terrible, quite terrible,' Darcy said with her usual over-dramatic airs. 'There I was, accidentally locked in the upstairs bathroom…'

'Fell asleep in a sunbeam, did you?' said Ginge slyly.

'I was locked in a bathroom,' Darcy said haughtily. 'Of course I was asleep! Why would I waste time not being asleep? The nephew let me out and oh, my poor dear Carol was quite dead on the floor, with the new Val McDermid novel unread on the couch. Unread! She'll be so distressed she never got to read that one, she'd been looking forward to it for ages.'

'Do you think the nephew did it?' Princess asked eagerly.

'I don't think he's much of a reader.'

'Did the murder, Darcy. Do you think he did your human in?'

'Not in the least,' said Darcy. 'He's a weedy sort of fellow, I wouldn't trust him to murder a mouse, let alone a human. Also, there was a distinct smell of peppermint around the body which did not belong to my Carol or to her horrible nephew. Someone else had been in the house!'

She licked her paws, and as she did so I heard Bootle's human say very clearly. 'I'll bet you the nephew did it. I didn't like the look of him at all.'

Oh, humans. You'd think they would recognise a red herring when they saw one.

Mmm, herring. I wonder if it's fish for tea?

It was a week before the next human was murdered.

Well, that's probably not true. I expect a lot of humans were murdered that week. But I only had interest in a very small circle of humans; one becoming smaller by the minute.

Tiff was tidying the bookshop at the end of a busy day of napping (me) and exchanging books for money (her). I was being helpful by rolling on everything I could find, and by licking bits of myself as and when required.

Suddenly, a blaze of a woman, all yellow hair and sharp perfume, came crashing through the door. I didn't recognise her without her cat, but Tiff knew her at once. 'Erin. What are you doing here?'

Oh, Erin. Tiff's favourite of the Feline Detective's Club. I never saw the appeal. Who wears perfume around cats? Now that I paid attention, I could smell hazelnuts and coffee, as well as her flowery chemicals. A haze of chickpea. A whiff of cat food; the expensive kind, but still tinned.

'Have you heard?' said Princess's human, throwing herself at the couch where, only moments before, I had been rolling on something crinkly. 'It's Leanne.'

That name was familiar. Was it from a book? Or a recipe, perhaps. I started thinking about cheesy corn bread, which I am definitely not allowed to eat, and spaced out for a little while, only to come snapping back to the conversation when Princess's human said the word 'Dead!' very loudly.

'How can she be dead?' said Tiff, horrified. 'She's not even thirty, she's a baby.'

'Hit and run,' said Princess's human.

'But,' said Tiff, and she had to sit down too, in a hurry. 'But that's two of us. In the same week.'

That was when I realised where I had heard the name Leanne before. She was Ginge's human. Two cats orphaned in the same week.

'Two isn't a pattern,' said Princess's human. 'Do you have anything to drink?'

'Tea,' said Tiff. 'I have tea.'

'Two of us dead in the same week,' said Princess's human firmly. 'Tea isn't going to cut it.'

I would have suggested milk, since this seemed to be a special occasion. (I'm very rarely allowed it unless Tiff has forgotten where she put down her cereal bowl.)

But no one asked me.

Frodo Baggins' human, Mel, was the next to die. It was few weeks after Leanne, in a 'freak accident' involving 'a kitchen knife'. This was all getting rather worrisome. Ginge had been adopted by his human's sister, and fell out of communication with the rest of us. Did his new human even solve mysteries? What was he going to do with himself?

Bootle's human took in Frodo Baggins alongside Bootle and Darcy, but that was hardly reassuring. What was going to happen if she got bumped off by whomever was murdering amateur sleuths? Would those wretched, pompous felines have to move into the bookshop with Tiff and I? Surely not.

Also, I did not want Tiff to die. I would never find a human as satisfying as her. There were no such humans alive in the world.

If we couldn't solve this mystery soon, we would not only run out of pet humans, but we would also lose any right to call ourselves detectives.

The only positive thing to come out of all this was that Tiff, Erin (Princess) and Kelly (Bootle/Darcy/Frodo Baggins) were now Zooming each other daily, and that gave the real detectives a chance to talk amongst ourselves.

'Something has to be done,' I informed my fellow felines. 'I hope you're all on your guard to keep your humans safe.'

'We're not dogs,' Darcy hissed. 'We do not guard. Are you suggesting that it's my fault Carol was murdered?'

'We don't know they were murdered,' said Frodo Baggins, who looked rather wide-eyed and shaky these days. 'Maybe none of this is true. Maybe they're planning a surprise party, or–'

Oh, dear.

'No time for denial,' I rapped out. 'We have to solve this one fast. Who are our suspects?'

'I think that should be rather obvious,' said Princess in a biting snarl. 'What do those three humans have in common? Us.'

'Are you suggesting one of the remaining humans is responsible?' asked Bootle, quite distressed. Understandably so, as that gave us each 3-1 odds that it was our human who might have been out there doing murders.

'No, wait,' said Darcy, giving Frodo Baggins a shove off the desk so she could lean in close for effect. 'Our humans solve crimes too. There's a long list of actual killers, and their families, who might hold a grudge against them for thwarting their evil shenanigans.'

'But not a grudge against all of them,' Princess insisted. 'Ours is a secret society. Who even knows that we consult each other?'

'We do,' I said heavily. 'The five of us. The three of them.'

'Six,' said Frodo Baggins, scrambling back up to the desk and shoving his bottom directly in Bootle's face. 'There are six of us, and three of them. You can't forget Ginge, just because…'

Why, no. We couldn't forget Ginge.

Tiff, Erin and Kelly were working on their own investigations. They had spent rather too long following the leads around Carol's nephew from the first murder, not knowing about the crucial peppermint smell that had assured Darcy he was innocent. Eventually, they discovered that he had an alibi and was independently wealthy enough that Carol's estate was more of a hassle than a benefit to his life.

No motive. Move on.

There were several suspects around the mysterious death of Mel, our third victim, and the human detectives spent a lot of time working away at that one, thanks to what they called 'the ABC theory' based on, I believe, a book by a certain well-shelved paperback author called Agatha Christie. Humans love their patterns. They had convinced themselves that if there was only one motive at play, and the other deaths were intended to confuse and distract the police, then the key murder had to be the third one.

Mel had several ex-boyfriends who seemed troublesome and/or potentially dangerous, but honestly none of them were remotely intelligent enough to plan something elaborate. Or to read a book.

Kelly, who had been generous enough to take in two of our three orphaned cats, was a touch flakier than the other humans. She insisted they should consider the possibility that their three dead detectives had been cursed.

The police, meanwhile, did not think any of the three deaths were murders at all. At least two had officially been ruled accidents with only Leanne's hit and run remaining an open case on the books. Needless to say, no one thought it was a good idea to suggest 'curses' to the police.

As for the feline detectives, we were convinced that it all came down to Murder #2. Ginge's human. I had been trying for days to inform Tiff of this vital information. I found screenshots she had saved of the Feline Detectives Club, and used claws and teeth to mark out Ginge as the most important witness.

Tiff was a bit cross, and withheld snuggles for several hours. I suppose I shouldn't have done that to her phone, but it's not my fault she doesn't print hardcopies.

I found a chart Tiff had made of the deaths, witnesses and suspects, and sat on it very thoroughly to get her attention. I was on the verge of drastic measures (it's amazing how efficiently a discreet bit of widdle in the right place can signpost a clue) when Tiff sat down at her table with a deep sigh and said, 'Mr Bramble, are you trying to tell me something?'

Finally! I leaned in, nuzzling her face with my whiskers, and carefully sicked up a bit of biscuit, directly on the chart where she had written the names Leanne and Ginge.

'You're the worst!' she declared, cry-laughing. 'But yes. You're right. You're always bloody right.'

Not long after that, Erin turned up in her shiny coffee-smelling sports car. Princess was in the back seat, in a designer cat cage, looking haughty. Tiff popped my own rather more loved and comfortable cat cage next to Princess, and hopped into the front seat next to Erin. 'We're not bringing in Kelly?'

Erin rolled her eyes and waved her takeaway latté cup dramatically. It smelled of caramel as well as the burnt nuttiness of coffee. 'Curses, Tiff. She's talking about curses. I can't share my car with that for two hours.'

'I mean,' said Tiff, sounding apologetic. 'I'm pretty sure my cat understands everything I say, and has opinions about the crimes we solve. So maybe it's not too far from that to curses?'

Erin scoffed. 'Obviously our cats understand us and help us solve crimes, that's not even a question. But curses are so not a thing.'

We help them to solve crimes? Honestly, humans. They really do think the world revolves around them.

Ginge's new human, Leanne's sister, was clearly fond of cats. She lived in a town with lots of good climbing trees. She also ran a cat café which sounds like it would be almost a better option than even a bookshop until you realise that a cat café involves cats. So many cats. Yes, you get humans coming in to pet you and feed you treats and admire you, but…I get that in my bookshop, and I don't have to share the territory with twelve other preening moggies.

'The smell,' gasped Princess, as Erin and Tiff carried us into the café, still in our cages. 'So many people all together. How can Ginge stand it?'

'He doesn't exactly have a choice,' I said, already checking the exits to see if we could pull off a competent jailbreak.

I would share my bookshop with him if I must.

Then we saw him.

Ginge sat on a beautiful, carpeted play palace, wearing a collar so fluffy that it might as well have been a cardigan. It sparkled. Collars are humiliating enough without involving both fluff and sparkle.

'He looks marvellous,' said Princess with an air of approval, as Tiff and Erin set us down near Ginge's perch.

'I'm embarrassed for both of you,' I informed her.

'Oh,' said Ginge. 'It's you two. What do you want?'

'We came to see if you are all right,' said Princess.

'We came to find out if your new human is a murderer,' I added.

'Well, that too.'

'I don't think she's a murderer,' said Ginge, licking his paws. 'Anyway, I don't do that any more. I'm a poet now.'

'You are?' said Princess.

I was shocked. Give up crime? This was Ginge, notorious solver of the Locked Car Boot Mystery, and the Smoked Eel Enigma. How could he possibly have given up his calling?

'Besides,' said Ginge. 'I like this human better than Leanne. She gives me raw chicken.'

Princess and I paused to salivate at the thought of raw chicken.

I glanced over to where Tiff and Erin had cornered Leanne's sister, asking her all kinds of 'friendly' questions. 'So you don't care if this new one–'

'Maggie,' said Ginge with a hum of contentment.

'You don't care if Maggie killed your human and two other humans from the Feline Detectives Club?'

'Not really. Like I said, I've moved on.'

'Why poetry?' Princess asked unexpectedly.

Ginge sniffed, and made a discreet sneeze. 'I have to put my keen intelligence to good use! Besides, the café already has a detective cat. He has precedence.' He nodded in the direction of an elderly Russian Blue, pretending to snooze in the corner. 'It was time to diversify. Would you like to hear one of my sonnets?'

'No,' I said.

'Yes,' said Princess, on the verge of swooning.

I left them to it. Tiff and Erin were still doing their thing. Ginge's Maggie looked annoyed. There was probably only a small window of opportunity before she threw us off the premises.

I discreetly unlatched my cage with one carefully-placed claw, and went to consult a cat about a murder.

Filibuster Shawshank was a long streak of light grey fur and gimlet eyes. He glared at me, tail flicking back and forth as I approached. 'Mr Bramble, I presume.'

He meant to intimidate me. That's my trick. 'Mr Shawshank,' I replied, having gathered some background from a frisky little kitten two tables back. 'I'm sure my old friend Ginge has updated you on the particulars of our case.'

'He didn't need to,' Shawshank sniffed. 'I hear things.'

'I'm sure you do. Tell me, one detective to another...do you have any ideas about the Feline Detective Club Murders?' It was important to name every mystery before some amateur came in and stuck you with something undignified.

'I have ideas,' he said with a yawn. 'I'm sure you wouldn't be interested.'

'From a master detective like yourself? I have so much to learn from you.' I batted my eyelashes at him and swished my tail. Yes, I'm a flirtatious little beast at times, but it gets the job done.

'Flattery,' he humphed. 'The solution is obvious. You don't need me to point it out.'

That was not good news. I had been hoping for a bolt out of the blue, a shocker of a twist. Not the obvious conclusion, the one that had been right there from the start. 'Which is?' I ground out.

Filibuster Shawshank nodded his silver head towards Tiff and Erin, who were now standing over my abandoned cage, looking frantic.

'Why,' he drawled. 'Those are your last humans standing, are they not? Easily enough to guess that one of them is the next victim…and the other must be the killer.'

When I told Princess what Shawshank had told me, she said I was being ridiculous, and started licking her white fur so pointedly that I knew it was useless to continue the conversation.

It couldn't, wouldn't be my Tiff. That left Kelly, who was currently in charge of three of my fellow detectives; and Erin, Princess's human. Tiff's favourite.

'Kelly's not picking up,' said Tiff, sounding distracted as we returned to the bookshop. Once there, Princess and I were both released from our cages while the humans toasted English muffins and made coffee in the only corner of the shop not reserved for books.

'I wouldn't worry about it,' said Erin, assembling cups and spoons. 'Do you have any syrups?'

'Some leftover vanilla, I think–'

'Aww, I fancied raspberry.'

'This is a bookshop, not a café!'

Syrups. I fell into a thoughtful repose. Erin liked her coffee sweetened and flavoured, because apparently humans don't value their teeth. She always smelled of something different. Caramel, hazelnut, vanilla, raspberry – peppermint?

I fixed my most accusing glare on Princess. 'Is it her?'

'I don't know what you mean,' she said haughtily, arching her back.

'Is it both of you?'

'Whoops,' said Erin, as water poured out of the electric kettle, gushing over my Tiff's shoes, and the faded carpet. 'Sorry! Accident.'

'Ugh,' said Tiff, reaching for a tea towel and then a mop.

Accidents, every single one of them.

There was the toaster, still merrily toasting those muffins. About to pop. I eyed the length of the electrical cord, just in time to see Erin lifting the toaster into the air–

Not in my house!

Tiff turned, just in time to see what Erin was doing. She yelled in alarm, sliding on the wet carpet as she tried to get away.

She didn't have to. I was there to save her. Cats can move fast when we have to. I leaped from the couch to Erin's arm, clawing all the way. She screamed and fell. The toaster fell too, but hit a dry bit of carpet, expelling its muffins across the floor in a shower of toast crumbs.

'What on earth?' Tiff yelled. Then, fierce and highly capable detective that she is, she burst into tears.

Kelly's brakes had been cut the day before. She managed to steer into a hedge, so was largely unhurt, as were the cats who had been travelling with her, on their way to a checkup at the v-e-t.

After Tiff reported her suspicions to her local police officer, that one who often came around to buy books for his mother even though his mother definitely had never read a book in her life, he flagged Erin's potential role in the investigation of the Accidental Cat Lady Deaths, now properly categorised as the Feline Detective Club Murders.

Half a fingerprint here, a lack of alibi there…it wasn't hard for them to assemble the case against Erin, once they knew where to look.

I blamed myself for not spotting it sooner, of course. No one knew better than I that Tiff had terrible taste in humans, and Erin had always been her favourite.

Tiff was keeping it all bottled up, so I didn't get the full story until Kelly came around to the bookshop for a visit. She brought with her all of the Feline Detectives Club cats (except for Ginge, now retired, and Princess, who apparently lived with us in the bookshop now).

I would never admit I was pleased to see Bootle, Darcy and Frodo Baggins, but it was nice to have an audience as I bragged to them about how I had solved the case, and saved my human from electrocution.

Princess never said a word against her human. She sulked a lot, these days, in the Mills and Boon corner.

'Erin was writing a book,' Tiff told Kelly as they cut into a decadent chocolate cake they had convinced themselves was necessary. 'The police found it on her hard-drive. She even called it *The Feline Detective*! All our stories, all our cases solved. But in her version, she claimed credit for all of them.'

'I can't believe she was willing to kill her friends for some book,' said Kelly, sounding horrified. 'I think I'd prefer to have been cursed.'

'Me too,' said Tiff grimly. She ate a biscuit. 'Damn it. Why didn't I think of writing a book?'

After the others had gone, I approached Princess, who was sitting on a stack of Melanie Milburnes like she owned the place. 'Would have been quite a book,' I said grimly. '*The Feline Detective*. With you as the star, I suppose.'

'I don't know what you're talking about,' said Princess, licking her paws. Still, she avoided my gaze.

I was going to have to keep my eye on that one. We were stuck with each other now, thanks to Tiff's ridiculously soft heart. But that didn't make Princess a bookshop cat, oh no. She had to earn that.

She also needn't think she was going to be allowed to help out, next time a juicy murder crossed our paths. When Tiff and I finally wrote our book, it would be called *Mr Bramble Investigates*, not "A Feline Detective, His Human and Their Sinister House Guest".

Possibly:

Cats Are Better Than Humans At Solving Murders
Like They Are Better Than Humans At Literally Everything Else
Why Yes, I Will Have A Plate Of Mince Thank You
A Bestselling Book Of Amazing Feline Detection Starring Mr Bramble.

Or something like that. I hope Tiff gets working on our book soon. I can't do everything around here.

La Gazza Ladra

a Phryne Fisher mystery

Kerry Greenwood

La Gazza Ladra

PHRYNE FISHER LOOKED OUT THE WINDOW AT THE SKIES OVER THE BAY AND sighed. She rose to her feet and opened it. It was a grey, autumnal day of light breezes, and a certain warmth had contrived to struggle through the clouds. Some sea air to clear the fogs in her brain seemed in order.

She felt unaccountably bereft this morning. Her adoptive daughters Ruth and Jane were at school, as was Tinker, her apprentice sleuth. Dot had been carried off to Collingwood by the sudden illness of her mother to be a ministering angel at the bedside, dispensing soup, hot drinks and Catholic sympathy. The Butlers were having a much-needed week's holiday by the seaside, and she was all alone in the house, save for Ember, Molly, and her locum housekeeper Mrs Frederick.

Downstairs the sounds of laundering could be discerned. There was no doubt that Mrs Frederick wielded a mighty broom. She was a lean, somewhat shrivelled individual with her hair tied back in a fierce bun. Industrious, assuredly; but her cooking was sufficiently dreadful for Phryne to make herself a note to increase the Butlers' salaries when they returned.

Toast, one felt, ought to be lightly browned. It ought not to be cremated. And last night Phryne, Tinker, and the girls had sat down to a dinner consisting of colourless, salty soup with no discernible flavour beyond a hint of unopened attics; a stringy cut of inferior roast beef with an overcoat of tepid grey, lumpy gravy; wilted, downcast spinach, cabbage and potatoes; and a granular rice pudding flavoured with ecru custard possessing all the appetising savour of thrice-boiled cardboard. Phryne barely nibbled at it, suppressed the girls' mutiny with a stern glance, and silently blessed Tinker's complete indifference to gross offences against haute cuisine. He ate everything on his plate and took his leave back to his shed. Mrs Frederick collected the dessert plates with an audible sniff and disappeared back into the kitchen. When the door was safely closed behind her, Phryne let out the breath.

'Miss Phryne?'

Phryne looked at Ruth with boundless sympathy. 'Yes, Ruth, I know what you are going to ask. But I would prefer not to load you up with housework this near the end of term. You have exams coming up, remember? Besides, Madam is sufficiently displeased with us as it is. If I tell her that she is being replaced as cook by a daughter of the house we'll never hear the end of it. However—' she inclined her head towards them, 'I am seriously regretting my decision to hire a replacement for the Butlers. You all behaved magnificently throughout that grotesque travesty of a meal. In consequence I will now allow you, in a barely audible undertone, to give your frank and honest opinion. Ruth? You first.'

'Miss Phryne, I think she does to food what Attila the Hun did to the suburbs of Rome.'

Phryne clapped her hand over her mouth. 'I see. Yes, I'm afraid you are right. Jane?'

Jane put her head to one side and thought for a long moment. 'I would diagnose revenge cookery. Owing to romantic disappointment, she takes out her frustrations by taking the finest ingredients and reducing them to swill unfit even for swine.'

'Perhaps you are right, Jane. Now, as a reward for good behaviour in the face of outrageous provocation, I will take you all to dinner tomorrow night at the *Windsor*.'

The girls expressed their appreciation and departed well content to their rooms. That evening Phryne had broken the news – that no dinner would be required on the morrow – and was rewarded with another sniff of doubtful import. That was for tonight.

Now, she felt at a loose end, and looked up with surprise as her bedroom door opened of its own accord. The newcomer was Ember: a kitten no longer, but a substantial full-grown cat built for endurance rather than speed. He looked up at Phryne with an interrogating eye. 'Mrowl?'

Phryne lay on her four-poster bed and extended a welcoming hand. Ember flowed rather than leapt onto the bed beside her and began to purr, sounding like a traction engine building up a head of steam for a grand excavation. Phryne took up her second-best hairbrush and began to brush Ember's coat with it. She had never particularly liked the plain wooden brush with the hogshair bristles; but it had turned out to be the perfect implement for Ember's gleaming, onyx coat. He lay on his side, extending his claws and spreading his paws like a kitten feeding from his mother. Much of Phryne's irritation with the world melted away. Cats were like that. Phryne admired the perfection of the feline form once more. She suspected that Ruth had been quietly supplementing Ember's diet. He was certainly putting on condition.

Tourmaline-coloured eyes opened again in interrogation, as if divining his mistress's silent criticism of his figure, and Phryne murmured soothing phrases to him in French, brushing all the while, and Ember's eyes closed again. After a quarter-hour of sybaritic indulgence, Ember quite suddenly jumped off the bed and alighted on the dressing-table.

To Phryne's utter astonishment, Ember picked up one of Phryne's new opal earrings in his paw and leapt down with to the floor with it held carefully in his mouth.

'Ember? Where are you taking that? That earring won't suit you, boy. And where are you going to put it?'

If Ember had been to a salon to have his ears pierced, Phryne did not want to ponder the implications. But before she could stop the cat's sudden egress Ember was off, and scampered down the stairs with a gentle skitter of paws. Phryne sat up and thought for a while. She then rose to her feet and addressed herself to her dressing table. She opened all the drawers and compartments and subsided once more onto her bed.

Some of her jewellery was still there. Her emerald necklace and matching gold earrings – the most expensive items in her portfolio – were still secure in their secret compartment. It would require far more sleight of paw than Ember had ever shown in the past to be able to unlock the secret spring built into the mahogany chest of drawers. Her garnet silver necklace, however, was nowhere to be seen. A few items of costume jewellery had also gone missing.

What on earth was going on? Did cats suffer from kleptomania? Phryne pondered for a long moment, took out a heavy necklace from her drawer and laid it on the dressing table. It was of little value, but brightly-coloured. It was reasonable to assume, surely, that cats were unaware of the relative intrinsic value of jewels. Perhaps this artefact: a leather cord from which depended a series of heavy stones: agate, amethyst, malachite, and catseye – might be a suitable distraction. It had been a ludicrously unsuitable gift from Lindsay Herbert, now long departed from her life. She had read of Lindsay's engagement in the newspapers, and she wished the happy couple many years of wedded bliss and the very best of luck.

She smiled in reminiscence, feeling that she had experienced the best of Mr Herbert. She had never forgotten how, not five minutes after proposing marriage to her, he had spoken blithely of some school chum being 'shackled for life' in matrimony. This, together with Lindsay's blithe assumption that when they were married she would give up her detective career, had reinforced Phryne's polite refusal of his offer.

She left the rather tasteless object on her dressing table and lay back on her bed to read a book. Sir Thomas Browne's sonorous phrases had always had a soothing effect on her.

> *The ferity of such minds holds no rule in Retaliations, requiring too often a head for a tooth, and the supreme Revenge for trespasses which a night's rest should obliterate.*

Excellent advice as ever, she mused.

Presently Ember returned, and accepted more caresses until the cat stiffened, looking hard at the dressing-table. Phryne laid down Sir Thomas Browne and watched as Ember leapt onto the dresser, carefully eyeing off the Lindsay necklace. He sniffed it, and to Phryne's astonishment ran out of the room and down the stairs. Presently he returned, and stood in the open doorway looking at her mistress with tail twitching.

'Ember, what's wrong?' she enquired. Phryne watched, enchanted, as the cat once more landed on the dressing table and opened her mouth. With all the delicacy of a watchmaker adjusting a mainspring, his jaws closed on the leather and took it in his mouth. He raised one front paw,

then the other, and slowly inched her way across the table. The heavy stones thudded against the polished wood. With a light bound the cat landed on the window-sill, the semi-precious gems still thudding against each other, and the wooden window-sill. Ember perched on the narrow sill, his head pushed forward towards the bay.

From the ground below came the sound of barking. Ember opened his mouth, and the necklace fell out of sight. At once Ember jumped down and curled up on the bed.

Phryne sprang to the window and looked down, just in time to see her dog Molly disappearing around the house, carrying the necklace in her jaws. Molly was possibly a Border Collie, though some of her ancestors had married for love rather than pedigree. Phryne closed the window and addressed herself to the complacent jewel-thief residing impudently on her bed.

'Well, sir? What was all that about?'

Ember stared straight at his mistress, folded his tail around his body and gave himself a wash. Phryne's reproof seemed destined to be ignored.

Thereafter, Phryne spent a busy few minutes in her jewellery drawer. She transferred as many items as could fit into the secret compartment and locked it again; all the while regarded with imperious attention by Ember. After she had locked the drawer she put on a coat and went for a fast-thinking walk along the beach.

Mrs Frederick's shift was to finish at four o'clock today, whereupon she presumably returned to her own house in order to commit yet more culinary outrages. The deal she had arranged with the agency was that Mrs Frederick would perform a six-hour shift, either starting at two in the afternoon if dinner was to be prepared; or at ten in the morning.

'Mrs Frederick won't be available for living-in, Miss Fisher,' Mrs Roberts had assured her. Once she had met the former, Phryne thanked whatever Powers there be for that. But this afternoon she would need to be home before four, if only for the sake of elementary courtesy. She considered omitting this, but decided with regret that it wouldn't do.

Phryne arrived home at five minutes to four to discover a considerable disturbance. There was Mrs Frederick, standing in the open doorway. Standing splay-legged in front of her, barking furiously, was Molly.

Phryne opened her front gate and looked hard at the housekeeper, whose normally impassive features dislimned into naked terror.

'Miss Fisher! Get that blasted animal away from me!' she screeched.

Phryne laid her hand on Molly's head. The barking subsided, but was replaced by ominous growls. Mrs Frederick smoothed down her blue overcoat and glared at Phryne.

'That bloody animal oughta be put down!'

Molly, sensing disapproval, barked again with a side-serving of more growls of menace and affront. And suddenly a great illumination descended upon Phryne.

'I think not, Mrs Frederick,' she stated. 'And now, before you go, you will turn out your pockets and your handbag.'

The housekeeper drew herself up, swelling with outrage. Her lined features flushed a mottled crimson. 'What? I have never been so insulted in all my life!'

'I rather doubt that, Mrs Frederick. But you can do it for me, or for the police. You are not leaving this property until you do.'

Mrs Frederick opened her mouth and closed it again. She thrust her grubby leather handbag at Phryne. 'Well go on, Miss High and Mighty. Search it, then! Be my guest!'

Phryne gave the unsavoury bag a brief inspection and handed it back. Blazing, furious eyes glared at her. 'Well? Satisfied?'

'Not yet. And now your coat. Take it off, please, and hand it over.'

Muttering incoherent oaths, Mrs Frederick struggled out of the coat and handed it over. Both pockets were empty. The housekeeper's face twisted in triumph.

But Phryne's inspection was not finished yet. She ran her fingers along the seams, turning the coat over and over. Phryne's unease deepened. If she had made a mistake, it was like to be an expensive one. Finally, her hands reached the stiff collar, and found what they were looking for.

'I see. Now, Mrs Frederick, I am going to take a small liberty with your coat. I am sorry about this, but not very. All I am going to do is take a few stitches out—'

Phryne removed her right glove and slipped a fingernail along the seam. She reached in and drew out a long silver necklace. In the pale afternoon sunlight, garnets blazed with a dark, blood-red fire.

'Et voilà! Here we have my garnet necklace. And now you are going to tell me why you stole it.'

All the fire seemed to have gone out of the housekeeper. 'I wanted something nice for myself,' she confessed. 'All my life I've slaved away for others. I didn't think you'd miss it.'

She seemed crushed now, and a good fifteen years older. Phryne's heart melted, recalling Sir Thomas Browne's sage advice.

'Mrs Frederick,' she said softly. 'You have some small talent for crime. Please don't indulge it any further. Now, have you taken anything else of mine while you were here?'

The housekeeper looked up at her in mute supplication and shook her head. 'Well, I am choosing to believe you. If you have told me the truth you will not hear from me again. Just don't come back. Ever. And—' Phryne reached into her purse and drew out a pound note. 'Here is something to tide you over.'

Tears streamed down the housekeeper's cheeks. She accepted the note and quivered. 'Oh, miss, I am so sorry. But how did you know?'

Phryne's mouth twitched. 'You had witnesses to your crime, Mrs Frederick. Never mind. I will only call the police if I find that you've taken something else after all.'

And that appeared to be that. Mrs Frederick shuffled off into the autumnal afternoon. Molly barked, and seemed desirous of further company. Phryne followed her into the back garden.

'Molly? Yes, you're a very good dog, but what is it now?'

Molly looked around to make sure Phryne was watching, and addressed herself to the potato bed. After a good minute's excavation, Molly stood back proudly and wagged her tail. There, among the rich loam and the germinating spuds, was the missing jewellery. Opal earring, mock-diamond tiara, and Lindsay Herbert's clunky necklace. Molly stood to attention. Well, she wanted to know. Am I a good dog?

'You are a wonderful dog, Molly. Well done, both of you.'

That night, as Phryne, Tinker, Ruth and Jane sat down in the palatial splendour of the *Windsor Hotel*, Molly and Ember lay sprawled on the kitchen floor and heaved contented sighs. Ember had eaten a good half of a baked salmon, and Molly, offered the run of the refrigerator, had opted for the roast lamb. They regarded each other with the complacent triumph of successful conspirators. It had been a very good day.

Thieves
and
Feathers

G V Pearce

The fairground wasn't very busy yet, at least not in the area around their little educational stall.

Most of the children were too excited to pay attention to anything that looked like learning, while their parents didn't need to find an excuse to rest just yet. Give them a few hours of walking around under the hot sun and they'd all be stopping in the shade to look at the pretty birds. It was always the same.

Harold considered himself to be an expert on the subject of human behaviour at the fair. After all, he did have the best view.

Every weekend this summer Harold and his colleagues would spend the day sitting quietly on their perches, while their handlers talked about their own work caring for birds of prey.

As if the public really cared about what two silly humans had to say; the birds were the real backbone of the operation. No one would stop to listen if they weren't there, looking impressive and beautiful.

Harold, as the smartest and second oldest bird, had elected himself leader of today's peculiar flock. In addition to himself there were two barn owls, a goshawk, a trio of bad-mannered ravens, and Eddie the eagle owl.

Glancing around, Harold saw that Eddie – the most senior bird in the rescue, and usually the most impressive – had fallen asleep in her water dish again.

The pose wasn't a dignified look for a bird that big, but Eddie just opened one eye to glare at him when he screeched a complaint.

No one appreciated the hard work Harold put in around here.

In fact, no one was paying attention to him at all.

'What does this say?' The handler named Austin said, apparently to himself, while he was poking around in the back of the van.

No sign of jewel thieves after

'Hmm, I can't read the next bit.'

Jack, the other handler, looked over. 'I don't know. I'm not in the habit of reading the newspaper lining the bird cages.' He gave a shiver of disgust. 'Certainly not after the birds have been in there. I doubt it's anything interesting anyway.'

On his perch Harold fluffed his feathers in agreement and turned his one-eyed stare in search of something more interesting than his handlers' usual Saturday morning bickering.

In this case, the 'something' was a shiny silver balloon tied to the wrist of a little girl who had stopped to look at their stall. Harold preened his flight feathers as an excuse to show her his best side.

'It says here that someone stole three million pounds worth of gems from that big house, you know, the one just down the road,' Austin was saying to Jack, despite the latter's complete lack of interest.

The handlers often talked at each other for hours like that. Harold had mostly learned to tune it out – unless they were talking about food it wasn't worth listening.

'And?' Jack replied, straightening the fliers on the table for the fourth time in ten minutes.

'Imagine having three million pounds worth of anything,' Austin sighed. 'Apparently, they were stolen eight months ago but the police don't have any leads. I wonder if it was an international heist, you know, like in the movies.'

Austin slammed the van door, startling the other birds for a moment.

Of course, Harold hadn't been surprised. No, no, he was always ready for anything. He was a brave and dignified bird. He'd only joined in with the panicked flapping as an excuse to mess up Jack's papers again.

It was important to keep the humans busy or else they'd get bored. Austin was definitely bored right now.

'Look, they had an opal as big as an egg,' Austin said, rustling a large dishevelled piece of paper in front of Jack's face.

Thirteen eyes turned to look at Austin in the brief hope that there might also be a real egg in the offering. Thirteen because Harold himself only had one eye, and Eddie was still asleep.

One of the ravens – seemingly disappointed at the lack of food – hopped into the air and flapped hard, catching a barn owl in the back of the head. The barn owl retaliated. Chaos descended. Typical Saturday morning nonsense.

Despite Harold's disapproving stare the raven didn't calm down until she was given a scrap of meat by Austin. Which had probably been the point. Those birds really had no manners.

'This newspaper is two years old,' Jack said, lifting the edge by the very tips of his fingers as he moved it away from his section of the table. 'Either the police will have caught those thieves by now or the gems are long gone.'

He waved the paper in Austin's direction. 'Also, please don't put dirty stuff from the van on the tablecloth, this thing cost a fortune. Oh, come on, Riley!' Jack cried as the younger barn owl snatched the paper and started to tear it apart.

Austin darted forward to retrieve it. 'Aww, I wanted to read the rest of that!'

Irritated by the behaviour of all involved, Harold returned his attention to the girl who had been shyly sidling closer while they were all distracted.

She was wearing a yellow dress covered in flowers and the look of a human trying to be brave.

'Hello, what's your name?' She asked him. 'I'm Lydia.'

Harold tipped his head, wondering whether she was actually expecting a reply.

'Hello, hello!' said one of the ravens. She never missed a chance to demonstrate her mimicry skills.

'Oh my word, that bird can talk!' An older human – probably the girl's mother – cried in surprise.

Rolling his one good eye, Harold waited for the girl's attention to switch to the show-off, but she didn't look away from him.

'Excuse me, mister?' She said to Jack. 'What's this one called?'

Before Jack had the chance to turn around, Austin had already bounded across the space to reply. He was just as much of a show-off as the raven.

'This is Harold. He's a harrier hawk, or a Montagu's harrier if you want to be specific,' he said, with an excited grin.

'Harold. That's a silly name for a bird,' Lydia replied bluntly.

Austin's grin faded.

'He should be called Silent Killer or Swift Wing or something,' she went on.

Harold ruffled his feathers and puffed up his chest. Yes, he should have a better name, the child was absolutely right.

'Well, it is a royal name,' Austin said, 'Harold, you know, the king who got shot in the eye with an arrow?'

'Someone shot this bird with an arrow?' asked an older man. He had his arm linked with the woman, so was probably the girl's father. 'I hardly think that's a suitable topic of conversation for a seven-year-old, now is it?'

Austin held up his hands defensively. There was still a bit of meat dangling between his fingers. 'Oh no, Harold wasn't shot with an arrow. He was found with birdshot injuries as a juvenile. The rehabilitation team think he fell victim to illegal hunting.'

Harold tried to grab the piece of meat, but Austin's hands were moving too much.

'So, which one was shot with an arrow?' The girl's mother asked. She'd lost interest in the raven's when she realised they only knew three words.

'None of these birds have been shot with an arrow,' Austin gestured to the top of his head as if he was wearing a hat, dropping the meat scraps onto the shoulder of his own shirt. 'I meant the king.'

'What, Elvis?'

'No, mum,' Lydia sighed, 'the king of England, we learned about him at school.'

'England doesn't have a king though. We've got the Queen.'

As Austin's shoulders slumped in despair, Harold almost managed to grab the meat, but the tether between his leg and the perch wasn't quite long enough.

'Oh no! Why is he tied up?' The mother shrieked. All around the stall birds flapped in alarm, even old Eddie who woke with a start and cry of her own. 'That's so cruel!'

'It's all right, those are just his jesses, madam. It's a safety precaution,' Jack cut in. He was covered in shredded bits of paper. 'It wouldn't be safe to have the birds loose in public – they might fly away if they're startled and get injured. They're very delicate.'

Harold gave him a look that was intended to convey the fact that Harold wasn't delicate at all, but as a bird it was hard to make that kind of expression. Jack didn't even notice the glare before he turned to look at the other handler with a frown.

'Austin, your shoulder,' Jack said, tapping his own. 'You've got something.'

'Oh, thanks.' Austin replied, absentmindedly brushing the meat away.
Harold watched one of the raven's grab the food as it fell.

He narrowed his eye. How dare they steal what was rightfully his? He was in charge here.

'Poor Harold,' Lydia said quietly. 'I bet you hate being tied up like that. I bet you want to be free.'

'I promise you, Harold is perfectly happy with us,' Jack said, holding out one of his informative pamphlets.

'I'm afraid that since he only has one eye he can't be returned to the wild. He wouldn't be able to hunt and feed himself.'

Preposterous! To demonstrate his perfectly workmanlike hunting skills, Harold snatched the flier from Jack's hand and tore a strip off with his beak.

Lydia laughed, but when Harold next looked up he found that she'd walked away with her parents to look at a booth covered in toys. For some reason she was trying to catch a yellow duck with a hook attached to it.

Humans were strange.

When Harold realised the duck wasn't edible, he lost interest.

Well, if Eddie could sleep the morning away, then so would Harold. It wasn't as if there was anything better for him to do.

'Psst!'

Harold opened his eye with a start, expecting to see a snake creeping up on him.

It was just the girl in the yellow dress again.

'Hello, Harold, look what I won!' Lydia said, holding up a shiny bag full of brightly coloured twigs and berries. 'It's an arts and crafts set! And look!'

She held up another object that looked like two twisty twigs stuck together. Then she clicked the two halves together and Harold finally recognised them. He held up a foot. He'd never liked having his talons trimmed but he knew the drill.

Instead of holding his foot Lydia took hold of his tether and started to cut.

The scissors struggled to get through the tough leather. Fortunately his handlers were too busy showing off the barn owls to a pair of young men in fancy dress to notice the several minutes of snipping noises.

'There! You're free!' Lydia whispered at last. 'You can go anywhere you want.'

Harold looked down at his leg, up at her, and then at his handlers. Jack had just retrieved a box of venison bits from the cool box. That seemed like the obvious choice.

Everything happened at once – Harold flew towards Jack's shoulder; Lydia screamed 'not that way!'; and a man dressed as a knight tried to 'save' Jack from the 'attacking' bird, knocking over the next stall in the process.

Or at least that's what they all told the security guards once the panic had died down again.

The first stall had collapsed onto the neighbouring tent, which in turn caused a chain reaction. By the time devastation was halted by a large enough gap, fourteen tents had fallen down along with several tables, and a bar stacked high with bottles of the handmade gin.

There was a terrible mess.

Half an hour went by before anyone noticed that Harold was missing. By then he was already on quite the adventure.

He hadn't intended to escape.

He was in charge, after all. But he'd been screamed at, almost hit by a man with a big metal glove, and then everyone had been shouting. It was only natural that he'd flown up high into the air.

Once he was up there he saw all the things he had been missing from the limited perspective of his perch. The fair was much bigger than he'd expected – at least a quarter of a mile full of interesting sights and smells.

Humans were sitting in metal boxes of various sizes, spinning or racing around, and they seemed to be enjoying it. Some of them were eating colourful clouds or drinking brown water that smelled like old hay.

He couldn't see the stall anymore, but he could see and smell something delicious.

For some reason humans rarely ate their food raw. When he'd been living with Angela – the woman who'd found him in that field all those years ago – she would often let him sit on his perch or in his cage in the kitchen while she 'cooked'. This odd ritual usually involved making various things very hot and mixing them together before you ate them.

Most human foods were too strange for him, but there were two he especially loved.

One of those beloved foods was called a *sausage*. He'd often seen people walk past their stall eating sausages, but those usually had the yellow stuff on them that made his tongue hurt. He'd tried to steal one or two in the past and regretted it.

Just below him a human was cooking dozens of those delicious sticks of meat on a big metal pan. Every so often, a different human took one of the sausages away wrapped in a bread bun and ruined it with the yellow stuff.

Well, the sausages in the pan looked perfect just the way they were. Harold didn't need the bread. He could just hold the sausage in his talons.

It was hard to land with the updrafts from the hot pan constantly pushing him back up into the sky. He soon realised that the only way to get within reach of the food was by sweeping low over the stalls and approaching the man from the side.

He hadn't hunted properly in years, but this felt just like chasing rabbits.

Except rabbits weren't usually armed with spatulas and towels.

Not in his experience at least.

Harold managed to dodge the angry man's wild flailing, but the situation was too dangerous to attempt a second pass at the sausages. He had been spotted and now the man was on his guard.

Oh well. Perhaps there would be another person cooking sausages somewhere.

As he scanned the area he saw a flash of Lydia's yellow dress.

The little girl was running headlong between the stalls with the bag she'd won clutched to her chest. Somewhere out of sight her mother was shouting her name and calling her a silly girl for causing so much chaos.

That didn't seem very fair. She'd only been trying to help after all.

Speaking of things that weren't fair – Harold spotted another sausage stall but someone was talking to the cook and pointing up into the air, directly at him.

Not long after an umbrella opened, hiding the food from view.

There really would be no sausages for him today.

Harold drifted lazily over the fair, landing from time to time on tall posts covered in twinkling lights, watching the humans do whatever strange things they felt like doing.

He wasn't sure where his handlers' stall was any more. He'd never seen Austin's van from above, and now that all the fallen tents had been righted he couldn't recognise any landmarks.

Beyond the fairground there were fields of wheat swaying gently in the breeze. The ears had almost turned that perfect shade of gold.

He had hunted in fields like that once.

In fact, he had hatched and fledged in a similar field. He'd even planned to eventually find a mate of his own to settle down. That future had disappeared a long time ago, along with his eye, but maybe this was a second chance.

There were mice scurrying around down there. He could hear them. He could see the plants shifting as they ran by.

Mouse wasn't as delicious as sausage, but a meal is a meal.

Harold dived towards his quarry.

He missed the mouse entirely, tumbling through the yellowing stalks of wheat with all the dignity and grace of a plastic bag caught in a cross wind.

Perhaps Jack had been right about his hunting skills.

Somewhere nearby a jackdaw was laughing at him.

Too embarrassed by his failure to challenge the other bird to a fight – and secretly a little worried that he'd lose due to his poor vision – Harold took to the air again, flying away from the sounds of the fair behind him.

On the far side of the field, there was a flash of yellow amongst green-gold stalks of wheat that were swaying more than the breeze would usually cause.

It was Lydia, her pace slowed to a stomping walk punctuated by muttered complaints.

'Why is everything always my fault?' she was saying, apparently to the rock she was kicking along the ground. Her voice switched to an approximation of her mother's shrill voice. '*Lydia, you made that man knock down all the tents! Lydia, you spoiled the Christmas party by letting the dogs inside! Lydia, you let the neighbour's goats into the garden! Lydia, you turned the lights off and let the burglars in! Lydia, Lydia, it's all your fault.'*

Her words faded away as she pushed through the hedge into the next field.

Harold banked sharply and turned to match her course.

He'd never be able to find Austin's van amongst all those tents, but he might be able to spot his aviary if he followed Lydia. She was a human, and humans all liked to live close together, so it was only logical that Austin's house would be near her own. How far could the van have travelled in just an hour? A mile? Maybe two?

He would be home in no time.

The sun was getting low over the trees, and Harold was just starting to admit to himself that he might be lost, when he smelled the one thing in the world that was better than sausages.

Bacon.

Harold wasn't supposed to have bacon very often because of something called salt, which was probably nothing but a cover for human greed. They wanted to keep the delicious crunchy lumps of meaty heaven all to themselves, he just knew it.

Angela had let him have a crumb of it once. He would never forget that taste.

The scent of it was drifting on the breeze, from a patch of warmer air just up ahead, behind a small collection of trees.

Circling lazily on the updrafts Harold spotted a house. It was much bigger than Austin's house where he and the other birds lived in the garden. There were towers and turrets for perching on; a perfectly square blue pond; and from one of the ground floor windows came the faint sound of sizzling, half drowned out by a woman saying a familiar name.

'Honestly, Lydia, you can't really blame them for being upset,' said a voice that was far more soothing than any of the other adults he'd encountered today. 'It sounds like the incident at the fairground was a heck of a mess.'

'Yeah,' Lydia replied sadly. 'Mum didn't have to bring up all that other stuff though. Okay, so I did bring the dogs in when it was snowing, and maybe I let the goats eat the grass because the mower was too heavy for me – but it wasn't my fault all those gems got stolen!'

'I know it wasn't,' the woman tried to interject but Lydia went on.

'I only turned off the outside lights so I could watch the bats hunting without the glare. I definitely didn't touch the alarm. I can't even reach those switches!'

Harold flew lower along the wall of the house. He couldn't see where the voices were coming from.

Lydia sighed. 'I wish there was someone who could help us get the gems back, then mum couldn't be mad at me anymore.'

On the second pass Harold finally spotted a woman standing close to one of the smaller windows, flipping rashers of bacon in a frying pan over a hot stove.

Bewitched by the smell he dived, aiming to land on the window ledge.

His one eye failed him again.

Harold hit the window frame, bounced off it in a mad tangle of wings and feathers, and came to rest inside on the kitchen table.

Lydia and the woman screamed in surprise.

The bacon hit the floor.

If only the room would stop spinning, Harold could have easily grabbed a piece. Sadly, the room continued to rotate slowly around him as he stared at the ceiling.

His wings were stretched out at his sides and his feet were in the air, which wasn't exactly the safest pose to be in near a stranger – and a not-so-stranger – but Harold just couldn't line up his thoughts properly to roll over.

'Oh my god, is it dead?' The woman murmured on his left. Since he had no eye on that side he couldn't see her.

'I think he's breathing,' Lydia said.

He croaked in surprise as a finger prodded him in the ribs.

'I guess you're alive then,' she said. 'Where did you come from?'

Harold turned his head to glare at her. That was a mistake. Somehow the room's spinning had changed directions.

She laughed. 'Silly of me to ask you, wasn't it?'

'I think that's the bird from the fair,' Lydia said. She was peering at him upside down from the other side of the table. 'I wonder how it got here?'

The woman was leaning over him now, holding one of those glowing plastic blocks that most humans seemed to be obsessed with.

There was a bright flash, so bright Harold could still see coloured circles even after he closed his eye.

'Oh no! I'm sorry!'

He tried to roll over but all he managed to do was flap weakly. This situation was getting to be even more embarrassing than the mouse incident.

Something pulled at his leg. He had to hope the source of the pulling was only the woman, and not a cat he'd failed to notice before he attempted the window. That would be the only way that his day could possibly get any worse.

'What's this? Oh, he's got a phone number written on this little strap!' She said, as if the details of his jesses were a source of delight. 'You are a pet, aren't you? I thought you were wild!'

Embarrassment was one thing, but that kind of insult could not be allowed to stand. With much flapping and scrabbling, Harold finally managed to roll over, fluffing his feathers like the true dignified professional that he was.

The effect was rather spoiled when he fell over again.

'Shh,' the woman said soothingly. She'd reached out one hand as if to pat him on the head, but he snapped his beak at her. He didn't need to be patronised.

Somewhere behind him Lydia gasped. Perhaps he didn't need to be quite so grumpy.

With her other hand the woman had been tapping at the plastic block with her thumb. Now it was making a noise like a very quiet, very strange bell.

'Hello?' The block said in a voice that sounded a lot like his own handler Jack.

Harold tipped his head. He'd heard this sort of thing before – one of the raven's could do a great impression of Austin shouting a rude word – but he always wondered how a box could be a mimic. It didn't even have a mouth.

'Oh hi,' the woman said brightly. 'Sorry to bother you. My name is Gwen, and I was just wondering if you're missing a bird? Quite a big bird?'

'You found Harold?!' Almost-Jack's voice shouted, the sound distorting so much that Harold flapped his wings in surprise.

The woman, Gwen, laughed. 'He's called Harold? Like the king? Oh that's perfect. I'm afraid he found me. I was cooking some lunch and he flew straight into the window frame.'

'I knew it was you!' Lydia whispered. 'Did you follow me home?'

Harold would have looked at her but he still didn't entirely trust the room not to start spinning again.

'Is he okay?' asked Jack.

Harold fluffed his feathers and shook out his tail. He was fine.

'Well, I'm not an expert but I think he might be stunned.' Gwen said despite Harold's efforts. 'It did take him a while to stand up. Now he's just sitting on the kitchen table, glaring at me.'

'He does that a lot,' Jack laughed. 'Do you think you could close your windows to keep him inside? That would make it easier for us to catch him. If you can give us your address?'

Well, that was his adventure over then. Growing bored of the humans' conversation, Harold stretched his wings, testing each joint in turn. Nothing was hurt, he was just a bit of a mess. He started preening, carefully smoothing out his flight feathers.

'Oh of course. I've got some bacon here, do you think that would help keep him calm?'

Harold looked up, suddenly interested again.

'Unfortunately, bacon isn't good for birds.' Jack said. He sounded a little apologetic but not nearly sorry enough for Harold's tastes. 'Just a dish of water should be fine, he only escaped this morning.'

That wasn't fair. Jack had no idea how bad Harold's day had been. He should be allowed a treat, surely. Just one little morsel?

'Okay,' Gwen turned to close the window, carefully stepping over the bacon still scattered over the floor tiles. 'Do you know Runwaithe Manor, the Spaulding's house? Oh, good. You'll have to drive around the back, I live in the old servant's quarters.'

While Gwen had her back turned to him, Harold shuffled to the edge of the table as quietly as he could. Jack would be here soon to take him back to the aviary. This would probably be his last chance to get any bacon for a while.

Wings half open he hopped down onto the floor, immensely proud of himself for moving so silently. His talons hadn't even clicked against the tile.

There were two rashers of bacon sitting in front of him: glistening, pink, and still slightly steaming. Heaven.

Harold had carefully reached out his beak, ready to tear off a chunk, when Gwen said, 'Hey! You aren't allowed that!'

Oh no.

He'd been spotted.

Thinking fast, Harold grabbed one piece in his beak, the other in his talons, and shuffled around looking for a way out.

Although the window had been closed, on the opposite side of the room a door still opened into another room, and some stairs. He could see a dim light shining from somewhere above. The stairs either led further into the house, or to the outside. It didn't really matter where as long as he could take his bacon with him.

Harold made a break for it.

Taking off while holding onto a greasy strip of bacon wasn't the easiest thing in the world.

This was especially true when there was a human shouting 'no, no, no!' and trying to block the only means of escape.

Still – motivated by the taste of the bacon in his beak – Harold had managed to get past Gwen, through the door, down the corridor, up three flights of stairs, and into a very strange set of rooms.

Everywhere he looked there were shiny glass cabinets, each one filled with glittering objects.

Sadly, it was rather difficult to navigate between unfamiliar and transparent obstacles, with only one eye and the view partially obscured by a waggling strip of breakfast meat. At least one cabinet door now bore the imprint of his face outlined in bacon grease and bits of wheat from his tumble in the field.

There had also been some rather loud crashing noises from inside those cabinets, but the sounds had mostly reduced to the occasional tinkle or thud now that Harold had found a nice place to perch.

He was sitting on top of a wooden cabinet that had been built into the furthest wall of the room. It was tall – so Gwen couldn't reach him – and there was an odd arrangement of wooden fruit in just the right place for him to rest his stolen bacon prize while he tore it apart.

'Oh, Gwen. Mum is going to blame me for this, isn't she?' Lydia asked quietly from just outside the doorway.

'Oh no!' Gwen cried as she stepped into the room. 'Oh no, the Spauldings are going to kill me! Look at all this mess!'

She was peering into the displays with one hand pressed against her mouth. Every so often she would step over a pile of glittering shards, or quietly murmur something to herself, but none of it seemed very interesting.

Harold ate his bacon.

Bacon was interesting.

The best thing in the world.

It wasn't his fault that those cabinets had got in his way, and he had no idea who or what Spauldings were. He was just a very happy hawk eating a very delicious treat.

He didn't notice the sun setting outside, or the sounds of vehicles pulling up on the noisy gravel driveway.

'Gwendoline?' A vaguely familiar voice called from downstairs. 'Gwendoline? Lydia? Where are you, you silly girl? Why is there a man outside looking for a bird? And why was the silent alarm activated? The police are going to be here any minute!'

'We're completely fine, don't worry about us,' Gwen muttered under her breath. 'After all, why be at all concerned about your assistant and your own daughter when the alarm is going off?'

Taking a deep breath she shouted back, 'We're up here, Mrs Spaulding! There's a big hawk in the gallery! It must have triggered the alarm! I'm afraid it's made a terrible mess!'

Harold had long since finished the first rasher of bacon, and had been leisurely working on the second, but as more people climbed the stairs he tried his best to eat faster. Jack would be here soon. Jack wouldn't be able to take his bacon away if he'd already eaten it all.

Outside the tall windows blue lights began to flash, reflecting brilliantly from the glass cases around the room and half blinding Harold's eye.

He tried to change position, but one of the pieces of the wooden fruit shifted under his talon with a click.

Harold lost his balance, the click became a clunk, and the whole cabinet he was sitting on swung out away from the wall.

'There you are!' Austin shouted from the doorway. Behind him stood

Jack, and two other humans that Harold recognised as Lydia's parents from the fairground.

Why were so many people in the room?

Why was Lydia's mother screaming like that?

Startled, Harold flapped his wings, knocking the last of his bacon into the space revealed by the moving cabinet.

It landed directly on top of the biggest, most delicious looking egg he'd ever seen in his life.

Harold was a simple bird. He didn't stop to wonder why the egg was sitting on a cushion of black velvet, surrounded by other bright shiny rocks. He didn't question the rainbow facets shimmering over its surface.

He was just going to eat it.

'Mrs Spaulding? Is everything all right up here? We heard screaming,' asked yet another new voice.

Harold pecked at the egg. The shell was very tough, much tougher than he would have expected.

'Oh, yes, of course Constable Fletcher, everything is fine,' Mrs Spaulding replied, her voice suddenly as sweet as honey. 'Absolutely nothing is wrong. Our alarm must have gone off by accident. Thank you so much for coming.'

Harold tried to turn the egg over with a talon. Maybe there was a weak point on the other side.

'Well, after you had that robbery two years ago—'

'Hey, isn't that the opal from the newspaper?' Austin asked, interrupting Constable Fletcher. 'The one that got stolen?'

Mrs Spaulding made a noise like a mouse squeaking in fright.

'I...I don't know what you mean!' She snapped.

'Yes, you do, mum,' Lydia said helpfully. 'You said that some mean men came in the night and stole all the gemstones.'

Gemstones? He'd been trying to eat a stone? Harold dropped the 'egg' in disgust and looked around for his strip of bacon.

'Okay, darling, be quiet now,' Mrs Spaulding hissed at her daughter through a fake smile.

Lydia was holding Gwen's hand and staring wide-eyed at her mother.

'Don't you remember?' Lydia went on. 'You said they took the rubies, and the sapphires too. But they were in the wall all along. You must be so happy!'

'Shut up!' her mother screamed.

Lydia squinted at her mother. 'Oh. Did you put them there?'

'Shut up, child!'

Harold flapped his wings at the noise and gave a warning cry.

He'd rather liked Lydia – she had set him free. She didn't deserve to be spoken to like that.

'Is that true, madam?' Constable Fletcher asked darkly, as he placed one hand on the mother's shoulder. 'I think we should have a chat about this back at the station, don't you?'

Behind the group, seemingly unnoticed by any of the other humans, Mr Spaulding – Lydia's father – turned and started to creep quietly down the stairs.

Now, that really didn't seem fair.

Abandoning the last scraps of bacon, Harold leapt into the air with a croak.

'Hey!' Austin shouted as the rest of the humans ducked out of Harold's way, conveniently clearing his path towards the fleeing man.

Harold wasn't sure what he had intended to do with Mr Spaulding once he reached him. Sadly, he never made it that far – Austin had grabbed him by the trailing strands of his jesses before he made it out of the room – but at least the commotion was enough to alert the other police officers who'd been waiting outside.

Which was fortunate since Harold had also startled Mr Spaulding rather badly.

The man's tumble down the stairs was cushioned by two unsuspecting Constables who had been running up towards the noise at the time.

There wasn't much to see after that. Partially because Constable Fletcher asked Austin to remove Harold from the scene, but mostly because Jack had slipped a hood over Harold's head to 'calm him down.'

Well, it wasn't as if Harold could give a witness statement, so – tired from all the fun – Harold closed his eye and was soon fast asleep.

He might have only dreamt the small hand stroking his back and saying, 'thank you,' but if he had it was a nice dream. He would have liked more bacon in it though.

'Hey Jack, look.' Austin read aloud as he waved a bundle of newspapers in front of Jack's face.

Fearless Falcon Foils Foolish Fraudsters

Harold irritably snapped his beak at them. He hated that headline. He was not a falcon.

'Yes, yes, we've seen it a thousand times,' Jack sighed. 'You don't have to read it every time you replace the newspapers in the transport cages.'

'I'm just proud of our Harold here, saving the day.'

'It's not even a good headline,' Jack went on, 'it's inaccurate. They could have gone for *Hero Hawk Harries Hopeless Hustlers*, that'd be alliteration and a pun.'

Austin groaned. 'No one but us would notice the pun.'

Opposite the charity's stall a little girl in a yellow dress seemed to be looking for something. Harold croaked to get her attention. She'd be more interesting than his handlers usual Saturday morning bickering.

Maybe she had some scissors with her.

He was about ready for another adventure.

Spam the Cat
and the Case
of the Missing
Person-and-A-Half

Elizabeth Ann Scarborough

Spam the Cat and the Case of the Missing Person-and-a-Half

FOR A CHANGE, MADDOG AND I WERE JUST HAVING FUN TOGETHER; friends enjoying a maritime festival. I rode on his shoulder, my paws and tail safely out of the way of big human feet. The music from the late-night main stage rock'n'roll band hurt my ears, but quite a few of the festival goers were dancing to it. The food booths were closed, unfortunately, but you can't have everything, and earlier in the evening we'd enjoyed fish (no chips for me) at SeaJ's.

Maddog told me there was a shanty sing in the evenings, and since both of us are pretty nocturnal, it was one of the few festival activities we could enjoy together.

Darcy, the lady who buys my kibble and pays my vet bills, likes Maddog although she doesn't know he's a vampire. Neither would anyone else who doesn't know him recognise him for what he is.

Vampires are supposed to be formally dressed and slinky, with slick hair and pale skin unless they've dined recently (or are of a race that does not do pale). They also have capes they fling around dramatically.

The only thing I'd ever seen Maddog fling is a fish net. He is shaggy-haired and forgets to get his beard trimmed. He usually wears an anorak or oilskins over a plaid flannel shirt tucked into Carharts and knee-high rubber boots. On official business, he wears his silver badge proclaiming him to be Vampire Peacekeeper south of the (Canadian) border. It is emblazoned with all of the popular religious symbols that most vamps avoid.

He's also a cryptozoologist, which means he likes to study cryptids, critters who are not widely acknowledged to be real.

Me, I'm a cat who just seems to bump into them. Cryptids, I mean. Although I guess you could say there's more around to bump into since the one that kidnapped Darcy a while back, accidentally turned my housemate and original mentor, Rocky, into a catpire. Now he's nocturnal too, and spends the day sleeping while hanging upside down in the corner kitchen cabinet.

Some cats hunt rodents, some hunt birds. Not me though, because humans seem fond of them. Besides, I have a ferocious mother eagle (a onetime client) who would take exception to me hunting birds the way Rocky now hunts the coyotes that used to terrorise him.

Like Maddog, I hunt cryptids, vampires of the antisocial sort, zombies, ghosts and once a Sasquatch.

Maddog calls me, jokingly, a purranormal investigator, and sometimes I act as his deputy, though I wear no badge.

We met when a rogue vamp, who Darcy met online, came to the Pacific Northwest where some popular books and movies had made it seem like vamps were in fashion.

He kidnapped Darcy. Maddog helped me un-kidnap her.

Since then he has also been a help to me when I need someone who can speak English to assist me in solving my cases.

But this was to be a night off, full of songs and, with any luck, food cats really shouldn't eat.

Many of the sailor songs were about getting drunk, being punished while getting drunk, getting tricked or kidnapped while getting drunk, the work they had to do between times they got drunk, and sometimes aquatic cryptids.

Maddog bellowed along in his deep voice, singing about going round the horn. I guess they had a lot of deer at sea, though I'd never seen any of our town deer show the slightest inclination to take a dip in the bay, the strait, or any of the other water surrounding our town on three sides.

I prowled the floor going from one pair of legs to another as many of the singers tried to entice me to sit on their laps. I purred along with some of the songs but have found my singing voice is not much appreciated by most humans.

I had returned to Maddog's lap and was just settling down for a nap when someone asked for a song called *The Eddystone Light* about a dysfunctional relationship between a mermaid and a lighthouse keeper and their unfortunate offspring.

Someone else followed up with a song about a sailor who wanted to mate with mermaids; then, as I was settling on Maddog's shoulder again as he prepared to leave, a fellow with a squeaky voice that was in no way melodious began a song I couldn't make much of since I buried my ears in Maddog's beard.

But then Maddog hijacked the song and his voice over-rode the so-called singer's. Afterward he apologised to the original singer with what sounded like humility, saying, 'Pardon me, but this song comes from my homeland, where there are a lot of selkies, and songs about them. I felt as though I was sittin' in my granny's kitchen with the neighbours gathered roond again.'

That was as good a time as I've had without the benefit of catnip.

But that was last year; and this year at festival time, I was seeing none of the same preparations. No tall ships in the harbour, no entrance tents erected outside the area that had become fairgrounds. I was disappointed but I knew how unpredictable humans can be. They must have changed their minds and turned off the fun.

So I was just going to sleep in, but my raccoon assistant detective, Renfrew, had other ideas.

'Come on out, Spam,' he called to me through my personalised cat flap in the kitchen door. Most of the other cats in the house were sleeping too though the television still droned in the living room. Someone had accidentally stepped on the remote so I heard a strange voice, not one of the announcers who talked on the Critter Channel.

Darcy always left the set on that channel when she went to Seattle. Little did we know she'd break her promise to return on the 12:10 AM ferry and instead be away longer than at any time since she'd been kidnapped by Marcel de Montreal, the Canadian vampire.

But I digress. Mrrhm.

I opened one eye and watched the door. I couldn't help it that my tail shook a little, even though it was only the raccoon and not some tasty prey. It's a cat thing, you know, like our primitive hunting instinct showing itself.

'Come on, cat, or we'll miss everything!'

'Every what thing?' I asked.

'The quiet! I've never seen anything like it in my whole life.'

'Like what? The Wooden Boat Festival? What do you mean quiet? Last year it was anything but.'

'No, really, really, cat, everybody is going – the deer, some of the other raccoons, squirrels, everybody. There are no people.'

'Where are they?' I asked, between yawns as I stretched from tail to claw tips. 'Last year the whole town was swarming with locals and visitors.'

'Don't know,' Renfrew said. 'Don't care. Hurry. There might be food!'

I yawned again. If there was food, there wouldn't be any left for me with Renfrew along. I decided to grab a bite on my way out.

Out the window the light had already started to fade. As I snapped up a few pieces of kibble, the corner cupboard door creaked open and Rocky somersaulted out, feet poised for a four-point landing which he did not make because his wings caught him first, half furled with their inverted scallops making him look like Batman's furry cat brother.

'Rocky's here,' I called out to Renfrew. To Rocky I said, 'There's something going on downtown. The animals are gathering.'

'Hmmmmrrr, how many and what kind of animals?'

Renfrew heard him and called out, 'Both dens of the coyotes from the Fort, I hear.'

Since he's become a vampcat, more or less by accident, Rocky was definitely interested in coyotes and grinned fang-ily.

We cut through the woods and peoples' yards, taking the shortcut to downtown, it was clear that business was not as usual. Cars were parked in driveways. The only voices were muffled, coming from indoors. Streets were empty, even of joggers and bikers.

When we reached Water Street, our main street that turns into a highway, the incoming lane was completely clear and the outgoing lane showed only a few straggling tail-lights. At the ferry dock, the boats wallowed in their berths, their windows reflecting the darkening sky.

I have to tell you, the walk down Water Street was eerier than Rocky in full blood-sucker mode. Nobody molested us, though I saw a cougar on top of the *Elevated Ice Cream* building, and a bear clutching a basket of cookies galumph onto the deck at *Courtyard Cafe* while Heidi, the owner, brandishing a broom, shooed him out of her establishment.

Rocky made a beeline for *Dogs Afoot* where the coyotes he had been promised were scratching at the screen door of the converted RV, trying to get at the hotdogs.

But most of the animals just played tourist, exploring the parts of the habitat usually too full of humans to suit them. A family of otters undulated across the road toward the water and Renfrew followed them. I kept strolling down the entire four blocks it took to reach the boat basin, now full of yachts that had docked for the show-that-looked-like-it-wasn't-going-to-happen.

A low moaning *mrrrrowwww* rode the wind to my pricked up ears. I trotted toward it, and the water, and as the noise continued, broke into a run. The other cat might be crying because he was hurt or stuck somewhere or under attack from one of the wild creatures to whom a housecat might look like a snack. I raced toward his cry. If I couldn't help him, I could find help.

The cat was stuck all right. He stood atop an arch of driftwood stuck into a sand bar that had otherwise disappeared in the rising tide. During low tide, this bar curves away from the shore into a long spit where it's fun to chase seagulls and annoy the ducks. But at high tide, the whole bar is covered and the gulls are flying while the ducks swim. Big black cats do not normally figure into the scene.

He let out another moan, this one ending in a pitiful mew.

I walked down the beach, and up to the spit. He was facing the other direction so I said, 'Hi, I'm Spam,' meaning to introduce myself and ask how he came to find himself in such a precarious position.

He jumped up, trying to see where I was but he missed his footing on the way back down and splashed into the water.

He surfaced, front paws flailing, cried, gulped, and splashed around. Few cats swim.

Fortunately for him, I am a fellow of many skills. Some of my best friends – or at least my most valuable confidential informants – are aquatic so it had behooved me to learn to deal with the wet stuff. Also fortunately, according to Maddog, I am of a breed descended from cats who reached American shores by way of Viking dragon boats where my forecats served as rodent exterminators. They didn't mind water but they had sense enough to learn how to get out of it.

I swam out to the flailing feline, and he tried to jump on my back and take me down with him. Instead, I grabbed him by the scruff of the neck and swam to shore with him in my teeth. His head stayed more or less above the water.

We both lay on shore gasping until I recovered enough to begin vigorously grooming him, which helped revive him.

He coughed up some water and a hairball as well.

'That's better!' he said.

'What were you doing up there anyway?' I asked.

'I was trying to see if Fergus was out there.'

'Who's Fergus?'

'My human. He's gone missing.'

'You think he's in the water?'

'I thought he would come here. He and I walked down here a lot. It was his favourite place.'

Before I could answer, a coyote streaked past, long legs pumping as it raced down the beach. Right behind it zoomed the distinctive bat-flap of Rocky's powerful wings.

'You'd better run you cat-eating son of a coyote!' Rocky laughed, but then landed beside us.

'What's this? A swim meet for cats?' he asked. 'I think I'll pass.' He twitched the whiskers on the right side of his nose. 'You've got a little seaweed or something stuck there, Spam-boy.'

The black cat looked like he was going to take flight. 'Wha – who's – what's that?'

'This is Rocky, one of my family,' I told him. He stared at the wings. 'Don't ask. You and I haven't formally sniffed rears yet–'

'Murray,' he said.

Rocky sniffed at him, got his nose wet, and backed off.

'Rocky, Murray was looking for his human before he fell in the water,' I said. 'Could you do a flap around this area of the Strait and see if you see him anywhere?'

'What? Swimming?'

'He has a kayak,' Murray said. 'I don't remember seeing it hanging on the side of the house when I left.'

Rocky was already airborne by then.

'Check with the birds!' I yelled after him. 'Ask if any of them have seen a human in the water, with or without a kayak!'

'You ask 'em,' Rocky yelled back. 'I don't speak bird!'

I didn't actually speak to many birds myself, though I had had a couple of uneasy encounters with that cranky mother eagle in the past.

'How long has your Fergus been missing?' I asked the black cat who looked more like a drowned rat. My fur fluffs up very quickly after wetting, another advantage of my breed.

'You want to find him too?' Murray asked, puzzled.

'We lost our human once too, and I had to go find her. Since then my friends and I have helped out with a few other cases. We're, you know, detectives like Midnight Louie and Joe Grey, Koko and YumYum.'

'Oh,' he said, clearly saying he had no idea what I was talking about.

'Most of them hunt criminals and murderers and that kind of thing, but in this town we seem to have a lot of supernatural types: vampires, as you can tell by looking at Rocky, though that was an accident; zombies and ghosts. Human detectives in stories are always complaining about people who want to hire them to find lost cats. It's a little more serious when a cat loses a human.'

Murray suddenly bristled into a wet ball. 'What's that?' he hissed.

Renfrew came barrelling down the beach, bobbing his ringed tail behind him.

'Hey, Spam, look what I found!' he called.

The setting sun glinted on something he carried in his paw-hands.

'Let me guess. Another shiny thing?'

'This one has a beautiful raccoon in it,' Renfrew crooned.

I glanced into it. 'No it doesn't. That's a beautiful cat.'

'No, it's a—'

'It's a mirror, Renfrew. You found a mirror.'

'Oh. Hey, I'm pretty cute! This might need a little wash though. Again.' He waddled into the surf and scrubbed the mirror with a vigour that would make a doctor happy.

'So, Murray, let's go back to your house and see if your Fergus is back yet?'

'You think he is?'

'I think even if he's not we might find clues about where he went. Does he have a cell phone? There's a way to use something called GPS to find him if he does, only I'd have to find out how to do that.'

'What if he doesn't? What if he never comes back and I'm left all alone?' Murray was one anxious kitty.

'Then we do what we're going to do anyway. Someone will have seen him. We'll ask around.'

Murray jumped into the air again, came down facing the opposite direction leaving me inhaling the tip of his tail. 'This way then. Come on.'

We chased each other out of the park and the boat yard and up the hill, but it's quite a hill even for a young cat.

'What made you look for Fergus on the beach?' I asked when we'd both taken a breather just to straighten the fur and lick off the dust.

'It's one of our special places,' he said. 'He would walk down here almost every day and we'd walk along the beach. Sometimes he'd carry me if there were too many dogwalkers around, but a lot of times we just sat on the gravel or a log and watched the water and the boats. I think he might have hoped he'd see his father.'

'On the water?'

'Well, yeah. They said Lochy was lost at sea but Fergus said that he can't have been. He was too at home on the water. So he kept looking for him, even after his mom gave up. She and Lochy didn't like each other any more, but until he joined the Sea Shepherds he still lived at home when their ship was in port.'

'What's a sea shepherd?' I asked, imagining sheep swimming through the waves.

'They try to stop other people from hurting sea animals. Lochy was really upset about them clubbing baby seals in Canada. Or whaling or catching dolphins in fish nets.'

'You seem to know a lot about that,' I said. Most cats I know wouldn't have taken the interest.

'Fergus asked him a lot of questions when he was home and that seemed to please him so he talked about it a lot. Jeannie, Fergus's mom, thought instead of being such a do-gooder Lochy should have been earning money as a fisherman or a boat builder or something.'

With that, Murray raced ahead and turned in to a driveway bordered by a few daisies and a lot of weeds. There were two deer in the yard grazing on the flowers of course. Deer aren't about to graze on something common when they can enjoy something beautiful.

I was going to ask if they'd seen Fergus, when I realised I couldn't even describe him and he probably hadn't stopped to introduce himself to them. Of course, they might be regulars to this yard. I reminded myself to try to snag a picture of Fergus when we went in the house. Of course, by the time I carried it in my mouth for awhile, he probably wouldn't be very recognisable and I couldn't exactly make 'lost' posters. Raccoon assistants, even with their useful paw hands, have their limits.

We trotted into the yard.

'You have your own entrance,' I said, spotting the cat door at the bottom of the people door. 'Me too. Lots of people around here don't let their cats out much because the coyotes used to be so bad.'

I thought warmly of Rocky. 'It's not been that much of a problem lately though.'

'No, Fergus's mom would never let me out but she's gone now.'

'She left?'

'Died. Cancer, her vet told Fergus. That's why I'm so worried about him. He's very sad and cries a lot when it's just me and him. I don't think he'd mean to leave me but he might just forget to come home.'

'Humans don't usually do that kind of thing,' I said, wanting to reassure him. 'He'd have to come back for his stuff and I'll bet that stuff includes you.'

I was trying to be as reassuring as possible, in spite of how I'd seen some people move house and just leave their cats behind – even locked in the old house.

'I hope you're right. He's my only human and I don't know what he expects me to do, with him running off like that. I blame the noise.'

'What noise?'

'Dunno. He said there was a noise. Apparently it's a dog whistle for humans except instead of making them come, it makes them stay home.'

'And people can hear it but cats can't?' Usually, according to Google, our hearing is way better than humans' or dogs'.

'I heard nothing but Fergus gave me a pet and said he hated to leave me but the song was calling him and there was something he had to do.'

'Mrt,' I said. I really felt a little miffed that if this was such an important song and all the people had to leave town, that cats couldn't hear it.

'Are you coming or aren't you?' Murray asked, stopping just inside his cat flap.

'Keep your tail on,' I said, stepping through.

There was a mail slot right over the cat door and I sledded down the opening onto the floor on a pile of mostly junk mail. It extended two or three feet into the room and a big muddy footprint in the middle of the pile indicated that the resident human also thought of it as junk – or maybe carpet.

'Your Fergus isn't much of a reader, huh?' I asked.

'No, but he swears at it and uses it for basketball practice,' Murray replied.

I could see that most of the mail was addressed to a Mrs Jean Finn.

Murray had no interest in the mail. Instead he walked into the kitchen, saying, 'I'm hungry. Fergus fed me before he got all weird and took off but – oh look! I didn't finish it.'

He applied mouth to sustenance while I looked around, searching for clues. I pounced on piles and scattered the junk mail enough that I could see where it was from or who was selling what, but nothing looked interesting. There was another smaller pile on the dining table so I jumped up on a chair and onto the table to check that out.

Nothing. Unless Fergus had gone out to sea to have his roof or windows replaced, or wanted to be cremated, or give money and vote for hundreds of different people, it was all useless as far as I could dig. I cut my mouth a couple of times tearing open envelopes.

Murray had finished his snack and was now curled comfortably in his large soft-looking if odd-smelling cat bed.

'You could help, you know,' I told him. 'It's your human who's lost after all.'

He looked up at me over his paws and yawned. 'But my bed is so comfy and it smells like Fergus and besides, you're the detective. You know more about finding clues than I do.'

'So you're not much of a hunter?' I asked, challenging. I might be the detective but if there were any clues, he'd know what was noteworthy and unusual in his home.

'Not nyow,' he said and yawned.

I gave him a 'Hsst!' and turned sharply. My tail connected with something under the pile of mail. I turned and saw I'd knocked over a brown wooden box. Letters were spilling out of it to join the junk mail under the table. Hopping down, I pawed through the new stuff.

'What's this?' I asked.

'Bills, I think. Our Mom kept them out from the junk pile. I sat down with Fergus to help him pay them and he did the right things – tore them open, ran his hands through his hair and said bad words, but then all of a sudden he pulled out something and – that's it!'

'What?'

'You're sitting on it – there, it's sticking out from under your tail.'

I tried to look under my tail but just ended up spreading the junk further. Finally I stood up and pounced on where I'd been sitting, capturing a letter half-stuffed into an envelope that was torn open.

'That's the thing,' Murray told me. 'Fergus forgot about the bills when he picked that up. He got all excited when he started reading it, then he began tearing the house apart, looking inside things and under things and behind things, in the closets, and all the clothes and in the laundry room and even Mom's sewing room where she quilts.'

For a great detective, I hadn't been very observant. I now saw evidence of Fergus's search. Coats and jackets were tossed onto the floor. The cushions had been pulled from the couch and Lay-Z-Boy chair and dropped back close to where they should have been. Even in the kitchen pots and pans and dishes and cans covered the counters, while the shelves were bare. The place had been tossed but I hadn't noticed. In my defence, I do live with fourteen other cats and a pretty messy human, so it wasn't that much different from normal to me.

Still, I decided I'd better look at the letter again.

I read typing pretty well but I didn't have much experience reading writing. We're very digital at Darcy's. Fortunately this was small block printed letters:

> SON,
>
> I MISS YOU SO MUCH. I HOPE YOU AND YOUR MOTHER ARE WELL.
> I NEED YOU TO DO SOMETHING FOR ME.
> IT'S VERY IMPORTANT OR I WOULDN'T ASK AND YOU CAN'T TELL
> YOUR MOM OR SHE'LL TRY TO STOP YOU.

I read the rest aloud to Murray, and he and I resumed the search that Fergus had abandoned.

We hadn't gone far, however, when Renfrew barged in the cat door, his rump scraping the sides and leaving them insulated with raccoon fur.

'Spam, this is a great day! I found two shiny things. The picture of the handsome raccoon and this cell phone someone must have dropped.'

'Where did you find it?' He was as likely to find it in an unsuspecting human's pocket as not. At the moment, however, humans, unsuspecting or otherwise, were in short supply.

'In the yard out there,' he said, waving his furry arm, with its handy little hand at the end, back toward the door.

'Can I see?' I asked.

'You'll find out whose it is and make me give it back.'

'If you found it in the yard it probably belongs to our client's family and could have a valuable clue.'

'How valuable?' he wanted to know.

'Not money kind of valuable. Information valuable.'

'That doesn't sound very shiny.'

'My paws are too big. Use those hands of yours for something besides washing stuff and stuffing your face.'

'Hey, cat, you got the order right! First wash your food and then stuff it in your face.'

Sometimes Renfrew missed the point entirely. 'Now look, here's what we need to do.'

Under the direction of my velvet paw, Renfrew made the phone give up the secret of its owner – Fergus – and its number.

While Renfrew's paws were flying I was surprised to hear a loud purr alternating with a sad mewing. Murray was kneading his bed and crying. I may have been a little rough on him. If we didn't find his Fergus, it would be the shelter for him, away from his cosy home and comfy bed and the humans who had loved him.

I bathed his head, giving his ears special attention, trying to comfort and calm him.

Two otters flowed in through the cat door.

'Word is you are searching for something at sea,' said the larger of the two. 'So are the merfolk and the finfolk. They are very unhappy–'

'Mad as wet werefish, I'd call it,' said the smaller one.

'We have mermaids around here too?' I asked. Vampires, zombies and bigfoots I knew about, but I hadn't spent enough time in the actual water to see much of anything natural, much less supernatural that lurked there.

'Aye,' said the larger one with a faint burr. 'Angry ones. They're all related, you know, them things that live in the sea but can turn human. Up north, in Alaska, some otters turn human sometimes too. (Humans get into everything!) The merfolk have tuned their songs to revenge frequencies until it gets sorted out.'

'Revenge frequencies? Did you otters figure that out yourselves?'

'We heard. We use bouncy sounds too, like dolphins and whales. We have a wetline to get the latest news in the water.'

At that moment the distinctive flap of Rocky's wings could be heard outside but instead of coming through the cat door like everybody else, he hung upside down in the picture window and gave me an upside down cat-bat grin.

Just as well, as it was getting crowded inside the house.

I ploughed through the accumulated junk mail on the table and jumped onto the window sill.

'Maddog's back.' Rocky told me. 'He wants you to meet him at the marina.'

Don't misunderstand. I am Maddog's favourite cat in the world. It's me he buys fish for at *SeaJ*'s and me he built the exclusive-access cat door for when he, Darcy, and I all decided that rather than being an indoor cat or an outdoor cat, I had earned the right to be an emancipated cat.

But ever since Rocky got turned, as vampires call it, when he fought off and exchanged chomps with the vamp who tried to invade our home, he and Maddog have shared a cross-species blood brotherhood; and other than me, Rocky is the only cat with whom Maddog talks. I scampered down to the beach in Rocky's jet stream.

'There you are, laddie,' my nearly-human friend said when he saw me. 'Just aboot to cast off. I was oot earlier in the wee boat and spotted something peculiar, but I could use your help.'

I leaped up onto his shoulder and rubbed cheeks and whiskers with him, giving his ear a lick for good measure.

He unwound the rope from the metal thingy that held the ship to the dock and we climbed aboard together.

'Wait! Detective, where are you going?' yowled Murray as his sleek black form bounded down the gangway. 'I thought you were going to find Fergus!'

I suppressed a growl but remembering his kneading and crying, felt sorry for him. 'This trip with my friend could be related.'

'Then I want to come.'

Behind him Renfrew charged toward us. 'Wait, Spam! You can't leave me!'

Maddog voiced no objections and tossed a half eaten apple to welcome Renfrew, and ran a quick stroke down Murray's back.

And then we set off, putt-putting out of the boat harbour and into the Bay, then up the Strait of Juan de Fuca as if we were heading for the ocean.

I asked Maddog where we were going and he said to Protection Island, once called Rat Island (which sounded more interesting to me). I had located it on the charts when I looked up between naps on another trip with Maddog, but all I remembered was that it wasn't far from our town.

It's called Protection Island because it's a safe place for the sea birds that nest there. Them and a lot of seals. And now, it seemed, another rare species had joined them.

'Hey, Spam, ask the man what all those boats are doing there!' Renfrew said.

Murray had apparently caught up on his napping because he stood with his front paws on the bow, scanning the weird spectacle of the little island surrounded by all kinds of boats – sailboats, rowboats, motorboats, a couple of fancy yachts and one tall sailing ship that had come to town for the festival that didn't happen.

'What are they doing?' Renfrew asked. 'Why are they just sitting there?' and then, 'Hey! Look on the island. There's shiny things over there.'

Maddog reached down and grabbed Renfrew's ruff to keep him from vaulting overboard.

'There he is!' Murray cried. 'There! That's Fergus's kayak.'

None of the boats had their motors running. They all just sat there letting the water wash them around while they stared at a collection of unusual looking birds, an awful lot of seals and three were-fish, mermaids that were human women from the waist up and fish all the way down their gleaming muscular tails. I would have to say they were all maybe were-salmon because their tails were copper coloured and their long hair was a similar shade.

The human boat owners and crews stood on the decks of their silent vessels, listening. And note by note, I heard what they were listening to. It was like the silent meow or a very internalised purr. It was there, and I felt it shiver the air around us. There was sorrow in it, also anger and blaming, as it beckoned and repelled at the same time. It seemed to be saying 'come near, stay where you can be seen but no closer.'

Of all the boats, only the bow of Fergus's kayak broke out of the ring and in a few strokes of the paddle nuzzled against the island. Murray yowled and I thought he would launch himself at the kayak. The three were-fish ladies watched him closely as if they were wondering what flavour he'd be.

Renfrew applied the conflict mitigation techniques he had learned while begging from previously unsympathetic humans. It probably wasn't his words, since there is no evidence that were-fish speak or understand raccoon, but what he did.

'I don't suppose any of you ladies lost this shiny thing, did you?' he asked suddenly, standing atop the boat's cabin to hold up his beach-combed treasure in one raccoon hand.

Their response was as weird as his question, and all three quickly looked down until one held up an ornately framed and handled, but broken, mirror. I've seen stuff on the iPad about mermaids since then, and apparently they are just about as conceited and vain as raccoons, though usually without the comic relief.

I couldn't figure out why they were so mad at everybody though. Was it because of the polluted oceans, some kind of environmental protest? They weren't wearing t-shirts with slogans or carrying signs. And yet they had stopped the festival and had become more personal, menacing all of these boaters with a dangerous combination of sonar and songs.

Finally though, Fergus spoke up.

'My name is Fergus Finn. I am searching for my dad, Lochlain. They say he was lost at sea but I don't see how he could have been. Before she died, my mom told me he was one of you – well, related. I didn't believe her then – she was on really strong pain medicine and I thought she was hallucinating. Seeing you guys, and you don't look like you work for Disney, I think you know, and I think that you wouldn't be here if there wasn't some connection.'

Murray's purr must have been loud enough for the mermaids to hear. 'That's my boy,' the black cat said, squeezing his eyes shut. 'If he were a cat he'd be a lion ! Or at least a tiger. Leopard at the bare minimum.'

Fergus didn't look especially catty to me but it was hard to tell with only his top half visible above the hole in the kayak. He did look a little like Murray around the head fur – his was curly and black with the same red brown highlights, and his skin was a similar gold colour to Murray's eyes, and the parts that showed from under his life jacket shone with sweat and salt water.

Humans like to think their animal friends look like them, though if that were true in our town all of the humans would have to be redheads. My old dad had been busy duplicating himself on every unfixed female in the vicinity so most of the cats within recent years looked like me, ginger, long-furred, rather large, and very fluffy of tail.

The fishy ladies were less impressed with Fergus than his feline friend though.

Their song escalated and changed. One sang to the other boats and they began leaving as quickly as they could without piling up.

'Aye, that's as well,' Maddog told me. 'They found the laddie and he it is, that they called for. They're throwin' the rest of us back but we willna leave until it's sorted.'

I was relieved by his decision. I needed a deck under my paws if I was to see this case to a satisfactory conclusion. Would Joe Grey quit now? I thought not. Nor Midnight Louie or my other mouser mentors.

The foremost mermaid amid the three stared hard at Fergus, her eyes bright and hard in the fuzzy dying light of what I'd heard Maddog refer to as 'the gloamin' – the overcast and twilit time that always made my paws itch to go hunting.

She was broadcasting her thoughts, not just for Fergus, but for all of us and her sisters and the seals, shaming the boy.

'Why seek your father now when you let him go to sea without his skin?'

Fergus looked thoroughly confused. 'What are you talking about – ma'am?' he added to be polite.

'When he was fished from the sea, he was naked except for a few tatters of soaking human rags. Where is his skin?'

'I, I don't know. Mom didn't–'

Maddog spoke up, 'Wouldn't the mother have hidden the skin to keep the father near, even before the laddie was born, ma'am?' Maddog said, his message a mixture of telepathy and a song similar to the one the mermaids had been singing but in a deeper tone.

I thought it was funny Maddog would call the mermaid 'ma'am.' From the waist up she looked like a thin teenaged girl. Her straight ginger hair, tangled with a little kelp, added to the resemblance, as if she were wearing some of those fake coloured strips of hair I'd seen sported by some of the younger females in town. Maddog looked old enough to be her great-great grandsire at least, but maybe he was deferring to her because we were in the water. She seemed to expect it – her expression was as stern as if she'd just caught him peeing on the rug.

'Yes, she did!' Fergus said. 'Dad wrote me that note, that I guess she'd hidden, but after she died I found it. Dad asked me to look for a seal skin that belonged to him and I *did* look for days and days, mostly out of curiosity since we heard months ago that he was lost at sea. And I mean, well, he's not going to need it if he's dead, is he?'

'Who said anything about dead?' the mermaid replied. 'The sea is his home so he can hardly be lost in it – but he cannot navigate well as a mere human.'

'He's alive?' Fergus asked. 'Nah, can't be. Hey, Dad! Dad? Are you back there hiding behind those seals? Not funny, man. Mom died last week, did you know?'

Murray ran back and forth across the deck, wanting to go to Fergus but there was all that water between Maddog's boat and the boy's kayak.

The daylight fled while all of this was happening, and when the mermaids started shielding their eyes, Maddog turned off his running lights.

So Lochlan Finn, rising from among the pod of seals clustered behind the mermaids, could have been mistaken for a ghost or a monster of some kind. Without his skin, I guessed, he hadn't been able to totally transform to a seal but neither was he still entirely human. He was, as an old song went that they sometimes played on the local radio station, caught between the devil and the deep blue sea.

Fergus probably turned as pale as his father appeared, started to say something, then horked over the side of his kayak though he didn't seem to bring up a hairball. Obviously the dad's transformation was not going to make for cosy family reunions.

But Fergus paddled forward to meet his father and they spoke softly though I heard what they said and so did Murray.

'Remember when you were a kid and I told you about this?' the father asked.

'You mean the turning into a seal thing? Well, yeah, but I thought it was like a fairytale. That's why I wasn't sure if you were kidding or not in your note.'

'I was not, son. There aren't so many of us as once there were, but the story is the same because it's true. We cast off our skins when we come ashore in human form to dance and sometimes to find mates. If a human takes a shine to one of us, he or she will take our seal skin so we can't turn back and return to the sea.

'Your mother hid mine very cleverly and I never did find it, but still the sea called me so I returned as a seaman instead of as a seal. I had a seal family when your mother took my skin, and I could not return to them. When I heard that men were clubbing seals for their skins, I joined the Sea Shepherds to do my best to protect my other family.'

'Yeah, but you abandoned us.'

'I would have come back. I had to as long as your mother hid my skin.'

Maddog was humming the tune of *The Great Selkie* to himself as he watched and listened.

I not only watched and listened but was captivated by the smell, I sniffed deeply the scent from the direction of the island – fish and seal and salt water but something else as well, something recently familiar. My upper lip curled in the flehmen response.

I was not the only feline sensitive to the smell. Murray's lip was curled too but his eyes closed blissfully and a purr throbbed through his body. I rubbed against his side. 'You know, don't you?'

'Now I do. I don't want to know though.'

'It's up to you, but look at them. Your family will never be happy the way things are – especially without the mom.'

'But, Spam, if Lochy has to turn into a seal and live in the ocean, and he gets his skin to go back, what about Fergus? What about me?' His purr turned into a yowl and his flehmen to the snarl humans sometimes mistook it for.

I had no real answer for him, but I felt very sad that the missing person case was turning out so badly for my client.

'I don't think Darcy would notice another cat at our house and if she did, it would be okay. You could come and live with me and my family maybe?'

'From having my own people to having to share one person with other cats?'

I shrugged my whiskers. 'It's not so bad.' But I knew for him it would be. 'And you know he can't stay like he is.'

'He shouldn't have left us!' Murray said, but wistfully. 'But – okay.'

I put a paw on Maddog's knee. 'I know where the skin is. Here's what we need to do.'

Maddog and Fergus loaded the kayak onto the boat. The mermaids and a small pod of the seals escorted the thing that Fergus's father had become, and they surrounded the boat as we docked.

The mermaids sang a new song. No lights blinked on as the humans tethered the boat to the shore, no human faces watched us, and no human voices interrupted the song of Lochlan's mer relatives, to ask what we were doing. Maybe it was because everybody knew – or thought they knew – Maddog. But I think Lochlan's mer kin had used their songs to conceal their presence from humans before.

When Fergus had boarded the boat back at Protection Island, the first thing he did was pick up Murray. Now Murray rode on his shoulder as we piled into Maddog's ancient truck. I thought maybe they would try to load the mermaids and Lochlan into the truck's bed but when I looked back, they had disappeared.

Maddog nodded to where they had been, giving Fergus an inquisitive look.

'Our house is on the cliff. There's stairs down to the beach,' he said.

We rode back to the house. Murray did not use his cat door to enter but clung to Fergus with all four sets of claws, as we walked inside. He didn't jump down from Fergus's arms, but mewed and looked away from his bed, leaving it up to me to walk over to it.

'Aye, Spam, I take your meaning,' Maddog said and added to Fergus. 'I don't suppose you checked your cat's bed for the skin?'

He and Fergus ripped the seam holding the bed together. Stuffed in the middle between the cushions was a gray dappled skin with fur stiff from being slept on. Its aroma was a milder version of what I'd smelled at the island. Like Lochlain and sort of like Fergus too, as Murray had said.

Murray cried but Fergus held the skin in the crook of his elbow between him and the cat who loved him.

I rode on Maddog's shoulder as we navigated the steep wooden staircase from the back yard of Murray's house down to the beach, where Lochlain, the mermaids, and the seals waited, their tails and flippers becoming agitated at our approach and churning up the water.

Fergus held out the skin to his father but then pulled it back as he reached for it.

'Tell me one thing, Dad. When do I start changing into a seal too? Or do I? Do I have to stay that way? If I do, what will happen to Murray and the house? I'll have to make arrangements.'

Murray head-butted him frantically, first on one cheek, then the other and let out a plaintive mew.

Lochlain shook his still-part-human head. 'No, son. My selkie secret is not the only family secret your mother and I didn't tell you.'

Fergus half turned his head away. 'What else?'

'Turned out we couldn't have pups of our own, so we adopted you.'

'So, I'm not going to turn into a seal too?'

'You'd have to ask your birth parents. Thank you for this,' he said, and pulling on his skin, slipped back into the water.

Renfrew had been running beside us all the while, tripping us on the stairs, and now he danced from one paw to the other on the shore. One of the mermaids extended her hand toward him and something she held on her webbed fingers glinted in the moonlight. She said nothing but Renfrew snatched the thing from her hand and spun around in circles. 'Thank you, werefish lady! I promise to keep it clean and shiny for you!'

But the mermaids already had disappeared beneath the now still water and all that could be heard was Murray's purr.

And that's how my first missing person-and-a-half case ended.

To Sniff Out a Thief

LJM Owen

To Sniff Out a Thief

SALLY ROLLED HER HEAD BACK AGAINST THE TOWERING BOOKSHELF behind us and murmured, 'What am I going to do?'

A small whine escaped my throat as I lay my head in her lap. Sally caressed my ears for a moment, then picked up one of the books lying beside us on the shop's wooden floorboards. She opened the front cover again and stared at the front page as if in disbelief.

'Who could have stolen them?'

The hint of fear in her voice made my stomach hurt. I decided not to make my usual visit to Nik after closing tonight. Sally needed me more.

First things first, I have to get her off the cold floor. After a long day of serving books and coffee to the Cherryvale Writers Festival crowd she needed a rest. I pushed my nose against her thigh and stood up, hoping she would follow.

The corner of her mouth curled up. 'All right, Baba, let's go home and get the kettle on.'

Once Sally had manoeuvred herself into a standing position, using the shelves and her cane for leverage, we locked *Cuneiform Café*'s front door and ambled to our cottage one street over.

I had hoped Sally would feel better after a strong cup of tea, but sitting next to her on the sofa I could still smell her distress. Such an unusual thing for her.

'I'm going to lose the shop.'

Her voice wobbled; I snuggled in as tightly as I could to reassure her. As she snoozed fitfully in front of the fire, I resolved to find the thief who had caused my Sally such misery. She had saved me; now it was my turn to save her.

Although I didn't understand what was so special about the books that used to be on the display stand in the middle of Sally's bookshop café – the ones she stopped to look at each day – I knew that she wanted those specific books and not the lookalikes that had replaced them.

Eve, who worked at the bookshop café with us, smelled of eucalyptus detergent, coconut shampoo and my best friend Nik. 'Surely the police can do something?' she said to Sally.

'Sergeant Plover took a report last night,' Sally said as we prepared to open the next day. 'She said it was unlikely she'd find them, especially now, with thousands of books floating around the writers festival.'

As they talked I sniffed each of the replacement books the thief had swapped for the ones that were important to Sally.

'Mr Lee's coming tomorrow to buy them. I can't see how I can possibly get them back in time,' Sally's voice cracked, 'if ever.'

'I'm so sorry Sally,' Eve said, setting out water and cups for the café.

'The sergeant said she'd check if there's any black market dealers in town, but–'

'Things always get nicked when the festival's on, you know that.'

'Yes, but not like this!' Sally's knuckles turned white as she squeezed the handle of her cane. 'This isn't like the two dollar paperbacks that usually go missing,'

Eve stopped moving boxes of cutlery to the countertop. 'What do you mean?'

'Those are opportunistic thefts, people nicking something they just came across. This was planned.'

I had finished inspecting the substitute books on the display stand. Four of them smelled as strongly of the shop as any other long-term shelf resident, and four held a tangy fresh mix of Sally, Eve, the shop and many outside smells.

'At least half of these replacement copies, these new or unsigned editions, have our stamp in the back,' she said. 'But half don't. So whoever did this went looking for copies of all eight books before coming in to swap them.'

My tail wagged with satisfaction that Sally had worked this out too.

'Meaning?' Eve said.

'Whoever did this has thought about it for a while. Long enough to find the substitutes, anyway.'

Eve started to move plates from the dishwasher to the food preparation bench. 'I see what you mean.'

'And,' Sally's voice grew stronger, 'how did the person who stole them even know they were valuable? The online bidders offered much more than they would have fetched at auction.'

'Well, Mr Lee would know?'

'Do you think he's stolen them to avoid having to pay me?'

'Maybe. Or one of the other online bidders? That Mr Chudders was upset you didn't accept his offer.'

'I've read some fairly damning things about how his company makes its profits,' Sally said. 'I didn't want my books bought with dirty money.'

'Anyone who saw the online listing could have known, I suppose, and decided to use the writers' festival as cover? Have you seen any of the bidders in the store? Or hanging around the festival?'

Sally finished counting the float into the till. 'I've never met any of them in real life, so I wouldn't know.'

And I didn't know what any of them smelled like, I realised.

Eve took a deep breath. 'Again, I'm so sorry Sally, but it's all covered by insurance, right?'

'No, that's the thing, they weren't.'

Eve stared at Sally. 'Isn't the shop insured?'

'Of course, but those particular signed copies weren't covered for the price Mr Lee offered. As I said, they'd normally go for much less at auction.'

'Oh.' Eve bit her lower lip. 'But you'll be okay, won't you?'

Sally leaned heavily on her cane. 'I think I'm going to have to close the shop. The boost from the writers' festival will only cover the business loan for about six months. After that...

Eve frowned. 'You never said things were that tight?'

'You have worries of your own,' Sally patted the back of Eve's hand. 'I didn't want to add to them.'

They had discussed Eve's 'troubles' before – something to do with horses. Horses were large, skittish creatures, far too pampered as far as I was concerned. I could imagine them causing trouble for someone like Eve.

Sally and Eve finished the last pre-open check and moved to the front door.

'Ready?' Eve asked.

'Ready.'

She opened the front door to the crowd gathered outside, who were eager for coffee and pastries to fuel their day of book festivities.

It was my time to catch a thief.

By two o'clock the shop was clear of festival goers and I felt ready to drop. I'd inspected over two hundred people and hadn't identified a single lead.

Wandering the aisles of books that morning, the shelves smelled only of the usual decomposing paper and ink. I had circled each group of chattering readers as they arrived and departed, searching for any hint of the thief. They smelled of sleeplessness and excitement, but not guilt or the missing books.

Given the deep furrows that lined Sally's forehead, I could see she hadn't made any breakthroughs either.

'It's quiet now,' she said to Eve. 'How about you take a break, come back at four and we'll close up then?'

'I don't want to leave you for the afternoon rush. I'll be back by three. How does that sound?'

I followed her to the front door.

'Are you going home with Eve?' Sally asked me.

I barked a yes. It would give me a chance to apologise to Nik for not visiting yesterday, and the stroll might jog my mind into thinking of a new way to find the book bandit.

She patted my head as I passed by. I stopped to lick it to reassure Sally I wouldn't be long.

Nik forgave me almost instantly, then coiled around himself and rested his black head on my flank for a nap. As we lay on his couch, something kept tugging at my nose.

What was it?

I sifted through the traces in the air around me: Nik, of course; enticing hints of meat from the kitchen; the overpowering perfume of flowers in the garden; coconut from the shampoo bottle in the shower; and the signature melange of *Cuneiform Café* clinging to Eve's clothes and handbag.

All to be expected, of course, but something was out of kilter.

I inhaled again, searching for the imbalance. It was something to do with the café…and Sally. There was too much Sally. Why was her scent in Eve's house stronger than usual?

I eased myself out from under Nik's head, careful not to wake him, and padded toward the hallway. Sally's smell was coming from one of the rooms down there.

Eve was in her dining room, talking on the phone '…it has to be cash…' She paused. 'Six o'clock tonight at my house.'

I tracked Sally's scent to one of the bedrooms, pulled the handle down with my teeth and pushed the door open. It was coming from the closet. Using my nose, I nudged the door open wide enough to get my head in.

The hinges squeaked.

I froze, but didn't hear anything to indicate Eve had left the dining room.

The smell was coming from a box on the floor. I prised the lid off with my teeth—

Oh no.

In a daze, I snuck past Eve and left Nik on his couch, then staggered through backyards to my own door flap and onto my bed in Sally's loungeroom. I tucked my head under my front paw and sighed.

I could save Sally after all, but it would mean losing my best friend.

I was back in the bookshop café by three o'clock, with a new plan. My one chance of helping Sally and not losing my friendship with Nik was for Sally to work out for herself where the stolen books were located. Perhaps if she confronted the thief they might return them and be forgiven. That's what happened whenever I stole one of Sally's pillows from her bed.

I could only think of one way to point Sally's suspicions in the right direction. I waited for everyone to be busy, carefully picked up a book from a low shelf and edged towards the cupboard under the counter where everyone's bags were kept. If I could get it in the right bag, and ensure Sally discovered it, she might suspect where her books had gone.

'Oh, how adorable! That dog is shopping for books!'

A reader had spotted me.

Eve swooped in and pulled the book from my jaws, her eyes narrowed.

'You left saliva on it, you silly dog. And bite marks. We'll have to discount it now.'

'Baba! What were you doing? No!'

Eve wiped the book off with her hand. 'Just a game.'

Her voice was brittle. I was sure she would keep a close eye on me now. My one idea for getting Sally to realise who was stealing from her had failed. Even worse, Sally suspected I had been a bad dog.

I had to choose – either help Sally retrieve her lost books or keep my friendship with the wonderful Nik. Sally had rescued me from the people who hurt my leg so badly it had to be removed, whereas Nik made every day special.

I flopped on my bed in the corner of *Cuneiform Café* with a whomp and waited for closing time.

Shortly after five o'clock, long after the patrons and Eve had left, Sally finally locked the front door and we began the walk home, our five legs and one cane drumming a distinct pattern on the concrete path.

I knew that Eve loved Sally, but that she also had a vindictive streak. Underneath, she was the same as the people that Sally liberated me from; I had seen it in the way she treated any humans she didn't like. Still, in the end, I had no choice.

I needed Sally to move faster than normal. I ran a few steps ahead, turned and barked at her.

'Baba! Shh!'

I barked again.

'Baba! What's wrong with you today?'

I walked toward her, spun on my back legs and padded urgently down the street once more.

Sally followed, her expression puzzled. 'I hope there's a good reason for all this fuss.'

I trotted to the gate at the front of Eve's garden, then down the path to her front door and began barking.

'Baba! Stop it!'

Eve flung the front door open. 'What's going on?'

She wobbled as I pushed past her into the house and ran down the hallway. I noticed Nik on the couch startle awake as I rushed through. I wanted to stop and make sure he knew I loved him, but there was no time.

Eve and Sally both followed me, yelling at me to stop.

Using my momentum, I shouldered the door to the room with the box in it open then scrabbled as hard as I could with my teeth and front paw to open the closet.

'Baba! No!' Eve grabbed hold of my collar and began to pull me back, but she was too late. I bit the lid of the box, pulling it with me as she hauled me out of the closet. My one front paw wasn't strong enough to hold my ground. All I could do was twist and shake, try to loosen her grip.

'Eve! Stop! Whatever this is everyone needs to calm down.'

Eve yanked even harder, choking me. She tugged again, lost her grip and flew backwards into Sally.

I watched Sally fall, almost in slow motion. A memory of the day she had stood between me and the people hurting me flashed through my mind. I needed to protect her now.

I jumped to place myself between Eve and Sally. As I did, my tooth stuck in the box's cardboard lid. It came with me as I moved, revealing the front covers of four of Sally's stolen books.

The look of shock and relief on Sally's face almost made my sacrifice worth it.

The look of horror on Eve's face, however, told me I had definitely lost my visiting privileges. She would never let me in the house to see Nik again.

'I'm so, so sorry,' Eve stuttered, standing over the fallen Sally. 'I didn't know…thought your insurance would cover…thought it would all be fine.'

'I have nothing to say to you,' Sally replied.

A contrite Eve helped Sally to her feet and ensured she made it to a comfortable chair in the loungeroom. 'Please forgive me, Sally. I honestly didn't think you'd get hurt.'

Sally's lips remained clamped shut. A low growl escaped the side of my mouth. Sally put a warning hand on my shoulder, asking me to remain calm.

Eve stared at Sally for a moment, sobbed once, covered her mouth with one hand, grabbed her bag with the other and ran outside as Sally pulled out her mobile phone.

Car tyres screeched out of the driveway as Sally dialled the police.

At six o'clock, as Sergeant Plover spoke to Sally in Eve's loungeroom, I spotted a man approach the front gate. He stopped when he saw the police vehicle, peered into the house, then turned and almost ran away. Eve's mysterious cash-paying visitor, I assumed.

'Are you sure you're all right? I can call an ambulance,' the sergeant was saying.

'I'm okay, honestly.'

Sally's voice and smell confirmed she really was fine.

'How are you feeling, emotionally I mean?'

'Hurt that Eve betrayed me, foolish that I didn't suspect her. But I'm glad to have the books back so I can still sell them to Mr Lee.'

The sergeant tapped a pen on her notepad. 'Do you know why she did it? Had she stolen from you before?'

'All I know is Eve came to town to start afresh. She'd had problems with betting on horses in the past, owed some money, but I thought she'd turned over a new leaf.'

So horses were behind this after all. I wouldn't've put it past them either, the oversized cossetted whinny machines.

'What will happen to Eve?' Sally asked, as I went to check on Nik.

He was staring at the stranger who remained in his house, his ears pivoting wildly as he tried to assess the meaning of the intrusion. I snuffled at the fur on his back, trying to comfort him.

'If we catch her she'll be arrested and charged. Will you be able to deal with her being here if she gets out on bail?'

'I don't think Eve will come back,' Sally said. 'Not after this. I think she'll run, head interstate to escape the mess she's made.' She paused. 'Baba, Baba!'

I touched my nose to Nik's and whined, hoping he knew how much his friendship had meant to me. I padded over to my human, tail between my legs.

Sally patted her lap, asking me to place my front paw on her knees. 'Baba, what's wrong? You're not in trouble. You're such a good girl!'

'I thought Baba was a boy's name?' the sergeant said.

'She's named after the Sumerian goddess of dogs,' Sally answered as she tugged one of my ears.

'Does Eve have any family in Cherryvale?'

Sally shook her head. 'She moved here on her own a couple of years ago.'

The policewoman jutted her chin toward Nik. 'The cat will need looking after.'

Sally kissed the bridge of my nose then raised her eyes to the tense curl of black fur on the couch. 'What do you think, Baba? Would you like a brother?'

I muffled my bark of joy so as not to startle the already-distressed Nik, and licked the side of Sally's face from jaw to forehead.

Sergeant Plover chuckled. 'I think that's a yes.'

Whimper's Brief

Craig Hilton

Whimper's Brief

LIFE WAS HARD, AND SOME DAYS WERE SO DAMN LOUSY HE COULD GROW teeth. One day, for instance, Whimper got bumped off the head of the queue. The brief runner, a mouse dressed in token scraps of clothing and the headband of his trade, had sprinted into the clamour of the main entrance lobby of the Magistrate's Chambers and bypassed him to slap his left hand on the right shoulder of the brief sitting next to him. An oink of pleasure, one greasy cheek puckering into a fat smile and he's suddenly cheated out of a paying client.

Picking up work as a legal representative by 'plying the rank' could make you a living fit for a Domestique but nothing more. It was a cut-throat existence, notwithstanding that it had been worse (they said) in years gone by, before the introduction of licences, when hundreds of half-baked briefs streetwalked in desperation for clients. So while the Freeborn class might operate through placed advertisements, or by retainers to well-to-do families, your everyday Domestique brief was consigned to sit in numerical order with his competition along a bench by the wall like motley birds on a fence.

And Whimper was now on that bench, and he was finally number one. The runner should have given the job to him; the twist of paper, hastily scribbled out jointly by the prisoner and the arresting officer at the scene and spirited with a set of young legs to the Chambers, ought to have been pressed into his own palm, not Kelly's. But there they were now, Kelly stooping to drop the runner the few copper coins for the service, and the grazed and grubby hands – lamp oil and muskmelon – pocketing them. And he just watched, with venom in his mind.

Dusk was near. Whimper may not get another case before nightfall, and his district after dark was very dangerous. Worse than the landlord or a three-day hunger. Under hooded lids he watched pig and mouse fade into the corridor's darkness, and then lifted his body onto wiry limbs and started off for the open doors. In his brain the wheels started turning, and by the bottom step his course was set.

The alleged offence – blasphemous affray – had been committed in a moon pool; that much he had overheard. So logically there were twelve possible destinations, one for each bailey of the old city. Count only the ones near Chambers and you had six. The brief runner had been eating muskmelon and handling lamp oil when he saw the arrest. Markets were at West Dockside and Tumbledown. Tumbledown was closer.

The cobblestones were warm from the oppressive heat of noon, although the slanting rays of sun were lifting now. Kelly would be tied up with his D904, and Whimper made good time. The dome of white came into view, and now the rat was pressing for a position under the eaves of the small pavilion in the milling throng slaking their thirst, carting water by the pitcher, laving away a day's load of dust and sweat.

Whimper stood with tail lightly off the ground to let a pair of nut-brown eyes scan the scene methodically. Citizens drew the clean water with love and faith, for it speaks of the Phoenix and the moon. Although Whimper could never decipher the ancient characters in the stone pillars, what he had read in the library suggested 'moon, corrupted from the Apostrian 'maug(h)in', meant 'clean water', and therefore the venerable moon pools of Delphi were masterpieces of sanitary engineering.

Which was straying from the point – his business wasn't there. He set off again at a fast run, a zigzag through chaotic streets, this time for West Dockside. Actually, he should have told Kelly to go bite his own head. Anger was boiling up in him as he reached the Ashment at the Array and turned right. With the long, straight run along the stone wharf past endless lines of barges, and with his breathing now deep and strong, and with the sun in his eyes and sweat beading into droplets, it became rage. Damn that pig! Damn him!

Right turn up Little Bollicutt Lane, through the mobs to the West Dockside moon pool. A little wider and more squat than the other, it was in the pale blue of shadow with a sunlit gold cap. A few figures were inside, but an armed constable barred the portal. Five paces behind him was the sergeant, who fixed a gaze on him and flattened his ears with a cougar's menace.

Whimper could also see a grey ram, and habit took him through the check-list: hopeless-looking, stooped, bloody-nosed, in a black belt, matching lime green jacket and rudely bespattered trousers.

'Excuse me, I'm Whimper – I've come to res... represent you.'

The ram broke into an open-mouthed grin and stepped forward. 'In thuh nick o' time, jus' as this here sergeant was gonna haul me – urk!' Whimper pulled out some folded pink paper and edged in to head them off.

'Sergeant...?'

'Pergi.'

He advanced cautiously. 'Sergeant Pergi, I'm Whimper, a legal rep, here to give legal representation. Here's my form and that's my licence number.'

'Yeah, yeah,' Pergi took it and waved him away.

'You fill in your bit there.'

'At the foggin' station.'

A dumbstruck pause. 'No. Here.' He tried further: 'The scene of the crime.' No response, and the passing ram cried: 'Can't you stop him?'

'Nope,' said the passing constable. Whimper darted to just inside the arch of the opposite portal, blocking their path and yelled: 'Miscarriage!'

That worked. The last rattle of armour reverberated from within the pavilion walls, and then all was silent but for the distant hubbub of the crowd cautiously re-entering the far end of the pool area. Sergeant Pergi's short, tawny whiskers were bristling.

'You want me to do this the hard way?'

'The right way,' said Whimper. 'Sir.'

'And if I just throw him in the lockup, whatta you goin' to do about it?'

'I'll go straight back to the Magistrate's chambers and file a wrongful procedure, Sergeant, uhh, 2117.'

'Y'know I can take your foggin' licence.'

'And I'll appeal, and win it back.'

It was a vivid image of a sparrow in the eye of a hurricane.

'Meanwhile Mister, umm, my client is entitled to legal representation.'

'Wait a minute, foggin'-wait-a-minute,' said Pergi in the suspicious drawl of a man beginning to smell a rat. He looked properly at the pink slip for the first time. 'This isn't your name. Who did you say sent you?'

'I'm here on the basis as a wandering brief.'

'But you said you came from the Chambers.'

'Yes but I'm here on the basis as a wandering brief.'

'It's ticked here that the brief runner was already in pay. Constable, do you remember the colour of his headband?'

The ram butted in: 'Look I don't care, really. A brief's a brief.'

'It's not that easy, Domestique.'

'That's right, it's actually quite complicated,' contributed Whimper, turning to face the ram. 'But I know my rights, sir. So how can I help you?'

'I wasn't fighting. I been set on and robbed! All my money and then they try to throw me in the pool. So I'm screaming and fighting, and that's when law arrives and everyone else buggers off and here I am!'

Whimper glanced up at Pergi with interrogation in his eyes, but the smile was undaunted. 'Subject involved in a blasphemous affray in a moon pool. End of argument. A moon pool should be a place of...' he searched for the word: 'Serenity.'

'BASTARD!'

All heads turned. There was a commotion in the nearby crowd, and out burst a furious pig in a blue-gold loincloth with a sheaf of assorted papers jammed under one arm. With wide eyes, wild breaths and pursed lips, he stormed up.

'What thef...' (remembered where he was) 'What do you think you're doing here, Whimper, with my client?'

'I salvaged him on a streetwalker basis. I've submitted the OP7 to the arresting officer.'

The pig pushed him aside and handed the sergeant (perhaps too forcefully) a wad of forms.

'I'm Kelly, I belong to the Jambonne family, I've been asked to represent one Dirk-Adam of the Lano family on a charge of blasphemous affray in the West Dockside moon pool, and here is my D904, which you will see is properly signed and stamped in all the appropriate places.'

The cougar took this in. Then Kelly quickly turned to his client and continued at this reckless pace: 'Right. Dirk-Adam, before we start, has Sergeant Pergi clarified with you the law under which you've been arrested?'

'No.'

'Have you come to an agreement with him as to the location the altercation started?'

'No.'

'Well now you've got two lines of defence for a start.' Then he was interrupted, and turned, glowering.

Whimper took in a deep breath. 'Kelly, I really am going to have to insist on this, but he's my client.'

'Like stink he is. We don't need your damn low-gutter tricks here.'

'Look.' He held a hiss of urgency to hide the pinch of guilt. 'What did you offer that runner to pick you out? A cut?'

'He was my own runner. He was wearing my colours.'

'Never!'

'Well he should've been. The contract's down.'

'No colours means no colours.'

'More to the point, Sheep here asked for me by name, didn't he?'

'I bet he didn't.' Whimper turned to the ram. 'Did you?'

'Lissen, I been arrested for been beaten up. Call that justice?'

'But did you request any brief in particular?'

'Okay okay, I guess I's started with you now, Mistuh Rat, so I might as well carry on with you.'

'You can't do that, sir,' said Kelly, 'and I've got the paperwork to prove it!'

'Anyways, Rat here's the on'y one who'll listen.'

'He'll listen, yes, but does he have the experience? Choose the wrong brief, Dirk-Adam, you could be looking at three months behind.'

'Three months!' and in the silence that followed all they could hear was the sound of Whimper choking.

Sergeant Pergi stood regarding them, almost licking his lips. 'Let me see if I've got this straight,' he began. 'The brief runner gave the note of invitation to you, the pig, and so you, the rat, get here first and take his case.' His smile was like curtains opening on a row of pearly white dancing girls. 'That sounds like a suspensible action.'

'Yes except–'

'Whimper of,' he looked down at the OP7, 'no family, I hereby suspend your licence to practice in the capacity as a people's legal representative in the City State of Delphi under the reign of Empress Alicia of Xanadu.'

Flailing for survival now: 'Sir, I dispute that.'

'Dispute it all you like. Now hand it over.'

Whimper looked at the wooden tablet in his palm before replacing it in his pocket. 'No, sir. I dispute that.'

'Do you refuse?'

'I dispute that.'

'Suit yourself. I'm arresting you for disobeying an order given within my power.'

Suddenly the bottom dropped out of Whimper's world; the shock hit him like a punch to the chest. There came the vague awareness of the pig snorting and sitting down suddenly on the lip of the pool with shoulders wobbling silently, and of numbness thawing into stinging pain. He clutched at what he knew.

'I want a brief.'

Pergi swept the horizon. 'Tough.' He grabbed rat and ram each by a shoulder and yanked them along.

'Oh sergeant, a moment if you please,' Kelly called. 'There's the small matter of the representation of my client.' He trotted up, still chortling.

'You and Dirk-Adam are not allowed to leave the scene of the alleged offence until I, the accused party's nominated representative, have examined the facts of the matter.'

Whimper muttered: 'For a start, he's been robbed.'

'Yeah, okay.'

'So he's got no money.'

Kelly's mouth moved a bit, but no sound came out. Then his head sank to his chest and he let slip an almost silent syllable.

A heavy, gloved hand fell onto his shoulder. 'You're under arrest.'

'Huh?' Eyeballs went round and glassy with panic, and his sweat suddenly smelled of fear.

'You said a foggin' rude word. Constable, you heard that, didn't you?'

The constable strode over. 'Heard what, sir?'

'The word *shit*.'

'Oh yes, sir. It was a definite *shit*, sir.'

Kelly closed his eyes and cursed quietly.

'He just did it again, sir.'

'I heard. What have you got to say for yourself, brief?'

'I...' Kelly's voice dried to a croak. He could hear and even smell the coolness of the water. 'I want a brief.'

Whimper snatched back his pink OP7 before the sergeant could react and made some hasty amendments. Then with half a smile he took out a second one, scribbled down a few details and passed them both to Kelly.

Their eyes met, and they nodded in understanding.

Kelly jotted a few details on them and returned one to Whimper.

'We've engaged each other,' said the pig. 'I'm his brief.'

'And I'm his.'

'Who's my brief?' said the ram.

'I am,' they chorused, faltering a little.

The sergeant looked away a while, to scenes of blood and slaughter. He turned back. 'Okay, right then. Whimper of no family, I've arrested you for disobedience. So when I tell you to foggin' hand over your foggin' licence, you foggin' well hand it over.'

The pig took a small run-up to this hurdle and was off. 'Apropos the contest between officer of the Imperial Crown and Whimper with regard to revocation of licence to practise law within the city-state of Delphi within said empire,' he said, 'my client did state three times that he disputed the charge. He will duly proceed to defend the charge in a forum of law, under Section Five of the Fifth Article of the Books of Assessment, at a cost to the Crown to be deducted from the budget of the station when he wins.'

He'd taken up the rhythm of an easy pacing back and forth, with arms by habit in the classic posture of debate. 'Essentially, to prove Whimper stole a client of mine you'll need my testimony. And as his official brief, I'm barred from giving it.'

Kelly flaunted a superior smile. 'And now if I trust you'll drop the suspension, there should be no problem with my learned colleague representing my own case.'

'Hrrr, go on, then. Two shits and a bastard,' said Pergi through his teeth. 'Let's see you get out of that.'

Whimper took the stand. 'I too will be brief. The... 'S' words... in all likelihood were a couple of sneezes, and the onus will be on you to prove they weren't.'

'Constable and I both heard it clearly. You're foggin' done.'

'But the words of two against two is fair refute. My own testimony, in combination with Dirk-Adam's testimony, will throw sufficient doubt on your own.'

'A prisoner can't give evidence.'

'Well technically he can, this time. It's Wilson's principle of non-exclusivity of a criminal law and a crown administrative law case – Section Eight of the First Article of the Books of Evidence.'

Whimper watched for an enlightened gleam (or any gleam) in the cougar's eye; he decided there was none. 'And similarly for the 'B' word, you, sergeant, will have to produce a witness to testify both that it was my client who shouted it, and that he was standing this side of the threshold when he did so. All I remember seeing was a crowd of people.' A demure grin. 'Might I take it now that you'll consider both cases dropped?'

The reply was strips of pink paper fluttering to the stone floor. Outside, hawkers were beginning to appear with their mouth-watering barrows of roasting skewers. Whimper noticed a lamplighter, a tall, red dog, was methodically making his way around the inside of the pavilion, pouring a gout of acrid oil into each fitting and planting there the seeds of flame. Soon it became easier to see, and then progressively more so.

The pig was speaking. After a moment it occurred to Whimper that now only Kelly had the valid paperwork for the case.

'My client, Dirk-Adam of the Lano family, has just told me how he was drawn into a fight – set upon if you like – and this occurred on the Bollicutt steps, outside the pavilion of the moon pool.'

Pergi was equal to this: 'When I apprehended Sheep, he was inside, right there,' he pointed, 'on the floor, in the middle of a fist fight.'

'Perhaps, Sergeant,' Kelly said, 'we'll find by the light of the lamps some spots of blood on the steps, proving conclusively that the incident occurred outside the pool pavilion enclosure. Is that not so?' He shared his lopsided, supercilious smile with the ram, who felt compelled to be helpful.

'Yes, it was definitely on the steps, sir, and there's more blood in 'ere, too, where they banged me 'ead on the trough.'

Kelly covered his eyes and groaned a little.

Then Whimper, who'd been building a line of defence in his head, moved up to speed and joined them. A fine opening remark stumbled on a sharp stomach pang from of the aroma of roasting meat, but he swallowed and started again.

'Sergeant, whereas it has not been demonstrated that Kelly used profane words within the boundaries of a moon pool, we have all distinctly heard you use them. And as to whether Dirk-Adam fought here, there is no such dispute that you have committed the offence of littering!

'If the mechanisms of the legal and penal systems are to be invoked, Kelly and I will be duty bound to clog them up with as much red tape as possible. Now on the other hand, assuming you want a quick result so you can get on to ridding the streets of the real villains, here's what I suggest you write down.'

He scrutinised the ram, running his fingers over him where needed. When the constable drew out a pad, he dictated: 'Subject noted to be bleeding from the nose; trail of blood from steps to edge of pool consistent with single source; subject bruised around the face but more so on the back of the neck; absence of bruising or abrasions on the knuckles; defensive injuries noted on forearms; quality and style of clothing indicates he was going to a celebration, in which case absence of money is significant; absence of linings to the pockets is more so.

'Conclusion: Evidence of an attack or robbery – high. Evidence of having gotten in even a single effective punch – nil.

'In addition,' and here he turned to face the sergeant directly, 'the murmur from the crowd was that it was a couple of the Whitpetter boys, and that they were heading for the *Two Anchors*. At the risk of telling you your own job, you could gain great advantage by asking Dirk-Adam for a description of the attackers and then seeing if they're to be found there. If so, and if they have any of his identifiable property (a pocket lining, perhaps) then you'll have picked up a couple of nice arrests and whatever's left of Dirk-Adam's money.

'But when you do collar them, please don't ask me to be their brief – I've had a very trying day, and I doubt I'd be able to represent them to the best of my ability.'

'Very well,' said Pergi. 'Fine. The charge against Dirk-Adam of the Lano family is dropped.' He paused as he scrutinised a piece of paper with evil intent. 'Now this D904 puts Kelly of the Jambonne family as his brief. So congratulations, Pig – you get the fee.'

Grinning, Kelly turned to Dirk-Adam, saying: 'Like the sergeant said, you're a free man. Well I know you'll want to find out how things go at the *Two Anchors*, so I'll just give you this small account, and I'll call round to your place during the week to collect it. The fee is two shillings.'

'Two shillings!' exclaimed Dirk-Adam. 'For five minutes' work?'

Whimper came forth helpfully: 'You'll find a lot of that's taken up by accounting fees, lodgement fees, interest. You'd have found Kelly's base rate extremely cheap, if you had been in a position to pay cash.'

'Yeah, yes that's right. If you'd had the money on you, it would only have been, say, a shilling,' said Kelly.

'Or less,' continued Whimper. 'Half a shilling, even.'

'Half a shilling,' concurred the pig, 'for a brief contract. If you could have paid me now, that is. But I suppose–'

'Wait a minute,' said Whimper in feigned surprise to Dirk-Adam. 'The belt you're wearing – that particular type of buckle. I know that sort. It's very clever. Designed so you can tuck a spare fourthbit into it for emergencies.' The ram's eyes went wide as he remembered he still had a silver fourpenny piece on him, and produced it with pride.

'There you are, mistuh. Ha'f a shilling. Paid in full.'

Kelly fumed. The sergeant and constable were heading out the doorway, so Dirk-Adam hurried after them, pausing only to cry out: 'And that was durn' decent of yah, Whimper, workin' me a reduction like that. I'm gonna tell all muh friends and they're gonna all ask fer you by name!'

Whimper took a final look at the rippling, sparkling, undulating, undiluted hue of deep magenta... then took his leave. He set out into the night alone, to avoid Kelly and follow the muse of life's damn perversity. Heaven's dome was smoky red and cast about with embryonic stars.

He slowed down by a hawker's barrow, still lost in the far distance. A knuckle prodded his back.

'For services rendered,' said Kelly, handing him a couple of juicy skewers, and making him stop and blink for a moment.

And now five minutes later, under a glowing, golden lamp, the three-quarter silhouettes of two untidy individuals could be made out enjoying the modest fare of the lower class.

'I still think you're a liar, though,' one was saying. 'That'll never change.'

'And you're still a bastard.'

Whimper chewed in silence, smiling inwardly.

Hauntings Inc.

Lindy Cameron

Hauntings Inc.

I KNEW IT WAS A DREAM, EVEN WHILE IT CLUNG TO ME LIKE THE CORAL snakes coiling from the luxurious locks framing her exquisite face. It was the ABBA T-shirt, at odds with the Hades-dark gaze, that gave things away – well, along with Magda Szubanksi's voice muttering something about lamingtons.

Wake up. I lifted an edge of my eye mask for a second. It was dark – but I knew this was not my beautiful house.

Sleep more. Dead tired; sore bum.

But how did I get here? Ah, eight hours straddling a Yamaha after a rare interstate job.

Where's here exactly? The Gatehouse Guesthouse at Jindalee Reach, on the Victorian coast.

And why? New clients: Elinor Blake and her drop-dead gorgeous (irrelevant) granddaughter.

Disturbance. Must've left the TV on coz Magda was now yacking about lost birds.

Rewind. New job. Nina. The Virgin Mary – What?

Sleep. Slipping back... into Medusa's embrace.

Then

Scaffolding around the Virgin Mary half-way up Yungarup Ridge could be a portent – menacing or benign – if one was open to such things. And while I'm often in pursuit of supernatural shenanigans, seventeen years of hunting had uncovered not even a whisp. Mary's dilapidated bespoke-framework of six pitchforks held together-apart by snaking barbed-wired was, therefore, merely peculiar.

The weird little dolls on the cemetery's cliff-edge grave, however, were something else. Three straw bodies, legs of chicken wishbones, heads of wax, eyes made of small copper nails, pushed only half-way in. Creepy. And sharp, as I discovered when the one I picked up drew blood. I sucked my finger and kept wandering.

A lemon-scented gum waved its branches in the gentle breeze that slipped through the cemetery. It was oddly quiet, given I'd earlier noticed a veritable choir of magpies, a kookaburra, and an old tune on a far-off radio. That was in the carpark. But here, among the stone-laden dead, there was barely a sound. A lesser woman might have been spooked but, as I said, the dearth of spooks is what fuels my business *and* was why I was here. Not here here, in the cemetery; but here, en route to my new client, and killing time coz I was early.

The oldest grave in the 'Old' Kooringa Cemetery – professionally unkempt and gold-coin-donation entry – was dated 1862 and held one Frank Surtees, sailor, drowned off Pelican Bluff, aged 24. The last internment was Angela Gale, spinster aged 93, in 1949. I assumed the latter was taken by old age, unless she too had gone swimming off the treacherous Pelican Bluff.

I knew the danger of the bluff because the cemetery map (an extra gold coin), which folded out to encompass the newer sea-level township below and Jindalee Reach above, was alive with adjectives: *Dangerous, Perilous, Hazardous*. The descriptors for the town's geo-features, all in italics and in colour, implied every single one should be avoided. Except Jerusha's Leap which, in itself, sounded ominous but was marked *Tranquil*; in lilac.

The boneyard part of the map looked more like an x-marks-the-spot of treasure clues with icons indicating the professions of the people at rest therein. An anchor for poor Frank Surtees, and a quill for Miss Gale; a tankard for Maybelle Anders, innkeeper, 1901; a horseshoe for James Kilgour, blacksmith, dead these 150 years.

The map also stated that the Blake family – the region's founding dynasty, and my new clients – rather than being buried alongside Frank, Maybelle and the other 147 historically deceased, were interred in a graveyard on Jindalee Reach. Well, the dead ones were.

I checked my watch. Time to go meet the live ones.

'George!'

I admit it – I jumped. And swivelled. Because – *hello* – I was the only one here.

The voice, raspy but young, repeated the name, stretching it across two syllables. 'Geor-orge.'

Oh, maybe it's a bird? A crow squawking–

'Is that you, Geor-orge?'

Nope. Okay, someone in the bush looking for their dog, or husband; or there's a kid behind a headstone trying to scare the tourist.

Little shit.

I returned to the parking area, straddled and kicked my Virago into action, and slipped my helmet on. It took five minutes to travel the last six hairpin bends of Yungarup Ridge to the scenic lookout, where I pulled up outside the high stone fence that hid the mansion on Jindalee Reach. I looked back over the quirky, vibrantly-coloured houses of the original hillside settlement which, like the cemetery, clung to the ridge face with its steep switchbacks and three terraced streets.

On this stretch of the southern coast of Victoria, the sea crashed into precipitous cliffs or surged into small bays – some sheltered, mostly not – where a few hardy towns had been built by even hardier seafarers and farming colonists on land they just decided was theirs.

I removed and placed my helmet on the tank between my legs, did a U-ey and rode through the huge open gates, by the small two-storey gatehouse, and on to Jindalee Reach and its 160-year-old mansion which was, I had read, a rambling–

Woah! I slowed to a crawl.

Stands of ancient she oak and paperbarks stood watch along the far east side of the plateau, while a western windbreak of gnarly moonah trees seemingly grew out of the end of the front stone wall and just kept on going – right over the cliff.

And there between the two, almost 30 metres away in front of me, and way too close to the edge of *the entire continent*, sat a sprawling many-storied marvel of a House – *Yes, house with a capital 'H' because turrets!* – of the kind every adventurous kid dreams of spending a mysterious holiday in.

I laughed at the hope I'd be greeted by a big scruffy dog and his four young human friends.

The House loomed on the brink of the Reach as if it had risen, according to its own rules, from the very ground itself. It was stone and red brick and timber, with wrought-iron balustrades, on *so many* verandas, and a widow's walk atop an obstacle-course of roof-levels, a mix of corrugated iron and tiles.

I followed the meandering drive alongside a pedestrian arbour of clematis in full bloom, which snaked all the way from the gatehouse to the House-house. Beyond its covered path was a host of smaller old buildings.

As I parked my bike and headed for the front door, I heard a sing-song voice calling, '*Hecketyhoo, Hecketyhoo, she's here at last, Hecketyhoo,*' and expected an excited girl on a hobby horse to come galloping into view but – nothing.

Before I got to use the owl knocker, the front door swung open to reveal a tall angular man with a flattop haircut, a lantern jaw and a diamond stud in his right lobe.

'Welcome Ms Arden, séance specialist and ghost buster.'

I smiled. 'And yet oddly, not here to bust anything.'

'True. I surmise this will be a curious weekend for you.'

Understatement. It was, after all, weird for a debunker to be hired not to discredit the thing their client was hellbent on doing. But even this was just another Thursday in the life of an investigator and exposer of alleged paranormal hooey; aka Lucy the Demystifier, Uncloaker, Raiser of the Veil, Looker Behind the Curtain.

Shut up!

"I'm the estate manager, Andrew Block. Just call me Block. If you'd like to follow me.'

'Righto, Block,' said I – Lucy Arden, Private Investigator.

Now

There were two voices: Magda S and Sean Connery. Must be an old TV talk show coz they never did a movie together. Did they? Suppose anything's possible in a dream.

'She's one of us, Finbar,' Magda's voice said.

'What makes you say that?' said 'Finbar' with Sean's voice.

'She's a ranga.'

I slowly opened my eyes. *Gah – why can't I see?* Oh. I was face down, head under the pillow.

'Go on Finbar, do it.'

'You know I can't without preparation.'

'Well, I could, but she might freak out.'

Why would Magda freak anyone out? Hang on a sec. There's no TV in this room.

It occurred to me maybe some kids had invaded my room, as they're wont to do when it's not appropriate.

Sure – kids with the voices of Sean and Magda.

'How about you sit close, so it's you she sees first and I'll tap her on the chin to wake her,' the Magda said.

Before *anyone* could do any chin-tapping I rolled over to confront my interlopers and came face to face with the Magda's chin-tapping – um – finger?

In a nanosecond I was vertical.

Feet on my pillow.

Back flat to the wall.

Arms outstretched, also pressed to the wallpaper.

Wits hanging from the ceiling like a startled cartoon cat.

There were no people in the room.

There *were* two creatures on my bed: one very-very VERY large and floofy ginger cat; and a gargantuan Huntsman spider.

The latter had tucked and rolled backwards when I flung the doona off in my bid to escape backwards to nowhere. The former hadn't moved an inch – except for a now-raised eyebrow.

What the hell kind of cat can raise an eyebrow?

And why can I see through said cat with the raised–

Holy snapping duck poo!

Sean Connery's voice said: 'Well that could've gone better.'

Magda's voice said: 'I hate it when they react like that.'

I looked about for the humans; the ones who were talking. There was no one.

My adrenaline was still arguing about flighting or fighting. But clearly, I couldn't run from the room while my wits were still AWOL, so I just stood there – twitching.

Get a grip. Dream. Ghost Cat. Hand-size Spider. Nightmare.

Or I'm hallucinating. Well, I was exhausted.

I shut my eyes and slid down the wall.

'She's going again,' said the Magda. The Spider. The talking Magda-spider.

Then

Where was I? Oh yes. Lucy Arden, Private Investigator. Spook Debunker.

I carry two business cards: one for everyday clients; and another for those folks needing a bit of intellectual biffo for odd predicaments of the supernatural kind. Regardless of the client's state of mind – sensible or spooked – I have serious personal bonnet bees about swindlers of any kind. It's my mission (when not engaged in the tedious surveillance of cheating spouses) to expose and discredit those frauds who aim to bilk the vulnerable and gullible. And, yes, even the stupid.

Con artists, charlatans, pretenders – look up your own thesaurus – make my hit list. Naturally, somewhere in my past, there's a good reason why it's my life's mission to expose those who prey on the emotions of the grieving and defenceless but, suffice to say, I am dedicated.

Sometimes the bad guys (gender irrelevant) in my clients' lives are dodgy plumbers, moneylenders or house cladders; other times they're psychics, spiritualists, mediums or clairvoyants.

I've only once been ineffective at reclaiming a client's money from a shifty tradesman or psychic; but had yet to fail in the de-haunting department. I am indeed Melbourne's primo ghost buster – in the sense that I smash any idea that spectres or ghouls are even a thing.

And, as an expert in proving the peculiar and spooky is merely odd and explainable, I find my clients are often the strangest things about the not-hauntings. They range from those freaked out by strange house noises, to people haunted by guilt or bad memories, or those desperate for an impossible connection to things lost. The latter are always disappointed. I was looking forward to finding out if my famously eccentric client, Elinor Blake, was merely odd or completely whackadoo.

Just-call-me-Block escorted me from the vestibule, down a wide hallway to a broad staircase of seven steps up to a landing from which a meandering carpeted corridor led along to another seven stairs on a bend. The hall continued on and around to the left but Block did not. He opened a heavy wooden door which revealed a latticed metal gate to a small lift. At his gesture, I stepped inside the tiny space and leant against the rear wall to assert a gap between my front and his back as we rode up two floors to–

Oh, my grandma's knickers!

It was one thing to realise a childhood dream of visiting a House like this but another thing completely to enter the physical manifestation of a place I'd visited in my dreams. Dreams of the asleep kind. Dreams I'd had all my life. Most recently… last week.

Don't be ridiculous. This is just hyper-effective déjà vu.

Scary vu is what it is. Don't think déjà vu pinballs around your brain with every new thing you look at.

'Are you okay, Ms Arden?'

I snapped my attention back to Block and nodded. 'Yes, it's just, this room looks, um–'

'Like a museum run by a lunatic?' Block finished.

'Familiar,' I said, at the same time as another voice said: 'I heard that, Andrew.'

'And magnificent,' I finished, as Block called out, 'Was not implying you are the lunatic, Aunt Elinor.'

I trailed after Block, my attention snapping this way and that like a red-dot watching cat.

Curated by a loon or not, this was a gallery of eclectic fabulousness. The timber-panelled maze of a room featured laddered bookshelves to a mezzanine level and up again to the vaulted ceiling all along its north, or landside, wall. The other side, judging by the natural light overhead, was obviously an island down the centre of a much larger space. It hosted random alcoves lined with bookshelves and set with club chairs and Persian rugs, or display cases full of – *oh, stuck insects; oh again, exquisitely carved scarab beetles* – or Wunderkammers loaded with the weirdness that such cabinets are known for. Pedestals and glass-fronted cabinets held skulls, both human and animal, antique pistols, gravy boats, and pocket watches; scary surgical instruments, botanical and mineral specimens, and feathers. There were orreries, sextants and compasses; steamer trunks and top hats; and everywhere small carvings of Ouroboros, cats and owls.

Against the wall at the end was a magnificent life-sized bronze statue of Medusa – with an exquisitely beautiful face crowned and framed by writhing snakes. I could not take my eyes off her.

Look away. Look away.

'Ms Arden, may I introduce you to–'

'Give her a moment, Andrew. She's being seduced.'

'Seduced? I'm what?' I forced myself to turn; not just to look away from Medusa but to physically turn from her, only to be blinded by the light that bathed another huge space and backlit everything in it. All I could see were the silhouettes of highbacked chairs, standard lamps, more statuary, and painting easels that filled the foreground. Beyond that was a mind-blowing view of Bass Strait through a panoramic window the height of a movie screen but much wider.

'Feel free to put your sunglasses on, dear, while your eyes adjust.'

I did just that and the instant polarisation revealed a woman, on the elderly side of mature, sitting on a chaise longue before a low table on which was a platter scones, cups and a large alpaca-shaped coffee pot.

The window, another six metres behind her, obviously extended back along the ocean side of the House; verifying the lunatic's museum was U-shaped.

Block tried again: 'Ms Arden, may–'

'Run along Andrew, we girls can muddle through. But if you see Nina, do tell her to hurry up.'

My client, Miss Elinor Blake, a study in relaxed elegance, smiled warmly as she reached for the coffee pot. 'Milk or sugar, dear?'

'Just milk please, Miss Blake.'

'Please, call me Elinor.'

I nodded as I took the cup. 'This room, your house, this view, it's–'

'Weird and wonderful?' She offered the plate of scones.

I smiled and took one. Using the tongs.

'We're waiting on Nina,' Elinor said, smothering the two halves of her scone in raspberry jam before handing me the little dish to do the same. 'I swear my granddaughter will miss her own funeral.'

A soft chuckle came from, I think, the other end of a burgundy-upholstered couch directly in front of the window. Whoever it was, was just out of view. As the sound drew no reaction from Elinor, I checked the portrait gallery on the wall behind her in case the paintings had suspicious eye holes. I realised my host, her arm extended with the whipped cream, was looking at me oddly.

'Sorry, I thought someone might be spying on us from a hidden corridor behind the paintings.'

'They'd have to be whippet-thin, or floating, as there's nothing beyond that wall but open air. There are many hidden passages throughout the house and grounds, Lucy, this was after all a smuggler's house, but not in the walls of Jericho's Folly, as we call my great-great-grandfather's, um, folly.'

'Smugglers! So I have walked into an Enid Blyton mystery.'

'Oh yes!' Elinor laughed, glancing towards the window couch. She returned her attention to me without comment. The hidden person, however, had quite clearly said: 'The Cliff House of Doom'.

'What shall we call our adventure, Lucy? The Smugglers one is already taken.'

'Five Hold a Séance at Jindalee Reach?' I suggested.

'Perfect. Except our practice séance will be a Secret Seven plot or, counting us, a Ten Again adventure. We're being joined by some Kooringa Councillors: the Mayor, Alistair Budwin; our GP, Dr Helen

Cooper; three new councillors; and, god help us – and I say that with some irony – Father John Carter, who wants to ensure we don't open a portal to hell.'

I shook my head. 'Forget Enid; that's a line-up for an Agatha Christie novel. Elinor, why on earth have you hired a debunker to not debunk your séance?'

Elinor waved a hand. 'Over Sunday brunch two months ago, Nina read aloud the article about you from the weekend magazine. That sparked Andrew's idea that our house is suitably spooky enough to host séances to raise extra money during the annual Medieval Fair.'

'Money for what?'

'To help fund our new Writers' House project, which in turn is aimed at keeping the wolf from our many doors.'

Elinor registered my expression and elaborated. 'Jindalee Reach is a money pit, Lucy. We are asset rich but cash poor. We've even been trying to sell some waterfront land down in the town but seven prospective and enthusiastic buyers inexplicably changed their minds.'

'But your Medieval Fair must bring in buckets with over a thousand people every year.'

Elinor nodded. 'But we are merely the hosts. Yes, the Kingdom of Aragul pay us for the use of our grounds and buildings, and we provide dormitory accommodation for those who don't want to camp, but we're always looking for innovative ways to capitalise on those crowds so we can continue to live in our own home.'

A little snort escaped before I corralled it. An almost-echo came from the couch. Elinor and I both glanced in that direction; she glared at – nothing; I caught sight of a fluffy ginger tail.

'Sorry,' I said. 'The idea that a séance is an innovative fundraiser–'

'Well, there must be money in it, Lucy. The magazine said you were busy debunking all those charlatans for relieving people of their hard-earned cash. Another scone, dear? Anyhoo, Andrew's original haunted house notion segued into Nina's idea of hiring you, partly, to make our séance as real as possible.'

I accepted the jam dish that followed the scone. 'They're never real, Elinor, hence the debunking.'

'You've never had a ghostly experience then?'

'Not in seventeen years of doing this.'

'I see. That's interesting.' Elinor seemed surprised but not disappointed.

'Have you ever been to a séance, Elinor?'

'No dear. I've never had the need. I feel like my forebears and late siblings are here with me all the time. I suppose it's the nature of this old house. So, Andrew is right about that at least.'

'You keep laying this idea on your granddaughter and nephew as if you don't approve—'

'Andrew is not my nephew; he's my uncle's very-young second wife's stepson from her first marriage. He spent his boarding school holidays here and had to call us something, so we became Aunts Elinor and Jerusha. He's now our estate manager, two days a fortnight.'

'You said partly for the séance?'

Elinor nodded. 'I did. You no doubt researched us and our town, before venturing all the way here from Melbourne.'

'Byron Bay.'

'Pardon?'

"I've just ridden down from Byron Bay.'

'Oh, my goodness, you must be exhausted. Were you holidaying?'

'A hexorcism in a hippie colony. It was a long ride, so I may need a nanna-nap before tonight's shenanigans.'

'Of course, dear. I'll ring for Andrew to show you to your room.' Elinor reached for a bell chord beside her. 'While we're waiting, what did you learn about us?'

I took a breath. 'Kooringa is famous as a haven for artists, writers, thespians and musicians – as befitting a town founded in the 1860s by an opera singer and her sea captain husband. Your ancestors, Isabella and Jericho Blake – who sound amazing by the way – earned a fortune from farming and trade, but the family always contributed to the rich cultural life of the town that grew up around this, their great house.'

Elinor raised a finger. 'Always, except for the two decades when Jason Blake was head of our family. The moment he died – and yes, somewhat suspiciously in a wild storm in 1983 – his sister Louisa and later two of his nieces, Jerusha and I, began restoring the family name to its previous benevolent reputation.

'In recent years, however, Kooringa has attracted a multitude of tree-and-sea-changers some of whom want to hijack our cultural endeavours for their own aggrandisement. You know, ex-big-city gallery owners, retired publishers and private school principals who've gathered into an expat clique hellbent on taking charge.

Of everything. Starting with possibly sabotaging our cultural committee.'

I gave Elinor an *oh-I-get-it* look. 'I'm not really here for the séance at all, am I?'

Elinor smiled. 'It *is* more your private investigator skills we need, but we needed a cover story for you being here. We actually have two cases that need solving, which is why our invitation was open-ended. Nina will fill you in on the main reason; but the other does involve some of those at this evening's gathering.

'You see, Lucy, our ulterior motive with this 'rehearsal' séance is to scare the bejeezus out of them.'

I snorted coffee out my nose. The invisible couch person guffawed. The ginger cat's tail swished to and fro. And Elinor paused, mid-lift of the Alpaca pot, and tried not to laugh.

I regained my composure with the aid of a serviette. 'What do you expect from me?'

'To observe, listen and later investigate whoever you think needs the dirt dug on them.'

Now

'If you'd care to open your eyes, we can explain.' Sean Connery's voice was soothing.

'Can't you do that with my eyes shut? I don't need to see through you to know I've either lost my mind or that ghosts are real.'

'I'm not a ghost, Lucy Arden. I'm a Pan*Dim*Be.'

I opened one eye. The cat – a ginger Maine Coon with regal snout and neck ruff – now seemed more translucent than see-though. Even sitting down, his polydactyl front paws stretched out in front like a sphinx, he was easily 35 cm high from the bed to the tips of his glorious, tufted ears.

'What the hell is a Pan*dim*be?'

'A pan-dimensional-being.'

'Sounds like a fancy word for a ghost. Or a nervous breakdown.'

'Finbar is not dead; so he can't be a ghost.' It was the Magda-Huntsman talking.

I opened my other eye. She was sitting near my right foot. I resisted the urge to flinch; or kick her off the bed. She was so – *by all the gods* – so very-very big.

'But you're not all *here*,' I said to him.

'I can be, it just takes some thought,' Finbar said.

I glared at him. 'Why the hell didn't you do that *thinking* before scaring me half to death?'

'Perhaps we thought a ghostbuster wouldn't be such a scaredy bat,' said the Magda-spider.

'Are you kidding me?' I pulled my legs up and sat with them crossed. On the pillow. Away from her. 'It's the whole talking spider and apparently-not-ghost cat thing that's weird.'

'Perhaps we should introduce ourselves.'

I waved consent.

'My name is Finbar Patrick O'Malley.'

'That's as Irish as a leprechaun,' I interrupted. 'Why do you talk like Sean Connery?'

'Do I?' The cat looked bewildered.

'We watch a lot of television,' the spider said. 'Love James Bond.'

As if that explained anything.

'And Thor, and Wonder Woman,' she continued, 'and *Midsomer Murders*, *Naked and Afraid–*' Finbar flicked his tail across my legs into the spider's face. 'And *Stha Twek*.'

'I am a pan-dimensional being, Lucy Arden. I can travel the dimensional spaces.'

The ferret of confusion in my mind took to running on its wheel. 'To go where? To do what? What does that even mean?'

'In 1873, the sailing ship I was on found a portal, which transported us here – just off the coast – into the middle of a terrible storm. I was the only survivor, rescued by Jericho Blake; Elinor's three-time great grandfather.'

'Were you a cat then?'

Finbar raised an eyebrow. 'Of *course* I was. Dimensional travel doesn't change who you are. Just how you are.'

I shook my head. 'Strange portal? Shipwreck? Are you sure you're not a ghost? And this is your delusion?'

'I am not a ghost, Lucy Arden. For someone who thinks the shades aren't real, you really want me to be one.'

'Because a 140-something year-old *PanDimBe* makes so much more sense.'

'And yet a ship's cat I was, on the *Lady Wiscasset* out of Maine, trading between the Spice Islands and Japan, when we were becalmed then drifted into the southern reach of the Dragon Triangle.'

My incredulous face prefaced my, 'The what now?'

'The Japanese call it *Ma No Umi* – or the Sea of the Devil. It's a major dimensional portal.'

'Like the Bermuda Triangle?'

'No, that's a gravity well,' said the talking bloody spider, with her red-orange abdomen, half the size of my palm, swaying behind her large thoracic-whatsit that held her eight bloody legs – giving her a full span, left-legs tip to right, of about 20 centimetres.

Help.

'Many vessels in the deep-deep there,' she was saying.

'And planes,' I said.

'Only low flyers. The gravity well has a magnetic lid to repel things above it. You'd be surprised how many broken aeroplanes are scattered in the space debris circling Earth.'

'How many portals are there?'

'Two large ones: one in the sea, one in South America; and lots of smaller portals everywhere,' Finbar said.

'Everywhere?'

The Spider waved a front leg seaward. 'Like out there near Emu Knot where Finbar and only half his ship arrived.'

I was so not going to ask why whateveri-it-was wasn't an emu.

'And in Jericho's Folly, in the main house; in the Cairo Museum, the *Windsor Hotel* in Melbourne, the Queen's bedroom at Buck–'

'Okay. I get it, Finbar.'

I turned my attention to the scary bloody Huntsman with the elegant – *shut up!* – orange and black legs who, I had to admit, was quite beautiful for a–.

What the hell? I am losing my mind!

'Are you a PanDimBe Tiger Huntsman then?' I asked her.

She rocked back onto her hind four legs and waved at me with all the rest of them. 'Do I *look* like a huntsman?'

My mouth tried very hard not to say so many things. I finally shrugged.

'A huntsman,' she repeated. 'A great big manly man with a beard and broad shoulders in a flannel shirt – with an axe?'

I laughed. 'Fair call.'

'We are Gresha,' she said. 'All of us. Cousins within the Gresha.'

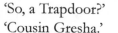

'So, a Trapdoor?'

'Cousin Gresha.'

'White Tail?

'Cannibal bastard. But still Gresha.'

'How do you distinguish between–'

'It's a human thing to want to make the difference.'

'Do you have your own name?'

'Allow me please,' Finbar said. The spider re-settled her front legs. 'Lucy Arden, I'd like you to meet Hecate Who.'

I inhaled deeply but quietly. 'It's a pleasure to meet you, Hecketyhoo,' I said. 'I think I heard–'

'My running noise,' the spider said gleefully. 'But my *name* has two parts: Hecate – like the triple goddess of witchcraft and the underworld; and Who, like the Doctor.'

'She thinks she's a Time Lord,' Finbar said.

I side-eyed her. 'Why?'

'Because I'm immortal and I regenerate.'

'Don't most Hunts– Gresha regenerate?'

'I am 75 years old.'

Finbar cocked his head. 'Slight accident with a portal while playing chasey in Jericho's Folly.'

'Did you two wake me up for a reason.' I asked. *Am I in fact awake?*

'Time to get dressed for the séance,' Finbar said. 'And to meet Nina in the Old Wing first.'

Ah, the gorgeous Nina Blake.

Then

'Are you suspicious of anyone in particular?' I asked Elinor.

'Dr Cooper suspects the Mayor of quashing our land sales; while I think two of the newbies are in cahoots with an outside developer.'

'So the doctor's in on your scheme?'

'Yes, but she's the only one. Helen and I have known each other since kindergarten.'

'Who is leading this séance?'

'I am.'

The voice came from behind me.

'Where on earth have you been, darling? Lucy and I have had time to solve the world's problems.'

Nina Blake moved to Elinor's side of the table. 'Time well spent then, Gran.'

Oh my. Oh. My. Goddess.

My brain began sparking in all the joyous places where cats and chocolate and *Dancing Queen* live.

Nina and I stared at each other in—

Wonder.

Well, that's what I felt, because Nina Blake was wildly familiar yet completely unknown to me.

And who the hell stole my breath?

Nina's face did that thing where it sort of pulls back the littlest bit when one is taken-aback but doesn't want to show it. I suspect my face had everything written all over it – in giant fluorescent type. I knew I'd never met her before but also knew, beyond doubt, I'd known her forever.

'And *there* it is,' said the annoying couch person.

'Sorry I'm late, Lucy. I'm thrilled you're going to help us find our friends.' She took a seat next to Elinor.

'Friends?' My gaze swivelled between the two women. 'What friends?'

'I was waiting for you, Ms Tardy Britches.'

'Charming, Gran.' Nina flashed her green eyes – *do you know how rare green eyes are* – at me. 'In the last few weeks several people on the Ridge have lost their pets.'

'I'm not a pet detective.'

Nina laughed. 'We know that, Lucy. But these are no ordinary animals; and have probably been abducted rather than just, you know, lost. Angel Lorrigan's diamond python disappeared from its enclosure; Michael Lowe's pair of talking sulphur-crested cockatoos vanished from his aviary; and three echidnas were definitely stolen from Liz Ward's sanctuary.'

'All natives,' I noted.

'We think someone's stealing them to sell elsewhere.'

'It's good you thought to employ me forever then, because that's no small job.'

Nor my field of expertise.

'Any suspects?'

'No, except we assume they must be local to even know about Angel's Igor.'

'You rang?'

I jumped at the extra voice in the room – behind me again.

'Oh do stop lurching around, Andrew,' Elinor said. 'Our guest had an awfully long ride here on her motorcycle, so please escort her to the gatehouse. We girls can get together again at about 4.30 to get organised for tonight.'

Nina stood, as I did. 'It's been lovely to meet you, Lucy.'

'Likewise, Nina.' I reached for her offered hand. 'And Elinor,' I barely managed, before the part of my brain that revels in wild thunderstorms, barrel rolls in a bi-plane, and singing *Bohemian Rhapsody* live on stage with *Queen*, also started dancing a tango. *Blimey!*

'I've never even been in a bi-plane,' I said. Aloud.

Nina tried not to smile. Elinor said, 'Pardon?'

'Sorry. Random thought – open mouth. Bad combo.'

'Love struck,' said the couch voice.

Oh. The couch *person*. The woman – in her fifties, maybe – with a spectacular mound of hair, and wearing a voluminous psychedelic caftan had finally slid into view. No one else paid her any attention. So neither did I.

Now

'You look fine. Time to go,' Hecate said, as I dragged a brush through my hair. My *red* hair, that she'd insisted on likening to *her* hairy red-orange abdomen.

'Shoes would be a good idea, Lucy Arden,' Finbar noted.

'Well, stop rushing me.' Black trousers, white shirt, comfy shoes. 'And why are we meeting with Nina beforehand?'

'Because we all have to tell you about Arlo and George. Come now,' Finbar commanded.

I don't know why, but I obeyed and took off after them – all the while saying, 'Wait a sec, stop wait,' – out of my room and down the stairs to the kitchen where there was now an open, hinged floor-door, revealing the gaping entry to—

I skidded to a stop.

'Hecate, jump on the light switch please,' Finbar said, truly invisible in the darkness below.

A vague idea of illumination pushed up at me. At least I could see the see-through cat again. 'We're gonna be late,' he said.

'Wait – give me a second. I'm still freaking out here.'

'Why?' Hecate asked, somersaulting back into the kitchen.

It was all I could do not to respond to my yammering pulse by grabbing the nearest plastic container and dealing with the bloody Huntsman like I always did at home: cover, contain, run for the front door, and chuck everything into the garden to add to Tupperware village under the snowball tree.

'Why?' I waved my hand at her, then both hands at each of them. 'Because, talking PanDim-Cat and Spider-Grisha thing-people are treating me like I *haven't* lost my mind.'

'Well, you haven't, have you?' Finbar said.

I'm sure my eyes were wild, because the ferret in my brain had left the wheel and was running loose in my cranium now.

'I think she's still scared of us, Finbar.'

'No I'm not,' I insisted. 'Ok, yes I am. But it's an irrational fear; I'm aware of that. I'm a thousand times bigger than you are. And yet here I am witless with absurd anxiety even though I know there's no reason to be afraid of you.'

'But you're a brave ghostbuster, Lucy Arden,' Finbar said, missing the point entirely.

Hecate, however, was wounded to her tiny core. 'Of me? Just me?'

Damn. Now I felt guilty for hurting a spider's feelings. I sucked it all up, like a good princess, and took the stairs, forcing myself to meet the Hunts– the Gresha's gaze as I passed her at so-many-eyes level.

I joined Finbar in the tunnel, whereon the biggest cat I've ever met led the way, his ginger butt swinging like a floofy duster.

Hecate joined us – cantering along the wall, at my elbow height. And I do mean cantering – not scary-spider-scuttling.

'Technically, Finbar, I courageously bust bogus mediums and fake psychics because, you know, there's no such thing as ghosts.'

'Oh darling, have we got a surprise for you.'

'What?'

'Nothing.'

'Finbar, you said you're not a ghost.'

'I'm not, Lucy Arden. I promise.'

'And you know me now, so how can you be scared?' Hecate veered higher, for a moment, to address me.

We came to a fork in the tunnel, the walls of which were carved rock, sometimes brick, and occasionally timber-lined, and lit by golf ball-sized globes every five metres. I was slightly miffed my first experience in a secret smugglers' tunnel was being hijacked by an impossible, and needy, talking spider.

Bloody hell.

I stopped walking. 'I'm sorry, Hecate. Have you seen the Alien movies?'

'Of course. Finbar and I love Jonesy the cat.'

'Good, so you know the face-huggers. When I was seven my shitty brother woke me one morning by putting a Huntsman on me. On. My. Face.'

'Oh no, what an awful thing to do to a Gresha.'

Finbar chuckled. 'Hecate darling, the awful thing was done to Lucy.'

'Oh. Right. I suppose those city Gresha can be uncouth.'

'Um–' I began.

'Remember that time when I was still learning to control my manifestations,' Finbar said, 'and I manifested right on top of you and didn't realise for half an hour.'

'Oh blerg. That was horrible. I couldn't breathe. So much fur. So dark. So – *oh*.'

I raised an eyebrow. 'I'm afraid *that* sp– Grisha back then didn't survive our encounter. I flung it from my face, it hit the wall–'

'La-la-la,' Hecate sang. 'Poor cousin.'

'Again, I'm sorry. But the point is I was traumatised not just by a spidery face-hugger but because I was responsible for Hunts-manslaughter.'

I swear Hecate waved her front leg – arm/appendage – as if she was giving me a there-there. 'So fear and guilt, and still scaredy.'

'Yes,' I nodded. 'Give me time.'

Steep stone-cut steps hidden *inside* a cupboard brought us – well Finbar and I – up to a landing where we next climbed a spiral staircase; while Hecate Who, the parkour stunt-Gresha, barely touched anything en route.

We emerged from behind a sliding bookshelf – *yes!* – into a ballroom-sized space with sheet-covered furniture around the edges, a pool table in the middle, and Nina Blake in silhouette at the panoramic windows.

'Come-come, Lucy Arden,' Finbar said, as if I was reluctant to cross the room.

'Wonderful,' Nina said. 'I see you've all met.'

I slowed when I got to five steps from the window. The view out – as in straight out – was stupendous: a rolling, heaving expanse of ocean in every direction, unobstructed all the way to the far horizon. Nothing between us and Tasmania. I gripped the back of a chair. I did not want to see down, because down was sickeningly vertiginous and that way madness waited.

'Uh-oh, scary heights,' Hecate said, planting herself on the window glass.

'Lucy dear, are you okay?' Nina asked.

'Yes. Fine,' I lied. 'But who the hell builds a house this close to a cliff edge, on the coastline of one of the most treacherous straits in the country?'

'Most perilous in the world. Bass Strait contains hundreds of shipwrecks.'

'The question remains,' I said.

Nina smiled. 'A crusty old mariner confined to land but determined to live out his days with salt-spray on his face.'

'What's wrong with a right-on-the-sand house? And why do we have to stand so close to the edge?'

Nina tucked a strand of auburn hair behind her left ear. 'Gran doesn't sleep well and often goes up to the Folly at night to paint. Lately she's noticed the Emu Knot lantern has been lit on moonless nights.'

I frowned. 'Is it not an emu or not a lantern?'

'What? Oh, Emu *Knot* – with a *k*. Come closer. It's okay, I won't let you fall.' Nina offered her hand, which I clasped. For dear life. And because I *really* wanted to.

'The window is closed,' Finbar said, jumping onto the wide sill. 'She can't fall.'

'Silly boy,' Hecate said.

I took the last step to stand beside the love of my life– *What?*

No. That *is* what it felt like.

That the love of my life – or all of my lives – was holding my hand. Against her heart.

'What the hell did your grandmother put in my coffee?' I asked softly.

'Must have put it in mine too,' Nina murmured.

'Magic mushrooms in the jam would explain – everything,' I said, waving my free hand between Nina *and* the talking animals.

'Why is everyone whispering?' Finbar asked.

'Love struck,' Hecate stated. Just like the woman in Jacob's Folly had done.

'Well pleflooffer,' Finbar exhaled. 'We have work to do.'

Nina let go of my hand, gave me a pair of binoculars and nodded towards a tiny island – more a rocky protuberance – about 200 metres offshore. 'Emu Knot.'

'Looks more like a wombat,' I said.

Through the binocs I could, however, see how the lumpy 'emu' on the islet once had a head. And beside those tumbled-down rocks on the east side was a small lighthouse. Or, rather, a conical-shaped stone thing maybe four-metres tall.

'Once upon a time that lantern was the only warning vessels had of a hazard close to shore,' Nina said.

'Wouldn't it still serve that purpose on a moonless night?' I swept the binocs right towards Whatnow Bay and the sea level township of Kooringa.

'There's a fully-fledged lighthouse on Kilgour Point,' Nina said, pointing vaguely in the direction of somewhere else.

'So?' I shrugged. 'Couldn't anyone boat out there and light the thing?'

'Not really. Emu Knot, which we own by the way, has only two possible approaches: a dangerous spot on the far side; or a direct line out from our dock, directly below Jericho's Folly. Boats can't pass across between the shore and the Knot, as there's a double rocky spine, eight metres apart, lying just below the surface that can only be seen at low tide.'

'So the mystery then, is *why* would anyone want to light a tiny lantern? Is this connected to either of the cases I'm here for, or is this a bonus mystery for the Fabulous Four of us?'

Nina laughed. 'Well you *are* here for a week at least.'

'You said *our* dock; does that mean *your* boat?'

'Yes. *Betsy* lives in Harrow's Cave, moored to a floating pontoon that moves with the tide.'

'Perhaps someone in your household takes *Betsy* for a spin. In the dark. In secret. To light a lamp. For no good reason.'

'It's not Nina; she's terrified of boats,' Hecate said.

'And she would've told us,' Finbar added.

'We have no live-in staff except during the festival,' Nina added. 'And Andrew was only here two of the many times Gran saw the light.'

'There's no moon this week,' Hecate noted.

'Lucky I'm here right now then,' I said.

Finbar thumped his back foot on the windowsill. 'We have to find Arlo and George'.

'Is George a red heeler?' I asked – and was suddenly the centre of everyone's attention.

'How do you–'

'Dropped into the cemetery en route, heard someone calling a George.'

'You *did*?' my three companions said in unison.

'Um – yeah. And then again, when I got to my bedroom. I opened my window to see who was calling.'

'And there was nothing there, right?' Finbar said.

'No. There was a kid called Timmy – in itself weird: *George and Timmy* – looking for his dog.'

'And you saw him?' Nina asked.

'Yes. He seemed surprised too. I told him my eyesight was actually pretty good for a 40-year-old even if he was a good distance away in the bush.'

'Haven't seen Timmy for a year. We thought he'd moved on,' Hecate said.

'I'd never actually met him,' Nina said.

'How do you know his dog is missing then?'

'Because George is *our* friend. And he's only been gone three days,' Finbar said.

'And two nights,' Hecate added.

'And Arlo?'

'Arlo is George's raven.'

'George the dog has his own raven?' I asked, with a prickly awareness I may never get my life back from crazy town.

'They're besties. Like Finbar and I.'

'Arlo can't fly,' Nina said.

'He can,' Hecate stated. 'Just short bursts. Mostly in panic.'

'We should go join Gran,' Nina said.

As we walked, I asked, 'Can Arlo and George talk to us, like you two?'

'George talks doofus,' Finbar said. 'Well, he's a dog.'

'Arlo is multi-lingual,' said Hecate. 'Speaks several Birds, and English with his voice; and whatever this is *we* all do, with his mind.'

'And who does he sound like?'

'Frank Sinatra,' said Finbar and Hecate.

'No – Elvis,' Nina insisted.

My gaze switched between the Gresha, the Maine Coon and the Human. 'Okay, to me you two sound like Sean Connery and Magda Szubanski.'

Nina's laugh was raucous and delightful. 'Gough Whitlam and Judy Dench.'

I snort laughed; not delightful at all.

I waggled my index finger between the talking creatures, who looked at each other and – I swear – came over all bashful.

'John Steed and Emma Peel,' Finbar mumbled.

'I honestly can't decide if I'm in a parallel universe or a lunatic asylum,' I admitted. 'When did you last see your friends?' I asked.

'Tuesday evening; said they had a lead on the Missings,' Hecate explained.

'And?'

'That's it,' Finbar said. 'George is rather excitable–'

'Understatement.'

'He came lollygagging up to us–'

'Bounding in thirty-three directions.'

'Hec, stop interrupting. George ran up, shouted: *We have clues. You'll never guess*, and ran off again, with Arlo riding him like a Bronco-bird.'

I looked at each of my companions in turn, and then again for good measure. 'So I have a missing friends case; a stolen snake, birds and echidna case; a likely unrelated lamp lighting mystery; and some suspect town councillors,' I said.

'Yes,' said everyone else.

'Okay, Let's make a start with the séance and see if we can't scare the truth – or wits – out of someone.'

More now than before

Two hours later – having met our co-conspirator, Dr Helen Cooper, in the fabulous hexagonal room set up for the séance – I was sitting on a purple velvet couch in said room, with Elinor and Helen. The latter, a charming woman with a snow-white bob, wasn't at all perturbed by

Hecate Who, who'd settled on the carved table beside her. She'd also stroked Finbar's ears before he morphed back into almost invisibility and was now just a slight shimmer of camouflaged cat against the also-purple drapes beside me.

I was assured that no one else in the room – even the not-nephew Block, whose idea this all was – thought tonight's entertainment was anything other than a run-through of something that might be a money-spinner for the Blakes. They all seemed delighted to be taking part in such a fun evening.

I'd been presented as the Expert Observer and politely introduced to the participants: Mayor Budwin, Father John, Councillors Barbara, Anton, and Gary. They had, in turn, greeted me with: a provocative and so not-sexy eyebrow raise; suspicion, because how could a mere debunker protect him from demon spawn; and either indifference or intense interest in my work.

Nina asked the councillors and Block to take a seat at the shrouded round table and join hands, as the lights appeared to dim themselves.

Nina began with a hocus pocus scene setter, which she'd apparently got from YouTube, as a slight whiff of clove and frankincense slipped into the room.

The participants suddenly became visibly nervous.

Good grief. It doesn't take much.

'I call on any restless spirits present to make themselves known.' Nina said. 'I am your willing vessel, if you would like to make contact with the living.'

Elinor's chatty couch friend from earlier in the day, wandered in late and prowled around in the almost dark, about two metres behind those seated, like she was stalking prey. Why that didn't distract everyone from their amusing nervousness, I don't know; especially as the woman was still wearing her tropical-strength caftan. Truth be known, she looked far more like a wacky clairvoyant than the gorgeous Nina, who'd simply donned a black cloak and dark eyeliner.

'Who first?' the woman whispered.

Nina nodded to the mayor, seated three chairs around from her, so Lady Obvious moved behind and touched him on the shoulder.

'Mother Budwin says he must stop watching the naughty stuff, or he'll go blind,' she whispered.

I slapped my hand over my mouth; Elinor bowed her head and quaked with laughter.

There was, however, no reaction from anyone at the table except Nina the Medium, desperately trying to keep a straight face.

'Alistair, Alistair,' Nina said.

The mayor was suddenly wide-eyed. 'Yes?'

'Amelia says you must stop watching—'

'What? I don't.'

'Your mother says it will harm your eyesight.'

Everyone except Father John snickered.

Nina glanced at me. 'Amelia also says stop acting like every woman wants to have sex with you. None of them do; but mostly it's just uncouth.'

The caftan queen moved again, this time behind councillors Barbara and Gary, who were sitting between Block and an almost-cowering catholic priest. 'Stolen things, Gary,' she said.

'Something is amiss,' Nina said, looking around the table – as if for a sign. Her gaze rested on the councillor. 'Are you up to no good, Gary Hilton?' she asked in a jovial tone.

'Me? No. Why?' The man seemed perfectly calm. As he should, given the obvious theatrics.

Nina shrugged, 'I'm getting a vague vibe of not-quite-rightness.'

'His watch is in Brian Green's gym locker.'

'Ah, I'm getting word,' Nina said, 'that your watch is in Biffo Green's locker.'

'Whoa. You're kidding?' said Gary. 'That bastard. But again, whoa!'

What the hell? Why is no one reacting to Lady La La? The lady who was now shaking her head at Barbara.

'Nefariousness,' she said. 'Snakes in Barbie's grass; her man choices are very spiky.'

'Barbara?' Nina said jovially.

'Yes, Nina?' the blonde said with matching amusement.

'I'm getting advice from beyond that you should perhaps choose you men friends more wisely.'

'Ha,' Barbara laughed swivelling her gaze between Gary and Block. 'Ain't that the truth.'

'Naughty Andrew,' Caftan lady said.

'Really?' Nina said, saying nothing else but she shot her not-cousin a serious eyebrow-raise.

I leant closer to Elinor. 'Have they all been hypnotised not to see your friend?'

'What do you mean, Lucy? What friend?'

'What do you mean, what do I mean? The woman with the Endora hairdo and the crazy caftan.'

Elinor was gobsmacked. To be precise she looked at *me* as if I'd unexpectedly turned into an alpaca. Or a pavlova.

'What?' I whispered. 'Say something, Elinor.'

'You can see her?'

Okay. My turn to look like I'd been smacked with a trout.

My blood also ran cold. Like ice. Like a sludgy, slurpy Slurpee.

'If you're all trying to con me, I swear–'

'Don't be silly, Lucy dear,' Elinor put her hand over mine. 'It's um–'

There was no way this adorable woman was trying to hoodwink me.

So what the hell was–

When I turned my hand over to clasp hers, Elinor's whole body jolted as if she'd seen – *I kid you not* – a ghost.

'Jerusha,' she said softly.

The crazy caftan creature faced us then abandoned her séance duties and rushed over to Elinor, where she dropped to her knees and they just *stared* at each other.

Elinor let go of my hand to reach out – and then looked frantically around.

'Hold Lucy's hand, Eli,' said the other woman; the other, probably, ghost woman. Who Elinor could clearly hear but not see, without me.

The me who really wanted to get the hell out of here now.

'Finbar,' I growled under my breath.

'I did warn you, Lucy Arden.'

Elinor was gripping my hand and grinning like a loon. 'You haven't changed a bit, Roosh.'

'Of course not, darling. I'm forever 60 and holding.'

'Helen, I can see my sister,' Elinor whispered.

'I gathered as much,' said a totally unflapped Dr Cooper.

In the meantime Nina – who'd clearly lost her audible conduit to the afterlife – *what are you thinking, Lucy?* – but had no idea why, was simply winging it.

'Father John the goodly spirits want me to assure there are no such things as demons; just lost souls. And many of those souls are living but have been abandoned by you and yours.'

'Finbar, perhaps you let Nina know she could wrap things up,' I said. 'We need to call an emergency session of Spooks R Us'.

Afterwards

Why we had to trek all the way up to Jericho's Folly after the ghostly revelations in the hexagon room, I don't know. Except that Elinor pretended she and Helen, the oldies of the gathering, needed cocoa and a chinwag after all that excitement. She tasked Nina and Andrew with politely getting rid of the guests. The not-nephew was clearly relieved when he learned he wasn't expected to join the gal talk. He had better things to do apparently and was happy to debrief the séance over brunch.

So, while Helen made cocoa in the Folly's kitchenette, in an alcove facing the sea, I sat between Elinor Blake and her twin sister who – sigh – had died in a hot air balloon accident right here on Jindalee Reach in 2001.

'Are you sorry now you didn't take my advice not to wear that ridiculous caftan?' Elinor said.

Jerusha Blake scowled. 'Don't you start.'

'I didn't realise, in all these years of just chatting, that you're stuck forever in whatever.'

'Well, it's not like there's an Afterlife Op Shop, sis. At first, I tried getting into something else, but I just kept falling through the clothes.'

'Why are you–' I began

'*Why* am I?' Jerusha frowned.

I waggled my head. 'Well yes, but specifically why are you here? Still. Is it unfinished business? Do we need to do something to release you?'

Jerusha eyes widened in horror. 'Of course not.'

Elinor squeezed my hand. 'We're all quite happily haunted, Lucy. Even more so now.'

I pulled a face. 'Did you invite me here to make *that* point. To debunk my debunking?'

'No dear. If I'm the first ghost you've ever met then the mediums you've taken down no doubt deserved it.

'You make me sound like a hitwoman.'

'A hitwoman?' It was Hecate speaking, as she and Finbar careened around the corner into view. She somersaulted two chairs; he passed right through an easel and a paint pot.

Nina arrived a moment later, still wearing her fabulous cloak and an expectant expression. 'Can you really see Aunt Jerusha, Gran?'

Elinor grinned, Jerusha nodded, Helen, carrying four mugs of cocoa, said: 'While I can still only *hear* half a bloody conversation.'

Nina and Helen sat in the chairs opposite us, and Finbar and Hecate on and at opposite ends of the coffee table.

I addressed Helen. 'Why did you not assume your friend was a complete nutjob then?'

A moment's dead silence was followed by everyone laughing like loons.

'Because–' Jerusha said, and then mindfully, I assume, moved the sugar bowl towards me.

'Oh. Okay, but why could I hear you as soon as I got here?'

'That's a mystery,' Finbar noted.

I needed verification on another matter. 'Everyone *can* hear and see the talking cat?'

'Yes,' said everyone. 'And Hecate,' Helen added.

'You couldn't *see* me at first though, could you?' Jerusha noted.

'No,' I admitted. 'And when I did, I figured you'd just been sitting at the other end of the couch.'

'Tell us everything you've done since you got to Kooringa,' Nina said.

So I did. And my time so far was analysed by all, until Elinor grinned. 'My sister wishes to speak.'

'That cliffside grave belongs to Timothy Barnett, who died in 1958 aged ten,' Jerusha said. 'His mother's been placing those weird little voodoo things there on his deathday ever since. My guess is pricking your finger allowed you to hear him, and later me; then the moment you shook Nina's hand, you could also see us both.'

'Even though *I* can't?' Nina noted. 'See her, I mean.'

'But you've always been able to hear each other?' I asked the three Blake women, who nodded.

Helen pouted. 'Must be a family thing.'

'Ooh, wait a minute.' I leant forward and held Nina's hand.

'*Oh my*, Aunt Jerusha,' she said, spilling tears of joy.

'You never know,' I shrugged and offered Helen my right hand.

'Well I'll be damned. Hello Roosh,' she said.

Lest you think I was just taking all of this in my stead – simply abandoning an adult-lifetime conviction that ghosts were nothing more than the manifestation of grief or the concoction of charlatans – I'll have you know that my mind was reeling. And rocking in so many directions I felt drunk. And stoned. And insane.

It was hard not to share the elation of the three live women holding my hands who were animatedly chatting with the dead woman none of them had seen for twenty years.

But hello: dead woman in a caftan on a couch!

Finbar, no doubt in an effort to help me feel less crazy, had 'manifested' enough substance as to be able to head butt my knees. As for Hecate Who–

Hello again! A PanDimbe and an immortal Gresha!

Helen had nipped off to the kitchenette to get the whiskey Elinor decided we'd all earned; while Nina and Finbar reported the things they heard when seeing off the guests.

'That Barbie was bossing the men around,' Finbar said.

'Which men,' I asked.

'Gary and Anton,' Nina said. 'She *is* a bossy piece of work.'

'She also said to Andrew: *it will stay undeveloped*,' Finbar said.

I shrugged. 'Do you think she's having an affair or whatever with Andrew?'

'Or reassuring him that whatever with Gary is nothing,' Nina said.

'It's like *Melrose Place*,' Hecate said.

'That's showing your age,' I said.

'Well I *am* ancient for a Gresha, Lucy.'

'That's peculiar.' Helen, holding a whiskey bottle and four shot glasses, was at the window.

'That describes the turn my life has taken in the last twelve hours,' I said.

'Has someone lit the Knot lamp again?' Elinor asked.

'Yes, but someone is also on the way to the Knot in a boat.'

In a flash our strange little clan of beings joined Helen to stare into the very dark night at – nothing.

No wait, there it was. Every few seconds, no doubt with the bump of an unseen wave, the limited starlight of a mostly overcast and moonless sky bounced off the dull hull of a rubber raft.

'I think there's two people in it,' Helen said.

'Is that your boat?' I asked.

'No, *Betsy* is a proper boat.' Elinor said.

I turned to Nina. 'Can you drive *Betsy*? Wanna go investigate?'

'Nina is terrified of boats,' Finbar stated.

'Doesn't mean her grandmother didn't teach her how to drive it,' Jerusha stated.

'For situations just like this,' Helen noted.

'To solve a mystery on an island,' said I.

'In the middle of the night,' Nina finished.

Elinor laughed. 'We *are* the Secret Seven.'

And now

Access to Harrow's Cave was down three levels in the tiny lift and along a short hall to a heavy wooden door, on the other side of which were seventeen stone-cut stairs descending to a smooth rock platform. The cave obviously went further back into the hillside under the house. The floating dock, and the boat moored to it, was currently level with the six-foot mark of a longer ladder going down into the water.

Nina and I used the rungs, Finbar and Hecate leapt and floofed, and moments later the tarpaulin was removed and stowed and we were untethered.

And clearly unhinged.

'Are you sure about this?' I asked Nina.

'I honestly – and I admit curiously – feel that anything I ever do with you, will be amazing,' she said.

'Oh, in that case,' I grinned, 'let's start with something stupid.'

'Make it so,' Hecate Who declared, as we slipped out into Bass Strait. 'Gaahh,' she added as the wind immediately caught and flung her into Finbar's voluminous, and now completely in-this-dimension, mane.

'Stay there,' he advised, standing boldly like the ship's cat he once was. 'Or you'll end up in the sea.'

It took five minutes to reach Emu Knot, because we kept the boat at a low throttle to avoid announcing our pursuit of the mysterious lantern lighter.

Nina semi-beached *Betsy*, I tied her to a rock ring behind the rubber raft, which was pulled right up on the sand, and we gathered onshore.

It was still a little windy, as Hecate emerged spluttering from Finbar's fur.

'Don't be such a drama queen, Hecate. You don't even breath through your mouth.'

'No, but I've got your furriness in my book lungs. And it tickles my pedipalps.'

'It's just as well our quarry can't hear them,' Nina whispered to me.

We made our way up onto the foreshore stones, then across a little grassy expanse, to the rising rocks of the seated emu's right leg. The ridge inside that leg gave us cover all the way along to the base of its neck, now only about two metres high, as the rest of it and the head were lying in a pile around the lantern. Once up there, I could see that the whole Knot was footy oval size, and there were two people standing twenty metres away on the ocean side.

'That's Andrew,' Nina whispered.

'And Barbie-ra,' said Finbar.

'And someone else coming from the other side,' I added.

It turned out to be two someones carrying three stacked crates.

'Smugglers,' Hecate said.

'But smuggling what?' Nina asked.

'Probably drugs.'

'Andrew's always been an opportunist, Lucy, but I doubt he'd smuggle drugs.'

A strange voice – right behind me – said, 'Smuggling friends.'

I swung around and got an excited face lick from a red heeler.

'Ranga Squad is in da house,' Hecate announced.

'You must be George,' I said to the boisterous dog.

'Yes-yes, good you here, stuck forever.'

'Two days, George,' Finbar corrected him.

'Baddies stealing friends. Other bads bring zotic friends here. There's a normus blue Gresha in a box, Hecate.'

'Zotic?' I asked.

'Exotic,' Finbar said. 'George, where is Arlo?'

'Sticking his beak in their boat.'

'Who *are* they?' Nina asked.

'Bad Block, kissy Barbara, numpties from way-out gianter boat.'

'Numpties?' I repeated.

'Friend stealing numpties,' George said, slobbering all over Nina, who said, 'Get off me, you drool monster. I've got to call Gran.'

We sat down so the light from her smartphone couldn't be seen by the bad guys.

'Gran, call Sergeant Ross, tell him to rope in the Kisler twins and their boats, and get out to the Knot with lights blazing. He's got some smugglers to arrest.'

A squawking and flapping heralded the arrival of a demented raven. He landed, ran up and down the emu's leg, picked up Hecate in his beak – dropped her again when she shouted '*not food*' – froze suddenly and said, 'Shit a brick!

'That sounds not good, Arlo.'

'Understatement, George. Who's the dame?'

What else could I say but, 'Lucy Arden. Private investigator.'

'Outstanding! Someone with skills. *To the rescue!*' He made come hither movements with his headed then flappy-jumped back the way we'd already come.

When no one followed, he said, 'I broke their boat. Have to rescue friends from the water. Now!'

Arlo led us towards the emu's bum, to avoid Andrew and his cohorts.

Nina grabbed my arm. 'I'll catch up in a minute. We don't want them to get off the Knot. I'll disable Andrew's boat; and get the keys from *Betty.*'

The she kissed me – right on the mouth – grinned and ran off into the dark.

Everything that makes up me began dancing a *pasodoble* to the Gypsy Kings; and right there, right then, I wasn't even sure whether they were performing in my mind or on the beach.

'Love struck,' Hecate said again.

'You shut up,' I said, and took off after the crazy raven.

As we rounded the end of the emu into the full-on sea wind, Hecate – howling her name into the night – was snatched up again, right off the rock this time. Finbar and I both raised an arm/paw but it was me–

Yes, dear reader, I caught her. A huntsman – in my hand.

And then – *by all the things sent to drive me completely mad* – I shoved the Gresha down my shirt front.

When we reached the smugglers' boat, we discovered that Arlo really had stuck his beak in it. It was deflating slowly and the crate bottoms were already in the water.

I began dragging them out to much muttering and complaints – while Arlo was busy telling everyone contained inside them that this human was helping.

'What the hell?' One – luckily just one – of the unknown bad guys was running towards us.

'It was sinking,' I said. 'I didn't want them all to drown.'

'Who are you?' he demanded, actually helping me.

'I'm with Andrew,' I lied.

'She is bloody not,' came a woman's voice. 'She's a bloody cop or something.'

'I'm a private eye,' I corrected Barbara who, I now realised, was dragging Nina by the scruff of her shirt along the beach from the other direction.

Smuggler Number One was suddenly armed – with a revolver.

What? This is Australia. Who carries a gun?

'Nina stuck a fishing knife in *our* boat. This is no accident.' Barbara then hollered. 'Andrew, get down here.'

I noticed Arlo loitering behind the armed thug, as a voice from the crate next to me hissed 'Let me at her.'

'Much as I'd love to let you out, Igor,' Finbar said, 'we all need to stay calm.'

Meanwhile, Andrew's first words on the scene were, 'Where on earth did that enormous cat come from?'

'Are you not more interested in why your cousin and the private dick are here?' Barbara asked in a tone that suggested Andrew's priorities were skewed.

'I'm here because it's my bloody island,' Nina said. 'And he's *not* my cousin.'

Barbara responded by shoving her to the ground, about two metres from me, whereon Andrew went and stood over her.

'What?' Nina asked him.

'You never liked me,' he said.

Nina threw her hands up. 'Are you kidding me?'

I casually put my hand to my throat, then down my cleavage. 'Hecate.'

329

'Yes, Lucy,' she *whispered* back; kind of unnecessarily.

'Six feet straight ahead. Alien face hugger.'

In the same moment that the fourth bad guy arrived at a run, so many kinds of hell broke loose it was difficult to keep track.

The beach was lit up by powerful halogen lights from a huge loval cruiser offshore, a uniformed cop followed in hot pursuit of Smuggler Number Two, Arlo leapt and flapped in Number One's face, while Finbar while launched a full body tackle and knocked the gun from his hand, and I pitched Hecate Who through the night sky right into Andrew Block's sooky face.

There was screaming. So much screaming.

And most of it coming from the not-nephew-cousin with the beautiful ranga Gresha hanging onto his face, laughing like the witch goddess for whom she was named.

CONTRIBUTING

AUTHORS

LOUISA BENNET

Louisa studied Literature at university and went on to learn Canine Linguistics from her golden retriever, Pickles, which is how she discovered what dogs really get up to when we're not around. Truth be told, Pickles came up with the story for *When the Chips Are Down*, and Louisa just transcribed it. (She's faster on the keyboard and less easily distracted by food or bad-tempered ducks.)

Louisa also writes crime thrillers as L.A. Larkin and runs courses on crime fiction and creative writing. Pickles runs courses on wee-mailing, duck toppling and drool management.

Monty and Rose also feature in the novels *Monty Dog Detective* and *The Nosy Detectives* (CDP).

LINDY CAMERON

Lindy, commissioning editor of this anthology, is also the author of: the Kit O'Malley PI trilogy, *Blood Guilt*, *Bleeding Hearts* and *Thicker Than Water*; the archaeological mystery *Golden Relic*; the action thriller *Redback*; and the sf novella *Feedback*.

She's co-author, (with Fin J Ross), of the true crime collections: *Toxic: Cold-blooded Australian Murders*; and *Killer in the Family*.

Lindy's also had the great honour of co-writing two short stories with Kerry Greenwood. Both feature Harriet Brookes: 'A Wild Colonial' for *Sherlock Holmes: The Australian Casebook* and 'The Saltwater Battle' for *War of the Worlds: Battleground Australia*.

Lindy is a founding member and National Co-Convenor of Sisters in Crime Australia, and the Publisher of Clan Destine Press.

KAT CLAY

Kat is a writer, critic, and content producer from Melbourne, Australia. Her short story 'Lady Loveday Investigates' won three prizes at the Sisters in Crime Australia 2018 Scarlet Stiletto Awards, including the Kerry Greenwood Prize for Best Malice Domestic.

She has previously been nominated for Aurealis and Ditmar Awards, and received an honourable mention in the Australian Horror Writers Association Shadows Awards for non-fiction criticism.

Kat's short stories have been published in *Aurealis, SQ Mag*, and *Crimson Streets*. Her non-fiction has been published in *The Guardian, The Victorian Writer,* and *Weird Fiction Review*. Her weird-noir novella, *Double Exposure*, was released in print and e-book with Crime Factory in 2015, and is available on most major eBook platforms.

LIVIA DAY

Livia (she/her) is a crime writer who lives on Palawa land, in Tasmania. Livia is the author of cozy mysteries such as The Cafe La Femme series: *A Trifle Dead, Drowned Vanilla, The Blackmail Blend* and *Keep Calm and Kill the Chef*.

Livia's new Fashionably Late series kicks off with *Dyed and Buried*.

JACK FENNELL

Jack is a writer, editor and researcher based in Limerick, Ireland. He is the author of two book-length studies of Irish genre fiction, *Irish Science Fiction* (2014) and *Rough Beasts* (2019); and editor of two short story collections, *A Brilliant Void* (2018) and *It Rose Up* (2021). He was also a contributing translator to *The Short Fiction of Flann O'Brien* (2013). His own fiction has appeared in the collections: *Hell's Empire* (2019) and *Chronos* (2018); as well as *Silver Apples Magazine*.

Jack teaches at the University of Limerick.

DAVID GREAGG

David is a registered wizard, and consort of Kerry Greenwood. He has published several books, including the ghost-written autobiographies of his cat, *Dougal's Diary* and *When We Were Kittens*; non-fiction for children, *It's True! Bourke and Wills Forgot The Frying Pan* and *It's True! The Vikings Got Lost*; and  fiction in collaboration with Kerry.

At various times David has been a medieval scholar, a mathematician, an accountant, armoured warrior, composer, conductor, impresario and tenor. No doubt the future will see him do equally unpredictable things.

KERRY GREENWOOD

Kerry is the author of more than 50 novels, a book of short stories, six non-fiction works, and the editor of two collections of true crime writing.

Her beloved Phryne Fisher series (21 novels and counting) has become a successful ABC TV series and movie – *Miss Fisher's Murder Mysteries, Miss Fisher and the Crypt of Tears* – which sold around the world. She is also the author of the contemporary mysteries featuring baker-sleuth Corinna Chapman.

Kerry is the author of several books for young adults; the ancient Egypt novel, *Out of the Black Land*; and the Delphic Women trilogy: *Medea, Cassandra* and *Electra*. Kerry has also co-written, (with Lindy Cameron), short stories for *Sherlock Holmes: The Australian Casebook* and *War of the Worlds: Battleground Australia*.

In the 2020 Australia Day Honours, she was awarded the Medal of the Order of Australia (OAM) for services to literature. In a previous life, Kerry was a lawyer and advocate in magistrates' courts for the Legal Aid Commission. She is not married, has no children, is the co-warden of a Found Cats' Home and lives with an accredited wizard (and other collaborator in fiction), David Greagg.

NARRELLE M. HARRIS

Narrelle writes crime, horror, fantasy, and romance. Her 30+ works include vampire novels, erotic spy adventures, het and queer romance, and Holmes/Watson romance mysteries *The Adventure of the Colonial Boy* and *A Dream to Build a Kiss On.*

In 2017, her ghost/crime story 'Jane' won the Body in the Library prize in the Scarlet Stiletto Awards, run by Sisters in Crime Australia.

Her recent works include *Grounded, Scar Tissue and Other Stories* (nominated for the 2019 Aurealis Awards for Best Collection), and *Kitty and Cadaver.*

Narrelle was also commissioning editor for *The Only One in the World: A Sherlock Holmes Anthology* (2021). Narrelle's next book is *The She-Wolf of Baker Street.*

CRAIG HILTON

Craig is a writer and cartoonist/illustrator based in Melbourne, Victoria, Australia. He is a full-time doctor and part-time cartoonist, whose work has appeared in the *Medical Journal of Australia, Australian Doctor* magazine and the *British Journal of General Practice.*

Working under the name of Jenner, Hilton is best known for the long-running daily comic strip *Doc Rat.*
But it was in the 1990s, in *The Ever Changing Palace*, a semi-professional magazine celebrating the American comic book series Xanadu, that the public first met the lower class detective rat Whimper.

MEG KENEALLY

Meg is the author of *The Wreck* (2020) and *Fled* (2019).

With Tom Keneally, she is the author of The Monsarrat series of colonial-era murder mysteries: *The Soldier's Curse, The Unmourned, The Power Game* and *The Ink Stain.*

She is co-editor with Leah Kaminsky of *Animals Make Us Human.* Her next novel, *The Last Queen,* will be out in 2023.

Meg is currently working on a history of Australian women.

C.J. McGumbleberry

C.J. is the super-secret alias of someone who is super secret, but who lives in the Pacific Northwest of the United States, who may or may not

have red hair, and who definitely absolutely just made his first short story sale to this collection.

With a penchant for nicknaming everything, you can be sure there probably is a dragonfly named Lizard in C.J.'s life, though he is neither confirming nor denying. C.J. invents the most amazing non-swearing swears you have ever heard.

Chuck McKenzie

Chuck was born in 1970, and still spends much of his time there. He's also spent a great deal of time in Covid-related lockdown, and while he'd love to say that this has motivated him to write again, mostly it's motivated him to slump on the couch, watching Netflix and eating chips.

'Time Spent with a Cat' is his first published short story since 2007.

Atlin Merrick

Atlin wrote this Ireland-set story about a minute after she unexpectedly moved back to the U.S. from Éire, because ain't that just the way things go. She's the author of two Sherlock Holmes books: *The Day They Met* (as Wendy C Fries), and *The Night They Met*.

Atlin is also the Commissioning Editor of Clan Destine's imprint

Improbable Press, which publishes genre fiction: adventure, mystery, contemporary supernatural, and romance.

Atlin lives in Oregon by way of New York, Melbourne, Dublin and London. Atlin thinks coffee is pretty.

Dr L.J.M. Owen

L.J. escaped the shadowy days as a public servant to explore the lighter side of life: murder, mystery and forgotten women's history. Her short story 'The Adventure of the Lazarus Child' features in *Sherlock Holmes: The Australian Casebook*. Her crime novels include *The Great Divide*; and Dr Pimms archaeological mystery series: *Egyptian Enigma*, *Mayan Mendacity*, and *Olmec Obituary*.

L.J. is the founding Director of the Terror Australis Readers and Writers Festival, a celebration of literature and literacy in Tasmania. She has degrees in archaeology, forensic science and librarianship, speaks five languages and has travelled extensively. Rare spare moments are spent experimenting with ancient recipes under strict feline supervision.

GV PEARCE

Gen is the author of the queer supernatural romance novels *Ghost Story* and *Strangest Day So Far*. Several years spent working in animal

welfare have left them with an endless supply of tales too ridiculous to be fiction. Perhaps one day they'll put those stories into a book. In the meantime, Gen can usually be found wandering the Yorkshire Moors in search of cool rocks, inspiration, and a decent cup of coffee.

VIKKI PETRAITIS

Vikki usually sticks to true crime and has written oodles of books in this genre, including one called *The Dog Squad* where she spent months

interviewing police dog handlers. She is also the maker of true crime podcasts with *The Vanishing of Vivienne Cameron* being downloaded all around the world.

Having taken on PhD studies in Creative Writing, Vikki has tried her hand at crime fiction, completing her first novel. For her story in this book, Vikki combined her love of dogs with her love of crime stories.

FIN J ROSS

Fin is a creative writing teacher, and a breeder of British Shorthair cats. She is the co-author, (with Lindy Cameron) of the true crime books *Toxic: Cold-blooded Australian Murders*, and *Killer in the Family*; and co-compiler, (with Willsin Rowe), of *Nifty Fifty: 50 Cryptic Crosswords with an Aussie Flavour*.

She's won eight category prizes in the annual Scarlet Stiletto Awards run by Sisters in Crime Australia.

Fin's historical novel, *Billings Better Bookstore and Brasserie*, is set in Melbourne in the 19th Century; and *AKA Fudgepuddle* follows the adventures of a demanding cat called Megsy.

TOR ROXBURGH

Tor is an amateur painter, a lover of reading and walking and music, and a podcaster. She lives and works in regional Victoria and co-hosts the *OK Smart Ass* podcast with Patrick Bonello.

She is the author of: *The Book of Pregnancy Weeks;* 12 teen romances; two guided journals; the epic fantasy, *The Light Heart of Stone*, and its sequel *The Rush of Stone*.

ELIZABETH ANN SCARBOROUGH

Elizabeth is the author of over 40 science fiction and fantasy novels, most notably the 1989 Nebula for Best Novel *The Healer's War*, the *Songs from the Seashell Archives* series and the Godmother series. She co-wrote 16 books with Anne McCaffrey including *Powers that Be*, *Power Lines* and *Power Play*.

The Spam the Cat series starring the intrepid tabby sleuth includes two novels, a novelette, three short stories, and a graphic novel (illustrated by Karen Gillmore). *Spam Vs. the Vampire*, the first novel in the series, has the late K.B. (Kittibits) Dundee as the primary author with Elizabeth as the secondary. Note: never co-write with a cat; they take all the credit.

Elizabeth and her feline supervisor, Cisco, live in a town in Washington State, surrounded on three sides by the Salish Sea, sometimes visited by pods of orcas, dolphins, and the occasional larger whale. Raccoons, otters, deer, coyotes, cougars and possibly Sasquatches also frequent the neighborhood.

Clan Destine Press Anthologies

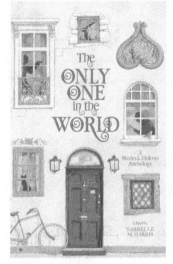

ISBNs: 978-0-6489586-2-8 (hc)
978-0-6488487-8-3 (pb)
978-0-6489586-3-5 (eB)

The Only One in the World

Since his first appearance in 1887, Sherlock Holmes has been the quintessential English sleuth, alongside his loyal companion and biographer, Doctor Watson.

But what if they had come from some other place in the world, or another time? How would they differ from Conan Doyle's creations? How similar might they remain?

Holmes and Watson are herein re-imagined in new cultural contexts, different genders and sexualities, and in stories rich in foreign detail that still reflect their origins.

Thirteen writers, from around the world, with cultural or historic expertise explore the possibilities with stories set in Germany, C17th England, Ireland, Australia, Russia, South Africa, India, Poland, USA, Ancient Egypt, Viking Iceland, and even the entire world.

You'll discover Holmes and Watson are not only unique in original canon, but the Great Detective remains singular in every world!

Stories by: Kerry Greenwood & David Greagg, Greg Herren, Atlin Merrick, Jack Fennell, Lucy Sussex, Jason Franks, Natalie Conyer, Lisa Fessler, Katya de Becerra, Jayantika Ganguly, LJM Owen, Raymond Gates and JM Redmann.

ISBNs: 9780648523635 (hc)
9780648523628 (pb)
9780648523680 (eB)

War of the Worlds: Battleground Australia

This rivetting anthology sheds fresh, antipodean light on HG Wells' original invasion tale, in stories that traverse the great southern continent. Home to the planet's longest surviving people and mysteries, Australia, it seems, was also invaded by marauding Martians.

In *Battleground Australia* we learn the war with Mars was not confined to England and did not end with all Martians destroyed by disease. In Australia some of the aliens survived and went underground, to emerge a century or more later.

With stories by some of Australia's best-selling literary, crime and speculative fiction writers:
Kerry Greenwood, Jack Dann, Janeen Webb, Sean Williams, Angela Meyer, Lindy Cameron, Jenny Valentish, Narrelle M. Harris, Lucy Sussex, Rick Kennett, Jason Franks, Dmetri Kakmi Bill Congreve, Carmel Bird, Jason Fischer and Kaaron Warren.